EVE AND HER SISTERS

Also by Rita Bradshaw and available from Headline

Alone Beneath the Heaven
Reach for Tomorrow
Ragamuffin Angel
The Stony Path
The Urchin's Song
Candles in the Storm
The Most Precious Thing
Always I'll Remember
The Rainbow Years
Skylarks at Sunset
Above the Harvest Moon

EVE AND HER SISTERS

Rita Bradshaw

headline

First published in 2008 by
HEADLINE PUBLISHING GROUP

1

Cataloguing in Publication Data is available from the British Library

Hardback ISBN 978 0 7553 3818 4

Typeset in Bembo by Palimpsest Book Production Limited,
Grangemouth, Stirlingshire

Printed and bound in Great Britain by
CPI Mackays, Chatham, ME5 8TD

Headline's policy is to use papers that are natural, renewable and recyclable
products and made from wood grown in sustainable forests. The logging
and manufacturing processes are expected to conform to the
environmental regulations of the country of origin.

HEADLINE PUBLISHING GROUP
An Hachette Livre UK Company
338 Euston Road
London NW1 3BH

www.headline.co.uk
www.hachettelivre.co.uk

Dedication

For my darling Mum. I know you're in a better place but I miss you more than words can say. You were the best mum in the world and such a special lady, with the biggest heart of anyone I've met. Give Dad a kiss for me, precious one.

And my Pippa, such a beautiful and faithful dog and so tolerant and gentle. It's not the same without your doggy smiles and dear old face.

Author's Note

A certain amount of artistic licence is necessary with a story such as Eve's, but where possible actual events have been recorded as faithfully as possible. For example, the pit disaster which begins the story occurred on 16 February 1909 and claimed the lives of 168 men and boys. The miners' local inspector, Frank Keegan, was acclaimed a hero for his part in rescuing twenty-six men; for any football fans, he was the grandfather of Kevin Keegan. Likewise, the hirings which took place at the annual Michaelmas Fair did happen. Folk were lined up like cattle at the market and inspected in much the same way.

For any of you who lament 'the good old days', spare a thought for the working class in the early twentieth century. Having said that, they could teach us a thing or two nowadays!

Love suffereth long and is kind.
1 Corinthians, 13:4

PART ONE

1909 – The Departure

Chapter 1

The moment Mrs McArthur from next door burst into the kitchen without even knocking once at the back door, she knew. A few seconds before, she had heard a man's voice in the McArthur's back yard shouting for Mr McArthur, and something in the tone had caused her hands to still on the dough she was kneading.

'Eve, lass. There's been a fall an' they reckon it's a bad one. Your da and the lads are down, aren't they? Quick, hinny.' Mrs McArthur didn't wait for a response but flew out of the house as fast as she had arrived.

The door hadn't closed behind the little woman before Eve was scraping the dough off her hands and pulling off her pinny. She ran into the hall without stopping to wash her hands, grabbing her coat and hat from one of the pegs on the brown painted wall.

When she opened the front door she saw people running in the direction of the pit, men pulling on their jackets and caps as they went and women carrying babes in arms with little ones hanging on to their mothers' coat-tails. In spite of the number of folk, an eerie quiet prevailed, only broken by the odd person or two banging on a front door to alert a friend or neighbour. If there was panic, it was of the numb, fatalistic kind.

3

Eve joined the tide heading for the pit gates, doing up the buttons of her coat as she went. She passed one or two women standing on doorsteps, and outside the corner shop a small group had gathered, not talking, just watching. All their faces reflected the same thing, silent pity laced with thankfulness it wasn't their man or child trapped hundreds of feet under the ground. This meant their menfolk worked at South Moor Colliery or even the West Shieldrow pit a mile north-west, not that one pit was safer than any other.

On reaching the colliery gates Eve joined the swell of people which was being added to minute by minute as word of the disaster spread. She saw Mrs McArthur and her married daughter, Anne Mullen, standing close together and she edged towards them. Anne had only got wed three months ago in November and Eve's eldest brother had been best man. As she reached them, Anne noticed her and reached out to grip her hand. 'Your da and Frank down, lass?' she murmured, her face chalk white.

Eve nodded. 'And William. He's just been made a hewer and they put him with Da and Frank.' The week before, William would have been doing repair work and therefore on a different shift. She remembered how pleased he had been when the deputy had said he could join his father and brother; the repair shift worked longer hours for a smaller basic wage than the hewers. She bit hard on her bottom lip to stop it trembling.

She had always been frightened this day would come. The West Stanley Colliery, or Burn's pit as it was known locally, had been the scene of an explosion over twenty years before and had taken the lives of her maternal grandfather and his three sons. Her parents had just got married at the time and they had taken in her grandmother, there being no other menfolk left. Grandma Collins had lived with them until the day she died, two years ago, and four years after the fever had taken Eve's mother. Eve had loved her grandma but the old woman's stories about the pit had regularly given her nightmares.

A snowflake drifted aimlessly in the bitterly cold air and somewhere behind her a woman said, 'We're in for a packet, you can smell the snow coming,' before becoming silent again.

Her grandma had viewed the pit as a live entity, Eve thought, her eyes fixed on the yard beyond the gates which fronted the lamp house and the first-aid post, the colliery office standing behind them. Her grandma had always maintained the pit was capricious at best and malevolent at worst, delighting in playing a deadly game with the men and boys who came to plunder its black gold. Certainly Burn's pit seemed no more inclined to give up its wealth than the other five collieries dotted about in the town of Stanley on the western edge of the Durham coalfield.

'Don't worry, pet.' Mrs McArthur turned to her, patting her arm for a moment before her eyes returned to the yard where her husband, along with the rest of the rescue team, were ascending the two flights of steps leading to the cage which would take them down into the bowels of the earth. 'Your da an' Will an' Frank'll be all right. It might not be as bad as they think, you never can tell.'

'You think so?'

The desperation in Eve's voice brought the older woman's eyes to her again. 'Aye, aye,' she said 'Don't fret.' And then she glanced at her daughter over Eve's head. Her look, had it been put into words, would have asked how much bad luck the Baxter family could be expected to bear. First the pit taking all the Collins menfolk years ago, and with Peter Baxter having been brought up in the workhouse as an orphan there was no kin on Eve's da's side. Then poor Molly, Eve's mam, dying of the fever like that before her rightful time, and old Ma Collins following two years ago which meant the running of the house was thrust on the shoulders of this little lass at her side, and her only eleven at the time. For sure, the lass hadn't had much schooling since then till she had officially left at Christmas when she was thirteen. And it was no good the School Inspector coming round shouting the odds in such cases, they turned a blind eye if they had any sense. With her da and two brothers to wash and cook for and her sisters to see to, the bairn's place had been in the home.

It was several hours later before news filtered through to the men, women and children at the pit gates, and then it was as bad as it could be. The explosion which had ripped through the coalface, snapping the props holding the roof like matchsticks and blocking the inroads and outroads to the section, had resulted in nearly two hundred men and boys being trapped below millions of tons of rock, coal and slate. The rescue teams were going to have their work cut out and it would be a long job, no doubt about it. Everyone knew what that could mean. Fatalities. Lots of them.

Eve watched as Anne clutched at her mother. 'He might be burnt, Mam. Doug might be burnt or gassed or—'

'Ssh, our Anne. Don't talk like that.'

'I can't bear it if anything happens to him. An' our Larry . . .' Her voice broke. 'Our Larry could be hurt an' all.'

'That's enough, lass.' At the mention of her son who had been working alongside Anne's husband, Mrs McArthur's face had twitched. 'The best place for you is home if you're going to talk like that, now then. It's no good thinkin' the worst, that don't help no one. Your da'll find them an' bring 'em up, you know he will.'

Turning to Eve, Mrs McArthur's face softened. 'Why don't you go home an' all, hinny? You can't do nowt here an' Nell an' Mary'll be back from school any minute. I'll come an' fetch you if I hear owt.'

Eve nodded. The crowd was not as large now as it had been at eleven o'clock that morning. Women had had to return home when children had become so cold they had begun to cry, and since the snow had begun to fall in earnest more had left. She herself was frozen to the marrow. When she tried to walk she would have fallen but for kind hands catching her as she stumbled.

Slowly and stiffly Eve retraced her footsteps. Once clear of the colliery she made for Clifford Road which led on to Murray Street where she lived. The house was a two-up, two-down terrace in a street identical to its neighbours and exactly the same as other clusters of streets built round the remaining five collieries at different points of the town. Probably as a result of the proximity of the six pits, Stanley had grown over the years and become much larger than the normal pit village but remained just as dirty. Smut and grime coated every building and the pavements and back ways bore evidence of the jet-black phlegm the miners spat to clear their sooty lungs. Today, though, with the snow settling thick and glittering like diamond dust in the dull light, the town appeared almost clean for once. The bitter cold even managed to dilute the smell from the privies in the back yards. These were full to brimming and due to be emptied the following day by the scavengers with their long-handled shovels.

Eve approached the house by way of the back lane. No one in the family came home through the front door and even in time of crisis the unwritten rule held. She pushed open the rickety wooden gate into the back yard and passed the brick privy and the small washhouse-cum-coalhouse next to it.

The back door, like that of any other in the neighbourhood, was never locked, and she stepped straight into the small scullery off the kitchen. Facing her was an old wooden chair without a back, on which boots were cleaned, and above this a row of pegs hung. In this confined space her father and brothers stripped off their filthy pit clothes each evening, whatever the weather, and washed in the tin bowl waiting for them on the backless chair which Eve had filled with warm water. When they had dressed in their spare set of clothing hanging on the pegs and come through to the warmth of the kitchen, she would take the pile of trousers and jackets out into the back lane and beat the coal dust out of them. Then they would take their place on the pegs ready for the next shift.

Eve paused, her eyes on the pegs. The sick fear she had been battling with throughout the long hours at the pit gates rose to the fore. *They had to be all right, they had to be. Anything else was unthinkable.* She crossed her arms over her middle as though she had the stomach ache, swaying slightly as she closed her eyes and prayed a frantic prayer consisting of muddled words and phrases. Her da, her lovely da. And Frank, he was only twenty-one, and William just eighteen.

After a few moments she raised her head, an inner voice telling her she had to be strong. She wanted to lay her head on her arms and give vent to the tears which had been choking her all day but she must not. She must not cry. If she cried, it would mean there was something to cry about and she didn't know that yet. She mustn't tempt fate.

She wiped her feet on the old cork mat, opened the scullery door and stepped up into the kitchen. Immediately the warmth from the range washed over her and again, as she glanced round the room, she wanted to cry. The open fireplace with its black-leaded hob, the oven to the right and rows of pans to the left, the gnarled wooden table covered with oilcloth beneath which six hard-backed chairs stood, the long wooden settle and her father's ancient armchair to one side of the fire – all took on a poignancy which she would have termed silly only yesterday.

She took off her hat and coat and threw them on the settle. The room was dark, the light almost gone even though it was only mid-afternoon. With the weather worsening outside, she lit the two oil lamps before seeing to the range fire which had nearly gone out.

The dough was ruined. She stared at it. But it would suffice for stottie cake, she couldn't waste it. She'd intended to make a pot pie for dinner with the steak and kidney she'd bought from the butcher the day before, but there was no time for that now before the girls got home. She'd make one tomorrow. Her da and the lads would likely need a good hot meal once they were home. For tonight Nell and Mary would have to be content with the last of the bread from yesterday, along with the remainder of the cheese and chitterlings. She had some pork fat on the slab in the pantry too, they could dip the bread in that if it was too dry. Tonight would have to be a make-and-mend meal, as her mother had been wont to say on the occasions she'd spring-cleaned.

Mam, oh, Mam.

The longing for her mother's arms about her hadn't been so fierce in years. Quickly she busied herself with practicalities. Taking the big black kettle from the hob she went into the scullery and out into the back yard, gasping as the cold and snow hit her. After filling the kettle she returned it to the hob. The fire was now blazing but she stoked it up still more, putting plenty of coal on. Her father and brothers being miners, coal was never in short supply.

Returning to the yard, she filled the scullery bucket with water. If the tap froze it took ages to melt with bits of burning paper pushed up the spout and experience had taught her that a full bucket was the minimum required for cooking, drinking and washing.

The kettle was boiling and the table laid for tea when her sisters came running into the kitchen ten minutes later.

'Hey, hey, hey!' Eve stopped them, pointing to their snowy boots. 'Wipe your feet, both of you. What do you think the mat's for in the scullery?'

'Is it true?' Nell, who was two years younger than Eve but a head taller and nearly double her size in width, which made her appear far older than her eleven years, had been crying. It was evident in her pink-rimmed eyes and red nose. 'The fall at the pit? Is it true?'

'Go and wipe your feet.' Eve ushered her sisters back into the scullery but as they went, she said, 'Aye, Nell, I'm afraid it's true. Now come and take your things off and sit down. Da and the lads are probably quite safe but we won't know what's what for a while.'

'Oh, Eve.'

'Now don't start blubbing, that won't help anyone and Da'd be mad if we gave way. You know he would. They'll be all right. I'm sure they will.'

It wasn't until her sisters were seated at the table drinking the hot tea she always served up in winter when they got home from school that Mary said, 'Mrs Price's husband is down the pit. Someone came to tell her and she went home. Flora Davidson, one of the girls from the top class, came to sit with us. She was ever so bossy.'

Eve nodded but didn't comment.

'Hannah Walton lives next door to Flora and she said when Flora an' her mam an' da came round for New Year's Eve, Flora kissed Hubert,

Hannah's brother, on the mouth. Do you think she would? Hannah said you can have a bairn if you kiss a lad on the lips. Is that how babies are made?'

'Shut up, you.' Nell poked Mary in the ribs and none too gently. 'Who cares about that when Da and the lads are stuck down the pit?'

'Shut up yourself.' Mary tossed her blonde curls and glared at her older sister.

With only sixteen months separating Mary and Nell, rows were common. It didn't help that the two girls were so different, and not just in looks; with Nell being big and beefy and Mary as fragile as thistle-down, folk would be hard pressed to see any resemblance whatsoever. But the real difference lay in their personalities. Earth and wind, her father called the two, but while he would come down hard on Nell, even taking the belt to her on the odd occasion, Mary got away with murder. It wasn't fair, Eve thought now, because Nell was all heart whereas Mary – as her detachment from the present calamity showed – was more interested in herself than anything else.

Her voice flat, Eve said, 'Eat your tea,' and placed the bread and cheese and chitterlings in front of her sisters.

Wrinkling her small straight nose, Mary surveyed the plates in front of her. 'You said we were having pot pie tonight.'

'I haven't had time to cook with what's happened. If you don't want anything, that's fine, but you'll go to bed hungry, all right?' Setting the pork dripping on the table, she added, 'You can dip your bread in that if you want.'

Mary pouted, a prelude to her crying, an action which normally served to get her what she wanted – at least with her father and brothers. Glancing at Nell's scowling face and Eve's tight one, she appeared to change her mind and reached for a shive of the bread. Eve forced herself to eat a little too, even though every mouthful seemed to stick in her throat. She could not afford to get sick. She had to keep things ticking over as usual. It was what her da would expect of her.

At eight o'clock she could stand her sisters' bickering no longer and sent them to bed. It was an hour before their normal bedtime and they went under protest.

Eve stood at the kitchen door and watched Nell's fat figure, candle in hand, waddling indignantly up the stairs to the room the three of them shared, and Mary flouncing after her. Eve pressed her fingers tightly to her mouth as if to forbid its trembling. Was it only last night the three of them had had a crack with da and the lads, laughing and joking after the evening meal? She swallowed hard. And now . . .

Whirling round she busied herself tidying the kitchen before starting on a basketful of ironing. Once that was finished and the oats were soaking for the girls' porridge in the morning, the urge to find out what was happening at the pit became overwhelming.

Hoping Mrs McArthur was back, she stepped into the back yard. The snow was inches thick and the air so frosty it took her breath away. The clouds had dispersed and the night was clear, the sky pierced with twinkling stars. Everything seemed clean and bright and new. They had to be safe, she told herself for the umpteenth time. It was inconceivable that on a beautiful night like this everything wouldn't come right. There had been other falls, other times when it had taken the rescue teams ages to reach trapped men and they had been alive.

The McArthurs' house was in darkness but a light showed from the kitchen window in the house to Eve's left where the Finnigan family lived. Mr Finnigan worked at the South Moor Colliery so he wouldn't know anything. She was about to go back into the house when the Finnigans' door opened and Mr Finnigan stood there in his shirt sleeves with a mug of tea in his hand.

'I thought I saw someone out here. Any news, lass?' he called softly.

Eve shook her head. She liked Mr Finnigan, everyone did. He was young and smiley and his wife had had twin boys the year before last and was expecting again.

'Let us know when you hear, and if you need anything in the meantime, you know where we are.'

The kindness loosened her tongue. 'Thank you.'

He nodded at her, taking a sip of the tea, and he was still standing there watching her when she opened the back door and stepped into the house.

In the kitchen she stood biting at her fingernails. Coming to a decision, she lit the candle in the lads' candlestick and made her way upstairs by its light to where Mary and Nell were sleeping. The lads' room was across the landing – her father slept in a big brass bed in the front room – and she gazed at the closed door for a moment before going into the room she and her sisters shared. She made her way to the double bed where all three of them slept. Bending down, she shook Nell gently, saying, 'Nellie, lass, wake up. Wake up.'

'Wh-what?'

'Look, I'm going to the pit to see if there's any news. I might be awhile so don't worry if you wake up and I'm not back.'

'I'll come an' all.'

'Don't be daft, I need you to stay with Mary.'

'Take my coat then, it's warmer than yours. An' me scarf an' all, an' Mary's. It'll be bitter.'

'All right.' Her voice soft, Eve added, 'I'm sorry I was moany earlier, I didn't mean it.'

Now it was Nell who said, 'Don't be daft,' her breath a cloud of white in the icy room by the light of the candle.

Tucking the eiderdown round her sister's shoulders, Eve smiled and left the room on tiptoe.

In the kitchen she pinched out the candle and then put on Nell's coat and her own hat and a couple of scarves. The last thing she did was extinguish the oil lamp before she left the house for the white world outside it.

Chapter 2

The last man and boy had been brought up. Of the one hundred and ninety-eight trapped miners, only thirty had survived. The miners' local inspector, Frank Keegan, was acclaimed a hero for his part in rescuing twenty-six men, but on the day of the funeral when the whole town turned out to pay their respects, people were not thinking of the living so much as the dead.

The day passed in a dream for Eve. She knew it was happening. She knew she would never see her father and brothers again but, like everything else, it did not seem real. Since the first day, a part of her had been expecting her father to walk in like he always did, his thick droopy moustache permanently stained yellow from the nightly soaking it got in Burton's bass, calling for his dinner, the lads a step or two behind him, pushing and shoving each other. There would be noise and bustle and activity; the house came alive when the menfolk were home. But it had not happened. It would never happen again.

The three sisters went to Mrs McArthur's after the funeral. Larry McArthur had made his last journey from the pit face to the surface held close in his father's arms. Unlike many, Eve's father and brothers included, he had not been burnt but merely looked as though he had gone to sleep. It had taken three men to prise the body from his father and Mrs McArthur had told Eve that when Larry was laid out in the front room, her husband had sat up all night stroking his son's face and telling him it was time to wake up. Anne's husband, too, had been killed and the day he had been brought up, Anne had found out she was going to have a child. She had now moved back to live with her parents, along with Mrs McArthur's younger sister, Alice Turner, and her three bairns. Alice's husband and son of fourteen had both lost their lives in the accident.

It was Alice who now left a group of mourners tucking into the ample spread Mrs McArthur had put on to come over to where Eve was standing, Nell and Mary pressed into her side. Without any preamble, she said, 'You're the lassies from next door, aren't you?'

Eve nodded. She had seen Mrs McArthur's sister several times at Christmas jollifications and the like, and thought her as different to her sister as chalk to cheese.

'Our Cissy tells me you've got no family to take you in, is that right?'

Again Eve nodded.

Bending forward slightly, her voice low, Alice spoke into Eve's ear. 'Don't think our Cissy will be able to help. She's got a houseful now, what with me an' mine and Anne coming home an' all, and family comes first at such times.'

'I know that.'

'Aye, well, just so it's clear. Cissy's got a reputation for being a bit of a soft touch, as I'm sure you're aware.' Hard eyes glanced at Nell and Mary before coming to rest on Eve once more. 'So, what are you going to do then?'

Eve's fair skin was scarlet but her voice was steady and her tone brought a flush to the older woman's face. 'I think that is my business, Mrs Turner.'

'Well! I was only inquirin' out of politeness.'

The three of them watched Alice stalk off.

'You've upset her.' Nell's voice expressed satisfaction.

Eve made no reply to this. Mrs Turner was nasty, as nasty as Mrs McArthur was nice, but her words had brought to the fore the fear she had been trying to put to the back of her mind for days. She had told herself she couldn't think of anything until the funeral was over, but she knew at the heart of her she had only been trying to put off the moment when she would have to consider their future. She could get a job, she had every intention of doing that, and she would work till she dropped but even the best paying job for a girl of her age wouldn't keep the three of them fed and clothed and with a roof over their heads. They had to be out of the house by the end of the week and the landlord had already made a concession in letting them stay that long. If she didn't do something, it would mean the workhouse for Nell and Mary, and she couldn't bear that. The bit of money the furniture would bring wouldn't keep them in lodgings for long; the only item of any worth was her da's big brass bed.

She hadn't been aware of Mr Finnigan standing behind them so when he spoke in her ear, Eve jumped.

'I didn't realise the three of you had no kith and kin to help out, lass,' he said.

She swung round to see him looking at her with the kindly expression he had worn since the accident. Flustered, she stammered, 'N-no, we h-haven't.'

'No one at all? Not even in distant parts?'

'Not that we know of.'

'Dear, dear.' For once he wasn't smiling. 'Well, I hate to echo that woman's question' – the way he spoke indicated that his opinion of Mrs McArthur's sister reflected Eve's – 'but what are you going to do? Do you have somewhere to go, a place to live?'

She stared at him miserably then shook her head.

The hazel eyes passed over each young face in turn, lingering for a moment on Mary who smiled at him. She thought Mr Finnigan was lovely and so did all her friends. He always had time for a laugh and a joke when he passed them playing, and more often than not he had a bag of bullets in his pockets which he'd pass around. To keep his attention, she said, 'I saw Archy and Stephen yesterday coming back from the shop with Mrs Finnigan. You can't tell them apart, can you?'

'No, you can't. Even I have trouble at times and I'm their da. You wouldn't think that, would you, that I wouldn't know which was which?'

Mary giggled. 'They look like you, Mr Finnigan.'

'Do you think so?' He considered this with a tilt of his head before smiling. 'Well, thank you, lass.' Turning his glance on Eve, he said, 'When have you got to be out?'

'Friday.'

'You've asked for more time?'

'Aye. It was supposed to be last Friday.'

'Ah.' He nodded. 'Look, lass, I might be able to help.' It was a conspiratorial whisper and instinctively the three girls moved closer to hear what he was about to say. 'It so happens the wife's mother cooks and cleans for the vicar at St Andrew's, big vicarage he's got, off Front Street. Do you know it?'

'Yes, I know it.'

'Well, her legs are so bad she's had enough. They're particular, she says, the vicar and his wife, and there's the odd evening when she has to stay late to serve dinner if they've got guests. It's all got too much for her. She's told 'em she wants to leave a couple of times I know of. I could ask her to put in a good word for you if you think it'd suit.'

'Oh, Mr Finnigan.' Eve's face lit up.

'Mind, I can't guarantee anything, you'd have to go an' meet 'em, but with Mam having worked for them for donkey's and her vouching for you I can't see there'd be a problem. Not with a nice little lass like you.' He grinned at them all, ruffling Mary's curls as he spoke.

'How–how much would I get?' Whatever the vicar paid, it wouldn't be enough to rent somewhere.

As though he'd heard her thoughts, Mr Finnigan's voice gentled still more. 'I don't know, lass, but the three of you'll need somewhere to stay. Now although I can't offer anything long term, not with another bairn on the way, I could see me way clear to letting you bed down in the twins' room. It'd be a squeeze with their cots but we could fit a double bed in, like as not. It'd give you a breathing space, maybe until Nell here starts work an' there's more coming in. When will that be, lass?' he asked Nell.

'Not for two summers, when I'm thirteen.'

'How old are you now?' He seemed surprised.

'Eleven, Mr Finnigan.'

'You're a big girl, I thought you were twelve months older than that. Still, it might not be a problem, come to think of it. The babbie'll be in with us for a good while once it's born. We'll manage somehow, eh?' He turned back to Eve on the last words. 'Well, what do you think?'

'Oh, thank you, Mr Finnigan, thank you.' It was too good to be true. 'But why would you help us like this?'

His heavy lids lowered but when he met her gaze again his eyes were clear and wide. 'It's what neighbours are for, and don't forget you'll be paying board and lodging so you'll be doing your bit.'

'But would it be enough? For the three of us?'

'Don't worry your head about that. You'll be getting rid of your furniture, won't you? Maybe there'll be a piece or two the wife can use. We'll sort something out anyway.'

The mention of Mrs Finnigan checked the flood of relief. 'But what if she, Mrs Finnigan, what if she doesn't want us to stay?'

Josiah Finnigan surveyed the young faces in front of him. Softly, he said, 'She will do what I say.'

Eve blinked. Had she offended him? But then he was smiling again and she told herself she was imagining things. She glanced at Nell and Mary but they were both gazing at Mr Finnigan, their faces expressing a gratitude that verged on adoration.

By Wednesday night it was done. Their double bed had been squeezed into the twins' room, and their personal bits and pieces and spare clothes lay neatly stacked in Eve's father's hefty studded trunk which fitted under the bed. Her mother's family bible and her father's harmonica were wrapped in a piece of towelling at the bottom of this; she hadn't been able to bear the thought of these being sold with the rest of the house's contents – although not all had been collected by Pott's Emporium. Mr Finnigan and his wife had expressed a liking for her father's brass bed and the kitchen settle, along with her mother's clock and the china dogs which had stood on the mantelpiece above the range. Mrs Finnigan had kept all the blankets and sheets too, and Mr Finnigan, being the same height and build as Eve's brothers, said he could make use of the lads' spare set of clothing and Sunday rig-outs.

Mr Potts had given her two pounds for what remained, and that, he had tersely remarked when Eve had nervously said she'd expected more, was generous. She knew he had had his eye on the brass bed and had been put out when she said it was spoken for and so she had said no more. Two pounds was not to be sneezed at. She stared down at the one pound note, ten shilling note and four half-crowns before wrapping them in a handkerchief and depositing it next to the bible and harmonica. She repacked the trunk and closed it quietly – the twins were already asleep in their cots – and pushed it further under the bed. She stood up, smoothed her skirt and picked up the candlestick but did not immediately go downstairs to where the others were sitting in the kitchen.

Mrs Finnigan's mother had sent a message late morning saying she had handed in her notice at the vicarage, and the vicar and his wife had agreed to see Eve tomorrow morning at ten sharp for an interview. If she could get this job and begin on Monday she could start paying board to Mrs Finnigan for the three of them straightaway. She would feel better about things then. Although Mrs Finnigan hadn't said anything, Eve knew she didn't like them being here.

Eve stared across the room at the sleeping children, the flickering candle throwing shadows on the walls.

Was it because of the twins, because it was such a crush in the bedroom now? To get to the cots you had to scramble over the double bed and there wasn't an inch of spare space to walk. Edging in through the door was difficult enough. She could understand Mrs Finnigan wouldn't like this, and her expecting another bairn and all.

Should she say something? Slowly, as if her thoughts were impeding her walk, she moved out on to the landing. But if she did and Mrs Finnigan said she didn't want them, where would they go? And Mr Finnigan was acting as though everything was fine; in fact he had been as skittish as a bit lass when he'd helped them move in when he was home from the pit, joking with them and teasing Mary until she'd laughed so much she'd been in danger of wetting her knickers. No, Mr Finnigan didn't mind having them there, you could tell that.

She had to get downstairs. Mrs Finnigan was about to dish up the evening meal. When she reached the kitchen door, Eve took a deep breath before opening it. She would try to make Mrs Finnigan like her and she would tell Nell and Mary to do the same. They had to be allowed to stay here until Nell was old enough to start work, then they could find a room somewhere. If they all did their bit in the house and took the load off Mrs Finnigan, that would help, wouldn't it?

Eve had lain awake most of the night but when she awoke to a still dark room, she realised she must have dropped off eventually. She lay for a moment wondering what had woken her and then realised it was someone going downstairs, probably Mrs Finnigan. No doubt she rose first and saw to the range and such before she started getting Mr Finnigan's breakfast.

Remembering what she had determined the day before, she roused her sisters without waking the twins who were snuggled under the blankets in their cots. The three of them struggled into their clothes, no mean feat in the cramped conditions and with the merest gleam of light from the street lamp outside the window to light their fumblings. Mary was as uncooperative as normal, trying to slide back under the covers and complaining about the cold the whole time she dressed. But

Eve was resolute they were going to start as they meant to carry on, and this involved Mary doing her bit for once. Mrs Finnigan had looked very tired last night, not that that was anything unusual for a miner's wife. In any pit house, come bedtime you would find a banked down fire, a kitchen table set for morning and an exhausted looking woman.

Mary was still grumbling about being woken up as the three of them reached the kitchen door. Eve caught hold of her sister's arm in the dark hall and swung Mary round to face her although she could hardly make out her features in the blackness. 'One more word from you and I'll skelp you, you hear me?' she whispered angrily. 'I told you yesterday you were going to pull your weight here, and you will.'

'I never had to get up so early at home.'

'This isn't home and everything's different, and you ought to be thanking your lucky stars you've woken up here and not in the workhouse.'

'You're nasty, our Eve.'

'And don't start blubbing, it won't work with me, not like it did with Da. You'll do whatever Mrs Finnigan asks you to do and you'll be cheerful about it.' Then she sighed deeply and, her voice dropping, she said, 'Come on, be a good girl. I know you're missing Da and the lads but so are me and Nell, have you considered that? We've all got to make the best of things. We want to stay together, don't we?'

'Aye.' It was sulky.

'Well then. Stop acting like a baby.'

She sensed rather than saw Mary's flounce. Her fingers itching to slap her sister, Eve opened the kitchen door. The slight figure of Mrs Finnigan was standing at the range stirring a pan of porridge, and like yesterday it struck Eve that Mr Finnigan's wife didn't look old enough to be married in spite of having two bairns and expecting a third.

Mrs Finnigan turned at their entrance, her small heart-shaped face expressing her surprise. 'What are you doing up so early?'

'We wondered if we could help, Mrs Finnigan.'

'Help? How?' Mrs Finnigan's voice was flat.

'I don't know. Getting the coal in, seeing to the breakfast, anything.'
When Mrs Finnigan said nothing, Eve continued, 'You and Mr Finnigan
have been so kind letting us stay but I know it will mean more work
and we don't want you to have to look after us. We'll all help in the
morning and Nell and Mary will do any chores you want doing once
they're home from school and at weekends, and me too once I'm back
from work. I can help with the twins if you like, I'm used to bairns.
Mary was only four when Mam died.'

As Eve had been speaking Mrs Finnigan's face had relaxed a little
but her voice was still stiff when she said, 'There will be more to do,
that's for sure.' She turned back to the stove.

'I know and we want to help, don't we?' She turned to Nell and
Mary, the former nodding vigorously and the latter less enthusiastically.
'We'll do anything. Before' – she had been going to say Mr Finnigan
but changed it to – 'you said we could come here, I was at my wits'
end, Mrs Finnigan. I couldn't see a way out, everything was black. But
now, well, we're so grateful.'

Again Mrs Finnigan looked at her, a long look this time. Then she
said, 'If you're going to be staying here I don't think we can stand on
formality, do you? My name is Phoebe. And the porridge bowls are on
the dresser.'

Ten minutes later Josiah Finnigan came downstairs, and Nell had just
finished telling them a funny story about something that had happened
the day before at school and they were all laughing. Eve's face was soft
as she looked at her sister. Nell was very good at acting the clown when
the occasion warranted it, and she had a way of drawing out the comedic
in the most ordinary happenings. Their father had always maintained
Nell could make the devil himself laugh if she put her mind to it.

Eve saw Mr Finnigan's eyes go to his wife who was still smiling.
Their gaze held for a moment and then Josiah said softly, 'This is nice,
everyone having a crack in the morning. I can think of worse ways to
start the day.' His eyes still on Phoebe, he added, 'That porridge smells
good, lass.'

'You'd better sit yourself down and have some then. Eve will pour you a cup of tea now it's mashed.'

As Eve did as she was told, she breathed out a silent sigh of relief. Mrs Finnigan was different to how she had been the night before and Mr Finnigan's face had shown he was relieved too. Everything was going to be all right.

By the time Eve left the house later that morning for her appointment with the vicar, her stomach was churning with nerves at the forthcoming interview. It didn't help that the day was dull and bitterly cold, the sky so low it seemed to be resting on the rooftops and the whole world grey. It had snowed on and off for the last few days, thawed, frozen, then snowed again, but overnight the frost had been severe and now the ground beneath her feet was a sheet of ice.

Mrs Finnigan's mother opened the door immediately when Eve walked round to the back of the vicarage and knocked on the kitchen door as had been arranged. 'Come in, lass, come in.' Mrs Preston was as small as her daughter but much older than Eve had expected, she must have had Phoebe late in life. 'By, it's treacherous out, isn't it? I won't be sorry not to have to turn out of a morning after the weekend, I tell you.'

The kitchen was large and well furnished and everything was spotlessly clean. Eve rubbed her boots carefully on the mat as Mrs Preston went on, 'The vicar is in his study. Mrs Cunningham, his wife, is out. She's often out. In fact she's rarely in.'

The sniff that followed this suggested Mrs Preston did not approve of the vicar's wife's absences but she said no more on the subject before continuing, 'The vicar said to show you over the house and explain what your duties would be, should you suit. You'll see him after.' Moving her head closer as though someone might be listening, she added, 'He's a grand man, the vicar. A scholar, you know? He likes everything just so and why not?'

Eve nodded. She didn't know what else to do.

'She, Mrs Cunningham, won't interfere with the running of the house so you'll have no worries on that score. She's chairwoman of umpteen different goings-on and a leading light in the town. A real do-gooder, you know what I mean?'

Again Eve nodded. She wondered why Mrs Preston didn't like the vicar's wife. Her tone had been quite different when she talked about the vicar, reverential even.

Ten minutes later they were back in the kitchen and Eve's head was swimming with the list of dos and don'ts Mrs Preston had impressed on her. The house was beautiful. Three of the five bedrooms were not used; the vicar occupied one at the front of the house and his wife one at the back overlooking the grounds. But the drawing room, dining room and breakfast room, along with the two bedrooms and the vicar's study – the only room Eve had not seen yet – had to be dusted and cleaned daily. She would be responsible for the laundry, ordering and buying food from the tradesmen who called at the vicarage every morning, and the cooking and serving of all meals apart from the late supper the vicar and his wife liked before retiring. This always consisted of cold meats, cheese and pickle and a light pudding which Eve must leave on covered plates on the cold slab in the pantry.

'The tradesmen?' Eve's voice was low, almost a whisper. 'How will I know what to buy? I don't know what the vicar and Mrs Cunningham like.'

'Don't worry your head about things like that. I'll tell you every-thing before you start. You'll soon pick up what you don't know.' Mrs Preston patted her arm. 'I've told the vicar he might have to be a little patient at first.'

This was clearly meant to reassure her. It didn't. Eve was feeling utterly overwhelmed.

'Now you must make sure you're here in the morning by six thirty, lass. You'll need to light the fires in the drawing room, the breakfast room and the vicar's study, and see to the range. The dining room you can leave till mid-morning. The house has to be warm by the time they come down for their breakfast at eight o'clock. They don't stand on ceremony when it's just the two of them but occasionally one of the married children come with their bairns and then they breakfast in the dining room. Everything has to be in covered dishes then, like the gentry do.'

And so the instructions went on.

When Mrs Preston eventually knocked on the study door and ushered her into the vicar's presence, Eve was half hoping she wouldn't be offered the job. She felt sick with agitation and fear, and now she had to face this paragon who was barely human, if Mrs Preston was to be believed.

Half an hour later when she left the study, she felt a little more re-assured. She had found the vicar to be a nice man, kindly. He had a funny, precise way of speaking and no northern burr to his voice, but he had smiled at her and had seemed concerned when she had related what had brought her here.

'Dreadful business, the accident. Dreadful.' He had shaken his bald pink head. 'And you say this neighbour and his wife have taken you and your sisters into his home? Christian charity in operation. Good, good.'

He had informed her she would begin work at a weekly wage of six shillings for a six and a half day week. She would leave the vicarage at two in the afternoon on a Sunday. She would eat her midday meal in the kitchen once she had finished serving in the dining room.

Oh, and he would review her wage once the initial trial period was over, he'd added as she left the room. He had not mentioned how long he expected the trial period to last, but Eve did not mind. She had a *job*, that was the important thing. Now she could give Mr and Mrs Finnigan payment for their board and lodging. She didn't mind what she did, how hard she worked or how long the hours as long as she and her sisters could stay together.

Chapter 3

It was a blazing June. Spring had been cold and wet with acres of mud, but with the arrival of the long days and short nights the essence of summer was suddenly everywhere and the temperature had steadily risen throughout the month. Now the sunshine and dry air created trembling heat hazes and by midsummer's day everyone was longing for a good thunderstorm to clear the air. None more so than poor Phoebe. Josiah's wife was now in her last week of pregnancy and constantly exhausted, her tiny frame dominated by her huge belly.

Eve had become fond of Phoebe whom she had found to be very childlike in spite of having just had her twentieth birthday at the end of May. Phoebe constantly needed her husband's approval in everything she did, and the more Eve had got to know the couple, the more she had been drawn to Phoebe and the less she had warmed to Josiah. She couldn't put her finger on why exactly. Josiah was always friendly and Mary blatantly hero-worshipped him, partly due, Eve suspected, to the little presents of sweets and chocolate he always seemed to have in his pockets for the child.

When she turned into the back lane her nose wrinkled at the stink from the privies. No amount of hot ashes could neutralize the smell of human excrement with the heat so intense. She thought of the Cunninghams' garden, the herbaceous borders full of lemon verbena, mignonette, lavender and all manner of sweet scented flowers, and the walls thick with climbing roses and jasmine. As had happened more often of late, her mind moved along an uncomfortable tangent. Why should families of ten or twelve be living in four rooms – two, some of them – with nowhere for the bairns to play but the narrow back lanes and alleys, and people like the vicar and his wife have all that space and a beautiful garden they rarely ventured into?

She knew what the vicar's answer would be should she put the question to him. She had got to know his opinion about lots of things over the last months by listening to snippets of his conversation with friends who called at the house.

The vicar was of the mind that God decreed one's station in life and if one was wise, one stuck to it. The poor, she had heard him declare when a group of them were discussing the Royal Commission's proposals regarding the workhouses, were naturally of lesser intelligence and morally and physically enfeebled. Therefore it was every good Christian brother's duty to treat them with kindness but firmness. She hadn't agreed with this. She was discovering she didn't agree with much that the vicar said.

She reached the gate leading into the Finnigans' back yard. Even after four months it still felt strange not to be going next door, into the house where she had been born. Another family were living there now, they had moved in the day after she and her sisters had moved out. McCabe was their name and they seemed nice enough, although apparently Mr McCabe drank like a fish on pay day and his wife or one of the bairns had to go and get him out of the Frog and Fiddler every Friday night.

She was about to thrust open the gate when Nell, who had been playing with a group of bairns further up the lane, called her name. 'Eve! Eve, I've been waiting for you to come.'

As Nell reached her, Eve said quietly, 'Why aren't you inside helping Phoebe with the dinner? I told you she's ailing, what with the baby an' all. She looked bad this morning.'

'It wasn't me, Mr Finnigan said to play outside.' Nell's voice was indignant. 'Phoebe was in bed when me an' Mary got home from school, an' her mam was here. She's took the twins home with her.'

'Is the baby coming?'

'No, least I don't think so. Phoebe's just feeling tired with the weather an' all, her mam said. We stayed in the house till Mr Finnigan got home. The dinner was all ready to put in the oven, Phoebe's mam had done it. Mr Finnigan said Mary would help him see to it and set the table and everything an' I could go out to play. It wasn't me who wanted to go, Eve.'

'All right, all right.' Eve was frowning but not at Nell. She wished Josiah would not persist in making fish of one and fowl of the other, but it was obvious Mary was his favourite. Maybe he thought the younger one needed a father figure more but it wasn't the case. In spite of her size and bulk, Nell was still just a bairn. He sometimes slipped Mary a Saturday penny or two too, and was forever playing little games with her like shuggy boats when he crossed his knees and stuck a foot out and Mary clambered on to his foot and he held her hands as he hoisted her up and down. Admittedly he would find it hard to do that with Nell but if he couldn't do it for one he shouldn't do it for the other. She was going to have to say something. What, she didn't know, because she couldn't afford to offend him.

'Come on.' She smiled at her sister, tweaking the end of Nell's snub nose. 'Let's go and see what's what but quiet mind, Phoebe might still be asleep.'

They entered the scullery noiselessly and on opening the kitchen door found the room to be empty. Thinking that Josiah and Mary might be upstairs with Phoebe, Eve said to Nell, 'Put the kettle on, lass. I'll just go and see how Phoebe is and then I'll make a pot of tea. And check the oven, would you? Something smells nice.'

She was still talking as she stepped into the hall. She was conscious of a sound, a sort of a scuffle, and as her head turned to the front-room door, it opened and Josiah stood there, Mary just behind him. 'Oh.' Eve blinked. 'I thought you were upstairs.' The front room was Phoebe's pride and joy and sacrosanct, only used on high days and holidays. The day after they had moved in, Phoebe had taken them into the hallowed interior and proudly shown them the stiff horsehair suite, walnut china cabinet and enormous aspidistra on its small table which stood in the bay, the lace curtains behind it starched into permanent folds.

Josiah smiled. 'I was showing Mary Phoebe's figurines in the china cabinet, they fascinate her. Don't they, Mary?' he added, turning his head.

Eve looked at Mary. She was standing quite still and she looked a little white. 'Are you all right, hinny?' she said gently. 'You look peaky.'

'She's got the stomach ache.' Josiah still kept his eyes on Mary. 'That's why I suggested we look at the china cabinet, I thought it'd take her mind off how she was feeling. That's right, isn't it, lass?'

Mary nodded.

'It's likely the heat,' he continued, stepping forward. Eve moved aside. 'It's getting everyone down. I'm all for a bit of sunshine but you can have too much of a good thing.'

He was still smiling and Eve didn't know what had caused the odd feeling inside her, an uneasy odd feeling, but then Nell called that the cow heel pie was in danger of burning and should she lift it out of the oven. In the ensuing bustle to save their dinner, the moment was put aside.

Later that evening as Nell and Mary were getting ready for bed, Phoebe began to have pains and the midwife was called. At five o'clock in the morning Eve was woken by a baby's cry. She had been dozing on the settle with a blanket over her after keeping the midwife supplied with hot water and numerous cups of tea most of the night. Josiah was snoring gently in his armchair in front of the range.

When the midwife appeared to summon Josiah upstairs, he put out his hand for Eve to come too, and so she walked into the bedroom with him to see Phoebe cradling her new son in her arms. He looked to be a tiny baby but he had a lusty cry and Phoebe and the midwife were smiling.

'Another boy,' Phoebe said softly, stroking the small downy head. As Josiah kissed her and sat on the side of the bed, she looked at Eve. 'Josiah was hoping for a little lassie this time.'

Eve was surprised. Most mining families wanted lads who could earn good money down the pit when they grew up.

Josiah shook his head. 'As long as you and the baby were all right I said I didn't mind.'

'But you would have liked a girl.'

'Only if she looked like you.'

He kissed Phoebe again and Eve smiled at them. 'He's a bonny baby. Have you got a name for him?'

'Josiah.' Phoebe's voice was firm. 'With the twins we felt it would be favouring one over the other if one had their da's name.'

Eve nodded her understanding. Phoebe looked exhausted and the bedroom smelt strongly of warm stale air and blood. It was making her feel a little nauseous and after clearing her throat, she said, 'Would you like a cup of tea and something to eat?'

'Just a cup of tea please.' Phoebe slid down in the bed a little and shut her eyes. 'Mam will be coming later before Nell and Mary leave for school. She'll see to me.'

After seeing the midwife out, Eve put the kettle on the hob and then walked into the yard where the pink light of dawn was streaking the sky. The air was cooler than in the house although the smell from the privies in the lane was strong. Again she thought of the Cunninghams and their world, a world devoid of the odours associated with human beings being crammed in together like sardines in a can. Everyone should be able to live like the vicar and his wife.

A blackbird's song pierced the early morning and a moment later she heard Josiah come downstairs. Turning quickly she went back into the house to make the tea, thinking as she did so, I must ask Mary if she's feeling well this morning, she looked peaky last night.

As it turned out, the morning proved so hectic before she left for work, it went right out of her head.

Nell cast a sidelong glance at Mary as they left the yard to walk to school. The dust was thick in the lane and she kicked at it with the toe of her boot as she said, 'What's up with you? You're quiet this morning. Don't you like the new babbie?'

Mary shrugged her thin shoulders. 'It's all right I suppose.'

'Worried it'll push your nose out of joint with Mr Finnigan?'

'No, he don't even like babies. He told me so.'

'Huh.' Nell's jealousy was to the fore this morning. She knew Mary had a shiny sixpence in her pocket that Mr Finnigan had given her because it had fallen out on the floor the night before when Mary had flung her frock down as she'd got ready for bed.

'It's true. He said you just shove milk in one end and it comes out of the other and that's all there is to babies.'

'What's the matter then?'

'Nothin'.'

'Nothing? Come off it, you're in a mood about something.'

'I'm not.'

Just the fact her sister had spoken quietly rather than snapping at her to mind her own business told Nell that Mary wasn't herself. As they came to the end of the lane and passed the Methodist chapel, her voice gentled as she said, 'You got belly ache or something?'

'A bit.'

'You should have said before we left. They'd have let you stay off school for a day.'

'I don't want to stay off school.'

'Well, if you've got the belly ache—'

'*I said I'd got it a bit, all right?*' Then, as if realising her voice had been

30

sharp, Mary added, 'You can come with me to the shop on the way home and get some sweets.'

'With the sixpence Mr Finnigan gave you?'

Mary nodded.

'He never gives me anything.'

'I've told you I'll share an' I will if you say nowt.'

'Why aren't you supposed to say anything to anyone when he gives you money? I don't see why it has to be a secret.'

Again Mary shrugged. Her voice low and without looking at her sister, she said, 'You promised, Nellie.'

'Aye, I know, but Eve's different, isn't she? It's not like letting on to Phoebe.'

'No one, Nellie.' They were approaching the school gates now and Mary sprinted forward. 'There's Hannah. I'll see you later at home time and we'll go to the shop.'

Later, once the register had been taken and the class were settled writing a story about an adventure they would like to have, Mary sat chewing on the end of her pencil. She shouldn't have told Nell about the sixpence being from Mr Finnigan but once she'd seen it, what else could she have done? But Nellie wouldn't let on, not if she knew she was going to get some sweets. She stared at the couple of lines she had written but her mind was a million miles away from what she was supposed to be doing.

She raised her head, glancing round at the rows of wooden desks and Mrs Price dressed all in black at the front of the class. The room was already warm and muggy and as her gaze went to the window she wished she was outside.

She hadn't liked what Mr Finnigan had done to her last night. It hadn't been like the kissing and cuddling or when he stroked her arms and belly when she sat on his lap and he moved her up and down over the hard thing in his trousers. Last night he had hurt her when he'd put his hand inside her knickers and pushed his finger into her private place. She liked being his special girl, she did, but this new thing had frightened her and last night she had been too sore to pee before she went to bed. She was still sore.

Tears smarted and she blinked them away. She wriggled slightly on the hard wooden seat, trying to get comfortable, but the ache between her legs was still there.

Why hadn't Mr Finnigan stopped when she had wanted him to? But he had said she would like it. She hadn't liked it, it had been horrible, and she had been glad when Eve and Nell had come and he'd had to stop. But he *had* given her a whole sixpence.

Her small fingers closed over the coin in her pocket and she felt the thrill of her wealth again. And he had promised to buy her an even nicer hair ribbon than Hannah's when it was her birthday in a few weeks' time. She cast a sidelong glance at her friend. Hannah's new red ribbon had been a bone of contention for days. And it was true what she'd said to Nell, Mr Finnigan didn't like babies and with the new bairn being another little lad she would still be his special girl.

'Mary Baxter?'

She became aware Mrs Price was frowning at her and quickly bent her head to her work. Mrs Price wasn't as nice as she had been before her husband was killed at the pit. These days she was moany and her face was all tight and not a bit pretty. Mr Finnigan said *she* was pretty, bonny he called her. Like the fairy queen in that fairytale he'd told them the other night.

The thought went some way to mollifying the aggrievement she'd felt after the fright of the night before, and with Mrs Price's eyes still on her she gave all her attention to the story and began to write.

The summer was a hot one relieved only by the odd shower or two which had barely dampened the thirsty ground. The water cart had been out often spraying the dusty dry roads. But now it was the last week of September. The fields of corn that Eve had passed on her way to work now lay fallow, and the mornings had become fresh with mists that hinted of chilliness. The field behind the Cunninghams' property saw flocks of swallows gathering to migrate, their screaming cries becoming more urgent as the month progressed, and the garden was full of bumblebees and butterflies making the most of the gentle sunshine of late summer.

The vicarage's apple and plum trees at the end of the garden were weighed down with fruit and the day before, the gardener had propped his ladder against the gnarled trunks and worked most of the day filling basket after basket with blushing apples and Victoria plums. To Eve's delight Mrs Cunningham had given her two baskets to take home that morning, on top of which she'd told her she could leave at midday rather than two o'clock as was usual on her half-day due to the fact the vicar and herself were going out to lunch after church.

As she walked home Eve found herself smiling in anticipation of the pleasure the windfall of fruit would give to the household. There hadn't been too much to smile about lately. The new baby had proved to be a fretful child who cried most of the night and Phoebe was exhausted and tearful. The twins were with Phoebe's mother more than they were at home, often staying overnight, and she knew for a fact that Josiah and Phoebe quarrelled once they were alone at night. She could hear them through the wall as she lay beside Nell and Mary trying to sleep. Mary . . .

She stopped for a moment, putting the heavy baskets down at her feet and flexing her fingers. She was approaching the grid of terraced streets of the town now; the nice part of the walk – as she always termed the distance from the vicarage to this point – was over. She stood gazing down the main street from which the terraces branched off on either side but she wasn't really seeing the town, her mind was occupied with Mary. She'd been worried about her sister for weeks but she couldn't put her finger on why. Certainly Mary was a bit up and down lately and moody with it, but then the child had always been something of an attention-seeker and with her blonde curls and big blue eyes people tended to indulge her. If she had asked Mary once over the last weeks if she was all right, she'd asked her a hundred times, and always the answer was the same. She was fine. Nell had assured her there was no trouble at school and Phoebe said Mary always did her share in the house without being prompted, but still . . .

Eve picked up the baskets and walked on. In spite of the September day having a definite nip to it she could feel the perspiration on her brow and her arms felt as if they had been stretched another six inches by the time she reached the back lane. She would be glad to get home.

The kitchen was empty; clearly the others weren't back from chapel yet. A new parson had started at the chapel recently after the old minister had retired and gone to live with his sister down south, and although he was nice enough, his sermons were twice as long as old Parson Riley's. Eve placed the baskets in a corner of the room and sank down on to a chair, only to rise again in the next moment. She'd brush her hair and change into her Sunday frock before everyone came back; she would be ready to help with the dinner then. Phoebe's mother had hurt her back at the end of last week and couldn't have the twins which meant everything was noise and activity once the lively two-year-olds were home.

She walked into the hall and reached the foot of the stairs before a sound above her alerted her to the fact she was not alone. She could never explain afterwards why she didn't call out and ask who was there; maybe in the back of her mind she imagined Phoebe might have stayed at home with little Josiah to try and get some sleep, but if so it was not a conscious thought. Whatever, she climbed the stairs soundlessly and when she reached the small landing the sound came again, a kind of grunt followed by Josiah's voice saying, 'That's it, that's it, keep going, lass.'

She might still have gone into the bedroom she shared with her sisters and the twins and begun to change, but for Mary's voice, small and flat, reaching her. 'My hand's aching.'

The door to Josiah and Phoebe's room was open a crack and she crossed the landing, her heart beginning to thump. She pushed it wide open. Josiah was sitting on the edge of the bed, his trousers unbuttoned, with Mary standing between his legs. Eve looked at the thing in Mary's hand; it seemed to have a life of its own because even as her sister saw her and sprang back from Josiah, it continued to twitch and move.

'No!' She didn't recognise the cry as coming from herself. Her fingers reached for the thick jug standing in a bowl on top of the small table by the door, and she threw it as hard as she could. Josiah was fumbling with his clothing and didn't see it coming. It hit the side of his head, sending him sprawling on to the floor where the water it had contained mingled with the blood pouring from the wound to his scalp.

Mary was screaming but as Josiah rolled over and then sat up, Eve didn't wait to see what he would do. Grabbing her sister's hand she pulled her out of the room and down the stairs. In the kitchen she had to shake Mary hard to stop her screaming and then the child burst into noisy sobs just as Phoebe and Nell and the twins walked in.

'What on earth . . .' Nell was open-mouthed. 'What's happened? I thought Mary stayed at home because she had a headache.'

Phoebe's face, too, was a study in surprise, but before Eve could answer she heard Josiah pounding down the stairs. He burst into the kitchen holding a thick wad of blood-soaked towelling to the side of his head, and immediately Eve sensed he was going to try and brazen it out. The gasps of shock from Phoebe and Nell and cries of fright from the twins at the sight of their father's blood-splattered clothes came in unison with Josiah shouting, 'Aye, you might well look like that. See what that little scut has done to me? She tried to brain me' – he pointed at Eve – 'and all because I found the other one pilfering when I nipped back from church to make sure she was all right. At our chest of drawers in the bedroom she was, bold as brass.'

'You liar.' Eve could hardly believe her ears. 'You were . . . I found you . . .' Her horror and disgust worked against her, the enormity of what she'd seen tied her tongue.

Josiah was quick to press his advantage. 'That's right, think up some story or other, but the truth of it is I caught her red-handed and you know it. I'd got hold of her and she was yelling her head off and the next thing I know Eve's joining in.' He was speaking to Phoebe now, who had the baby in her arms and the twins pressed into her skirts, wailing. 'Hit me with the water jug and damn near did for me an' all. Look.' He moved the towel to expose a deep cut at the side of his head which immediately oozed blood.

'I wish I had done for you.' Eve found her tongue, her voice harsh. 'You're filthy, filthy. He was making Mary . . .' She didn't know how to explain it, couldn't find the words to describe what she'd seen. She had always known that lads were different to lassies, of course, and she had seen the twins' naked bodies and little Josiah's too, but never a full-grown man's genitalia. Her father and her brothers had been private in their habits. She knew her mother had often washed the backs of the menfolk when they'd had their washdowns in the old tin bath in front of the range, but she and her sisters had not been allowed in the kitchen until the menfolk were clothed again. And from the time her mother had died she had prepared the bath and then left the kitchen until she was called once they were dressed. That this thing males had between their legs could assume such a monstrous size was outside her comprehension. 'He was making Mary do something to him,' she finished thickly. 'Wasn't he?' She turned to her sister, holding her arms as she looked down into Mary's white face. 'Tell them, lass. Tell them what he was making you do.'

Mary stared back at her. She had stopped crying now but her eyes were luminous and glittering and she looked scared to death. 'I — I can't.' And she began to sob again.

Her voice quieter, Eve said, 'It's not your fault, hinny. All right? It's not your fault, it's his.' Straightening, she looked steadily at Phoebe. 'He was making her touch him there, making her hold his . . .' She gestured with her hand.

Josiah attempted to look outraged. 'What did you say?'

Undeterred, Eve glared straight into his red face. 'You were and you know it. You're disgusting. Now I know why you wanted us to come and live here.'

'You ungrateful little scut.' Josiah looked as though he wanted to

36

strike her and Nell must have thought so too, because she moved quickly to stand with her sisters.

'He's been giving Mary money. We've bought sweets with it.'

Nell's whisper made Eve stare at her. 'What did you say?'

'He's given her thruppenny bits, sixpences an' all. She said it was a secret and she couldn't tell. He told her not to tell.'

Phoebe appeared transfixed by what had been said. She had not moved or spoken, and now her eyes went to her husband once more. And it was to his wife that Josiah said, 'They're lying, damn 'em, but now I come to think of it there might have been money missing from my pocket now and then. Perhaps they're all in on it, the thieving. Likely it's been going on since they came. I can't find me granda's pocket watch for a start, happen that's been sold or put in the pawn.'

'You're lying.' Eve's voice was stronger, it rang in the kitchen. 'We haven't taken anything and you know it. You've been interfering with my sister and I'll have the law on you.'

'The law, is it?' He advanced a pace but although Nell and Mary cowered, Eve faced him, her eyes blazing. 'We'll see about who calls the law in, girl. First the thieving and then attacking me like that. I'll see you go down the line for this little lot, you see if I don't. And then them two will be for the workhouse. Thought about that, have you? And they can rot there for all I care. Last time I try to help anyone, that's for sure.'

An unnameable sensation was flooding through Eve. Never before had she wanted to inflict harm on another human being, but the urge to tear and rake at Josiah's face, to annihilate him from the face of the earth, was so strong she could taste it. Her rage was scorching and she could see Josiah had read what was in her mind and it disconcerted him. He stepped back, glaring at her. 'It'll be my word against yours, remember that, and I say she and maybe the pair of you too have been stealing from us. We took you in out of the goodness of our hearts, got you a job at the vicarage, treated you like our own, and this is how you repay us.'

'You're unnatural, twisted.' The words were fired at him. Eve seemed to have grown inches, so rigidly did she hold herself. 'To make a little bairn do that. What else have you done—'

'Stop it.' Phoebe's voice was thin and piercing. It brought all eyes to her. 'Stop this.'

'He's lying, Phoebe, I swear it.'

Phoebe's eyes flickered as they met Eve's.

She knows. Eve stared at Josiah's wife. The reaction, slight as it had been, betrayed Phoebe's knowledge of the truth.

But then Phoebe shook her head. 'You're wrong. This is a mistake.'

'I know what I saw and it's not a mistake. He was—'

'No.' Phoebe's face was drained of colour and she was speaking through stiff lips but her voice held a sharpness which belied her slight, girlish exterior. 'Whatever you think you saw you've put the wrong interpretation to it.'

'That's right, it wasn't like—'

'This is a respectable home.' Phoebe cut through Josiah's blustering as though he hadn't spoken. 'We're respectable people. My mam and da' – she took a gulp of air – 'they're respectable too. I've got bairns. I won't have our good name dragged through the mud.'

'You can't be taking his side.' Eve stared at the woman she had come to know and have affection for over the last months. She was shocked and hurt but above all angry. 'You can't, Phoebe, not after what he's done.'

'He's my husband.'

'He's a pervert. A man who likes little children, little girls. He's sick, dirty.'

Again Phoebe's eyes flickered. 'I won't have you saying these things.'

'But you know it's true. You do, don't you, Phoebe?'

'No.' Even Phoebe's lips were white. 'No, I don't, and I won't have us cut off and shunned by everyone, I won't. I-I've noticed things going missing. House-housekeeping money out of my purse.' Josiah was staring at his wife but Phoebe did not glance his way.

Harshly, Eve said, 'You're making this up.'

'If you go to the police station I shall swear it's true.'

'You'd really do that?'

Phoebe's chin rose. 'Aye.' Her eyes never flinched from Eve's as she repeated, 'Aye, I would really do that. And with your attack on Josiah you would most likely be facing a prison sentence, and Nell and Mary, like Josiah said, would be put in the workhouse.'

Eve attempted to say something but the words stuck in her throat. She felt sick with disgust and disillusion.

The look on her face caused Phoebe's countenance to crumple and her voice held a pleading quality when she next spoke. 'Please, Eve, for the sake of the bairns.'

'Whose bairns?' Eve's voice was no longer like that of a thirteen-year-old girl's but someone far older. 'Your boys? And what of Mary? She's a bairn too.'

'You heard what she said.' There was relief as well as bravado in Josiah's voice. 'We're on to you and the best thing you can do is clear off before you find yourself in real trouble.'

Phoebe turned her head and looked at her husband. The look shocked Eve as much as anything that had gone before. She would not have thought gentle Phoebe capable of such hatred.

'Please, Eve, please don't make me tell no one.' Mary was tugging at her sleeve, whispering. 'I couldn't bear it, I couldn't. Don't make me. I'll run away, I will.'

'It's all right.' She patted her sister's thin arm, her mind racing. She couldn't bear the thought that Josiah was going to get away with what he had done, but what was the alternative? If Phoebe stuck to her guns, it would be their word against the married couple's, and with Mary and Nell having bought sweets for who knew how long, it wouldn't look good. Oh, why hadn't Mary confided in her? How long had it been going on? What had he done to her? How could Phoebe lie for him when she'd looked as though she hated him? Eve felt sick, bewildered. If she reported Josiah to the law and it went against her, who would take care of Mary and Nell? Phoebe was right, it would be the workhouse for them, the very thing she had fought against all along. Looking at Josiah's wife, she said, 'You'll live to regret this day.'

A spasm passed over Phoebe's face but she did not answer.

'Go and get your things together.' Eve pushed Mary and Nell in front of her as she spoke and then turned to tell Josiah what she thought of him one last time, but as she did so he sat down suddenly on one of the hard-backed chairs, saying, 'I feel bad.'

That gash would need stitching. The thought brought little satisfaction, she wished him dead, but as she followed her sisters out of the kitchen, she noticed Phoebe made no move towards her husband.

She hoped the pair of them drowned in misery from now on. As she climbed the stairs her eyes were dry but her heart was weeping for her sister. For that man to take a little lass who had just lost her da and brothers and betray her trust the way he'd done was wicked, evil, and Phoebe was as bad. Protecting him like that, she was as bad as him.

The anger kept her going while they packed their belongings into three parcels she made by ripping and knotting the sheets off the double bed. Apart from telling Mary and Nell the large trunk was too heavy to carry and they would have to send for it later when they were settled somewhere, Eve said nothing. For once her sisters were silent too. It was as though the three of them had agreed by unspoken consent that any questions and answers would be kept for when they had left the house. The only sound in the room was Mary sniffing.

When they were ready, the bible and her father's harmonica at the bottom of her parcel, Eve squared her shoulders. She didn't know where they were going to go or how they were going to manage without a penny to their name but they couldn't spend another night under this roof. Anything, *anything* would be preferable to that.

'Here.' She stripped the blankets from the bed, folded them and gave one each to Mary and Nell and kept a third for herself. 'We'll likely need these and they're ours anyway.'

They picked up their parcels and went down the stairs. Phoebe was standing in the hall. 'Where are you going to go?' she asked quietly as Eve met her eyes.

Eve did not answer this. What she did say was, 'I shall send for my father's trunk later.' She reached for her hat and coat hanging on one of the pegs in the hall and passed Mary hers. Nell had kept hers on since coming home from church.

'Here.' Phoebe held out a handful of coins. In answer to Eve's raised eyebrows, she said awkwardly, 'It's your wage for last week which you gave me on Friday. I – I thought you'd need it.'

Eve stared at her. She was not going to refuse the money, they would need it. Besides which, she had earned it. She took the coins without comment, slipping them into the pocket of her coat.

'Are you going to the vicarage?' Phoebe was blocking their path to the front door. 'Because if you say anything about Josiah to the vicar I'll do what I said, Eve. I mean it.'

Still Eve said nothing, staring into the face of the woman she had thought of as a friend until today. Phoebe's tone became soft, almost wheedling. 'Try to understand.'

'What do you want me to understand?' Eve pushed roughly past her and opened the front door, gesturing for Nell and Mary to step down into the street. 'That you're protecting him knowing he's done such a terrible thing? Because you do know, don't you, Phoebe? Am I supposed to understand that you're prepared to lie, to see me in gaol and Mary and Nell in the workhouse rather than speak the truth?'

Phoebe's face was stiff, her voice low but hard now. 'We took you in when you had nowhere to go. Don't forget that.'

'And you were paid for your trouble. You had the best of my parents' things and my wage each week. You haven't lost by it.'

They exchanged one last look and then Eve turned and followed Mary and Nell. The door banged shut behind her as she joined them on the pavement.

Chapter 4

They had reached the end of the street before Nell said, '*Are* we going to the vicarage, Eve?'

Eve shook her head but did not speak. Most folk were home from church now and although the street was not as crowded with bairns playing their games as on a weekday, there were still enough around to gape at them as they walked along carrying their parcels. She purposely did not glance at the houses they passed. She didn't want to risk catching anyone's eye. As they turned into Front Street and the Methodist chapel came into view, she saw Mr and Mrs McArthur standing talking to the new parson at the door to the chapel and kept her head down, breathing a sigh of relief once they were out of earshot. She didn't know what she would have said to anyone if they had stopped her. She needed to think things through before she talked to anyone.

'Where are we going then?' Nell's voice was small and choked.

'Don't cry, not now, neither of you.' Eve glanced at them once before staring ahead. Their frightened faces pained her. 'Wait till we get clear of any houses and into the country and then we'll talk.'

'Why aren't we going to the vicarage?'

Eve swallowed deeply. The question was understandable but all she wanted was to get somewhere quiet and find out exactly what had gone on with Mary. She was sick with fear at what Josiah might have done. As calmly as she could, she said, 'There's no point, Nell. The vicar – well, I know his views. He wouldn't take us in. He would be of the opinion the workhouse is there to cater for such a situation and we should be grateful for it. He's on the Board of Guardians.'

Nell said no more.

They walked steadily for some time and it said much for Mary's state of mind that she never spoke once, not even to complain her legs were aching or her parcel was heavy. The late September sun had little power to it and the walk in the fresh air would have been enjoyable under normal circumstances. Small flowers starred the green banks on either side of the dusty lane they came to, blackbirds and starlings squawking and quarrelling over the ripe blackberries covering the hedgerow. It was the sight of the berries that prompted Eve to say, 'We'll stop here for a bit. Are you hungry?'

Her sisters nodded warily. It was as though they weren't sure if hunger were permissible at such a time.

'We'll pick some blackberries in a minute, but first' – Eve plumped down on the grass, putting her parcel behind her and patting the bank either side of her – 'we have to talk.'

Mary started to cry but she sat down. Eve put her arms round her sister as Nell joined them. 'Don't cry, hinny. This isn't your fault, none of it, understand? It was him. He was wrong to do what he did. I have to understand what happened though, Mary. You must tell me it all, from the beginning. It's important.'

Eve only had the sketchiest knowledge of the facts of life. Her grandma had already died when she had begun her monthlies and so her father had taken her next door to Mrs McArthur. That good lady had told her enough to comprehend what went on between a man and a woman and that it was vitally important to keep yourself to yourself until you were wed unless you wanted to end up in the workhouse with your belly full. Neither of her sisters had started their monthlies yet though, and Eve had never been so thankful for something in her life. The possibility of Mary's small child's body carrying a baby was unthinkable.

By the time Mary had finished speaking, Eve and Nell were sick to their stomachs, but a thin feeling of relief undergirded Eve's revulsion. Some of the things Josiah had made Mary do to him were nauseating, but as far as she could ascertain he had not tried to violate her apart from once. Returning to this, Eve said gently, 'When Mr Finnigan put his hand inside your knickers and hurt you, are you sure he didn't do it again? Or anything else like that to your private place?'

Mary shook her curls. 'He tried to but I cried and shouted and carried on and said I'd tell, and so he stopped.'

Eve stared at her sister. She felt disconcerted by the matter-of-fact way Mary had spoken and she could tell Nell did too. 'But he wouldn't stop doing those other things?'

Mary wriggled. 'He said I was his special girl and he was nice sometimes. He-he gave me lots of things, sweets, money an' that. Like Da and the lads did.'

'But this was different, Mary. You do see that, don't you? Da and the lads . . .' She didn't know how to put it. 'They didn't want you to do things that were wrong like Mr Finnigan. They loved you properly. They didn't make you do anything you didn't want to do.'

Mary stared at her, her big blue eyes shaded by their thick lashes. 'Aye, I know.'

She had to ask. 'Why didn't you tell me what was going on, or Nell even? Did you think we'd be cross?'

Again the wriggle. 'He said it had to be a secret and if I told we wouldn't be able to stay and we'd be out on the streets. He said no one else would take us on and . . . he wanted to look after me. He said . . .'

'What? What did he say?'

'He said he loved me more than Phoebe an' the bairns.'

'Oh, hinny, hinny.' Eve pulled Mary into her and hugged her fiercely.

The three girls spent that first night curled up together on a bed of bracken and moss in a sheltered spot under the thick hedgerow, wrapped in their blankets. Although the day had been mild it had become bitterly cold in the early hours, and Eve had awoken long before dawn. She lay stiffly in the darkness, trying to control her shivering so as not to wake her sisters.

She and Nell must find work soon. Somewhere far away from Stanley where no one would be aware of Nell's real age. Her sister could easily pass for thirteen and that would have to be their story from now on. Mary looked exactly what she was, a bairn, but if she and Nell could find employment they could rent a room somewhere. She was used to making a penny stretch to two; somehow they would manage. They'd have to.

Worry about the future gnawed at her, along with hunger pains. The blackberries had been welcome but hardly filling. She must find a village shop once it was light and get something for them to eat, a loaf of bread and perhaps a bag of pig's chitterlings and some cheese. Thank goodness the weather was holding; if it had been raining she didn't know what they would have done.

They had to find work and somewhere to stay quickly. Panic threatened to overwhelm her. If it wasn't for Mary, she and Nell could likely go into service, but no big house would set them on with a child in tow. But they couldn't be separated. Whatever it took, they couldn't be separated. She had let Mary down once, she wouldn't do it again.

Hot tears seared her cold face and for the umpteenth time Eve asked herself how she could have been so blind to what had been going on. She would never forgive herself, and if her da and the lads were here they wouldn't forgive her either.

Over the next little while this was a constant refrain at the back of Eve's mind. She had never travelled further than the outskirts of Stanley before and had no idea where to make for or the best place to find work. This, added to the guilt she felt about Mary, made each day harder than the one before.

The first three days the weather remained clement and they were able to buy food from the villages they passed through. Every morning they found a stream to wash and drink from but although they looked presentable, there were no jobs to be had. Every night they found as sheltered a spot as possible and put on every item of clothing from their parcels, huddling together under their blankets but waking cold and damp. The fourth day was one of drizzling rain. Thankfully a farmer's wife took pity on them and let them spend the night in the hay barn. In spite of the rats and mice scurrying about, it was the first time they'd slept soundly since leaving Stanley, but when Eve woke in the morning it was to the knowledge their money was all but gone and they were no nearer finding work or lodgings.

The farmer's wife appeared at the bottom of the hayloft as they prepared to climb down. She shook her head at Mary's cough which had got worse each night they had slept in the open, her eyes sweeping over them as one by one they climbed down the ladder to stand in front of her. 'Ee, you shouldn't be traipsing the countryside, now then.' She patted Mary's blonde curls, adding in an aside to Eve, 'They'd be fed and clothed in the workhouse, lass. There's that to consider with the winter coming on.'

Eve stared at the round, kindly face. The farmer's wife meant well, but she'd rather see them living the whole winter rough than go into that place.

The woman sighed as she took in Eve's expression. 'Aye, well, I can see you've made up your mind so I'll say no more. Come away into the kitchen and have a bite afore you go, the three of you.'

Mary and Nell looked eagerly at Eve but she pressed her hands on their shoulders in silent warning. 'I'm sorry but I can't pay you much. Maybe just a hot drink if you'd be so kind?' she said flatly.

'A hot drink?' The farmer's wife smiled. 'Aye, I can do that right enough, lass, and a bit more besides, but no more talk about payment. I've got five bairns myself and a couple of grandchildren. I wouldn't like to think of any of them out on the road without a soul to help them on their way.'

The kindness was too much. As they followed in a small procession across the farmyard which smelt strongly of cows and manure, Eve swallowed against the lump blocking her throat. It wasn't raining but the sky was grey and overcast and it was cold, a north-easterly wind chaffing her face.

'Wipe your feet there.' A huge cork mat lay at the threshold of the great stone-floored kitchen and they did as they were told, then stared open-mouthed at the room in front of them: the whitewashed walls, shining copper pans, dresser laden with brightly coloured crockery and two black settles strewn with red cushions. But it was the long wooden table that held their eyes. The remains of what clearly had been breakfast had not yet been cleared away and the big loaf and pat of butter and plates holding traces of fried bacon and eggs made their saliva flow.

A roaring fire was blazing in the enormous range between two big bread ovens, and now the farmer's wife said, 'Have a warm while I clear away these dirty dishes. My lot are messy eaters, bless 'em.'

'Let me help you.'

As Eve made a move, the farmer's wife flapped her hand. 'I'm all right, lass. I made a pot of tea before I came for you. There's three mugs on the dresser and milk and sugar on the table. Sort yourself out and I'll get the bacon on. You all like bacon and eggs?'

Eve was so hungry she had to swallow twice before she could say, 'Yes please.'

Once they were seated at the table sipping the hot, sweet tea, Eve glanced at her sisters. Their faces held the rapt look hers probably did. The only time they had had sugar in their tea at home had been on high days and holidays, and it had always been porridge for breakfast. Over the last days she had been too worried about money to even buy milk, they had slaked their thirst at the streams they'd found, and each

47

mouthful of food had been chewed slowly and carefully to make it last. She knew Mary and Nell had been constantly hungry although they hadn't complained.

They had had two cups of tea by the time the farmer's wife slapped three plates of bacon and egg in front of them, after which she cut thick slices off the loaf of bread and spread them liberally with the rich golden butter. 'Help yourselves, there's plenty more where that came from.' She glanced at them in turn. 'This'll keep you going for a while, eh?'

Eve's voice broke as she said, 'Thank you, thank you very much.'

The farmer's wife busied herself about the kitchen until they had eaten their fill and were sitting back in their seats, replete for the first time in days. She joined them at the table, pouring herself a cup of tea and sitting down before she said, 'So, where are you heading for?'

Eve stared at her helplessly. 'Anywhere we can find work.' When they had knocked on the farmhouse door the previous evening she had told the farmer's wife her father and brothers had been killed in an accident at the pit the week before and as it was a tied house they'd been turned out on their ear. It was stretching the truth a little but now she elaborated on this, saying, 'Nell and I have been used to domestic work in the past but we don't mind what we do.'

'Aye, well, it's a town you need, lass. You won't pick up much in the country, not now the tattie pulling is dwindling and all the part-time work. You heard of the Gateshead hirings at the Michaelmas Fair?'

They shook their heads.

'That's your best bet, to my mind. You get all sorts there, wanting this an' that. Course there's never so much doing as in the summer but there's always domestics wanted, some to live in and some out.' Her gaze rested on Mary for a moment. 'It might be a mite difficult for you to get somewhere living in, mind.'

'That wouldn't matter. If Nell and I were earning we could rent a room.'

The farmer's wife didn't comment on this but her face expressed doubt.

Refusing to have her hope squashed, Eve said, 'When is the Michaelmas Fair?'

'Why, today, lass.' The farmer's wife seemed amazed she did not know this. 'In Saltwell Park. They do the hirings near the bandstand.'

'Could you tell us how to get there?'

'Aye, I can do that. It's a bit of a walk, mind, but you'll be there midday if you put your best foot forward and likely there'll be folk hiring until twilight. Now, do you want another cup of tea afore you go?'

Eve stood up, Mary and Nell following her lead. 'No, but thank you. We'd better go.' She glanced at their empty plates. 'What do I owe you?'

'I told you, lass. Nowt. Now you get off and good luck. I'll be saying a little prayer for you the day.'

Their stomachs full and the farmer's wife's good wishes ringing in their ears, they began at a brisk pace. It was an hour before the rain began, but when it did it was nothing like the drizzle of the day before. Long before they reached the outskirts of Gateshead they were soaked through to their skin, the biting wind whipping their sodden clothes about them and their faces blotchy and numb.

Fear had taken hold of Eve. She didn't mind being wet, not for herself, and Nell was as strong as an ox, but Mary was different. She herself was thin − scrawny, some of the unkinder lads at school had called her − but Mary had a fragility that, combined with her blonde curls and translucent skin, made her fairylike. And her cough was worse. Much worse. Handing her parcel to Nell, Eve turned to Mary. 'Climb on my back and I'll give you a piggy but don't strangle me, mind.'

Mary didn't need to be told twice. Nell held out her hand with a resigned air and Mary gave her her parcel before scrambling on to Eve's back. She buried her face in Eve's neck, seeking her sister's body warmth like a small baby animal.

Once they were on their way again, Mary shut her eyes, trying to imagine she was home and warm and safe. The rain gusted against them but she was protected to some extent now and felt a measure of comfort.

She wished she was back at the Finnigans'. She coughed, wincing as her chest hurt. She hadn't liked what Mr Finnigan had made her do but she missed Hannah and her friends. And it'd been warm there and Phoebe's meals had been grand. She hated being cold and wet. She hated it when they'd had to sleep outside. Most of all she hated this tramping about from place to place. It was all right for Nell, she didn't mind walking.

She coughed again, and when Eve said, 'You all right, hinny?' she mumbled a reply.

Nell had been nasty to her this morning. Resentment against her sister flared. All she'd done was to whisper to Nell that she didn't want to go to Gateshead and she didn't see why they couldn't go back to Stanley and Nell had nearly bit her head off. And saying that this was *her* fault. Hurt at her sister's hard-heartedness brought tears pricking at the back of her eyes. It wasn't her fault. Eve had said it wasn't. Nell was horrible and she'd always been jealous because Mr Finnigan hadn't made a fuss of her.

She glanced at her sister trudging along at the side of them, burdened by the weight of their things. Rain was dripping off Nell's nose and her felt hat hung limply round her face. When in the next moment Nell stumbled and nearly went headlong, Mary smiled to herself.

Nell caught the smile and knew exactly what Mary was thinking. She would have liked nothing more than to take her hand and wipe the smile off her sister's pretty face, but of course she couldn't. She ground her teeth and marched on. She wasn't sorry she'd gone for Mary earlier, she was sick to death of her. Mary was bone selfish and always would be. Look how she'd lorded it over her when Mr Finnigan had given her those hair ribbons for her birthday, twirling them in front of her nose. Mary always had to be the centre of attention, it'd been the same since she was a toddler.

She shouldn't have said what she'd said, though. The guilt she'd been battling against since she had lost her temper with her sister rose up. Mr Finnigan had been wicked and Eve would go barmy if Mary told her what she'd said. She hadn't meant to lose her rag but Mary's griping had made her mad. Mary knew full well they couldn't go back. She just hoped they found work at the hirings; Eve's money wouldn't last for ever.

Eve was thinking the same thing. She had been amazed at how expensive buying their food had proved, she could have made three or four loaves of bread for the price of one in a shop. But it was her inability to provide a roof over their heads which was her main worry. And here they were looking like drowned rats and Mary's cough like a bark now – that'd put folk off. And how many people would come to the hirings on a day like this? The weather would be bound to put potential employers off. Mind, it might reduce the number of folk who were seeking to be hired too. She hoped so, they needed every advantage they could get. If she and Nell could get work, they could manage for a week or so until they got their wages and could look for somewhere to stay. There must be another kind farmer round this area somewhere who had a barn they could sleep in, or even someone with a tin shack on their allotments. Her da had had an allotment at one time and the little hut he'd made there had kept the rain off. Anything was better than nothing. She would beg, plead, anything.

She hoisted Mary further up her back. It felt as though it was breaking. But everything depended on their finding work. There had to be one person in the whole of the north-east who would give them a chance. Didn't there?

They reached Saltwell Park just before one o'clock, the bad weather having hampered their progress. After getting directions they made their way past the bowling green and the avaries full of twittering birds. The rain had at long last let up, a weak sun occasionally popping its head out from behind the grey scudding clouds, but the day was cold. September was all but over, winter was round the corner.

They heard the music from the fair's merry-go-round before they saw the bandstand, but on turning a corner, green lawns stretched in front of them and the sprawling stalls of the Michaelmas Fair met their eyes.

Setting Mary down, Eve took her bundle from Nell and made Mary do the same. There weren't many people walking round the fair, no doubt due to the morning's rain, but she saw a line of folk standing by the bandstand and her heart sank. There were several men and quite a few women and girls of her age or older, and even a couple of families at one end. More people than she had hoped for certainly. They approached the bandstand and joined the line next to one of the families. The woman glanced at them and nodded, but she did not speak. Eve realised no one was talking.

About twenty minutes later a stout gentleman dressed like one of the gentry approached the line. He walked down it slowly and then stopped in front of the man of the family next to them. Eve received a surprise when the man spoke because his accent was broad, coarse even. 'How many of you are there?'

'Six, sir.' The man's eagerness was pitiful.

'I'm looking for a labourer who isn't afraid of hard work and a woman who's experienced in the dairy.'

'That'll be us, sir. Fifteen years we've been with Farmer Armstrong, Wickham way, and the wife in the dairy all that time along with helping the missus in the house. The master died three months ago and the son's selling—'

'Yes, yes.' He was impatient. 'And your lads?' Hard eyes weighed up the couple's children. 'How old are they?'

'The youngest is six, sir, and the oldest'll be thirteen next summer.'

'So they could be put to use when they're back from school.' It was a statement, not a question. 'Religion?'

The man glanced at his wife and hesitated. He was obviously trying to work out what the farmer wanted to hear. After a moment it was the wife who ventured, 'Church of England, sir.'

The farmer nodded. 'Good, good. I can't abide this so-called Nonconformist claptrap and the Catholics are worse.' The small eyes in the fleshy face studied the family again, for all the world as though he was buying cattle for his farm. 'There's a two-roomed cottage, clean and dry, and a sack of tatties each week, along with plenty of logs and bits of wood for the range. You'd get ten shillings to start with.'

Eve stared at the farmer. Ten shillings a week for this man and woman working all hours and their children too once they were home from school? Surely he would ask for more. And then the man's voice came, quiet and servile. 'Thank you, sir, and you won't regret it. By, you won't. It's grateful we are and—'

Again he was silenced by a wave of the farmer's hand. 'It's Willow Farm, Felling way. I'm Farmer Burns. Be there tonight by seven o'clock and one of my men will be waiting for you. Do you understand?'

'Yes, sir, I understand.'

'You have furniture, I take it?'

'Aye, the wife's sisters have it in their houses but I can get a flat cart from—'

'Seven then. Prompt.' With that he walked off, the tails of his coat flapping.

Once the farmer had disappeared, the wife said in a low voice, 'Ten shillings, Jim.'

'It's better than nowt.' The man's tone had altered, it was harsh, choked. 'He knows he's got us over a barrel. It's the worst time of year to get the push and at least there's a house. We'll manage. It'll be better than at your mam's. Not that I'm not grateful to her but with her only having the two rooms and your da and Don on shift work, it's been murder.'

'Better than the workhouse.'

'Aye, lass. Better than the house.'

The two looked at each other for a long moment and then gathered the children together and walked slowly away.

Eve glanced at her sisters. They both looked blue with cold. She supposed she did. She bowed her head, she had a great desire at this moment to cry but she must not. Fumbling in the deep pocket of her coat she found the cloth bag holding what remained of the six shillings. Extracting a thruppeny bit, she pressed it into Mary's hand, saying, 'Go and buy yourself a mug of soup at one of the stalls. It'll warm you and stop that cough. And bring me back the change, mind.'

Mary was off in a trice and as they watched her go, Eve touched Nell's arm. 'It's her cough . . .'

'I know, I know, don't fret. I'm all right. That breakfast will do us the day, eh?'

As she had done often over the past days, Eve thanked God for Nell. The two sisters smiled at each other but said no more.

The afternoon wore on. By four o'clock their numbers had been considerably reduced but no one had stopped in front of them, not even for a moment. One or two people had turned their heads as Mary had coughed but their faces had expressed all too clearly what they were thinking. A cold, silver twilight was beginning to fall and the lights from the stalls were brighter in the gloom when yet another man approached the remaining hirelings. No one had shown any interest in over an hour and now Eve felt the stir of hope move down the line. The other family had disappeared a little while earlier after one of the children had been sick, and of the three men and six or seven females – two older women and several girls who looked to be sixteen or more – standing there, Eve knew they all presented a better picture than she and Nell did.

The man was young, tallish, and although his coat and trousers looked to be of good quality he wasn't got up like the farmer had been or some of the other men who had stopped in front of the line. He walked slowly and she saw straightaway he was looking to hire a female because he didn't even glance at the men. He stopped in front of one girl – a pert piece, Nell had termed her a little while before – and spoke to her for a minute or two before moving on. And then he was about to pass her and Eve felt a wave of terror encompass her. This was their last hope, it was nearly dark, and if he walked away what were they going to do? Against everything she had observed during the afternoon, she spoke first, saying, 'Please, sir.'

He turned, his face expressing surprise. 'Yes?'

She didn't know what to say now that she had got his attention. Only the knowledge that she had to try or they were lost forced the words out of her dry mouth. 'We . . . my sister and I are looking for work, any kind of work.'

He nodded, his gaze moving to Nell and then back to her before falling on Mary.

In answer to the unspoken question, she found herself beginning to gabble. 'This is my other sister, she's small but she's stronger than she looks.' Mary chose that moment to cough convulsively but, ignoring her, Eve carried on, 'My da and brothers were killed at the pit and it was a tied house so we had to leave. We didn't have anywhere to go and so we're looking for work.' She had already said that. Desperately she searched her mind for something to say that would keep him in front of them.

'How old are you?'

She didn't falter as she said, 'Fifteen, sir, and my sister's thirteen.'

His face expressed his disbelief but his voice was flat when he said, 'And the bairn?'

She could tell the truth about Mary. 'She was ten in July.'

'You say you had nowhere to go?'

'No, sir.'

'So where are you staying at present?'

For answer, she said, 'Last night we slept in a barn.'

He didn't speak for a moment but looked the three of them over again. Eve could tell he was uncomfortable and wanted to move on but she had run out of words.

'I was only looking for one domestic to work in my inn.'

'I see.' Her voice had a dull note to it.

'Isn't there somewhere or someone who could take the child off your hands? Your sister and yourself would find work then.'

'I don't want her off my hands.' She had answered more sharply than she'd intended. Weakly now, she added, 'We're staying together, the three of us. We-we'll find somewhere.' She didn't know why she had said that, perhaps it was because he was looking so ill at ease. She almost felt sorry for him.

He nodded, turning from her and walking on. Her shoulders slumped but then she brought herself straight as he swung round and came back. 'There's only one attic room at the inn for the three of you and I can't offer much but if you are both prepared to work then perhaps I can take you on.' He was speaking quickly as though he was already regretting the offer. 'My mother isn't too well, you see. Up until now she worked in the kitchen. I take it you can cook?'

'Aye, yes. My mam died years ago and I was running the house up until – until the accident.'

'I'm talking about cooking for more than a handful of people. Can you do that?'

She nodded vehemently. 'Yes, sir, and Nell can help.'

'And you say you're used to running a house? Washing, ironing and the like? There's a daily who comes in but my mother did her share too. I'm not sure how she will be over the next little while. She may not get better.'

'We can do it, we'll do anything.' Nell chimed in, her round face alight. 'Won't we, Eve?'

The shadow of a smile touched the young male face. 'It's long hours and hard work but there'll be as much food as you can eat and a warm bed at night. Like I said, I was only looking for one person so the most I can offer is five shillings.'

Five shillings. A shilling less than she had been earning at the vicarage and for that he got Nell too. But the three of them would have their meals and a roof over their heads. For that she would have worked for free. Her face beaming, Eve said, 'Thank you, sir. We accept.'

His smile widened. 'Oh, you accept, do you?' It was as though she had said something amusing. 'Where are your things?'

Eve nodded at the bundles behind them.

'That's it?' The smile had left his face. He didn't comment further, saying quietly, 'I've some business to attend to but I'll be leaving at six o'clock. Meet me by the Dog and Duck. You know where that is?'

They shook their heads. 'We come from Stanley,' Mary piped up, deciding she had been ignored too long. 'We don't know where anything is.'

'I see.' He was smiling again. He looked nice when he smiled, Eve thought. 'And what's your name?'

'Mary Baxter.' Mary beamed at him. He was a nice man.

'And I'm Eve, sir, and this is Nell. But we'll find the Dog and Duck easy enough.'

He nodded. 'My name is Travis, Caleb Travis, and I'm no sir, all right? Till six it is then, and don't be late.'

'We won't, s— Mr Travis.'

They watched him walk away and then Eve grabbed her sisters' hands and held them tightly for a moment. 'Pick up your things.' Even to herself her voice sounded gay. 'We're going to have a bite to eat, would you like that? And not soup. What about pie and peas and a hot drink to go with it? We're going to be sleeping in a bed tonight.' And they all laughed, although Eve found she could just as easily have cried.

Chapter 5

What the dickens had possessed him? Caleb Travis's face was grim as he left the noise of the Michaelmas Fair and made his way out of Saltwell Park. On reaching the back yard of a fishmonger he knew, he tipped the fishmonger's lad a couple of pence for keeping an eye on his horse and cart and climbed up into the narrow wooden seat. His mother would have a fit when he walked in with those three lassies, one nowt but a little bairn. He didn't believe the other two were the age that thin one who was as straight as a pit prop had said either. Three of them, dear gussy. He groaned in his throat. What on earth had he been thinking of to take them on?

Pulling his cap down low over his eyes he scowled as he clicked at the horse to walk. He had come to the hirings intending to look for a competent cook and in his mind's eye he'd decided a woman of middle age, someone who'd perhaps fallen on hard times, would be able to take his mother's tongue in her stride. And the devil himself needed all his gumption when his mam was in full flow. He'd often thought over the last six years since his da had died he'd done it on purpose to escape the nagging and complaining he'd had to put up with at home. Fourteen he'd been then, and ever since he'd shouldered the responsibility for keeping the inn up and running but never a word of appreciation from his mam. And he wouldn't have minded that so much if she'd tried to be civil, but it wasn't her way. Mind, with the customers, butter wouldn't melt in her mouth. Aye, she could be sweetness and light when it suited her.

He drove into the town and stopped at a butcher who could be relied on for good meat at a knockdown price when bought in bulk. Then he did the rounds of the other shops and once his purchases were complete he returned the way he'd come. The whole time his mind had been preoccupied with the mess he had got himself into.

But how could he have walked away? he asked himself for the umpteenth time. It was clear they were desperate. And complain though his mother most assuredly would, she was getting double the work for the price of one. Not that she would see it that way because it wouldn't suit her to. If he had come back with the paragon of all domestics, she'd have found fault somewhere. Well, he'd taken his mother on more than once over the last six years and no doubt he would do so again, and probably before the day was out.

When the horse lumbered to a halt in front of the Dog and Duck he didn't see them at first, the night being so dark, and for a moment he felt relief. Then a voice out of the shadows called, 'Mr Travis? Is that you?'

'Aye, it's me. Let's be having you, we've a mile or two to travel yet afore we're home.'

The three of them came hurrying to the cart and with a nod of his head, he said, 'There's room for one beside me and two in the back.' When Eve was sitting beside him, he turned his head to Nell and Mary. 'You'll need to hold on to something once we're clear of the town. Some of the potholes are so deep you can see Australia.'

He heard the little one giggle and the sound brought an answering smile to his mouth. Poor little mite. He doubted she'd had much to laugh about the last little while. She'd looked blue with cold standing there in front of the bandstand, they all had. His thoughts brought a warmth to his voice as he said, 'Off we go then.'

They had left the town behind them and were travelling on the country road which led to Wrekenton when Eve said, 'Where is your inn situated, Mr Travis?'

'Didn't I say? We're making for Washington, lass. It's about six or seven miles to my place. Do you know Washington at all?'

'I've heard of it.'

'Aye, likely you would have with your da being a miner and Washington being in the centre of the Durham coalfield. Sad to say there's a few in the town who've been through what you have, the pit taking their menfolk.' Realising he had been less than tactful, he forced a cheerful note into his voice. 'My inn's on yonder side of Washington, the Fatfield side. My grandfather used to cater mostly for the keelmen and pitmen, we still do to some extent. But the town's changed since his day. Much bigger now. We've got the old village but there's New Washington, we'll pass that on the way through. Several good shops there. The Co-op stands on the corner of Front Street and Spout Lane, grand shop, the Co-op. Most folk in New Washington work at the Usworth colliery or the chemical works or brick works. Aye, it's growing fast, Washington.'

'Is it bigger than Stanley?' asked Mary from the back of the cart.

'It'd swallow it whole, like a whale with a minnow.'

His voice had been jocular but when the child's voice came small and uncertain, saying, 'Will we get lost?' Caleb could have kicked himself.

'Not a bit of it,' he said quickly. 'Don't you worry your head about that. And if you do lose your way, you just ask for the Sun Inn, all right? Everyone knows the Sun Inn next to the smithy.'

'Why is it—' Mary's voice stopped abruptly as though someone had dug her in the ribs.

Pretending he had not noticed, Caleb said, 'Why is it called the Sun Inn? I don't rightly know. Perhaps my grandfather liked the sun, eh? That'd be reason enough, I suppose.'

They clip-clopped on in silence, passing through several small hamlets where lights shone at cottage windows and the odd dog or two barked. By the time they reached the straggly outskirts of New Washington, the lamplighter had been busy, and they could see rows of houses and other buildings and shops. Caleb pointed out one or two places of interest like the Co-op before they turned off into Spout Lane, passing more terraces and then allotments, followed by still more houses. And then they came to Washington itself and the village green.

The horse knew exactly where it was going and turned off into a large yard, beyond which loomed the Sun Inn. 'Here we are then.' Caleb jumped down from the cart and then helped Eve to get down. Mary and Nell joined them. 'Wait a minute while I see to the horse and put this stuff away and then I'll take you in.'

Once he had the horse out of the shafts he led it into a stable, re-appearing a moment later and proceeding to carry the contents of the cart into a large shed next to the stable, which he then locked. It was dark in the yard, the cobbles beneath their feet gleaming greasily in the thin light coming from the back of the inn.

Caleb was panting when he joined the three girls standing exactly where he had left them, their parcels of belongings held in front of them. 'Follow me.' He led the way down a passageway at the back of the inn, which led to the back door. He opened it and stood aside and they trooped into a large scullery with three deep stone sinks facing them. Two massive work tables took up most of the floor area, and on the far wall, three rows of shelves held bowls and plates and lethal-looking knives, along with wooden boxes full of vegetables, fruit and potatoes. 'Most of the food apart from bread and pastry and the like is prepared in here and carried through to the kitchen. The meat is kept in cold storage out there' – he indicated the yard with a jerk of his head – 'and brought in daily.'

Without waiting for any comments, he continued through the scullery and opened another door into the kitchen of the inn. It was even bigger than the farmhouse kitchen and the range was huge, with two hobs and two enormous ovens, but what the three girls noticed more than anything else was the warmth. A long table ran down the centre of the room, with three smaller ones set against the far wall, along with shelves holding shining copper pans, rows and rows of crockery and dishes, cutlery boxes, folded linen, tin bowls, rolling pins and a hundred and one other things. One of the smaller tables held large containers of flour, sugar, dried fruit and rice, another tea, coffee and cocoa, among other things. Caleb opened a door to reveal a deep pantry, its shelves stocked with food and the large cold slab holding joints of cooked meat and various cheeses. 'I think I've shown you everything you need to make the meals but it will be up to you to order and re-stock in plenty of time. Two girls from the village serve table and help me behind the bar should I need it, you won't be out front at all.' His glance moved from Eve to Nell and then back again. 'Any questions?'

Eve's brain felt addled. Hesitantly, she said, 'How will I know what to cook?'

'The girls will bring the orders through.' Taking in their faces, he said, 'Look, I'll explain everything tomorrow. We're just serving cold meat and cheese and pickles tonight like we've done since my mother fell ill, but I shall lose customers if that carries on much longer. I'll show you the room and you can get settled in and then come down and get yourselves something to eat and drink. Then I suggest you get to bed. It's an early start here. I shall expect you down ready to work at six in the morning and most nights it'll be well after ten before you're able to leave the kitchen.'

Eve nodded, trying to hide the panic she was feeling. 'How many people stay at the inn?'

'Guests you mean? It varies. We've four rooms on the first floor, but it's rare they're all taken at the same time. The daily sees to them. Our main trade is with folk wanting meals at lunchtime and in the evening and we're always busy then but not overly so. You'll manage. My mother and I have rooms on this floor at the back of the inn but you'll be in the attic.' He paused. 'I've done the best I can with the room but it'll be a squeeze with the three of you.' He didn't add here that when he and his mother had discussed a resident cook he had wanted to put whoever they hired in the least used guest room but his mother had thrown a blue fit. Consequently he'd spent the last couple of days clearing the attic of cobwebs and years of dust and making a rough base for the straw mattress he had lugged up the stairs, along with a couple of bits of old furniture. Glancing at Mary, he added, 'I might be able to fit a pallet bed in for the bairn tomorrow.'

'Oh, we'll be fine, fine. Please don't concern yourself about that.'

'You haven't seen the room yet,' he said with grim humour.

Eve looked at him. He wasn't particularly good-looking, his face was too square and rugged to be called handsome but his eyes were lovely. A deep dark brown with thick lashes, but it was more − her mind searched for the word she was looking for to describe their expression and then she found it − more the kindness in them that was so appealing. And it was this kindness that made it easy for her to say quietly, 'We were at our wits' end today, Mr Travis. I don't know what we would have done if you hadn't taken pity on us because we'd little money left and Mary's cough is bad. I'll be forever grateful to you.'

It was with obvious embarrassment that Caleb waved his hand and turned away, saying, 'Believe me, lass, you'll earn your keep here, it's no picnic. Now follow me and mind your step when we get to the first floor and the staircase to the attics. It's narrow and steep.'

On leaving the kitchen they found themselves in a long, thin passageway. Almost opposite the kitchen door was one leading into the inn's bar and lounge and they could hear talking and laughter. The next moment it opened and a young, bright-eyed girl stood there carrying a tray full of used glasses. 'Oh.' She was clearly taken aback. 'You're back then. We've orders for cold meat and cheese.'

'You know where it is.' Caleb turned to Eve and Nell. 'This is Cassie, she helps out front. Cassie, these are the new cooks, Eve and Nell.'

The girl nodded, her large blue eyes sweeping over them. 'Pleased to meet you.' Then her gaze returned to Caleb. 'I've told me mam I'm working late tonight, as long as you need me.'

She likes him. Eve stared at the pretty face. But then who wouldn't?

'Thanks, Cassie.' Caleb spoke quietly, almost flatly. 'But I think we'll be all right.'

He doesn't like her, not in that way. Eve didn't know why this warmed her but it did.

The girl tossed her head of thick brown hair. 'Well, the offer's there,' she said pertly, flashing him a smile.

Caleb led them along the passageway to a staircase with open treads. At the top of this was a wide landing, the polished floorboards and white walls making it appear light and airy. They passed four closed doors, two on either side, before reaching a door at the end of the landing which Caleb opened. 'Like I said, mind your step.'

The stairs were very steep, the rough wooden treads going up almost vertically like a ladder, and Eve was glad of the handrail fixed to the rough wall. The stairs opened straight into the attic and Eve saw it was barely a room. The floor area was huge, she reckoned it might cover the whole of the inn, but most of the space was unusable, being barely high enough for a bairn to crawl in. The part where they were standing was better but even here Caleb was having to bow his head. A wooden base with a double mattress on it was standing in front of them, along with a chest of drawers and a hard-backed chair. A row of pegs had been nailed to one of the roof beams to hang clothes on. Some attempt had been made to make the space more homely, there was a thick clippy mat on the floor and a brightly coloured patchwork quilt covered the bed.

Placing the oil lamp on the chest of drawers, Caleb said quietly, 'I told you it would be cramped with the three of you.'

'It's lovely.' Eve turned quickly to the other two. 'Isn't it?' she added meaningfully.

'Aye, lovely,' said Nell.

Mary gazed about her. 'Are there mice?' She was terrified of mice and had gone hysterical the night before when she had seen a rat in the hay barn.

Caleb laughed. 'You can always rely on the truth from bairns. No, I've never seen evidence of mice up here. We have the odd one or two downstairs but the cats usually see to them.'

'You've got cats?' Mary's face lit up. 'Are they nice and friendly?'

'Not to the mice.' Caleb laughed again and Mary giggled. 'But they'd be pally enough with you, especially if you start off right by giving them a titbit of chicken. But don't tell anyone I told you that. They're supposed to earn their keep mousing.'

Mary decided she liked Mr Travis a hundred times more than Mr Finnigan. 'I like it here,' she said, in the manner of one bestowing a compliment.

Caleb grinned. 'Well, thank you, ma'am.' Turning to Eve, he said, 'This is your oil lamp but there's candles on the chest of drawers.' He pointed to them. 'I'm sorry there's no natural light up here but keep a candle burning all night if you want. There's plenty in one of the cupboards in the kitchen. Just help yourself when you need them.'

'Thank you.' Eve hesitated. 'When . . . when will we meet your mother, Mr Travis?'

'Tomorrow will do.' He turned to the head of the stairs. 'I'll see you in the kitchen at six o'clock and go through everything with you then, all right?' His eyes went from Eve to Nell and they both nodded. 'And we'll have to see about a school for Mary. Which school did she attend in Stanley?'

It was Mary who answered. 'The penny Methodists.'

'The penny Methodists.' He looked at Eve. 'There's a Church of England school not a minute or two away in the village. Would you have any objection to her attending that?'

'No, not at all.'

'I'll see to it tomorrow.'

Once they were alone they stripped the quilt off the mattress and then made up the bed with the sheets and blankets which had been folded in a pile beneath it. The quilt was very thick and heavy and Eve thought it was just as well, the roof space was icy cold. But they'd be fine snuggled together, warm as toast, she assured herself. She brushed Mary's hair to order before they went downstairs to the warmth of the kitchen and found something to eat. They would only be up in the attic to sleep anyway and the kitchen was lovely and warm.

They were lucky. In the moment before the three of them trooped downstairs, Eve turned and looked at their new home. If Caleb hadn't offered them work, things would be very different tonight. And then she picked up the oil lamp and carefully led the way down the vertiginous staircase.

'You've done what? Are you mad, boy?'

Caleb stared at the mountain of flesh that was his mother. He had always thought that fat people should be jolly, it went with the roundness and soft flesh somehow, but not so his mam.

'Don't call me boy,' he said tonelessly. 'I've told you before.'

'Oh aye, you've told me.' Mildred Travis glared at her only child, her pale, almost opaque eyes made more colourless by the redness of her complexion. 'Told me lots of things, you have, like how you were going to Gateshead to bring back a woman to see to the cooking. And what do you do? Bring back three waif and strays and one of 'em a bairn. A *bairn*. I'd as soon have had that Cassie mooning about the kitchen than this.'

'You said you'd have Cassie in the kitchen over your dead body when she offered to help out.'

Mildred snorted. 'Help out! There's only one person she wants to help out and it's not by cooking neither. Brazen, she is. She's got her eye on this inn when I'm gone, that's the truth of it. If you were a miner with your backside hanging out she wouldn't look the side you were on.'

Privately Caleb agreed with his mother but he would rather have cut out his tongue than admit it. 'You didn't want Cassie in the kitchen, you can't have it all ways. The lassies might be on the young side but don't forget there's two of them and we're paying for one.'

'Aye, and feeding two of 'em an' all, along with a bairn.'

'They're getting five shillings for a seven-day week and sixteen-hour days, half a crown each. By, Mam, you can't begrudge them their grub. It's nowt short of slave labour.'

Mildred had a blue woollen shawl crossed over her enormous breasts, and when she tucked the ends of it behind her, the long sleeves of her voluminous nightdress flapped. 'Don't talk to me like that. I'm your mother.'

'None knows it better than me.'

'And I'm bad. You heard the doctor, there's something wrong with me heart and my back's none too good an' all.'

'Aye, well, I've been telling you for years to cut down on the food and stout.'

'*It's nowt to do with me weight.*' Mildred reared up in the bed like an angry whale. 'Did Dr Stewart say that? Did he? No, you know damn well he didn't.'

'Nor is he likely to with the two shillings he gets every time you call him when you have a turn. He might be a quack but he's not daft.'

'Ooh, to call Dr Stewart a quack.'

Caleb had had enough. The blazing fire burning in the grate was making him feel hot and nauseous and reminding him he hadn't eaten since breakfast and it was now well past midnight. The inn was closed, all was quiet and he wanted nothing more than a plateful of cold meat, cheese and pickles and his bed. His tone harsh, he said, 'Do you want to see the girls in the morning or not? They're working here, Mam, whether you like it or not so let's be straight about that. You can either get their backs up from day one or be civil, it's up to you, but if you choose the former path it'll be you that suffers, no one else, so please yourself because I'm past caring.'

'Your father would turn in his grave if he could hear you speaking to me like this.'

67

He doubted it. He rather thought his da would buy him a drink and pat him on the back. 'Be that as it may, you've got the choice. If Dr Stewart is right and you're going to be in that bed awhile, we need someone to work the kitchen. Cassie and Shirley have still got to be paid and as you pointed out before I left for Gateshead, we're not made of money. The lassies are the best I could get.'

Mildred stared at her son. The best he could get? She doubted it. More likely he had felt sorry for the lassies if they'd been turned out on their ear. She knew her Caleb, he was weak, like his da. A soft touch. And there was a certain type of woman that picked up on that a mile off. Cassie Palmer, for instance. She'd tumble him and get her belly full as soon as say Jack Robinson and then turn the screws so he walked her down the aisle. She knew lassies, oh aye. And Caleb was like any young man when the sap was rising. But she'd see these three he'd picked up. She'd do that. And if they didn't suit she'd make their lives so miserable they'd be glad to leave. She had her ways. 'I'll see them.' She stared fixedly at her son and felt a stab of fury when he refused to be intimidated. 'But I'll speak as I find, I always do.'

Caleb said nothing to this; he turned and left the room without speaking. On the landing he paused and pressed his first finger and thumb into the corners of his eye sockets, letting out his breath as he did so. Then he went slowly down the stairs to the kitchen.

'So you're the lassies me son's been telling me about.'

Eve, Nell and Mary were standing at the bottom of the bed in Mildred's room. They were all feeling surprise at the sight of the hugely fat woman in front of them, but mixed with Mary's amazement was awe that anyone could have so much money that they could eat themselves so big. And the room, it was bonny. Her blue eyes took in the furnishings, the roaring fire and the open box of chocolates on the bed of Mr Travis's mother.

'How do you do, Mrs Travis.' Eve spoke first and Nell and Mary followed suit.

'Not too good, girl, but then you know that.' Mildred glanced at Caleb who had positioned himself behind the girls. He stared back at his mother, his eyes betraying nothing of what he was feeling. 'So introduce yourselves, one at a time.'

They did so, Eve speaking first and Mary last. Mildred watched them carefully as they spoke. So Eve was the thin one, as plain as a pikestaff but for her green eyes, and Nell was the plump one with blue eyes and a spotty face. But the little 'un, now she was a mite different to the other two. Bonny, she was. If the bairn's blonde curls and dimples had been on one of the older two she might have had cause for concern. Fifteen and thirteen they said they were? Aye, and pigs fly. She'd bet her last farthing they were a couple of years younger. But that didn't matter. Not if they worked hard and kept their noses clean. All things considered, this might not be so bad after all.

Leaning against her pillows, Mildred folded her hands over the mound of her stomach. 'Me son tells me you were turned out of your place a few days ago. Is that right?'

'Yes, we were. My da and brothers were killed down the pit and it was a tied house.'

'Aye, I've heard the same before. It don't pay to live in a tied house but then beggars can't be choosers, I suppose. So, it would likely have been the workhouse for you without my son here.'

'*Mam.*' Caleb glared at his mother.

'What? I was only saying. The lassies know how fortunate they are you gave 'em a chance. Isn't that right?'

The opaque eyes were as hard as glass as they demanded an answer, and Eve realised Mrs Travis was nothing like her son. 'Yes, Mrs Travis.'

'Aye, to be sure. Good food and a warm bed at night isn't to be sneezed at. And you are used to cooking for a good number, I understand?'

Had they said that? Eve cleared her throat. 'We're good cooks, Mrs Travis. I'm sure we can satisfy.'

'That remains to be seen.'

Eve didn't know how to answer that and so she said nothing. It was Mary who broke the silence by saying, 'This is a lovely room, bonny.'

Mildred's eyes fastened on the young face. 'You think so?'

Mary nodded enthusiastically, ignoring Eve's warning glance to keep quiet. She was fed up with being told to say nothing lately. 'Like a princess's room.'

Mildred stared at her for a moment before bursting into a laugh that shook her rolls of fat and disclosed a set of uneven blackened teeth. 'A princess's room. Did you ever hear anything like it?' She glanced at Caleb who was smiling. 'And what am I then, pray, if this is a princess's room?'

Mary looked at the huge woman in the bed and Eve and Nell held their breath. 'You're too old to be a princess but you could be a queen and that's even better.'

Mildred's chest heaved with her laughter and she had to wipe her eyes before she said, 'You're a rum 'un and no mistake. A queen! You'll go far, lass, with a tongue dripping in honey.'

'Come on then, I'll show you the ropes.' Caleb decided now was a good time to leave. The meeting had gone far better than he could have hoped for, mainly because of the bairn's ease with his mother which frankly amazed him. And his mam seemed to have taken to the child which amazed him still more. She wasn't a one for bairns, his mam. She hadn't even liked him.

Mildred was still smiling as Caleb ushered the girls out of the room and just before he shut the door, she said, 'Caleb?'

'Aye?' He turned to look at her.

'Give the little 'un a chocolate.' She took one from the box and handed it to him. 'Tell her the queen sent it.' She was still laughing when he shut the door.

Chapter 6

It took Eve and Nell a week or so to feel they were beginning to keep their heads above water, and by the end of this time several things had become clear.

Caleb – as he insisted he be known, saying Mr Travis made him feel as ancient as the hills – had been right when he'd said they would earn their keep. They were on the go from dawn till dusk and then some, eventually falling into bed each night too tired to think. In spite of this they were agreed they had fallen on their feet. There was food in abundance, they were warm and dry and Caleb was not mean in his dealings with them. He wasn't mean with anyone. He was, all three girls decided, a lovely man and they could understand why Cassie and Shirley were always giving him the eye.

Mrs Travis was a different kettle of fish. Early on Eve and Nell had agreed they didn't think they could ever come to like Caleb's mother. The more they had to do with her, the more this proved right. Mary, on the other hand, was often in Mildred's room once she was home from school, an arrangement the old woman actively encouraged, much to her son's continuing astonishment. The old woman clearly genuinely liked the child.

Eve suspected the attraction on Mary's side could be down to the supply of chocolates and other sweets Mildred consumed in vast quantities, but, whatever it was, she was grateful for it. It kept Mary out of their hair when they were working and the relationship boded well for their being kept on at the inn, should Mrs Travis recover fully. Not that there seemed to be any sign of this. Caleb's mother appeared to be enjoying her role as an invalid to the full. That, and rubbing Caleb up the wrong way. Every morning he took her a bowl of hot water so she could wash herself and change her nightdress. He emptied the slops and saw to any little jobs she wanted doing, but invariably returned to the kitchen with a grim face. Eve found it puzzling that a mother could treat a son like Caleb so badly, but Mildred was a funny kettle of fish in more ways than one.

Mary seemed to have adapted to her new life with ease. She no longer spoke of Stanley with longing and on the surface showed no ill effects from her mistreatment by Josiah Finnigan. She had reverted to being the somewhat aggravating and forward little madam she'd been before their father and brothers had died, and although this caused altercations with Nell whenever the two sisters were together for more than five minutes, it went some way to reassuring Eve that all was well.

As the weeks rolled by they settled into life at the inn as though they had always been there. Nell turned twelve at the end of November, and Eve fourteen the following month. The jollifications over the festive period made life hectic, but once the New Year was over, Eve and Nell found they were managing their days much better. And then towards the end of a bitterly cold January that had seen snow up to the window sills and drifts eight feet deep in places, violence erupted in the Durham coalfields as the miners went on strike. The men were angry their officials had agreed to eight-hour shifts and round-the-clock working.

Eve and Nell had experienced their father and brothers being on strike in the past. Inevitably it had meant a period of pulling their belts in even tighter and making do on scrag ends and spotted vegetables while they got further and further behind with the rent, but this time they saw things from a different angle. When the miners were making half a bitter last all night and the waggonway workers and keelmen were having their shifts cut, the pub's takings took a nosedive.

It was this situation which played a part in turning Eve's dislike of Mildred Travis into something far stronger. The incident came about one morning in the second week of February. The snow was still deep in places and there had been a hard frost during the night. When Eve looked out of the scullery window into the yard, the white world outside the warmth of the house held the glinting sparkle of diamond dust. She stood for a moment gazing out, her soul soothed by the beauty the normally ugly view held. There had been mornings like this at home when she had escaped the confines of the house for an hour and gone for a walk in the countryside surrounding Stanley, sometimes running and running for the sheer joy of it until she had to stop with the stitch. One time when William had been on night shift he hadn't gone straight to bed on returning home but had offered to come with her. The world had been quiet and the air biting and he had talked as he never did at home. Of leaving the pit, of travelling for a while, seeing new places and meeting new people. He had been bright, William. Intelligent. All his teachers had said so, one even going so far as to say it was a crime he was going to follow his da down the pit. She remembered she had looked down at his hands as he had waved them expressively. They had still been boy's hands, a trace of childhood dimples over his knuckles remaining . . .

'Oh, William, William.' She turned sharply from the window, a physical ache between her breasts. Pray God he was in the world of light and colour he had craved. She couldn't bear to think he was lying under the ground in the dark, that that was all there was. Life couldn't be so cruel.

'You all right, lass?' Nell turned from the porridge she was stirring on the hob as Eve came into the kitchen.

73

Eve nodded, fighting back tears. 'I'll take Mrs Travis her water while you get her tray ready.' Caleb was suffering with a heavy cold which had seen him retire the night before after several hot whisky toddies. She was not surprised he wasn't downstairs yet. Occasionally, when he was particularly busy or had had words with his mother the day before, she would take Mildred her bowl and bring out the slops after stoking up the fire. It wasn't a job she relished but she did it for Caleb.

When she reached the bedroom she knocked and waited a moment before entering, her voice determinedly bright and cheerful as she said, 'Good morning, Mrs Travis. It's a beautiful day.'

'Oh, it's you, is it?' Mildred was sitting up in bed, a white linen cap on her head. 'Where's Caleb?'

'He's not well, he'll be along later.'

'And Mary?'

'It's a Saturday. I've let her sleep in for a while.' She placed the bowl on a side table next to the bed with the bar of soap and towel she fetched from a drawer, and bent to retrieve the chamber pot from under the bed. The smell hit her and she had to swallow hard before she could say, 'I'll empty this before I see to the fire.'

'Do it now. The room's freezing.'

The room was as warm as toast. Admittedly it wasn't at the furnace level Mildred usually insisted on but the fire had been well banked down the night before and sufficient heat had escaped to ensure that, unlike every other room in the inn, there was no ice coating the inside of the window. Eve didn't argue with Caleb's mother, though. Setting the pot down by the bedroom door she approached the grate and proceeded to rake out the glowing hot coals and add more wood and coal. The fire immediately began to blaze and crackle.

'I'll say one thing for you, you know how to make a good fire even if your pastry is wanting.'

Eve ignored this. Her pastry was fine, everyone said it melted in the mouth. Everyone apart from Mildred Travis. She dusted her hands on her apron but before she could leave the room, Mildred said, 'I suppose there was never a shortage of coal in your house, not with it being free, but that's not taken into consideration when they decide they're going to strike.'

She was in one of her awkward moods. Eve looked into the red face in which all the features looked squashed by the flesh surrounding them. 'They are striking because of round-the-clock working and—'

'I know why they're striking. I'm not stupid, girl. I'm saying it shouldn't be. They do an honest day's work for an honest day's pay and they should be content with their lot in life. What would happen if those in the inn trade suddenly decided not to open their doors, eh? You answer me that? There'd be stones through the window and lynchings but we're all expected to put up with the miners walking out whenever they feel like it.'

What a truly stupid woman she was. Knowing she should keep quiet, Eve couldn't help saying, 'The two things are not comparable.'

'Not comparable?' Mildred hitched herself further up her pillows, her chins wobbling. 'And why is that, pray?'

Eve's cheeks were burning but not because of the warm room. 'Because they are very different occupations,' she said flatly.

'Oh aye, I'll give you that. One can be done by morons but the other takes some intelligence.'

Perhaps it was the earlier thoughts of William, William who had loved books and poetry and who had been thirsty for knowledge that made her lose restraint. Approaching the bed, Eve glared at the woman now looking at her with faint disquiet. 'You don't know what you're on about.'

'*What?* What did you say to me?' Mildred spluttered.

'I said you don't know what you're on about and it's true. My da and brothers had more intelligence in their little fingers than you have in the whole of your body.'

'How dare you!'

'You can't compare the work in an inn to what my da and brothers

75

had to do every day of their lives and you know it at heart. You're just being nasty. You woke up this morning and wanted to hurt someone, that's the truth of it.'

To say that Mildred was surprised by this milksop – as she had privately termed both Nell and Eve – confronting her was an understatement. For a moment she was lost for words and then her voice came like a bark. 'That's it, you're out on your ear, girl. You can pack your bags this minute and be off.'

'What the hell is going on?'

Neither woman had heard Caleb. Mildred didn't waste a second. 'This . . . this kitchen scut has had the effrontery to insult me. Telling me I don't know what I'm talking about and that I'm stupid.'

'I didn't say that, not the stupid bit.' Eve's face was now as white as lint but she wasn't going to be dismissed without telling Caleb the truth. 'Your mother was on about the miners' strike and she called them morons. I said' – she took a deep breath as she recalled exactly what her temper had prompted her to say – 'that my da and brothers had more intelligence in their little fingers than she has in the whole of her body.'

Caleb stared at her in amazement.

'There, by her own mouth she's hung herself.' Mildred was triumphant. 'To be spoken to like that by the likes of her in me own house. I want her out within the hour. Do you hear me, boy? And without a reference an' all.'

It was with some effort Caleb dragged his eyes away from Eve. He would have bet good money she didn't have it in her to stand up to his mother like that, but perhaps he should have known. Beneath that quiet, gentle exterior she had guts, did Eve. Look how she'd stopped him in his tracks that day at the Michaelmas hirings. He had had no intention of taking her and her sisters on but somehow she'd accomplished making him do just that. They said still waters ran deep and it was the case with this lass for sure.

Bringing his gaze to his mother, he said, 'We will discuss this later.'

'Will we, by blighty! We'll discuss it now, not that there's anything to discuss. I've said my piece. She's out where she belongs, in the gutter. That'll give her something to think about.'

'Eve, go and help Nell in the kitchen.' He didn't look at her as he spoke but kept his eyes on the furious woman in the bed. It was only when he heard the door click shut that he moved, coming to stand close to his mother. 'You have to open your mouth to wound, don't you? Always to wound. That little lass has worked her socks off since the day she stepped foot in this place and all for a measly half-crown a week. Well, I tell you something, Mam. If she agrees to stay after what you've said the day, she'll be getting more than that.'

'You'd do that? You'd take the part of a kitchen scut against your own mother?'

'Can't you see beyond the end of your own nose? She does the work of two women. Oh, Nell is willing enough but she needs to be told, directed. It's Eve who runs the kitchen. And you might not like to hear it, Mam, but things are running smoother than they have for a good few years. We both know you should have got someone in there a long time ago. You weren't up to it and the result is this.' He gestured at the bed.

'Listen to me, Caleb Travis.' Mildred's voice came slow and deep. 'You take the part of a skivvy against your own mother and I'll never forgive you. Never. And you know I don't make idle threats.'

'That's up to you, but aren't you forgetting something? If Eve goes, the other two go with her and that'll be the end of Mary keeping you company. You thought of that?'

It was clear from his mother's face she hadn't. 'The bairn would stay here with me if it was put to her.' Mildred recovered immediately. 'She's not daft, she's as bright as a button.'

'You'd do that? Purposely split them up after everything they've gone through to stay together?'

'Don't you look at me like that. You wouldn't be taking this stand if I was on me feet.'

'Oh aye I would. This has been coming for a long time and you know it as well as me. And let me make it absolutely plain for you, Mam. If that little lass goes, I go. And, like you, I don't make idle threats. We both know my feet have been itching for a while now but you're my mother and you need me here and so I've stayed. But enough is enough. And if I stay it will be as master in my own home. No more "boy". You hear me, Mam? Now I'm going to see if I can talk her into staying and you'd better pray she agrees.'

Mildred said nothing but her face spoke volumes, the pupils in her colourless eyes black pinpoints of fury as her son left the room, quietly shutting the door after him.

Eve was sitting on one of the hard-backed chairs at the kitchen table, Nell patting her shoulder ineffectually when he entered the room. He could see immediately she had been crying but she rose to her feet, her face white and strained but her voice steady when she said quietly, 'I'll go at once of course but please don't dismiss Nell too. She and Mary need shelter this weather.'

'I'm coming with you. We both are.' Nell looked at Caleb. 'And your mam asked for everything she got.'

He made no comment to this, indicating for them to be seated. 'You've been here over four months now, is that right?'

Her green eyes huge, Eve nodded.

'Then I think it's high time we looked at your wages again. I'd like to pay you more but how about if we double it for now? Five shillings each a week.' His gaze included Nell for a moment. 'You both earn it, I'm well aware of that.'

'But . . .' Eve couldn't go on, waving her hand helplessly.

It was left to Nell to say, 'But your mother? She won't stand for it. She don't like me and Eve, it's only Mary she's got time for.'

'My mother is aware of the offer.'

'I . . . you . . .' Eve tried to articulate what she was feeling but all she could say was, 'You don't have to pay us any more money. We don't expect . . . You've been so kind.'

'Five shillings a week each or nothing.' A small smile touched Caleb's mouth. 'Deal?'

'Deal.' Again it was Nell who spoke when Eve couldn't.

'Good.' He nodded briskly. 'And I for one would like a cup of tea. I've got a mouth on me like a badger's backside and my head feels like it's going to explode, but at least the cold is gone.'

PART TWO

1912 – Mary, Mary, Quite Contrary . . .

Chapter 7

'And where do you think you're off to, madam? There's a pile of tatties a foot high waiting to be scraped over there and they won't do themselves.'

'Oh, *Eve.*' Mary gave a little toss of her head which set the daisies on her straw hat bobbing. 'Kitty and her mam an' da are going to Girdle Cake Cottage and they said I could go with them, been's it's my birthday.'

'And you accepted the invitation without a thought of asking me if it was all right you went? Even though Saturday is our busiest day, especially at the height of summer?'

'It's my *birthday,*' Mary pouted. 'I didn't think you'd mind.'

Nell's birthday – hers too, come to it – had passed unacknowledged. Mary was well aware of that. And since she had left school for good at the end of the summer term a week ago and started work in the kitchen, she had tried to sneak off more than once. Nell was serving in the front of the inn – an arrangement which had come about through Shirley leaving to get married at the same time as Mary had begun work in the kitchen – so at least Eve was spared one of the lightning rows between her two sisters which were becoming more bitter by the day. She drew on her limited store of patience. 'You can't take off whenever you like, Mary. You know that. How many times do we have to go over the same ground?'

'I didn't think you'd *mind*, not on my birthday.' Mary's big blue eyes filled with tears. 'Please, Eve, please. Just this once. *Please?* I so want to go an' I've been looking forward to it.'

Eve stared at her sister. She knew she was being manipulated but the underlying guilt at the back of her mind which had never gone away since she had found out about Josiah Finnigan made it hard to say no. Girdle Cake Cottage on the north bank of the river some miles away was a pretty little tea room, a very popular venue in the summer months. Folk travelled upstream from Sunderland by boat to have their tea and then returned on the tide, so there were always new faces to see and a lot happening. And Mary craved such excitement. Eve didn't know why her sister was so restless and skittish – flighty, Nell called her – but as Mary had got older and the prettiness had turned into a beauty that even now, at thirteen, caused heads to swivel, Eve had become more anxious about her. 'You say Kitty's mam and da are going?'

'Aye, yes.' Sensing victory, Mary turned on the charm which nearly always worked with everyone, except Nell. 'Please, Eve. I'll love you forever.'

'Go on with you.' Laughing now, Eve flapped her hand. 'But you make sure you're back by five o'clock, Mary. I mean it. I'm going to be run off my feet in the meantime.'

'I will, I promise.'

A butterfly kiss touched Eve's cheek and then in a twirl of ribbons and lace Mary was gone. Eve watched her sister cross the yard, calling out something to Caleb who was unloading some meat for the cold store as she went. She looked much older than her years. The ever present worry turned into fear. And she was so beautiful. Fresh, lovely. This past year Mary had shot up and filled out but it wasn't so much this that made Eve feel she wanted to keep an eye on her sister every minute of every day. Eve frowned to herself, turning away from the scullery window and returning to the dressed crab she had been preparing at the work table. It was something about the way Mary was with people. Eve did not think 'with *men*'. She would not allow herself to think men. Mary was gay and coquettish with everyone, it was just her way. And she had always loved plenty of attention.

'Where's she off to?'

Caleb had come in without her hearing him, and Eve swung to face him. 'Kitty's parents have offered to take the pair of them to Girdle Cake Cottage for her birthday,' she said quickly, sensing he wasn't best pleased. Then, as his face relaxed, she added, 'Why? Where did she say she was going?'

He smiled a little sheepishly. 'Her exact words were, out to tea with some fine gentleman.'

Eve shook her head, laughing. 'You know what she's like.'

Aye, he knew what Mary was like. And how he was going to keep his hands off her until she was sixteen and he was able to make his feelings plain, he didn't know. But he would have to. In spite of her silliness and flirty ways she was still nowt but a bairn. Three more years. He screwed up his face against the thought of it. And her living in the same house.

'What's the matter?'

Eve was staring at him with some concern and uncomfortably he explained away his grimace by saying, 'A tooth's giving me some gyp. It catches me now and again, that's all.'

'Oil of cloves is good for toothache. I've got some in the kitchen somewhere. I'll sort it out for you.'

'I'd as soon have a cup of tea if it's all the same to you.'

'Come on then.' Smiling, she washed her hands in one of the deep stone sinks and then followed Caleb into the kitchen. He was sitting at the table and at the sight of him her heart flooded with the feeling she was finding more and more difficult to hide. She had first become aware of it a few months after they had been at the inn. They had been alone one night, Nell had begun the first of her monthlies and had retired early to bed with tummy ache. They had been sitting very much like this, having a cup of tea and a slice of cake together, and she had asked him if he would help her send for her father's trunk which they had left with a neighbour. One thing had led to another and she had found herself telling him the whole story bit by bit, even the fact that she and Nell weren't as old as she had claimed.

He had been very kind and gentle with her, drying her eyes when she had cried over Mary and telling her it wasn't her fault. The next day he had gone himself to fetch the trunk and when he had returned she had noticed the knuckles on his right hand were raw and bleeding. He never told her exactly what had happened, merely stating that Josiah Finnigan wouldn't touch another bairn for many a long day. It was then she had known she was falling in love with him and the feeling had grown month by month until now it was such a part of her she couldn't imagine feeling any other way. It was hopeless, she knew that. Caleb did not love her and never would but he did see her as a friend and confidante and with that she was content.

No, not content.

The ridiculousness of such a thought made her movements abrupt as she mashed a pot of tea and brought out a fruit cake she'd made the day before. How could she be content, loving him as she did? One day he would take up with a lass, there had been more than one who had thrown herself at him since she had known him but none had lasted long. But there *would* be a lass he wouldn't grow tired of, a girl who would capture his heart. But she'd face that when the time came.

If only she had something about her. She sliced the fruit cake and put two thick shives on a plate and pushed it towards Caleb. Nell would always be plump but as her sister had matured, the wealth of her bust and the generous curve of her hips had drawn some lads' eyes to her, and Nell had an easy manner, she was witty, warm. Mary was already a beauty. Tall and slim, with a mass of golden hair, she'd have the lads falling over themselves to walk out with her. But she herself had neither Nell's womanliness nor Mary's beauty. She wasn't ugly: perhaps it would have been better if she had been because her plainness made her un-noticable. At least ugly people got a reaction of sorts. And she had long since ceased hoping her small breasts would bud into something fuller. Tall and thin, she had no shape at all.

'This is grand.' Caleb had already finished one slice of cake and now reached for his mug of tea. 'You're a canny cook, Eve Baxter. Everything you make melts in the mouth.'

'And you've a silver tongue, Caleb Travis.'

'Not so. Even my mother has been forced to concede your fruit cake is second to none.'

'Not in my hearing.' Since the time she had stood up to Mildred a state of war had existed between them and would until the day one of them died. Only the fact that the trouble with Caleb's mother's back had proved to be a permanent thing which confined her to bed most of the time had enabled Eve to stay at the inn. She had little to do with the older woman, rarely venturing into Mildred's room. She cooked her meals but it was Caleb or Mary who served them. Eve knew that had she been forced into greater contact with Mildred she would not have been able to stand it. Mildred was a spiteful woman, cold and calculating, and she knew from various comments Mary had let drop during the last three years that Caleb's mother had done her best to turn Mary against her.

Mary herself was well aware of Mildred's strategies and found them amusing, taking everything she said with a pinch of salt whilst being careful to keep the older woman happy. Mary benefited from this in various ways. Mildred had given her the odd trinket or two, along with a fine brooch which had been Caleb's grandmother's. Barely a month passed without Mary receiving a monetary gift from her benefactor for some little thing she had her eye on. Things she made sure Mildred heard about.

'What would we do without you, Eve.' Caleb took another big bite of cake. 'You walked into this kitchen and took over as though you'd been born here. I think that's what really riles my mother. She'd have felt better about it if you'd struggled.'

'I did at first.' And at his raised eyebrows, 'No, I really did, Caleb, but I suppose I'd been running things at home for so long and then with working at the vicarage I'd got used to cooking for a lot of folk when they had their dinner parties. I was off school more than I was at it when I was a bairn.'

'But you can read and write well.'

Eve shrugged. 'I suppose so.' She did not add that the older she had become, the more she understood the thirst for knowledge which William had displayed and lamented her lack of schooling. In spite of being a kind man, Caleb was solid working class. She had heard him speak scathingly of the suffragette movement, especially in the wake of the trouble last year when women had smashed windows in government buildings and business premises. And when more violence had erupted a few weeks ago in June he had expressed the view that a woman's place was in the home and not meddling with matters they did not, *could not* understand.

It had been one of the few occasions in the last three years when he had made her truly angry. The outcome of the somewhat loud and terse discussion which had followed had been an agreement between the two of them to disagree. She knew that if she said now that reading and writing well was not enough for her, that she wanted to learn so much more about so many things it made her head whirl when she thought about it, he would not understand. It was fine for a woman like Marie Curie to win her second Nobel Prize for her work on radium in Caleb's eyes. She was one of the gentry and furthermore a foreigner. But an English working–class woman? That was different altogether. It was even more galling to admit that had he for even the slightest moment been attracted to her, she would gladly have put aside any longing for self-betterment like a shot.

'What's the matter?' As she lifted her eyes from her cup of tea, she saw that his deep brown gaze was fixed on her face. 'My mother hasn't upset you, has she?'

'Not at all,' she answered truthfully.

'What is it then? Something's put that look on your face.'

'I can't help my face, Caleb.' Her earlier ruminations gave the words an edge and quickly she added, 'I suppose I worry about Mary when she's out, that's all. She's too impetuous and she's not a little bairn any longer.'

'What do you mean?' It was sharp.

'Just that she's growing up fast. I know some girls look older than they are but it's not just that with Mary. It's her manner, the way she is. And she attracts folk to her.'

'Has she said anything to make you concerned?'

'No, no, she hasn't.' She was sorry she had said anything. Caleb had always assumed the role of a big brother with Mary and Nell and she knew he was protective of them all.

'She hasn't mentioned anyone's been after her? A lad? She's far too young for anything like that, especially after what happened in Stanley. She's still a child at heart.'

'I know that.' She smiled at him, but he wasn't looking at her. His eyes were fixed on Mary's old straw bonnet which was hanging on the back of a chair. His mother had presented Mary with a new one for her birthday.

She stared at him, taking in the look on his face. Her heart began to race, a little whimper deep inside crying, no, no, it's not true. No, not Mary. She must be imagining things.

And then his eyes left the bonnet and he raked back his hair. He stood up and finished the last of his tea in one gulp. When he glanced at her, it was the old Caleb again. 'Well, between us we can keep an eye on her, eh? Likely it'll be easier now she's working here all day although if I know anything about Mary, you might have to crack the whip now and again.'

He grinned at her and it took more effort than he would ever know for her to smile back and say, 'I've bought one special.'

'I'd best get on.' He turned at the door. 'What time did you say she'd be back?'

'I didn't.' She kept her face blank and her voice even. 'But I told her to be home by five, there's plenty to do.'

He nodded. His voice thoughtful, he said, 'I might take a wander later and make sure she's not late. What do you think?'

'I'm sure Mr and Mrs Lindsay will look after her. They're nice people.'

'Aye. Aye, you're probably right.' He nodded again. 'You usually are.'

She didn't want to be right. She didn't want to be reliable Eve with, as Caleb often said, an old head on young shoulders. It was with gritted teeth she returned to the scullery.

'You're barmy. You know that, don't you? She'll take advantage. Now you've let her get away with it once she'll be off every Saturday afternoon. You mark my words, Eve.'

'No she won't. I made it plain I'm allowing it this once because it's her birthday.'

'Suffering cat tails.' Nell closed her eyes for a moment. 'Her birthday. The whole inn's heard nowt but her birthday for the last week an' more. Anyone would think she was five years old.'

'Don't start, Nell.'

'*Me* start? That's rich. I bite my tongue every day, lass.'

'I know she can be difficult—'

'Difficult? That's the understatement of the year. Look, Eve,' Nell bent forward, facing her across the kitchen table, 'she's got to pull her weight now she's left school. I'm out the front now and you can't do the lot out here. It was never supposed to be that way. She knows that well enough too.'

'It isn't. It won't be.'

Nell shook her head slowly. 'How often in the past twelve months have you took your half day? Just answer me that.'

Eve flushed. 'What's that got to do with anything?'

'It was arranged with Caleb we'd have Sunday afternoons off, me one week and you the next so there was always someone in the kitchen, but I can count the number of times you've took yours on one hand.

You're daft, our Eve. When are you going to learn that by being as nice as you are, you just get walked over?'

'Who's walking over me now? Mary or Caleb?' She was smiling as she said it, trying to diffuse the situation, but Nell was having none of it.

'There's more to life than these four walls and the folk in 'em. The world doesn't revolve around the Sun Inn, Eve.'

'I know that, Nell.'

'I'm not sure you do.' Nell picked up the four steaming bowls of soup Eve had ladled out and placed them on a large tray, along with shives of thickly cut, crusty bread. 'I'd better take these through. Oh, by the way,' she said over her shoulder, opening the door into the passageway, 'one of them lads from Glebe's pit, Toby Grant, has asked me to walk out with him.'

Eve stared at her sister in surprise. 'What did you say?'

'That I was too young to have a lad yet. And he said he was going to keep asking me every week until I decided I was old enough. Saucy devil, he is.' And with that Nell let the door close behind her.

Mary was not home by five o'clock. She wasn't home by six. And at seven Nell took over in the kitchen while Eve and Caleb went looking for her.

It was a lovely summer's evening. The July day had been hot, and as they left the inn behind them and walked along Washington Lane towards Fatfield, they passed pale shimmering fields of freshly mown hay which made a mosaic against grain fields which had mellowed to the bronze of harvest. The still air was heavy with the scent of eglantine and hedgerow flowers, and Eve thought that but for the churning worry about Mary she would have taken this evening and Caleb's un-expected company as a precious gift. As it was, Caleb strode along with a frown on his face and twice she had to ask him to slow down so she could keep up with his long legs.

'She wants a good hiding, that's what she needs,' he muttered as he measured his footsteps to hers for the second time. 'You're too lenient with her, Eve. She gets away with murder.'

'Me?' The unfairness of it was too much. 'I'm hardly the only one. You spoil her to death and so does your mother.' He had given Mary a beautiful little music box that morning which had a ballerina that twirled and danced when you lifted the lid. But then they had all given Mary gifts. Even Nell had bought her three fine lawn handkerchiefs in a little box, saying, 'Here. You've made such a song and dance about it being your birthday, none of us could forget it, more's the pity.' That was the thing with Mary. She was selfish and fanciful but you couldn't help loving her even as your fingers itched to slap some sense into her.

'Aye, well, it's going to stop. She has to learn some responsibility. She's left school now, she has to understand that.'

'I couldn't agree more.'

'She'll do the work she's getting paid for, same as everyone else. The running of the inn only works if everyone does their bit.'

'You might have to inform your mother of that. She'll still expect Mary to spend most evenings with her.' Mildred and Mary would sit looking through Mildred's *People's Friend* or *The Lady* magazines whilst munching their way through a box of chocolates more often than not.

'I'll see to my mother,' he said grimly. 'Have no worry on that score. We're not having a palaver like this every other week. Mary will knuckle down and toe the line, same as everyone else.'

Before the revelation of that afternoon, his concern would have warmed her, now it was tying her stomach in knots and only confirming her fears. But Mary was still so young, she told herself for the umpteenth time that day. And whatever Caleb's feelings were, he had made it plain he considered her sister had a lot of growing up to do. By the time he felt able to say anything, things could have changed. *He* could have changed.

They had almost reached the quaint whitewashed riverside tea room before they spotted Mary. She and Kitty were standing in a group of people which included Kitty's parents and they were laughing and talking animatedly. As Mary caught sight of them, Eve saw her say something to Kitty before she darted to meet them, calling, 'I'm sorry, I'm really sorry but Kitty's mam's sister and her family happened to come along and they've been talking and the time just went.'

Eve glanced at Caleb. She had seen his eyes scan the group which consisted of Kitty's parents and a younger couple, along with the other couple's six children, ranging from a babe in arms to a girl with bright auburn hair who looked to be Mary's age.

She knew what he had been fearing. She, too, had been worried that Mary might have been talking to young men. The Girdle Cake was renowned for being a trysting place, among other things. But it was with quite a different voice to the one with which he had been speaking as they'd walked that he said, 'We were concerned, it's after seven. You promised Eve to be home by five.'

'I'm sorry, really I am.' Mary's face was alight as it always was when she had been out somewhere enjoying herself. Linking her arm in Caleb's with an ease Eve envied, she said, 'I'll work extra hard tomorrow to make up. How about that?'

Caleb shook his head but the action was more rueful than angry. 'I told you, it's not about that. We were worried.'

'But I was with Kitty and her mam an' da.'

'You might have got separated.'

The two continued talking as they began to walk and Eve fell into step slightly behind them. Mary had barely glanced at her, her sister's apologies had been for Caleb, and now Nell's words came back to her. 'When are you going to learn that by being as nice as you are, you just get walked over?' Well, she was beginning to learn. Aye, she was. And in spite of all his ranting on the way here, Caleb had said nothing to Mary about letting her down in the kitchen. She had worked like a Trojan all day but that was nothing compared to one look from Mary's blue eyes.

And then she caught the thought, hating herself for feeling jealous of her baby sister.

But Mary was not a baby any longer. She glanced at her sister's profile. Mary's beautiful face was bright and teasing and as she said something, Caleb threw back his head and laughed. Nell was right. There were going to have to be changes made at home and she, for one, was going to have to do her share in rethinking a few things.

Chapter 8

It proved to be a difficult summer. Mary did not take kindly to having her freedom curtailed. She had been used to being Mildred's pet lamb and doing as little as possible once she was home from school. Now she was a schoolgirl no longer and although she liked receiving a wage, she didn't like the work which went with it. More than once the kitchen was rocked by the rows inside it but Eve stuck to her guns. She asked no more of Mary than she had asked of Nell when Nell had worked with her, but Mary was convinced she was being victimised and Mildred did nothing to pour oil on troubled waters.

Nell's support and – surprisingly – Caleb's got Eve through more than one sticky patch, however, and by the time the beech trees surrounding the village turned from copper to orange and the birds were once again gathering in flocks as they sensed the approach of winter, Mary seemed to have accepted her lot and harmony was restored. Most of the time.

October was a wet month and November one of hard frosts by night and icy mists by day, but the bad weather seemed to curb Mary's restlessness and she appeared more content as Christmas approached. She took her half-day when it was her turn on a Sunday and made it stretch a little, leaving to meet Kitty before lunch and only returning in time to go to bed, but Eve did not mind this. She knew where Mary was and she trusted Kitty's parents to see Mary home safely. Besides, she was now in the habit of using her own free time too. In the summer she would walk for miles, not returning until ten o'clock when twilight was falling. Now, as the days got shorter, she still made sure she left the inn after lunch and walked for most of the afternoon, unless the weather was really bad, knowing that once she was home again she would invariably start work. She could have gone up to their attic room and read one of the magazines she treated herself to each week since the events of the summer, but reading by the light of the oil lamp in the freezing room had proved no pleasure.

Late one Sunday afternoon, as the cold winter sun was setting, casting fleeting wisps of silver and feeble glimmers of yellow into the pearly grey sky, she came across Caleb a mile or so from the village. He was leaning against an old five-bar gate at the entrance to a barren field. It had snowed lightly during the day and a whisper-thin layer had settled in the ploughed furrows; the field was devoid of life apart from a huge oak tree standing in magnificent solitude in the dying light, several crows outlined against the bare branches. Their raucous cries must have disguised the sound of her footsteps because as she reached him, he jumped violently, dropping something over the gate. He turned to face her, his attitude almost shamefaced.

'Eve.' Aware his face had turned a ruddy red, Caleb tried to salvage something from the situation, saying, 'You surprised me. It's those fairy feet of yours.'

'You draw.' She couldn't believe her eyes.

Her amazement as she gazed down at his open sketch pad did nothing to alleviate his hot colour. 'It's nothing.' Hastily he bent down and reached under the gate, drawing the pad to him and closing it and then stuffing his piece of charcoal into the pocket of his coat. 'Where have you been walking?' he asked inanely. 'It's a lovely afternoon, isn't it?'

'Can I see?'

She held out her hand as she spoke and as he gazed into the clear green eyes he considered exceptionally striking, he knew she wouldn't take no for an answer. Another girl might have allowed herself to be deflected when confronted with his obvious reluctance, but not Eve. Cursing himself for not keeping a better watch out, he said curtly, 'I scribble a little, that's all,' as he passed her the sketch pad.

He watched her as she opened the pad and proceeded to examine the drawings on each page. She took her time, pausing for a full minute on one drawing he had made of her and Mary and Nell. He had been particularly pleased with that sketch, feeling he had caught the essence of each girl in the portrait. Mary's beauty and vivacity, Nell's solid warmth and Eve's mercurial plainness which at times transfigured into something lovely.

When she came to the view in front of them, she turned and surveyed it whilst dropping her glance to the sketch pad several times. 'I can't believe you can draw like this,' she murmured, a break in her voice. 'This is wonderful, they are all wonderful. You have an incredible talent.'

The colour which had begun to die down surged into his face again, his voice gruff as he said, 'It's nothing.'

'It is *not* nothing.' She lifted shining eyes to his and no one could have called her plain in that moment. 'Why have you never said? I had no idea.'

He shrugged. Her admiration both warmed and embarrassed him. From a young lad he had viewed his desire to draw and paint as something faintly girlish, not manly, and certainly if any of his peers had found out, he knew his life wouldn't have been worth living. If he had tried to explain to anyone how the different shades of bark fungi or the thick masses of old-man's-beard festooned on bramble bushes made him itch to get out his pencil and capture what he saw on paper, he would have been a laughing stock. Landscapes, people, droplets of freezing winter rain chilled by a bitter wind and encrusting wild haws with ice, they were all equally fascinating. But lads played football in their spare time, or joined the Boy's Brigade or played marbles and suchlike in the back alleys. Lads didn't draw pictures.

'How long have you been doing this?' Eve asked softly.

'As long as I can remember.' He paused. 'But I'd prefer it not to be known, all right? It's just something I do for my own pleasure, that's all.'

'Does your mother know?'

His mam? He almost laughed out loud. He remembered the one time he had shown her something. He couldn't have been more than six or seven, and he'd been as pleased as punch with a drawing he had done of some wood anemone poking their coy heads round the bottom of an old tree. He had felt he had caught the delicate white flowers perfectly as they had danced in the March breeze. She had stared at the drawing before she had ripped it in two, her voice strident as she'd said, 'If you've time to waste on such nonsense, you've time to help your da more. Flowers indeed, a lad of your age drawing flowers. By, there's times, m'boy, when I wonder what I've bred when I look at you.'

Aware of Eve's eyes on him, he said flatly, 'No, my mother doesn't know. Like I said, no one does and I'd prefer it to stay that way.'

'I won't say anything, of course I won't, but if I could draw like this I'd be shouting it from the rooftops.'

Again her enthusiasm warmed him and now he smiled. 'Thank you.' He took the pad from her and thrust it into the deep pocket of his old coat. 'We'd better be getting back, it's nearly dark and I can smell more snow in the wind. We've been lucky up to yet but it's going to come and come hard by the look of it.'

They had walked some distance before she said in a small voice, 'Do you really see . . .' She hesitated. 'Us like that?'

He glanced at her but her head was lowered and he couldn't see the expression on her face. 'Like what?'

'I-I don't know how to explain it. I mean you captured Mary exactly, she looks beautiful, and Nell too, she was just right, but . . .'

Her voice trailed away and he waited a moment for her to continue. When she didn't speak, he said, 'But what?' He didn't understand what she was getting at. 'What do you mean, Eve?'

'I'm not . . .' She paused again. 'Were you being kind when you drew me?' She kept her head down as she spoke.

'Kind?' He was genuinely puzzled. 'I draw what I see, Eve. That's all. That's the only way I *can* draw.'

Her voice little more than a whisper, she said, 'I know what *I* see when I look in the mirror and it's not like you drew me. I wish it was,' her voice broke for a moment and he felt a stab of acute embarrassment, 'but it's not. I think you were being kind.'

'Why would I when I didn't think anyone would ever see the picture?' he asked reasonably, trying to disguise the immense pity which had sprung into being at her words. He'd had no idea she saw herself in such a negative way.

'I don't know.' She cleared her throat. 'But . . . thank you anyway.'

'You don't have to thank me for seeing you as you are.' He knew his voice was too hearty but he didn't know how else to pass this off. He had never credited Eve with being concerned about her appearance. She was so practical, so down to earth. This new side to her had thrown him and made him realise he didn't know her as well as he had thought he did.

They walked back to Washington in silence. Caleb felt he ought to make conversation but for once it was beyond him. As they reached the inn and walked into the yard, the snow began to fall, big fat feathery flakes which immediately settled on the cobbles. 'Looks like we're in for a packet.' Caleb glanced up into the laden sky. 'Beautiful, though, isn't it?'

'Yes, it is.' His artist's eye would have more of an appreciation of beauty than most men's. The thought was like a knife turning in Eve's breast. She had no chance with him and it was no good thinking otherwise just because he had drawn her so sensitively. Whatever he said, that had been Caleb being kind. Perhaps he had thought an ugly ducking between two swans would be too cruel, not that he had made her – or Nell – a swan exactly but he had certainly attributed something to her face she had never seen.

Caleb opened the scullery door. Slamming the lid on her thoughts, Eve went past him into the inn. She took off her coat and hat and shook them after she'd wiped her feet on the big cork mat. As she opened the door into the kitchen, warmth and the comforting smell of food hit her, but in the next second she was aware of Mary and Nell facing each other across the kitchen table, both their faces scarlet with temper.

What now? Feeling she couldn't stand one of her sisters' rows tonight of all nights, she was about to say something to that effect when Nell said hotly, 'Here they are. Now you tell them what you told me and see if they believe you.'

'Why should I bother? I'm sure everyone will think the worst, they always do.'

'What's going on?' Caleb moved forward, his gaze going from one girl to the other. 'What's the matter?'

Nell was so angry she was shaking. 'Mary had a gentleman caller a little while ago and he was forty odd if he was a day. Came into the inn as bold as brass asking for her with his arms full of flowers and chocolate.' Nell jerked her head across the room and there on one of the smaller tables lay a beautifully wrapped bunch of what looked like hothouse blooms and a large box of expensive chocolates. 'I asked him what business he had with her and he looked me up and down as if I was something he'd trodden in and told me to be quick and fetch her. Well, we had a few words' – Nell's tone left the listeners in no doubt as to the nature of the exchange – 'and it appears he'd been told that m'lady here was the daughter of the innkeeper and seventeen years old to boot. Now who do you think could have told him that?'

With one accord they all looked at Mary who glared back defiantly, her face burning and her breast heaving. Such was the expression in her eyes she did look far older than her years.

'I set him right but he wouldn't believe me, not till I fetched madam and made her spell it out. Then he presented her with the flowers and chocolates and was out of the door like he had the hounds after him.'

'You made me look a fool in front of everyone.'

'*I* made you look a fool?' Nell was apoplectic. '*I* did? You did that all by yourself, Mary. It wasn't me who started shouting and screaming in front of everyone. Went for me like a fishwife, she did. Toby and one of his pals had to drag her off me in the end. The whole village'll be talking about it tonight.'

Eve had been stunned at first but now a burning anger was rising as she looked at Mary. Her sister was showing no sign of shame, just the opposite in fact. Striving to keep calm, she said, 'What have you to say for yourself?'

Mary shrugged but said nothing. She glanced at Caleb and then looked away quickly.

'Did you tell this man you were seventeen years old?'

'I might have done, I can't remember.'

'And that you were the daughter of the innkeeper?'

'I said Mildred was widowed and that she was an invalid. He-he must have assumed I was her daughter, I suppose.'

Nell gave a 'Huh!' of disbelief, but Eve raised her hand before Nell could say anything more. 'Sit down, Mary. We're going to get to the bottom of this.'

When Mary continued to stand, her eyes narrowed and her full pink lips drawn tight, Caleb made all three girls jump as he barked, '*Your sister said sit!*'

Mary sat, and Eve nodded for Nell to do the same as she sat down. Caleb continued to stand just inside the kitchen door, his face white and his eyes dark with rage.

'I want you to tell me the truth, Mary, and I shall know if you are lying. Don't think I won't go and see Kitty and her parents because I will; this man, too, if I need to.'

'You don't know who he is.' It was sulky and still defiant.

'Believe me, I'll find him,' Caleb cut in and such was the tone of his voice that Mary's brittle façade began to crack a little. For the first time she looked frightened.

'So? Where did you meet him?' Eve said quietly. 'And when?'

'In the summer.' Mary tossed her blonde curls.

'At Girdle Cake Cottage?' It had to be.

Mary nodded. 'And then he used to come to Flannigan's later on.'

'Flannigan's?' Eve's voice was puzzled.

'Flannigan's Temperance Bar,' said Caleb grimly. 'It's on the south side of the river downstream from Fatfield Bridge. It's another tea room, like the Girdle Cake, but not so popular.'

'And you arranged to meet this man there?' Eve's stomach was turning over. 'By yourself?'

'Not by myself.' Mary's bravado was returning. 'With Kitty and her cousins who live in Biddick. They're older than us. We told her parents we were meeting them and going for a walk, things like that. And we did go for a walk sometimes.'

Things like that. Please God, please, please don't let her have done anything foolish with this man. 'What is his name and where does he live?' Eve asked flatly.

Mary's eyes flickered. 'I don't know.'

'Don't be so stupid, of course you know.'

Her tone brought Mary sitting straight and stiff, and her fingers fiddled with the lace collar of her dress as she said, 'His name, I know his name but I don't know where he lives. Only that it's Sunderland. What does that matter anyway?'

'And his name is?' Moments ticked by. 'Mary, we're sitting here until I get his name. Even if it takes all night.'

'Nicholas.' Mary glared at her. 'Nicholas, all right?'

'Nicholas what?'

'Nicholas Taylor.' And then in a rush, Mary said, 'But he's nice, a gentleman, he owns his own firm and everything. He's rich. He wears lovely clothes and has a great big house.'

'Is that what he told you?' Eve didn't dare look at Caleb.

'It's true. He's always buy—' She stopped abruptly.

'Yes?' Eve stared at her sister who was now looking down at her hands. 'What were you going to say?'

'Nothing.'

'He has bought you things, that was what you were going to say, isn't it?' Eve's voice had dropped into a low, flat tone. 'What things, Mary? Where are they?'

Mary stared at her sulkily, and this time when Caleb barked, 'Answer your sister,' she did not flinch but merely tossed her head, her blue eyes shooting daggers at the three of them.

'I know where she'd hide them.' Nell stood up and as she did so Mary sprang to her feet.

'Don't you dare! Anyway, you don't know.'

'Of course I know. Not everyone is as stupid as you. I know you put things under the floorboard on your side of the bed but I don't go poking and prying.' Nell turned to Eve. 'I thought it was stuff Caleb's mam had given her, like that brooch and the hairbrush with the engraved handle.'

'Go and fetch whatever is there. And you, Mary, sit down.'

'They're *my* things.' Mary stamped her foot, her blue eyes flashing. 'I'll get them.'

'You won't.' Eve nodded her head at Nell who left the room. 'You'll stay exactly where you are until we sort this out.'

'I hate you.' Her voice high, Mary repeated, 'I hate you all. You and Nell are jealous. You haven't had a lad after you and that awful pit-yakkor asking Nell out—'

'Toby is a nice lad.' Eve made her voice calm and controlled to hide the hurt that had speared her. 'And don't call him a pit-yakkor.'

'Why not? That's what he is. Smelling of the pit and his fingernails always dirty. Well, I don't want someone like that.'

'*You are thirteen years old.*' Eve took hold of herself once more, taking a deep breath. 'Thirteen, Mary. You won't be walking out with anyone, be he pitman or prince, for two or three years yet.'

'I will, you can't stop me. You don't own me, no one does.'

'Don't be such a silly girl.'

Again Mary stamped her foot and now her voice was loud and strident as she cried, 'I'm not a silly girl and I'll do what I want. I'm not at school anymore. And you, all dried up and only just turned seventeen.' Her eyes wild, she swung her gaze to Caleb, saying, 'It was her birthday last week but she said she didn't want anything said, no fuss made, as though she was seventy instead of seventeen. Well, I'm not going to end up like her. I want—'

'*Shut up.*' Caleb approached the angry girl, and such was the expression on his face that Eve rose to her feet and stood in front of her sister, saying, 'Caleb, Caleb, calm down.'

'You go behind our backs doing goodness knows what and then bite the hand that feeds you. And Eve *has* fed you, make no mistake about that. But for her you could well have found yourself in the workhouse, do you realise that? It would have been easy for her to get set on somewhere without you hanging round her neck, but she chose to look after you. She didn't have to but she did it. Because she loves you. Have you ever thought of that? She loves you although for the life of me I can't see why.'

Mary stood open-mouthed. This was Caleb and he had never spoken to her in such a fashion before. Caleb was hers, she had always known that. He wasn't like Mr Finnigan, he had never tried to touch her or kiss her, but nevertheless, he was hers. Her eyes filling with tears, she muttered, 'You all hate me.'

'Of course we don't hate you.' Eve's voice was shaking, for a minute she had thought Caleb was going to hit Mary. 'But can't you see you have plenty of time in front of you for lads and all that kind of thing? And this man is old, Nell said so.'

'He's not old. Not really.'

'He's too old for you. You shouldn't be thinking of lads at all. Is–is Kitty seeing someone too?'

'Kitty?' There was a note of scorn in Mary's voice. She thought of

104

how Kitty had cried when one of Nicholas's friends had tried to put his hand inside the bodice of her dress. 'No, Kitty's not seeing anyone. She comes to keep me company, that's all, because her mam thinks we're together so she can't stay around the village.'

She had got it planned down to the last detail. 'And her cousins? Do they meet anyone? Any lads or – or men?'

Mary shrugged. 'I don't think so.'

'You don't know? You must know if you're with them.'

'We haven't seen Kitty's cousins recently.'

'How recently?' Eve's stomach was turning over.

Again Mary's eyes flickered away from hers.

'Mary? Answer me. How long has it been just you and Kitty going to meet this man?'

'Eight weeks or so.' And she was glad about that. She had never liked Fanny and Sally. They always whispered about her, she could tell. Digging each other in the ribs and giggling behind their hands. She knew Nicholas's friends had got fed up with them because he had told her so. It was much better when it was just her and Nicholas and Kitty. Kitty hadn't minded waiting by herself while she and Nicholas had gone into the woods a way. It had hurt a bit, the first time, but he had said he loved her. The next time he had taken a room at one of the riverside inns for an hour. She had enjoyed that.

As Nell entered the room, Mary glared at her sister, but Nell wasn't looking at her. 'There's some bits here that haven't come from Mrs Travis.' She put the bundle she was holding on the kitchen table and unwrapped the blue cloth.

Eve stared at the bracelet and pocket watch lying amid the items Mildred had given Mary. There was a fine pair of kid gloves too, and a silk scarf in peacock blue. 'He's bought you these?' She raised her eyes to Mary. 'The jewellery and gloves and scarf? You've accepted these from this man?'

'Yes.' It was a snap. 'Why shouldn't I?'

'I shouldn't need to tell you that. You will return them.'

'I will not return them.' Mary reared up, two spots of angry colour in her cheeks. 'They're mine.'

'This man thought you were seventeen years old, a woman. Old enough to accept presents from an admirer. You will not keep them. You know you were wrong to accept them, Mary.'

'They're mine,' Mary repeated, her words coming slowly now. 'I won't give them back. You can't make me.'

'You have no choice in the matter.'

'I won't forgive you.' Mary stared at her and the words she said now were coated with bitterness. 'I mean it, Eve. I won't forgive you if you do this to me.'

'It should be your sister saying that.' Caleb had had as much as he could stomach. 'And as for returning them, I shall see to it personally. I want a word with this Nicholas Taylor who owns his own firm and for his sake I hope meeting him in tea rooms was all you did.'

Mary lifted her chin, her eyes meeting his. 'It was. Of course it was. He's a gentleman like I said.'

He hoped so. Hell, he hoped so. His guts writhing, Caleb glanced again at the jewellery lying on the blue cloth. If this man had touched her he would kill him and be damned.

'I'll go into Sunderland tomorrow.' He spoke to Eve.

'I'll come with you.'

'There's no need, you are better placed here.'

'I'm coming with you.' She had seen what was in his face and she didn't dare let him go alone. 'She's my sister, Caleb.'

There was the sound of two sharp knocks and then Cassie stuck her head round the kitchen door. The girl's bright eyes flashed over their faces before she said to Nell, 'I know you said to hold the fort but it's busy out there. You'll have to come.'

'She'll be out in a minute.' Caleb's voice was dismissive. Cassie's gaze was burning with glee and curiosity about the scene in the inn earlier, but she knew Caleb well enough not to argue. When the door had shut again, he said, 'Can you work in here with Mary tomorrow, Nell?

I'll get Cassie's mother to come in and help out front. She's done it before. I'm sorry but I see no other way if Eve's coming with me.'

Nell nodded. The sight of the jewellery and gloves and scarf had shocked her to the core. She knew Mary was a selfish little madam who could lie through her back teeth when it suited her, but *this*. She thought back to the man who had come into the inn. He had been very well dressed and attractive in a way, but old. Old enough to be Mary's father and then some.

'Where does this man live?' Caleb looked at Mary.

'I told you, I don't know. Sunderland.'

'How do you arrange to meet him if you don't know where he lives?' Caleb asked, his tone biting.

'It's always on a Sunday afternoon near Flannigan's. I couldn't go on my last half-day because I was in bed with that bad cold and cough. Kitty had said she'd go and tell him if I couldn't come, but she didn't. I suppose Nicholas was worried and that's why he came looking for me.' And now they had spoilt everything. Seeing Nicholas was the only thing she had to look forward to. She hated it here, hated her hands always being red and sore from peeling all the vegetables and washing up and the hundred and one other jobs she had to do each day. And she loved that bonny little watch. It was hers, she'd never had anything so nice and Eve had no right to take it. Nicholas would think she didn't care for him anymore, he'd never come to Flannigan's after this. Again, but weakly, her voice scarcely more than a whisper, she muttered, 'I'll never forgive you if you go and see him.'

'Don't you understand what could have happened with a man of that age, what he wanted? He's not a young lad wet behind the ears.' Caleb stopped, shaking his head. Of course she understood. Hadn't she made it clear to him on more than one occasion that she would be willing? He had tried to convince himself that her coquetry meant nothing. That she was a young lass, a beautiful lass who was awakening into woman-hood. That the invitation in her eyes was an innocent realisation of her prettiness. Finnigan, the swine, had finished her childhood all too early but Caleb had been determined she would have nothing to fear from him, that he would show her what real love was when she was old enough to be his wife.

'He was nice.' Mary's voice ended on a sob. 'And he loved me. He wanted to give me nice things, there's nothing wrong with that. I hate you, I hate you all.'

'Mary,' Eve searched for the right words, 'did he try and do anything? You know what I mean.'

'No, I've said, haven't I?'

Eve wanted to believe her. More than anything in the world she wanted to believe that this man had been genuinely in love with a girl he had thought to be seventeen and that his intentions had been honourable. She glanced at Nell and Nell's face reflected the same doubt she was feeling. When she looked at Caleb, her heart rose into her throat at the pain and anger she saw there and she knew he was fearing the same thing. More for his sake than anyone else's, like an actress taking her cue she obeyed the inner voice that told her she had to bring some normality back to the situation. They might be wrong. Pray God, oh, pray God they were. Her voice assuming a calm she did not feel, she said quietly, 'Then we have to trust you are telling us the truth until we speak to him and he can verify what you claim. But it was silly, very silly to meet this man secretly. You put yourself in considerable danger.'

Mary looked at her, a long look. More than anything else it confirmed to Eve that her suspicions were right but following the course she'd determined on moments before, she rose briskly to her feet. 'The inn won't take care of itself. Nell, go and join Cassie and I'll help Mary in here.'

Caleb watched Eve organising everyone. He wanted to shout at her to stop being so damn cool and controlled, to yell or lose her temper, anything that showed feeling, but that wasn't Eve. And yet . . . His mind caught at the memory of her face that afternoon, a memory that now seemed to have happened in another lifetime. She did have feelings but she buried them deeper than most. He must remember that in his dealings with her. But for this present situation . . . He groaned inwardly. Had Mary let this man touch her? However she acted and however old she appeared, she was still just a young girl. This man had turned her head with his talk of being a fine gentleman with money to throw around. He would go mad, stark staring mad if she had let herself be used.

He left the kitchen and went back out into the yard. He lifted his face to the snow-filled sky as he had done a little earlier, but this time his eyes were closed. He let the snowflakes settle on his face and hair.

Did it bode well that this man had come looking for her? Did it mean he held her in some respect? Or had he simply assumed no one would be any the wiser because he'd been told her only parent was a bedridden invalid? That might be nearer the truth.

But he would have known, wouldn't he, loving her as he did, if she had slept with this Nicholas? He would have sensed it, felt something was amiss. And he hadn't. She had seemed the same. Beautiful, bright, even angelic looking. Everything he could ever want.

He opened his eyes, wiping the snowflakes from his face. He knew why Eve had insisted on coming with him tomorrow. She was worried he might do something silly when he found this Nicholas Taylor. She was right, he might, if the man's answers were anything but what Mary had indicated. They would have to see, wouldn't they? But he was ready for anything.

He remained standing in the yard for some time. When he moved, it was not to go into the inn but across the cobbles to the meat store. It was icy inside and a grim place at the best of times. Shutting the door, he stood in the darkness, and for the first time since his father had died, Caleb cried.

Chapter 9

'And you say Caleb and Eve are going to Sunderland tomorrow to try and find this man?' Toby Grant's rough face was concerned as he looked at Nell. The two of them were standing at the far end of the long wooden counter which ran down the width of the inn, Nell on one side and Toby on the other. Cassie was serving customers some distance away and they could not be overheard, although the other girl constantly looked their way.

Nell nodded. Leaning forward, her elbows on the polished wood, she murmured, 'I'm worried, Toby. About what Caleb might do. You saw that man, he's a gentleman, he's got a bit of money behind him. If Caleb loses his temper, it could mean him going down the line if the man turns nasty.'

'But there's nothing to say this man did anything except buy her trinkets. There might be nothing to worry about, lass.'

Nell looked at Toby. It had been after he'd first asked her to walk out with him that she had truly noticed him, but since then she had come to see beyond his nondescript looks and short, thickset body. Mary always called him a pit-yakkor and she knew her sister used the term of abuse to rile her. But Toby wasn't a pit-yakkor. His un-exceptional appearance hid an intellect that was keen, and as well as being bright he had a ready wit and a capacity for kindliness that was very attractive. His family were known for being God-fearing and hard-working, but she considered his father and three older brothers somewhat narrow-minded. Toby wasn't like them. The more she'd had to do with him, the more she had come to feel she liked him. She liked him very much. But he always gave folk the benefit of the doubt. And while this might be commendable in some instances, she knew her sister had been up to no good.

'I know Mary,' she said in a voice heavy with meaning.

'Right.' Toby stared at the girl he had fallen in love with the first time he had seen her. He had lost count of how many times he had asked her to walk out with him, but he knew she was weakening. She had turned fifteen in November but she was no silly bit lass who did nothing but giggle and act coy like some he could name. And lately she had begun to confide in him, treat him a bit different to the rest. His voice low, he said, 'Look, lass, whatever happens it's out of your hands. If this man has been . . .' He paused. 'If he's taken advantage of her, then you can't change things.'

'But Caleb would go for him. There'd be hell to pay.'

'Aye, well, let's just hope this bloke's got enough sense to deny every-thing then.'

Nell blinked. She gave a small laugh as she said, 'I suppose that's one way to look at it.'

Toby was recalling the sense of amazement he had felt when he had first realised the three new lassies at the inn were sisters. For the life of him he could see no resemblance. He liked Eve, she was tall and as thin as a lathe but she was nice enough and he knew Nell loved her. But Mary. If ever there was a lass who needed a firm hand it was that one. Pretty as a picture she might be, but he, for one, wouldn't touch her with a bargepole. He'd nearly come to blows with one of his brothers when Mick had called Mary a whore in the making, but privately he could see what his brother meant. The way she looked at you, the air she had, it was as knowing as time itself. And yet Nell and Eve were so different. Still, that was the way of it in families sometimes. He had an aunty on his da's side who was never talked about but he understood from one of their neighbours that Aunt Delia was no better than she should be. She'd left her man and four bairns and run off with a tinker, so he'd been told, and the tinker hadn't been the first man knocking on her door when his uncle had been down the pit working.

'Try not to fret, lass.' There was a silence between them as he watched Nell bite her lip. He knew she was angry and upset in equal measure and he hated seeing her like this. Nell was made for laughter, it was in her wide-lipped mouth, her big hips and plump, high breasts. She was what his mam would call salt of the earth and she never let anything get her down, but this, this had knocked her for six.

'I can't help it,' she muttered after a few moments.

'You don't think Mary's in the family way?'

'What? No, no, it's not that. No, I don't think that.'

'Well, if what you suspect is true, that's something to be thankful for. It's a whole new ball game with a bairn on the way.'

There was another silence before Nell said, 'You must think we're an awful family.'

'Don't talk such rubbish.' Looking Nell straight in the face, Toby said, 'Lass, you know how I feel about you, I couldn't have made meself any plainer. I'll wait forever if I have to but I will wait. I won't be going anywhere.'

As they continued to stare at each other, Nell put out her hand and placed it over his on the wooden counter. 'I'm glad. It's my half-day next Sunday.'

It took a moment for what she had said to register, but then his unprepossessing, big-nosed face lit up. 'Nell, oh, Nell.'

The snow was thick when they came down for breakfast the next morning, but not so deep they couldn't make the journey into

Sunderland as Eve had secretly hoped, even though she told herself it would only have delayed the inevitable anyway. Mary had fallen into a sullen silence, speaking only in monosyllables when pressed, and no one dallied over breakfast. Caleb had informed his mother what was happening when he took her her hot water for washing. He had returned from Mildred's room with a face as black as thunder and no one had asked him what had transpired.

Once Cassie and her mother had arrived and Nell and Mary were ensconced in the kitchen with a list of the day's requirements, Eve and Caleb set off in the horse and cart. Caleb had insisted on wrapping a thick rug round her before they left and Eve was glad of this as the journey lengthened. The heavy blue-grey sky promised further squalls of snow before the day was out and it was bitterly cold, the frozen landscape through which they were travelling glitteringly white.

Caleb hadn't said two words other than to inquire if she was warm enough, but as they were approaching South Hylton the sound of a woodpecker's rapping, crystal clear on the still air as they passed the depths of a wood, brought his head tilting. 'Life goes on.' He looked at her with a wry smile. 'Nature doesn't stop whatever the problems us foolish human beings are struggling with. That's why I admire it, I suppose.'

'That and its beauty I suspect.' Eve was so glad he was more like himself. If he was talking, that had to be a good sign.

He nodded. 'Look at that beech tree. It must be all of one hundred and twenty feet and it's as lovely in winter as it is in summer. It's thought that groves of beech trees once provided the inspiration for Gothic architecture, did you know that?'

Eve shook her head, fascinated he was talking like this.

'You can see why in the winter when the strength and power of their mighty form is best displayed. The strange smoothness of the bark, the way the silver-grey glimmers in the light—' He stopped abruptly, shaking his head with a self-deprecating smile. 'I'm rambling. Sorry.'

'You're not,' she protested. 'It's interesting.'

'Interesting.' His voice had a harsh note to it now. 'Did you have an inkling of what was going on?'

'With Mary and this Nicholas fellow? Of course not. Neither did Nell, I've asked her. Mary kept us all in the dark. We had no idea she was doing anything other than seeing Kitty on her time off. If I'd have known I'd have done something.'

'Aye, I know. I knew that. I'm sorry.'

'Do you think what happened before, with Josiah Finnigan, led her to this?' It was the thought which had kept her awake all night. She hadn't protected Mary then and she hadn't protected her now. 'Changed her in some way, I mean?'

Caleb shrugged. 'I don't know.' Then seeing her face, he added quickly, 'I shouldn't think so, no.'

He did think that and she couldn't blame him. She thought the same herself. Nell was of the opinion that with or without Josiah, Mary would have proved wayward, but then she and Mary had never got on. Oh, Mary, Mary. Her fingers knotted together under the rug, Eve kept her eyes straight ahead, not wishing to see the condemnation she was sure was in Caleb's face. And what if anything happened to him because of her? That was the other thing that had haunted her during the night hours. He loved Mary. She knew he did. And being the sort of man he was, he would want to kill Nicholas Taylor if he had interfered with her. But she wouldn't let that happen. No matter what she had to do.

Seven hours later they were on their way home and Eve had had to do nothing. All their inquiries had proved fruitless. No one knew of a gentleman called Nicholas Taylor. Caleb had torn about like a man possessed, they had neither eaten nor drunk anything all day, but although he had left no stone unturned, it seemed Nicholas Taylor had vanished. Whether the man had given Mary a fictitious name or whether he lived elsewhere they did not know, but one thing was for sure. There was no Nicholas Taylor, gentleman, owner of his own firm, in Sunderland.

Eve's relief made her feel faint on the way back. It was either that or the fact she had eaten no lunch and Caleb had dragged her from pillar to post all day.

Caleb, she knew, was upset at the outcome although he had not expressed this in words. He had not said anything at all for some time. When he did speak his words brought Eve sitting straighter. 'I shall return tomorrow, I'm not leaving it like this. This man can't vanish into thin air. He's somewhere.'

'Return? To Sunderland you mean?' Eve asked anxiously.

'Where else? I might get a lead from someone.'

'But we would have found him if he had his own business, Caleb. And if he doesn't, he's one of hundreds, thousands.'

'Business or not, I'll keep looking. Maybe he was exaggerating, maybe he just works for someone. The next step is to check that out.'

Eve shook her head slowly. 'You can't ask the name of every man in the town, Caleb.'

'I'll find him somehow. I'll track him down.'

'No, you won't. We have to face facts. He either gave Mary a false name or he lives elsewhere or both. It's like trying to find a needle in a haystack, a needle that doesn't even want to be found. He-he knew what he was doing.'

She glanced at Caleb's profile. The dark, heavy sky was nothing to the expression on his face. 'He's gone now and he won't show his face again. And Mary said nothing happened, remember.'

'Do you believe her?' He looked straight at her.

'Yes,' she lied, knowing it was what he wanted to hear. 'I believe her. She just liked the presents, that's all.'

He relaxed slightly. 'I wish I could have got my hands on him for two minutes. I'd give him presents all right.'

She said nothing to this. 'The best thing we can do now is to get back to normal. It would be prudent for us all to keep more of an eye on Mary, but apart from that, we need to try and put this behind us.' The words sounded hollow even to her own ears. Every time she let her mind relax, pictures of Mary with this man Nell had described came flooding in. But how could she have known what Mary was up to? She had thought she was with Kitty and Kitty's parents, and at thirteen she couldn't keep the girl locked up in chains. Even though that was exactly what she *did* feel like doing. She'd never know a moment's peace now.

They travelled on in the silent snowy world, the snow thick on the branches of the trees bordering the lane and the horse's breath a misty cloud in the bitter late afternoon. As they approached Washington, Caleb said softly, 'You haven't eaten all day, I'm sorry. We should have gone somewhere for a bite.'

'That's all right. It was more important we did what we did.'

'And I'm sorry we missed your birthday too. Why didn't you want to make it known?'

Eve had hoped he would have forgotten what Mary had said. 'I don't like any fuss, that's all.'

He smiled but not unkindly. Shaking his head, he said, 'You're a strange lass.'

She smiled back but inside she was crying. He saw her as a strange lass and he was right. No one knew she was strange better than she herself.

'Don't take on, hinny. Likely they won't come across him and this will be nothing but a storm in a teacup.'

Mary was sitting on Caleb's mother's bed. She had brought Mildred's afternoon tea tray with two hefty slices of cake and a couple of the little pastries Mildred loved, but she had barely shut the door before she had burst into tears.

Wiping her eyes, she said again, 'I hate the pair of them, I do, and Nell too. They're all against me. And keeping the things he gave me. That's nothing less than stealing.'

'I know, I know.' Anything that drove a wedge between Mary and the other members of the household and made the girl more hers suited Mildred. She had been a bit put out when Caleb had told her what had transpired; Mary hadn't mentioned a word to her about any suitor. Carefully now, she said, 'And he was a gentleman, this Nicholas? Respectful?'

Mary knew what she was asking. She also knew that for all Mildred's championing of her, Caleb's mother was straight-laced. 'Aye, he was.' Sniffing, she added, 'I'm sorry I didn't tell you about him. I was going to when I had the chance, I promise, but Eve's kept me so busy the last weeks I've hardly had a chance to draw breath.'

'Oh aye, I know, you don't need to tell me. Never has liked you coming in here, that one hasn't. Like I've always said, she's jealous of you, lass. Nell is, an' all. You're bonny and different to them, different as chalk to cheese, and it gets up their noses good and proper. And don't you fret about the little watch, I'll get you something to replace that. All right? I'll get in touch with my nephew, him that works in that little shop in Gateshead I told you about, remember?'

Mary didn't, but she nodded anyway, her face brightening. She tended to shut off when Mildred went on about her extended family but she had learnt that as long as she nodded in the right places, Mildred was none the wiser.

'It's only a small shop but what they call exclusive and they have some nice pieces in there, according to my sister. I'll tell her what we want and she'll see to it he sorts something out. It'll be your Christmas box from me, lass.'

'Oh thank you, thank you.' Her eyes shining, Mary beamed.

'And, lass,' Mildred lowered her voice even though there was no chance they could be overheard, 'any time you want to tell me something you don't want them others to hear, you come and see me, be it about lads or anything else. That sister of yours can't stop you having lads, now then, just because none would look the side she's on. Nasty bit of work she is, I've always said it.' She paused. 'Caleb said this Nicholas was getting on a bit, is that true?'

'Not really, it was Nell who told them that.' The more she had thought about Nicholas over the past twenty-four hours, the younger he had become and the more dashing. 'He's probably a bit older than Caleb I suppose, but we never discussed his age.'

'Well, that's nowt. So about middle twenties? Something like that? Twenty-five or –six thereabouts?'

That was stretching Mary's imagination a bit too far. Prevaricating, she said, 'I don't know, it's hard to judge some people's ages, isn't it? But he was lovely.'

'Aye, well, it don't matter anyway. They've treated you shabbily, hinny, but don't you fret. If you spit in the wind you'll get your own back, that's what I always say. They'll get their comeuppance, sure as eggs are eggs.'

Mary helped herself to a chocolate from the box on Mildred's bed. She wished Mildred *was* her mam like she'd told Nicholas. She wouldn't have to do any work at all then and she could lord it over Eve and Nell and treat them as they deserved. And Caleb talking to her the way he had! She'd make him pay for that.

A sharp knock at the bedroom door preceded Nell opening it to say curtly, 'You're needed in the kitchen, Mary.'

Mildred sat up straighter in the bed. 'She's talking to me and it's a private conversation *if* you don't mind!'

'She was delivering your afternoon tray and there's work to be done. And I do mind. I mind very much when she's shirking.'

Mary stared at her sister and with Mildred at her side dared to say, 'Do the work yourself if you're so bothered. I'm busy.'

Nell stared at the grossly fat figure in the bed. She didn't doubt Mildred had been tickling Mary's ears and making her feel sorry for herself. She was sick to death of the pair of them. 'If you don't come this minute I'll tell Eve when she gets back.'

'May I remind you your sister is not the mistress of this establishment.' Mildred glared at Nell. 'She takes too much on herself, you both do.'

It cut no ice with Nell. 'It's a good job we do, isn't it?' she declared boldly. 'You wouldn't have such an easy time of it if we didn't. And you,' her glare was more ferocious than anything Mildred could muster as she looked at Mary, 'you get your backside back to the kitchen or I'll drag you there.'

Mary only hesitated for a second. She knew Nell was quite capable of carrying out her threat. She slid off the bed and flounced past her sister into the passageway. Before Nell closed the door, Mildred spoke again, her voice holding the same imperious note. 'I shall have something to say to my son about you. Your feet aren't so far under the table as you'd like to think.'

For crying out loud! This old biddy was waited on hand and foot while she sat in that bed weaving her web like a great fat spider. She was as much responsible for what had happened as Mary, more so. She had fed Mary with fanciful ideas along with her boxes of chocolates from the minute they'd stepped foot in this house. The strain of the last hours and not least her worry as to what was happening with Eve and Caleb in Sunderland made Nell lose all restraint. From where she stood with her hand on the doorknob, she said, 'You complain all you want, missus, and see if I care. And don't think Mary's going to have time to spare to sit and chat with you either. If she thought she was hard done by before today, she'll soon learn she was in clover in comparison with how it's going to be from now on.'

'How dare you speak to me like that.' And then as Nell made to shut the door without answering, Mildred added, 'I know your little game, you *and* your sister's, so don't think I don't, madam. You've set your stool out good and proper, the pair of you. Think you're in clover here, don't you? Well, Caleb's not as daft as he looks, think on that. He wouldn't take either of you as a wife, not in a hundred years.'

For a moment Nell was lost for words. She was barmy, Caleb's mam. Stark staring barmy. Who had been talking about Caleb or being wed? And then unwittingly she did something which confirmed to the woman in the bed that the suspicions she'd had for some time now concerning Mary's sisters were right. Nell laughed. A full hearty laugh. And then she shut the door on Mildred's outraged countenance.

She was still smiling when she walked into the kitchen. 'What were you laughing at?' Mary asked aggressively as she took a loaf of bread out of the bread oven, slamming it on the kitchen table. 'I can't see anything funny in this place.'

'Go careful with that, it'll be nowt but crumbs.'

'I said what were you laughing at?'

'Your friend in there. Daft as a brush, she is. She's of the mind me and Eve are after Caleb.'

Mary took another loaf out of the oven before she said, 'She's half right then.'

'What?' Nell stared at her sister.

'Oh, I know you're satisfied with your pit-yakkor but Eve likes him. She'd like nothing better than to be Mrs Travis.'

Nell snorted. 'Don't talk soft.'

'I'm not talking soft.' Mary brushed her hands down her apron. 'She's always liked him. Right from when we came here.'

'As a friend, aye. We all like him as a friend.'

'Not as a friend.' Mary stared at her sister, a hard look. Like the night before, she appeared far older than her years. 'I'm telling you she likes him in that way.'

'Has she said that?'

'Of course she hasn't said that but I can tell. I can always tell who likes who.'

There were occasions when Nell experienced the weird notion that she was the younger sister and not Mary. This was one of those times. Almost against her will, Nell found herself saying, 'Does Caleb like her back?'

Mary smiled scornfully. 'Don't be silly.'

She was a nasty little so-and-so at bottom. Nell stared at Mary's beautiful face and in that moment she could have slapped her. In a voice throaty with emotion, she said, 'I don't believe for a minute Eve likes Caleb in that way. You're just telling lies same as you always do. You wouldn't know the truth if it rose up and bit you on the backside.'

Mary shrugged. Tipping the loaves out of their tins on to the table she didn't look at Nell as she said, 'Please yourself what you think, I don't care, but I'm telling you she likes him and he'll never like her in a month of Sundays. She'll spend her days working her fingers to the bone for him and his mam, like you will for that pit-yakkor, given half a chance. But whereas Toby might do you the dubious honour of giving you his name, Eve'll end up a dry old maid.'

Her voice trembling, Nell said, 'You're spiteful, our Mary. There's something in you that's plain cruel.'

For a moment she thought Mary's face was going to crumple but then her sister tossed her head. 'Why? Because I don't want to end up like the pair of you? I'm not going to be worn out and bitter by the time I'm thirty, Nell. I've seen what's expected of miner's wives and I don't want that sort of life, and I don't want to slave here for ever either. And I won't. I won't.'

'You just don't want to work at all.'

'No, I don't.' Defiantly Mary faced her. 'I want to dress nice and have pretty things and go places, what's wrong with that? You only have one life and I don't want to waste mine in this dirty backwater where everything revolves around the pits. I hate the pits, I hate them. They took Da and the lads and every week there's some accident or other. If I have to stay here I'll go mad. But I won't stay here. I have no intention of staying.'

Nell stood open-mouthed. This whole conversation with Mary had surprised her but nothing so much as the authority with which her sister had spoken the last words. This was no idle fancy spoken in the heat of temper. In fact, Mary wasn't angry. More impassioned. 'Where do you think you're going to go?'

There was a pause before Mary said, 'Somewhere. I don't know. But it'll be a long way from here, that's for sure.'

'But-but you're thirteen.'

'I don't mean tomorrow, Nell.'

It was sarcastic and Nell flushed. 'I know you don't mean tomorrow,' she said sharply, 'more's the pity. You cause more trouble than a cart-load of monkeys and you couldn't care less. Talk about selfish. And the way you are about Eve! She's been so good to you but you don't see it, do you? You take and take and take. You make me sick and that's the truth.'

Mary stared at her. 'You've always hated me.'

'Don't be daft.' There was something in her sister's face that suddenly made Nell feel acutely uncomfortable. 'I don't.'

The stricken look faded and Mary's demeanour changed. 'But I don't care. I don't need you or Eve or anyone.'

'I don't hate you,' Nell repeated. 'I don't like you sometimes I admit, but I don't hate you, you're my sister.' She drew in a long breath before she said, 'If you're determined to go when you're older I suppose that's up to you but in the meantime couldn't you try and fit in here? It would make things easier for everyone, including you. And . . . and don't say anything to Eve about leaving. She loves you. We all do,' she added a little lamely.

Mary bit on her lip but any reply she would have made was lost as they heard the back door open, and the next moment Eve and Caleb came into the kitchen.

Chapter 10

On the surface the next eighteen months were mostly ones of peaceful co-existence for the occupants of Sun Inn. The year 1913 came and went, and as 1914 dawned the threat of civil war in Ireland and the grim prospect of war in Europe as the arms race gathered momentum barely touched the lives of the little community in Washington. It was incidents like a pit explosion in Wales when walls of flame and deadly methane gas took over four hundred lives, or the more militant suffragettes burning down a church in Scotland that were talked about.

The possibility of wars far away over the water were too remote, too distant to impinge on the lives of ordinary working men and women for more than a minute or two. But the rich owners of the collieries doing nothing about working conditions and spending nothing on safety, and the fight for women to have recognition within the law – these things were real. Who hadn't lost a member of their family or a friend at some time or other to the pit? And what woman alive didn't sometimes feel resentful that the scales were so firmly weighted on the side of men? There was unrest of some sort or other all over the country, and it began to gather steam as spring struggled to make itself felt.

March came in like a lion and went out like one too, with icy buffeting easterly winds and sleet, and occasional flurries of snow. An infant spring advanced through April although the month was cold and rainy, and even May was on the chilly side, frosts refusing to give up their grip on the north-east every night. Then in the last week of May the weather changed for the better. Everywhere in the lanes and fields of Durham the scent of wild flowers in profusion filled the air, stitchwort, white dead-nettle and other flowers of mid-spring joined by emergent yellow buttercups, cow parsley, hedge mustard and cowslips.

In the town of Washington, the sudden appearance of days of constant sunshine and dry air brought a sigh of relief. The sun began to accomplish the long awaited job of baking the thick mud in the back lanes and dirt streets. Once again the housewife could let her clean washing blow on the line in the fresh air rather than having it draped over a clothes horse in the kitchen, thereby turning the room into a steam parlour. It had been a long, hard, relentless winter, but it was over.

Along with the arrival of summer came changes in the lives of Eve and her sisters. At the beginning of June, in the week that saw railway and mine workers join builders on strike and two million men and boys laid off, Nell married her Toby.

It was a small wedding at the local parish church with a breakfast at the inn afterwards. Nell, decked in white, was rosy-faced and happy, and Toby was like a dog with two tails. Caleb gave the bride away and Eve and Mary were bridesmaids in simple dresses of deep blue. The day was a torment for Eve. Not only was she losing Nell who had been her best friend as well as her sister, she was acutely aware of the marked contrast between herself and Mary in their identical frocks. But she could do nothing about that. Not for the world would she have upset Nell by refusing to be her bridesmaid, and not by word or gesture did she reveal how she was feeling. She smiled and chatted her way through the day until the time came when Nell and her new husband left the inn for the two-up, two-down house they were renting in Spout Lane. They had only been able to furnish the kitchen and one bedroom and now that Toby was on strike there would be no spare money at all. Nevertheless, there had been no question of Nell suggesting to Toby that she continue at the inn once they were wed. Nell was marrying a miner. She knew he was of the opinion no man worth his salt would allow his wife to work outside the home.

Up in the attic bedroom that would now be just hers and Mary's, Eve helped Nell gather the last of her things together. Once everything was neatly packed in the big cloth bag, Nell straightened. Careless of her wedding finery she pulled Eve to her, hugging her hard and with tears. 'I'll miss you so much. You will come and see me often, won't you? It's barely a five-minute walk. Promise me you'll come, Eve.'

'Course I will and you know where we are too. You can come for a cuppa or a bite to eat anytime.'

'Aye, I know. Oh, lass, I wish you were coming an' all.'

'I don't somehow think that's what Toby's got in mind.'

They smiled through their tears, Nell giggling weakly. 'I hate the thought of leaving you here by yourself.'

'Don't be daft, I'm not by myself.' But she knew what Nell meant and already she felt lonely.

Mary appeared in the doorway, as beautiful as a summer's day, her blonde hair flowing down her back. 'Toby said to hurry up. He's champing at the bit down there.'

'Aye, I'm coming.' As she reached Mary, Nell hugged her, too, but briefly. 'You two look after each other. All right?'

Mary stared at Nell, and Nell stared back at her. The exchanged glance declared they were both remembering what had been said the night Eve and Caleb had gone looking for Nicholas Taylor. 'Have you said goodbye to Caleb's mam?' Mary asked into the pause which was getting uncomfortable.

'No.' Nell picked up her cloth bag. 'And I'm not going to either, vicious old biddy.'

Mildred had forever alienated Nell by assuming she was *having* to get married when Nell had told her of her wedding plans at the beginning of the year. There had been a heated exchange which had culminated in Nell telling Caleb's mother she would never set foot in her room again. She never had.

'I think she's got something for you. A sugar bowl and spoon.'

'She can stick her sugar bowl and spoon where the sun don't shine 'cos I don't want it.'

'Nell, perhaps it would be better to accept the olive branch if she has got something for you?' Eve said quietly.

Nell turned and looked at her sister, her beloved sister. She didn't want to hurt Eve but it had to be said. 'I don't have to try and pacify her or put up with her whims and fancies anymore,' she said simply. 'She's a hateful old woman and the only person in the world she likes is Mary. You know that as well as I do. And I loathe her, lass. That's the truth of it.'

'She's old, Nell.'

'So are lots of folk but it doesn't make them like Caleb's mam. She would have been a nasty bit of work when she was young and she's a nasty bit of work now. She looks on gentleness and kindness in a person as weakness and she despises them for it.'

'Charming.' Mary was visibly affronted. 'So I've got neither of those qualities then according to you if she likes me so much.'

'I didn't say that. Now did I?'

'Not in so many words, no, but that's what you meant.'

'Don't tell me what I meant.'

'And don't treat me as though I'm half sharp, Nell.'

The conversation was brought to an abrupt halt by the sound of Eve laughing. As her sisters' eyes swung to her, she shook her head at them. 'At least some things never change. The sky could fall in and the earth swallow us up but still you two would spend your last seconds arguing.'

Nell and Mary smiled sheepishly. Eve walked over and put her arms round them and the three hugged, Nell and Mary united for a rare moment.

They filed downstairs and joined the wedding party in the main room of the inn. Eve watched as Caleb's gaze immediately went to Mary. It had been the same all day, he hadn't been able to keep his eyes off her. She couldn't blame him. Mary looked enchanting. The cut of the bridesmaids' dresses which the three girls had sewn themselves, along with Nell's wedding dress, showed Mary's tiny waist and full high breasts off to best advantage, and the cornflower blue exactly matched her eyes. She always looked fetching whatever she wore but today she was exquisite. And to give Mary her due, she had tried to stay in the background and let Nell have the limelight, Eve thought. She had noticed that and had made a mental note to thank her sister once they were alone.

Nell and Toby were making the short journey to their rented house in Caleb's horse and cart which had been decorated with wild flowers and greenery. Even Rosie, the horse, had a topknot of bright flowering whorls of bird's-foot trefoil, the yellow and golden-orange pea-like flowers dazzling in the sunshine. Amid somewhat ribald shouts of encouragement to Toby for the night ahead from his pit mates, and general good wishes from the rest of the wedding party, the couple climbed into the seat of the cart. Then Caleb led the horse out of the inn yard and through the village centre; everyone followed, throwing rose petals and clusters of creamy white blossoms from dogwood and elder. Once the horse and cart had turned into Spout Lane, the wedding guests shouted their goodbyes, and Eve's last sight of Nell was her sister's radiant face as she turned to wave.

'He'll make her happy, lass. Have no doubts about that.' Mrs Grant, Toby's mother, was standing by Eve and Mary as they watched the cart disappear into the distance. 'Fair barmy about your Nell, my lad is.'

'I know that, Mrs Grant.' Eve smiled through her tears. 'And she loves him very much.'

'Aye, Jack for a Jill, they are. Course it's not the best start with the men coming out on strike the very week they get married, but you come from mining stock, don't you? You know all about strikes and what have you.'

Mary had not joined in the conversation, standing slightly apart from the other two women. Now she made a small sound in her throat. It could have meant anything but Eve realised Toby's mother had got the measure of Mary when she looked at her and said, 'A working man has to do what he can to try and force a decent wage out of them owners, m'girl. Don't be mistaken about that. And there's nowt wrong with a man providing for his family whatever job he does. You'd be quick to complain if there was no coal for a fire, now then.'

'She didn't mean anything, Mrs Grant.' Eve glanced at her sister, willing Mary to say something conciliatory to the irate woman but Mary just stared back at her in the aloof way she adopted sometimes.

'I know what she meant, lass. She's never considered my lad good enough, we all know that. Why, I don't know, because like I said, you come from mining stock. Still, I don't want to cast a pall on the day so we'll say no more about it.'

Oh dear. Eve searched for the words to pour oil on troubled waters as Mary turned and left them and made her way back towards the inn, but before she could speak, Mrs Grant patted her arm. 'Don't you fret, lass. I know you're of the same mind as Nell and she's a canny little body without any airs and graces. I shouldn't have spoken out today of all days, but my lad is a good son and he'll make a good husband an' all. It gets up me nose to see him looked down on by a bit lass like your Mary.'

'I'm sorry, Mrs Grant,' Eve said helplessly.

'Aye, well, like my Seamus always says, it takes all sorts.' She smiled at Eve. 'He's always telling me least said, soonest mended an' all, but I think that's easier for men than women, don't you? Me, I like to call a spade.'

Eve nodded. She could see why Nell got on like a house on fire with Toby's mother. They talked for a minute or two more and then, the wedding guests having dispersed, Eve said goodbye to Toby's mother and returned to the inn. Mary was sitting in the kitchen with Caleb as she entered, a fresh pot of tea on the table. Eve could see immediately from the expression on Caleb's face that Mary had been putting herself out to be nice. Sometimes when her sister was in what she and Nell had always termed Mary's bratty moods she would hardly speak for days on end and then Caleb was always subdued and on edge. But the smile slid from Mary's face as she saw her, and her sister's voice was sharp when she said, 'Been having me over with Mrs Grant then?'

'Of course not.'

'There's no of course about it. I know what she thinks of me, same as she knows what I think of them. Ignorant, loud-mouthed lot.'

'You can hardly call the Grants that, Mary.'

'Why not? Just because Nell's took up with one of them?'

Eve sighed. This was Mary, as mercurial as quicksilver. She had been as nice as pie all day but something had got under her skin. And then she felt she had her answer as to what the something was when Mary said, 'And as for her lumping us with them, you might be happy with that but I'm not. All they can talk about is the pit, religion or Toby's da's allotment.' Her lip curled in a sneer. 'They're pathetic, the lot of them, and she dares to have a go at me! And you, apologising for me.'

'I said you didn't mean anything, that's not the same as apologising.'

'But I *did* mean something. Why should I pretend to be over the moon about Nell marrying a miner and a miner who's out on strike to boot? She could have got far better than him.'

'Toby can't help the strike.' Caleb entered the conversation, his voice low, almost soothing. 'It's one out, all out. You know that. His life wouldn't be worth living if he didn't go along with the others and the union. He's only doing what he has to.'

Mary turned her great violet-blue eyes on Caleb. 'So you're sticking up for Eve and the Grants? Is that it?'

'You know I'm not. It's not a question of that.'

A catch in her voice, Mary said, 'It sounded like that to me. I'm the odd one out here, I can see that.'

'I'm going to change out of this dress.' Eve left the kitchen, she couldn't bear to witness what would inevitably occur. Mary would pout and toss her curls and maybe even force a little tear or two, and Caleb would soon be eating out of her hand again. She didn't understand how a strong, sensible, good-looking man like Caleb, a man who could have any one of a number of lassies round about, could allow himself to be manipulated so. And then she shook her head at herself. Of course she understood it. She endured all manner of agonies of mind to be near him, didn't she? And whereas Caleb might not be deliberately playing with her feelings like Mary did with his, it all boiled down to the same thing: love made one foolish. Mary knew Caleb cared for her; they had never discussed it but Mary knew he was in love with her all right. And one day, when Caleb made his feelings plain and brought his love out into the open, she would have to endure seeing them walking out together, getting wed, having bairns.

Eve closed her eyes for a moment before ripping off the blue frock and throwing it on the bed. Hastily she pulled on her everyday dress and tied her big serviceable apron round her waist. Wedding or not there was work to be done and it wouldn't do itself. But one thing she had become clearer about over the last months. When the day came and Caleb wed her sister, she would leave Washington. Nell was settled, there would be nothing to keep her here. She would come and visit, she couldn't bear the thought of losing touch with either of her sisters, but to stay and deliberately torture herself was not an option.

Chapter 11

When war was declared on 4 August as Britons returned from the annual Bank Holiday, the announcement after weeks of uncertainty was met in many quarters by cheering and singing the national anthem. It was generally agreed by all classes that the Kaiser needed teaching a lesson and the English were man for the job. Maniac he was, the Kaiser, and cruel with it. Look how he'd treated the poor Belgians. Such things couldn't be tolerated in a civilised world and he'd better learn that and fast. Thousands of men and boys volunteered. When the British Expeditionary Force landed in France in the middle of the month, folk everywhere were predicting the war would be over by Christmas. Still more young men, desperate to do their bit before it ended, enlisted in their tens of hundreds.

By the time the reality of a bloodbath at the French town of Mons hit the newspapers, followed by the Russian army suffering a terrible defeat on the Eastern Front at Tannenberg and the British army calling for five hundred thousand more men, the war had taken a back seat in Eve's eyes. In the middle of September, Mary didn't return from her half-day off with Kitty. When Caleb knocked the family up at eleven o'clock, he discovered Kitty hadn't seen Mary all day. Furthermore, Mary hadn't kept her company for some weeks. Kitty thought Mary had a beau but she had been very cagey about him. At midnight Eve found the letter Mary had left for her on the bed in their attic room. It was short and to the point.

Dear Eve,

I'm sorry but I can't do this for one more day. I've met someone, he's not from these parts but he's rich and he wants me to marry him. We are going away together and I won't be coming back, not until everything's settled. I'll try and send word when I can to let you know I'm all right, but the thought of another winter in Washington isn't to be borne. I'm not like you. I hate it here and I'll never be happy while I stay. You won't be able to find me so don't waste time looking. Thank you for all you've done for me. I know it doesn't seem like it but I am grateful.

Your loving sister,

Mary

'But where could she have gone?' Eve looked at Caleb. He had come running upstairs when she had called his name and had just finished reading the note she'd thrust at him. 'We have to find her before she gets too far.'

He remained quite still for another moment and then lifted his eyes to hers, his face chalk-white. His voice deep and bitter, he said, 'This is no sudden decision, Eve. She's thought this through. She'll be long gone.'

'But we have to try.' Eve's heart was pounding like a drum and she felt sick. For a moment, just the merest fraction of a second, she'd felt a bolt of elation shoot through her as she'd read the scribbled words. Now the guilt was crucifying. Her own sister, her baby sister. How could she be glad she'd gone? What sort of a person was she? But she wasn't glad, she told herself feverishly. She would do anything to get Mary back. Anything. They had to search for her until they found her.

After a sleepless night Eve and Caleb knocked on Nell's door first thing in the morning to impart the news. Nell and Toby were having breakfast, and when Nell revealed the conversation she'd had with Mary after the first fiasco, Caleb and Toby nearly came to blows when Caleb shouted at Nell for not speaking sooner.

'And what good would that have done?' Nell rounded on Caleb as she pushed Toby down in his seat at the kitchen table. 'I told you, she was determined to go. It was just a matter of when, you couldn't have stopped her. What were you going to do? Treat her like a prisoner the last couple of years? Lock her in a room? Not let her leave the house? Eve would have been worried sick the whole time if I'd said anything and it wouldn't have made any difference.' She stepped closer to Caleb, her voice harsh as she said, 'You have never seen her for who she is. Oh aye, she's as pretty as a picture and charm itself when she wants to be, but she's selfish through and through. She always has been. But you've never seen that, have you?'

Caleb stared into the angry face of Mary's sister. He wanted to shout at her that he knew exactly what Mary was like, that she was everything he had ever wanted and always would, but he did not. Neither would he admit to himself that Mary going like that, without a word to him, without even mentioning him in the letter she had left for Eve, had been a body blow. She had walked away from him without a second thought and it had left him feeling like murder. If he could get hold of this man she'd flown off with he would kill him. He would kill them both. No, no, he wouldn't hurt a hair on her head, would he? Suddenly he didn't know himself and it was frightening.

'Nell, all that doesn't matter now. We have to find her.'

Nell looked at Eve and for a moment she wanted to shake her until her teeth rattled. Her voice still harsh, she said, 'Why, Eve? So she can run away again in a month or six or a year? When are you going to wake up to the fact that she is as she is and not as you would like her to be? She was born wayward and you know it.' As Eve made a movement of protest, Nell continued, 'Oh, I know all that with Josiah wasn't her fault but, that apart, she's got a way with her and you know it. That man, Nicholas whatever his name was, he was old, Eve. Too old to be satisfied with a kiss and holding hands from a young beautiful lass like Mary. You know it and I know it.'

Caleb stood up suddenly and as he did so Toby rose too, but Caleb did not speak or turn to Nell but walked straight out of the house.

Her voice quiet, Nell said, 'He doesn't want to hear the truth because he's under her spell too. You do know that, don't you? That he only ever had eyes for her?'

Eve looked at her sister. There was a question in the words that she pretended not to understand. 'He's always looked after her,' she said flatly. 'He's looked after all of us.'

'None of us need looking after, Eve.' Nell sat down with a little thud in the chair next to her sister. Signalling with her eyes for Toby to make himself scarce, she waited until he had left the kitchen before she said, 'Mary said something else that time, something I couldn't say in front of Caleb. She said you were in love with him. Are you, lass?'

Eve remained completely still for a full ten seconds. Then she lifted her face to Nell. Nell read what was there and her voice was soft as she muttered, 'Oh, lass, lass.'

'He mustn't know, no one must know. Promise me, Nell.'

'They won't from me, lass. I'd as soon cut out me own tongue. But I wish from the bottom of me it weren't so, lass.'

'Nell, I felt . . . When I knew she'd gone, when I read the letter I felt . . .'

'Relieved? Pleased?'

Eve nodded, her face awash with tears. 'Only for a moment but it was there. How could I think like that?'

'Oh, lass, don't take on so. If you want the honest truth, I feel like that meself and I'm not in love with Caleb.' Nell grimaced but Eve couldn't smile. 'Look, lass.' Nell took her sister's hands in her own, squeezing them as she said, 'She was always going to go. Like that letter said, she could never be happy here. She wants – well, I don't know what she does want but it's not here. Bright lights, nice clothes, living in a grand house, that's her. And likely she'll get it an' all, looking like she does.'

'Nell, she's working class. Her voice will always give that away as soon as she opens her mouth. Lassies, even ones as beautiful as Mary, don't marry into the gentry.'

'There's working class that have pulled themselves out of the gutter and rub noses with the nobs. Look at the Jefferson chemical works, he had nothing to start with but now he owns half of the town and his wife's the daughter of a miner.'

'And for every Jefferson there's a hundred men who'll just take advantage of her. If . . . if what we suspect is true and she allowed that Nicholas man liberties, she'll probably allow this other one the same thing.'

'You can't do nowt about that.' Nell shook Eve's hands. 'You can't, lass. Like I said to Caleb, you have to see her as she is, not as you'd like her to be. The thing is you've been part sister, part mam to her, to both of us. It's been harder for you to accept that side of her because of it. You've not been able to see the wood for the trees.'

Eve smiled shakily. 'You're a wise old bird on the quiet, Nell.'

'Aye, that's me. Like my mother-in-law said the other day, I'm sixteen going on sixty. But she meant it as a compliment. I think.' Nell made a funny face again and this time they both laughed.

'I like Toby's mam.'

'Aye, so do I. She's not as straight-laced as the menfolk, I don't have to watch me ps and qs with her in the same way I do them. Mind, they're nice enough, I'm saying nowt against them. They're just a bit stiff and proper what with Toby's da being a lay preacher an' all, and one of his brothers being a deputy at the pit. They feel there's things to live up to, I suppose.'

'But Toby isn't straight-laced.'

'Oh no, my Toby's all right.' They were simple words, but the look on Nell's face as she spoke her husband's name told Eve there was nothing wrong with Nell's marriage. And she was glad, so glad for her sister, even as she wondered what it must be like to be adored.

When she left Nell's house a minute or two later, Caleb was nowhere to be seen. On the way back to the inn in the warm September sunshine, Eve made up her mind on a number of issues.

She would leave no stone unturned in trying to find Mary, but if it was to no avail then she would have to accept the wisdom in what Nell had said. Mary had been determined to go, that much was for sure, and perhaps they all had to come to terms with the fact that Mary had chosen her own path. It was just that fifteen was so young. Eve bit down hard on her lip, sighing.

She would continue as she was at the inn, she could do nothing else. And maybe, now that Mary had made it so clear she could not live in Washington, Caleb would begin to accept there was no hope in that direction. Time healed and changed things. Didn't it? Aye, it did, and that's what she had to believe over this.

She glanced down at the frock she was wearing. It was a little faded, being one of two work dresses she wore in the kitchen. She would buy some nice material when she next called at the haberdashery in New Washington and make herself a couple of new frocks; it was long past time she did so. She nodded mentally to the thought. However things turned out with Mary, whether they managed to find her and bring her home or she came back of her own accord, it was time she started to take care of herself. She would never be a beauty and she wouldn't pretend to try, but she was young. She wasn't nineteen yet. She had got into the habit of not bothering with how she looked, feeling it was pointless, but that was self-defeating. Nell had said she'd been part sister and part mother to them and she was right, but the time for that was over.

She thought back to something Caleb had said a month ago when they had been discussing something or other. 'An old head on young shoulders, that's what you've got.' He had smiled at her, shaking his head as though it was something to be faintly ashamed of. No, not ashamed of exactly, she corrected herself in the next moment. But to be pitied almost. Well, she didn't want his pity. Her chin came up and her green eyes with their short dark lashes narrowed. She would prefer anything, even him actually disliking her, to pity.

When she walked into the kitchen of the inn she could hear the sound of raised voices from the direction of Mildred's room. There had been no point in waking Mildred the night before to tell her about Mary, and when she had taken Caleb's mother her bowl of hot water for washing that morning Mildred had merely grunted and rolled over in bed. Then she and Caleb had left for Nell's. But it was clear he'd come back and broken the news.

She walked along the passageway and was about to enter the room, Mildred's door being slightly ajar, when the sound of her own name spoken with some venom caused her to freeze.

'You blame me for spoiling the lass, I know, but it wasn't me who's driven her away but that Eve.' Mildred fairly spat her name out. 'I got her measure the minute I laid eyes on her. Eaten up with jealousy against the lass, she is, and is it any wonder looking like she does? One as bonny as a picture and the other like a scrag end.'

'Shut your mouth.' Caleb's voice was low and deep. 'I've told you, you'll go too far one day.'

'Me go too far? And what about her? Keeping Mary working from dawn to dusk and never a kind word, I'll be bound. That bonny little lass was made for better things than being a kitchen maid and you know it. No wonder she couldn't stand it. And you say *I* encouraged her? I just tried to make her life bearable, that's all. But that, that *scarecrow*—'

'Another word and you'll regret it, Mam. I'm warning you.'

Eve turned and fled on silent feet through the house and into the yard. The sun was still shining, the air mellow and warm. She stood for a moment gasping, as though she had been held under water for a long time. A *scarecrow*. Was that how people saw her? Was that how *he* saw her? She felt herself diminishing, shrivelling into nothing as the world around her seemed to get bigger and she smaller.

She stood for some minutes, her hands clenched at her side as she struggled to control the desire to curl up in a little ball and die. The words Mildred had spoken whirled about in her head as she stared before her dry-eyed. And it was the fledgling individual deep inside her who had strived for life that morning, the girl who had thought she could maybe, just maybe, become more than friend to him at some time in the distant future, that she addressed when she muttered bitterly, 'New frocks. Huh.'

Exactly two weeks later Caleb walked into the kitchen and told her he had enlisted. Eve stared at him, too shocked to react.

He pulled out a hard-backed chair from under the kitchen table and sat down, staring across the kitchen but not at her as he said, 'I have to get away, Eve. I'm sorry but I have to. I know it's not fair leaving you to cope with the inn and Mother and all, but I'll get someone in to run things. It won't all be on your shoulders. I'll make sure of that, I promise you.'

She sat down too because her legs felt too weak to hold her but still she didn't speak. She could not.

'I'll be in a battalion of the Durham Light Infantry alongside other lads from the north-east, so the sergeant said. Course there's training first. That'll be for a few weeks.'

'When . . .' She had to clear her throat. 'When do you go?'

'For training? In the next week. Apparently there's some hoo-ha about the poor state of training accommodation and more centres are being built, but I've got one the other side of Newcastle. I should be able to nip back when I get leave.'

For the first time since Mary had left, there was life in his voice. Suddenly Eve wanted to hit him. She stood up and walked over to the range and adjusted the big black kettle on the hob. 'Do you want a cup of tea?' she asked flatly.

'Please. I'm frozen. I know it's only the first week of October but there was sleet in the rain earlier.'

She didn't care if it was sleeting. She didn't care about anything except that he had chosen to go to war and he could be crippled or blinded or killed. She kept her back to him as she got out the big brown teapot and warmed it through with hot water. It took enormous effort to keep her voice calm when she said, 'Why didn't you tell me you were thinking of enlisting?'

There was a pause and she nerved herself to turn and face him. He was looking slightly sheepish. 'I suppose I thought you'd try and talk me out of it. I know I'm leaving you in the lurch to some extent and I'm sorry about that, truly I am.'

The fact that he obviously thought she was more worried about taking on extra work than about his safety made her voice sharp. 'But you just went and did it anyway.' Because of Mary. He loved Mary so much that going away to be shot at and goodness knows what was preferable to staying and being reminded of her.

He nodded. As she turned her back on him again, he said quietly, 'I had to get away, Eve. I couldn't stay here.'

'You've said.'

Silence reigned until she had mashed the tea. She brought the teapot to the table, along with two clean mugs, and then fetched the milk jug. His voice small, Caleb said, 'I'll see about getting someone in tomorrow—'

'*I don't care about that.*' It was too revealing. Moderating her tone, she said, 'It's not that, Caleb. I could run the inn myself with all you've shown me over the years as long as you get someone else for the kitchen. It's just that now, with Nell not here and Mary having gone . . .'

'You're lonely.' His voice was soft and slightly surprised. 'Of course you are, I should have realised. The three of you have been together for so long and suddenly – oh, Eve, I'm sorry, I didn't think.'

Not about her, no. His whole being had been tied up with Mary and, to some extent, how he was feeling. Men were selfish. She looked at him, loving him, as she thought, you really are the most blind, stupid man. 'It's all right.' Better he thought she was missing her sisters than suspect the truth.

'Nell isn't too far away and perhaps in the circumstances Toby might be agreeable to her helping out for a bit.'

Eve shook her head. 'I don't think so.'

'Well, I can try. I could put it to him in terms of asking a favour, how about that? We'd pay her of course, but I won't labour on that. I'll stress the family angle, all right?'

Eve wanted to fling her arms round him, to tell him that she couldn't bear the thought of him going, that if he got sent over the water to fight she would never know a moment's peace, day or night, that she loved him more than life itself. She lowered her eyes in case he could read what was in them. 'Two sugars?'

He didn't answer this. What he did say was, and in a voice that was nearly her undoing, 'I should have thought what your sisters' going would mean to you. I'm a fool.'

By the time Caleb was ready to leave Washington for the training camp, a new set-up reigned at the inn. Much to Mildred's fury, Eve was now in the position of innkeeper. Caleb had made her fully conversant with the financial side of things and what was entailed in running the inn as a whole once she had said she was prepared to take it on, declaring he would far rather have her taking care of things in his absence than some stranger he would have to draft in.

A middle-aged widow and her young daughter who had just left school had been taken on as cook and kitchen maid. They now occupied the attic room, Eve having taken over one of the bedrooms on the first floor at Caleb's insistence. In addition to this he had employed a man from the village to work in the front of the inn with Cassie. This meant there was a male presence behind the bar and someone to lift the heavy barrels and work in the meat store when required.

Nell had been unable to come back and work at the inn, not because Toby had forbidden it but because she had just found out she was expecting a child in the spring. On hearing the news, Eve had already determined a portion of the increased wage Caleb was paying her for her extra responsibilities would find its way to the young couple. They had so little, the strike in the summer having taken its toll on their meagre circumstances. She knew she would have to be tactful in what she did because Toby was a proud individual, but as a delighted aunt she could buy all the baby would require quite openly, along with slipping Nell some shillings to supplement her house-keeping on the quiet.

The morning of Caleb's departure was a difficult one. Eve kept telling herself he was only going to training camp but the spectre of France still loomed large. 'You'll write?' she said quietly, once he had come into the kitchen after saying farewell to his mother. She had decided she would say her goodbyes with others present and Ada, the new cook, and her daughter Winnie were busy pummelling dough at the table.

'Of course.' He smiled at her but she could tell he was itching to be off. She doubted the last minutes with Mildred had been particu-larly uplifting. 'But I'll be back soon for a visit no doubt. We get leave, you know.'

She nodded. Now she was actually faced with the moment of his departure, words failed her. A glimmer of what she was feeling must have shown in her face because his smile widened as he said, 'It's only training camp, woman. Don't worry.'

And then her heart stopped beating and the world stood still as he bent and lightly kissed her forehead. 'I know I can rely on you to take care of things, Eve,' he murmured.

For a second of time she was enveloped in his body warmth, so close she could smell the soap on his skin and the faint odour of tobacco on his tweed jacket. She knew it was the kiss of a friend and meant nothing but it was more than she had ever expected. She murmured something, she could never afterwards remember what, and then he was saying goodbye to Ada and Winnie and picking up his bag.

Despite all her good intentions to stay in the house, Eve followed him into the yard and then the street beyond. 'Be careful, won't you?' she said in a small voice.

Caleb nodded. It was a frosty morning, the sky a pearly white and the air crisp and cold. 'You too.'

And then he turned and walked away from her. Eve watched him go, her arms crossed and gripping her waist against the pain in her breast. In that moment she knew that if she could have wished Mary back and married to him so he was safe, she would have done so.

PART THREE

1916 – Homecomings

Chapter 12

'You-you can't mean it.' Mary stared beseechingly at the man who had just risen from the bed.

Clarence Harley-Shawe walked over to the chair where he had laid his clothes an hour previously. He pulled on his trousers before he glanced across at her. Mary was sitting up among the ruffled covers, her hair hanging in tumbled disarray about her shoulders and the dark pink of her nipples vivid against the whiteness of her breasts. Once the sight of her thus would have stirred him but now he had become tired of her charms. He had taken her tonight because he had nothing better to do before he joined his friends at the gambling house. That was the truth of it. And now he wanted rid of her once and for all.

'Please, Clarence.' As her eyes met his, Mary's lips trembled. 'Tell me you don't mean it.'

'Bernard isn't so bad, is he?' He reached for his silk shirt. 'And he is enamoured of you, m'dear.'

'Clarence, *please*.' She began to cry.

'I suggest you consider his offer. You won't get better.'

'But what of us? I–I thought you loved me. You said you loved me. And we've been happy, haven't we?'

It was a great pity when beauty went hand in hand with empty-headedness in the fairer sex. For months now he had found her tedious in the extreme. Without looking at her, he said, 'The lease on this apartment runs out at the end of the week and I shall not be renewing it. It has . . . served its purpose. If you wish to be kept in the manner to which you have become accustomed I suggest you are generous with your favours to Bernard when he calls. Do you understand, Mary?'

'I can't believe you are saying these things.'

'Oh come, come, m'dear. You are a sensible girl, you know how it is. We had a pleasant time together and you were well recompensed for your efforts to make an old man happy, but I have a wife and other obligations which need more time.'

'You haven't been to see me for over a week, how can you say I've taken too much of your time?' She reached out imploringly. 'Please, Clarence, don't do this thing. I care for you, you know I do. I can't bear to think we won't see each other again.'

Why the blazes he had been tempted to bring her to London with him he didn't know. If only he had left her where he'd come across her, all would have been well. But she had fascinated him in those days. Part girl, part woman. Shy one moment and then as brazen as any of the whores he'd enjoyed in his time the next. And so he had set her up in this apartment and showered her with enough pretty things to keep her happy and life had been satisfactory for a while. But now she bored him to death. It served him right for taking a mistress out of his class. Girls like Mary were all right in the whorehouses but he liked a mistress who could discuss politics and current thinking in the aftermath of their lovemaking. A woman with intellect who could stir more than his nether regions. If this girl did but know it, she had been fortunate he hadn't ended their liaison long before now.

He buttoned his coat and reached for his top hat and gloves, but before he could cross the room and make his escape, Mary had crawled across the bed towards him and flung herself at his feet, holding on to his legs. 'Please, please, Clarence, you can't do this thing. I'm not – I'm not a . . .'

'A whore, m'dear?' Her tears were mingling with liquid from her nose and mouth and his distaste was great. He removed her fingers from the fabric of his trousers and pushed her away before stooping and wiping the dampness from his clothes with a fine lawn handker-chief. Irritated beyond measure now, he said, 'But a whore is exactly what you are. You know it, Bernard knows it, so do the rest of my friends. Frankly, you can count yourself fortunate that Bernard asked for you when I expressed my desire to be rid of the situation. But this is too bad, you are forcing me to say things I never intended to say. Why cannot you say goodbye with dignity and let us end it like that? Bernard is a good man.'

'He's fat and bald and has smelly breath.'

'He is a Sir and he has connections.' It was sharp and cold. 'And you are an ignorant girl with little to commend you. Remember that when you make your decision. It is easy to fall back in the gutter, m'dear, but it will be almost impossible to climb out of it again if you bite the hand that feeds you. The finer things of life come at a price, so pay it.'

As she went to clutch him again he thrust her from him so violently she went sprawling backwards, banging her head on the dressing-table stool. 'Goodbye, Mary.' He did not look at her again as he strode out of the room, nor did he heed her cries to stay. He wanted only to be gone.

Mary heard the door to the apartment slam and it was only then she became quiet. She picked herself up from the floor, reached for her silk robe on the end of the bed and wrapped it round her nakedness. He had gone. He had gone and he wouldn't be coming back. The thing she had been dreading for months now had come upon her. She had known he was tired of her, he had made little effort to hide it even though he had still expected her to service him as willingly as ever when he had called to see her. Sometimes he had barely stayed half an hour whereas before it had been the whole night on occasion.

147

Drying her eyes, she walked across to the long walnut dressing table and righted the stool before sitting on it. She stared at herself in the mirror. It hadn't been like this at first. At first he had made a fuss of her, petted her. Not that he was ungenerous even now. This beautiful apartment, her clothes, her horse and carriage and the little maid who came every day at six in the morning ready to run her bath and went home at night once she had served the dinner, it was all paid for by Clarence. And she had been grateful.

She stared down at her smooth white hands and manicured nails, picturing them for a moment as they had been when she had first left Washington. She didn't want to return to being a skivvy. She *wouldn't*. No matter what. But Bernard Vickers? Shuddering, she stared into the large blue eyes in the mirror. He was repulsive. But rich. Richer even than Clarence.

She turned and glanced round the room. The silk sheets, the elaborate decoration and fine furniture, she had got used to this. She couldn't do without it.

After more than ten minutes she stood up. She had never fooled herself that she loved Clarence although she had told him she did of course. But she had liked him. And she had liked the lifestyle he had been prepared to pay for. Could she grow to like Bernard Vickers? He must be twenty years older than Clarence, seventy if a day. One of his grandsons had recently got married at the Abbey amid much pomp and ceremony.

Leaving the bedroom she walked into the high-ceilinged hall, past the door leading to the drawing room which had made her gasp when she had first seen it and into the dining room where she had been eating her evening meal when Clarence had arrived unexpectedly. The remains of the duck with orange and the lemon soufflé which had been her pudding she ignored, reaching instead for the bottle of wine on the table and filling her glass to the brim. She drank it straight down and then poured herself another. Clarence had said Bernard would be calling to see her later when she must have her answer ready. How much later she didn't know, but she did know she would need fortifying before she opened the door to him.

The diamonds in the bracelet she had on sparkled as she put her glass down. She touched the jewels lovingly. Clarence had bought her this for Christmas only three weeks ago and she had fooled herself into believing that he still cared for her. She had been clutching at straws, she knew that now. She had known it then.

It was nearly midnight when she heard the knock on the door. She had changed the sheets on the bed and had a long bath, sprinkling her favourite perfume in the water. Now, wearing nothing but a whisper-thin black negligée and with her hair brushed to gleaming silk, she walked into the hall and opened the door, a welcoming smile on her face.

Chapter 13

'So what do you reckon then? Think we're going to knock them Germans into next week like the old generals want?'

Caleb shrugged. 'I wouldn't hold your breath.'

'Oh, I shan't hold me breath, mate. Not me. I've been in this war too long to do that. Now Kitchener's gone, there's no voice of reason left, if you want my opinion.'

Caleb didn't particularly, but he liked Algernon Griffiths or Big Al as he was generally known and so he let him talk on. Al liked to talk, and there were few enough pleasures left in the world for sure. Caleb had first met Al when they had been up to their waists in mud and crawling with lice in the trenches some months back in January. Now it was the beginning of July and they'd looked out for each other since then. Algernon had one of those naturally optimistic natures that refused to be downcast for more than an odd minute or two, whatever the situation.

'The corp says we're going to be part of the offensive on the Western Front. The generals have been planning it for months. Always worries me when I hear that. If they've had it in mind for months then ten to one the Germans know about it an' all.'

'You could be right.' Caleb adjusted his pack which weighed a ton. He and his battalion were marching at a smart pace, some of the men singing music hall tunes and accompanied by the odd mouth organ here and there as they walked in the dead of night. They could see points of flame stabbing the darkness miles away where British shells were falling.

They were passing through a small French town and officers in staff cars slid past, the motorcycles of despatch riders scooting by. It was good to be walking briskly for a change after all the time in the trenches. They passed a French sentry who raised an arm in salute, calling, '*Bonne chance, mes camarades.*'

'Aye, the same to you, chum,' Al yelled back. 'With knobs on an' all.'

'He was wishing us well.'

'I know that, I'm not as thick as I look.'

'That'd be impossible,' Caleb agreed, straight-faced.

'The corp reckons this assault on the Somme is the biggest battle of the war up to yet. Umpteen divisions of our lot and the Frenchies on a fifteen-mile front. If it's anything like them poor blighters at Gallipoli had to put up with, it'll be another disaster in the making. I had a cousin in that lot and he wrote his mam they had to skedaddle with their tails tucked atween their legs. Mind, they did get ninety thousand men out of there without losing one, so that's something.'

Caleb nodded. He wasn't interested in a retreat which had happened six months ago. As Al elaborated on the mistakes that had been made in Gallipoli, he let his mind focus on the letter he had received that morning which was tucked in his tunic pocket. He had come to rely on Eve's letters like the bread he ate and the water he drank. They provided a link with a world that wasn't bloody and soul-destroying, a world where normal folk still went to bed at night in a real bed and got up in the morning to a cup of tea at their own fireside.

She had written the usual stuff. Nell's little lad was walking already and into everything, and the next one was due in a couple of months. He could see Nell churning them out like clockwork every year, the way she and Toby were going.

His mother was the same as ever and sent her best. By that he took it to mean his mam was driving Eve mad and had sent no message to him at all.

She had acquired a dog, a stray, she thought. She'd found him skulking in the yard one night and took him in for a meal and he'd stayed ever since. Sensible dog, he thought, a smile touching his lips. Obviously knew when he was on to a good thing. If he came back in the next life as a dog he'd make a beeline for Eve's door. And it wouldn't hurt for her to have some protection when the inn was closed either. More than once over the last months he'd worried about that.

'. . . an' about damn time, that's what I say, eh?'

'What?' Caleb became aware that Al was waiting for an answer and he hadn't heard a word. 'Sorry, you can't hear yourself think with them bawling out "Pack up your troubles in your old kit bag".'

'Better than "Keep the home fires burning". They've done that one to death the night.' Al hoisted his pack further up his back. 'I said it's about time they tightened up the call-up net, in my opinion. Our Ellie's written the government's going to conscript all men between the ages of eighteen and forty-one, married or not, 'cos they can't get enough volunteers. Now I'm not saying everyone should've been as barmy as me an' you and put their hands up for this lot from the start' – Caleb knew that was exactly what Al was saying, having listened to his views on what he called the lily-livered blighters back home who were sheltering behind their wives' skirts – 'but a blind, deaf an' dumb man knows we're not going to win this war without every last jack man mucking in.'

'I suppose so.'

'You know so, man. We all do. Our Ellie says some of the women have taken to handing out white feathers to blokes who are weak-kneed, shaming 'em like.'

Poor devils. As Al talked on, Caleb's mind returned to Eve and home. He realised the two had become synonymous in his mind. And it was funny, but he could picture Eve in his head as clear as day whereas when he tried to conjure up Mary's face, it was indistinct, blurred. It hadn't been that way at first. It had been after Ypres when most of the men he had joined up with had been cut to pieces by German guns or had their insides burnt away by choking chlorine gas that he had realised he hadn't thought of Mary in days. He still loved her, he would always love her, he told himself firmly, but the ache of her loss which had paralysed him at first was easing. The blood and guts of trench warfare had seen to that.

'Looks like we're nearly there,' Al said as they heard one of the officers up front shouting orders.

'There' turned out to be astride the River Somme in Picardy. After making their way to their positions, they waited for morning. At 7.30 a.m. the artillery barrage was lifted and Caleb and Al and forty-four divisions of British and French soldiers went over the top. Caleb and Al, along with every other British soldier, were carrying entrenchment tools, two gas helmets, wire cutters, two hundred and twenty rounds of ammunition, two sandbags, two Mills bombs, their groundsheet, haversack, water bottle and field dressing – almost seventy pounds of equipment each. They staggered into no-man's-land at little more than a slow walk, their orders to seize four thousand yards of enemy territory by nightfall.

In the first five minutes Caleb lost his friend and most of his battalion, cut down by relentless machine-gun fire. He saw Al fall, his face blown away, and within seconds there were heaps of dead and dying. The noise, the screams, the thunder of guns was numbing, he couldn't take in the horror of the slaughter he was seeing. They were being mowed down indiscriminately, officers and men together, but still they had to go forward into the guns.

He didn't pray, he didn't think, he didn't do anything except stumble forward in the noise and din and falling bodies, the smell of gunpowder and blood and mud sticking in his nostrils. The German defences were formidable and deep, even the capture of the first and second lines brought little advantage and no respite from the guns. They had been assured the bombardments by the air force in previous days had destroyed the heavy barbed-wire obstacles in their path, but more soldiers were getting tangled in the wire, hanging like screaming puppets until they were blasted into oblivion.

At midday the attack was suspended so the stretcher-bearers could work in no-man's-land. The German guns were silent, and the men sat in small stunned groups in the trenches. Caleb looked round him. Every man was blood-splattered, filthy, the whites of their eyes showing stark in their grimy faces. Al was gone. He couldn't take it in. And how many others? Hundreds, thousands. Why was he still alive? Lots of those men had had wives, bairns. Al and his Ellie had three. Why was he alive and they had gone?

Someone passed him a mug of tea and he drank it without tasting it. He felt tired, bone tired. They had marched all night and fought all morning. What was Eve doing right now? In that other world that he hadn't valued until he had left it. He shut his eyes but he could still see red, a red the colour of blood, behind his closed eyelids.

The British artillery fire resumed at four that afternoon even though there were still wounded to be retrieved from no-man's-land. The toll rose swiftly until nightfall. Caleb was amazed to find himself alive at the end of the day.

That night he sat dozing on and off in his dugout, wondering when his turn would come. He wouldn't survive. No one could survive this slaughter for long. He hoped when he went, it would be like Al, blown away into oblivion in a moment of time. One searing shaft of pain and then nothing. There were too many lads who'd been maimed or burned or blinded. *Blinded.* His stomach muscles clenched. Left helpless like a baby, needing someone to lead you for the rest of your life. He wouldn't be able to tolerate that, he'd have to end it.

He'd write to Ellie. He nodded mentally to the thought. Tell her Al hadn't suffered, that he'd been joking and laughing till the very end which had been quick. Al would have wanted him to do that and it might give his wife some comfort in the midst of her mourning.

Would there be one soul who would genuinely mourn for him? He doubted his mother would waste a tear, they'd never got on. He'd often thought it was funny that his da, who'd been a gentle, kind man, should have been taken, whereas his mam had gone on and on. Only the good die young. He'd heard that phrase bandied about a lot in the last months, but certainly it applied to his parents.

As dawn broke he reached in his haversack for his sketch pad and pencil. Working swiftly, he drew a picture of Al as he had often seen him in the evening when his friend would take the small picture of his wife out of his tunic pocket and stare at it for a long time. Al's face had lost its habitual toughness at those times and Caleb had realised he was seeing the husband and father rather than the soldier. The picture finished, he wrote a quick letter and put the two together in an envelope. He'd see it was put with Al's effects which were being sent to his wife. He'd do it this morning before he went over the top again. Just in case. He went to put the notepad away and then paused.

He would write to Eve. It hadn't been long since he had written but that didn't matter. The desire for a link with home was strong this morning.

A tiny movement on the perimeter of his vision caused him to glance up. A small bird was perched on top of the dugout, looking at him with bright black eyes. It was a beautiful little thing and as he stared at it the tiny head tilted for a moment before the bird flew off.

Well, how about that. Caleb glanced round to see if anyone else had noticed but his comrades were fast asleep.

Feeling the need to share the wonderful normality of the incident, he swiftly captured the little bird on paper before beginning to write beneath his sketch, 'You'll never guess who came to see me this morning . . .'

When he had finished the letter he read it through, realising he had said far more than he had intended. He had told her about Al and the letter he had written to Al's wife, about the mindless madness of the last hours, of the ache in his heart for England's green countryside.

Would she think him weak, womanly? He read the words once more. But it was how he felt. He would give the rest of his life for a day spent tramping England's countryside with his sketch pad. A muscle in his jaw working, he put the letter in an envelope and addressed it to Eve. He would send it. He could trust Eve to read it and not think the less of him. She would understand. She was like that.

His sergeant, a rough diamond, appeared round a curve in the trench, rousing the men who were still sleeping. When he reached Caleb he stood for a moment. 'Get any sleep, Travis?'

'Some, Sarge.'

'I was sorry Griffiths bought it yesterday. He was a good lad, was Griffiths.'

'Aye, he was, Sarge. One of the best.'

'We go over in fifteen minutes so get yourself something to eat.'

'I'm not hungry, Sarge.'

'I didn't ask if you were hungry or not. I told you to get something to eat. All right?'

'Aye, Sarge.' Fifteen minutes. Fifteen minutes before likely as not he'd be blown to smithereens. What did it matter if he went to meet his Maker on a full stomach or not? Nevertheless, he did as he was told after dropping the letters into the mail bag. Sergeant Todd was a good bloke who was easy to talk to but no one in their right mind would consider disobeying him.

Fifteen minutes later Caleb was in position. The deafening explosions meant the sergeant had to bellow at the top of his voice when the moment came for the men to go over the top.

Caleb began to stumble forward as shells screamed and men shouted in a repeat of the day before. Then to his horror he found he'd blundered into a tangle of barbed wire. Panicking, he tore at it with his hands. He didn't want to die like this, caught like a lump of meat on a skewer. And then he was free again and the relief was almost exhilarating.

The barrage from the German guns was fierce but still they advanced inch by inch. Men fell to the right and left of him and once or twice the force of the shell which had blasted them knocked him off his feet but only for a moment or two. He didn't know how far they had advanced or how much time had gone by when they reached the abandoned dugout. The sergeant was in front of him and as he reached him he bawled at Caleb and the privates behind to get into the trench, which they did gladly.

A shell burst overhead and a shower of wood, dirt and clay rained for a moment or two. It had hit the far end of the trench and he could see a couple of men frantically digging out another who had been buried. The sergeant had joined them and was yelling orders. They went over the top again and now it was mayhem, men being killed indiscriminately by not just the German artillery but their own. Caleb was firing his pistol but he had no idea if his bullets reached their targets, and then there was a period of face-to-face fighting before once again the Germans retreated a few hundred yards. He knew his steel blade had taken at least one of the enemy out, he had seen the man's eyes widen and the blood spew out of his mouth as he'd sliced into his chest. Five years ago he would never have dreamed he would stick a bayonet into a man's belly with as little feeling as if he was swiping at a fly. What had he become? What had they all become? Living pawns in a macabre game played by the old generals.

And then he knew he had been hit. He felt no pain, just the impact of what registered like a giant fist full of heat. He hit the ground and lay for a moment, stunned. And it was when he went to pull himself up like all those other times he had been knocked down that the pain made him cry out.

'Stay put, lad.' Sergeant Todd's face was thrust close to his. 'I'll be back for you in a while.'

He nodded. He didn't believe him. It was the sort of thing you said to give someone hope, knowing the odds were stacked against them. He'd done it himself. They both knew that stuck here like a broken doll he'd likely be blasted into smithereens within minutes. He looked down at his legs. Hell, what a mess. He screwed up his eyes against the pain.

Could he crawl back to that trench? When he tried to bend his knees the pain was so unbearable he fainted. When he came round he was aware of indistinct figures some way in front of him, lunging and turning as they fought. Everything in him shrank from lying here waiting for a German bayonet or bullet to finish him off. Steeling himself, he brought his torso off the ground with his arms and began to drag himself round, his legs trailing behind him.

How many times he passed out before he reached the dugout he didn't know. He passed bodies and bits of bodies, pushing them aside as they blocked his path. He had almost reached the trench when the weakness overcame him. He lay a couple of feet away, unable to move. And then a head appeared above the parapet and a pair of arms reached for him, dragging him unceremoniously over the edge. As he hit the ground, agony exploded in every cell of his body and he knew no more.

Chapter 14

'He's alive. Here.'

As Mildred handed her the telegram which had come that morning, Eve drew in a long shuddering breath. Gathering her wits, she read the few words which stated Private Caleb Travis had been injured in the course of duty and shipped back to England to a hospital down south. The words swam before her eyes but conscious of Mildred's hard gaze she forced herself to say quietly, 'I'll make arrangements to go and see him.' *He was alive.* She had thought . . .

'See him? It's over two hundred miles away, girl.'

'What's that got to do with it?'

'Who'll take care of things here while you're gallivanting?'

Eve took a step backwards, her face now looking as hard as Mildred's. 'Nathaniel is more than able to take over and Ada needs no supervision in the kitchen. She's more than competent.'

'And me? What about my needs? Who'll take care of me?'

'Ada and Winnie—'

'I don't want either of them numbskulls bumbling about in here. It's took me long enough to get you to do things right.'

'That's up to you. I'm going to see him so you have the choice of Ada and Winnie or nothing.'

· Mildred glared at her. 'I'll see my day with you, girl. As God is my judge. Taking advantage of a poor invalid.'

Eve turned away. She had heard it all before. Countless times. Mildred's threats and rages had little effect on her these days. 'Eat your breakfast,' she said tonelessly.

Out in the passage she stood for a moment, clutching the telegram to her breast. Then she made herself walk into the kitchen. Ada and Winnie were waiting for her as she had known they would be. 'He's alive,' she said. 'But hurt. He's in a hospital in Oxford.'

Ada's brow wrinkled. 'Oxford? Isn't that down south?'

Eve nodded. 'I shall need to make arrangements to go and see him. Will you be able to cope if I go? With Mrs Travis, I mean? She's already playing up about me going.'

'Oh aye, lass. Don't worry about that. She don't bother me none. I can give as good as I get.' Ada's eyes narrowed. 'Sit down,' she said, 'before you drop down. You look bad.'

She felt bad. Weakly, Eve murmured, 'I'm all right.'

'Aye, and I'm a monkey's uncle. Here,' swiftly Ada poured her a strong cup of tea with plenty of sugar, 'get that down you, lass. You've had a shock.'

As she sat down at the table, the big shaggy dog who had been lying on the clippy mat in front of the range fire immediately came to her side, whining as he pushed his head into her hand. Eve patted him and took a sip of the scalding hot tea, her mind racing. She would have to travel by train and she had never ventured on one before. How would she go about it? And she would have to find somewhere to stay in Oxford, at least overnight. The prospect was daunting but not as daunting as staying here and doing nothing.

Five days later she was standing outside the hospital in Oxford. Caleb's letter had arrived that very morning just as she was about to leave for the train, and she had read and re-read it countless times on the journey south. It had been different to the ones before it, and not just because of the beautiful little drawing of the bird. The others had been more in the nature of reports, stating where he was and what was happening around him. This one revealed his thoughts, the inner man, and because of that it was infinitely precious.

She had checked the visiting times earlier and now she made her way through the hospital corridors as the nice lady on the end of the telephone had directed her. When she reached the ward she took a deep breath before entering. There were a few visitors dotted about the ward but many of the beds had no one sitting by them. Several beds had curtains drawn round them and although perhaps half of the men were sitting up, quite a few were lying still. The highly polished floor, clinical cleanliness and strong smell of antiseptic emphasised the fact she had stepped into another world as she walked over to the nurses' station.

'I'm looking for Caleb Travis,' she said a little nervously to the somewhat severe looking sister who had raised her head at her approach. 'I understand he's in this ward.'

The sister smiled a tight, prim smile. 'That's right. And you are?'

'His housekeeper.' She had decided on the journey that housekeeper sounded better than trying to explain she managed Caleb's inn for him. 'His mother is an invalid so she asked me to come in her place.' Another necessary embellishment.

'I see.' Piercing eyes looked her up and down. 'I understand Mr Travis's home is a good distance away.'

'In the north-east, yes.'

'You know Mr Travis is still very poorly?'

Eve's heart missed a beat. She nodded. 'What exactly are the nature of his injuries?' she asked quietly.

'His legs took most of the damage but there was an injury to his chest too which affected his breathing for a time. I'm happy to say that has now settled down.'

Eve stared at the emotionless face. What did 'most of the damage' mean? 'He will get better? I mean he will be able to walk normally in time?'

'Dr Reynold is very pleased with how the last operation went.'

The last operation? 'How many operations has he had?'

'Mr Travis was operated on immediately he arrived here to remove shrapnel from his chest. Once it was considered safe to do so, Dr Reynold operated again, this time on his legs. Unfortunately there was a slight complication with the right leg which necessitated a further operation yesterday.'

'I see.' No, no she didn't. Telling herself she couldn't be palmed off, Eve said again, 'He will be able to walk, won't he? In time, I mean. Once his legs heal?'

The sister hesitated. 'The right leg was a cause for some concern but like I said, Dr Reynold was pleased with how the operation went yesterday. You can rest assured he has done all he can to save the leg.'

The colour drained from Eve's face and now the sister lost some of her stiffness. She rose swiftly and came round the desk, taking Eve's arm as she murmured, 'There, child, don't worry. I'm sure it will be all right. The next few days will tell. But he is young and fit and that is in his favour.'

Caleb. Oh, Caleb, Caleb. 'Can I see him?'

'Of course, but you do understand he mustn't be upset? We need to keep him positive. Dr Reynold is of the opinion that the patient's state of mind has a bearing on his recovery.'

Eve's shoulders straightened. 'I won't upset him.'

'Good, good. Come this way.' The sister led her to the first of the beds with the curtains round it. Popping her head through the slit, she said, 'Mr Travis has a visitor, nurse. Have you finished?'

'Just finished, sister.'

As the sister drew the curtains, a small plump nurse bustled out carrying a bowl and towel, smiling at Eve as she passed. Eve couldn't smile back, her eyes going to the inert figure in the bed. Caleb had a huge cage over his legs and he was lying flat with his eyes shut. His face was as white as lint. As she moved forward, he opened his eyes and to Eve's huge relief his voice sounded the same as ever as he said, '*Eve*. I didn't know it was you. I thought it was the hospital padre again. He keeps checking to see if I'm still alive.'

'Go on with you, Mr Travis.' The sister's voice was disapproving. 'The Reverend Briggs is concerned for all our patients, as you well know. He likes to have a cheery word now and again.'

Eve sat down on the chair by the bed as the sister returned to the nurse's station, glad of the moment or two to collect herself. She wanted to take his hand but fearing he might think she was too forward, she contented herself with smiling and then saying softly, 'How are you feeling?'

'Not too bad.' He smiled faintly. They both knew it was a lie. 'How did you get here?'

'On the train. It was quite an adventure.'

'Who came with you?'

'I came by myself.' She smiled again.

'By yourself?' He stared at her. Then reached out his hand which she gripped, her heart thudding, as he said, 'Bless you, Eve. That was kind of you. But you shouldn't have come all this way by yourself.'

'I wanted to.' His hand felt cool although the ward was warm. 'Everyone wanted to know how you were.'

He closed his eyes for a moment but his voice was strong when he said, 'A lot better than some of these poor devils, I can tell you. There's one man who's lost an arm and both his legs.' He paused, his voice low when he added, 'And some of them are ill in their minds, you know? They wake up screaming, they think they're still out there.'

'Oh, Caleb.' She stared at him, aghast.

'But I'm all right. Just tired.'

Just tired. Remembering her promise to the sister, who was watching her with eagle eyes from behind her desk, she swallowed hard. 'I've brought you a couple of things. Some fruit and those toffees you like. And Ada's sent one of her fruit cakes.'

'Any brandy?' he asked, straight-faced.

He was still holding her hand. She wondered if he realised. 'You're not allowed brandy.'

'I know.' He grinned at her. 'I was hoping you didn't.'

She smiled. Did he know there was a possibility he might lose his leg? He couldn't, could he? He was too cheerful. And then she swallowed again when he said very quietly, 'What have they told you?'

'That you've had three operations, one to remove shrapnel from your chest and two on your legs.' As she looked into the deep brown eyes she suddenly realised she was mistaken, he knew all right. Quickly, she said, 'I got your letter this morning, the one in which you drew a picture of the little bird.'

He stared at her for a moment. 'That seems a lifetime ago.'

'You said you were longing for the time you could walk the lanes around Washington again. That time will come, Caleb.'

'You think so?' His eyes were holding hers, watching her.

'I know so.' She nodded. 'Without a doubt.'

He squeezed her hand, shutting his eyes again. His voice was barely audible when he murmured, 'I was feeling very low today, Eve. Like . . . like giving up.'

She didn't know what to say. She would have given the world to be able to put her arms round him and kiss him, to comfort him. But all she could do was sit and hold his hand.

And then his eyes opened. 'But you came and now . . . now I don't feel like that.'

Her voice thick, she said, 'I'm glad.'

'When do you have to go back?'

Making her mind up on the spur of the moment, she said, 'Not for a few days.' They could manage at the inn. They would have to. She would get a message to them explaining how things were here. She couldn't leave until she knew. Until *he* knew. Ada and Winnie would understand.

She stayed until the end of visiting time although they didn't talk much after that but he didn't let go of her hand. When the bell rang he still didn't let go, not even when she stood up and said, 'I have to go, Caleb.'

'You'll come tomorrow? Please, Eve?'

She didn't think visiting was allowed on Thursdays but she didn't intend to let that stop her. 'I'll try.'

'Good.' He smiled at her, squeezing her hand again.

Warning herself that this meant nothing, that any familiar face from home would have worked on his vulnerable state of mind in the same way, she gently extracted her fingers from his. 'I'll have to go. The sister is looking daggers at me. I'm the last visitor left.'

'That's Sister Shelton. Her bark's worse than her bite.'

'I'd rather not suffer either.'

She was rewarded by a grin. 'I'm glad you came, Eve.'

She nodded, her voice soft. 'So am I. Goodbye, Caleb.'

She stopped at the sister's desk on her way out. 'When is the next visiting time?' she asked quietly.

'Normally Saturday between three and four thirty but we make allowances in certain circumstances. You are the first visitor Mr Travis has had. I presume he has no friends or relations in these parts? No one who can easily pop in?'

'No, sister. There's no one.'

'When do you have to return home?'

Eve hesitated. 'I want to stay until the doctor is sure he's going to be all right. I'll get lodgings somewhere.'

The sister nodded, her starched cap rigid. 'Then we'll see you at the same time tomorrow afternoon.'

'Thank you.' Eve relaxed. 'Thank you very much.'

The tight face softened just the slightest. 'We always put the patient's best interests first.'

'Yes, I can see that.' Eve smiled and walked away, her heart singing. He would be all right. She'd make him all right.

Eve stayed in Oxford for a full week. At the end of that time

Dr Reynold pronounced himself satisfied that both legs were healing nicely. The patient would never win the Olympics, he remarked jocularly to a prim-faced Sister Shelton, but there was no reason why by the end of the year he shouldn't be walking without his sticks. Not if he was sensible. And they would see about moving him closer to home now he was out of danger. Would the patient like that?

So it was that when Eve took her leave of Caleb on the day she was returning to the north-east, he was a vastly different individual to the dangerously ill man of a week before and looking forward to his transfer to the north. 'They reckon a week or so if it can be arranged and then I should be moved to Newcastle or Sunderland.' He smiled at her, his eyes bright. 'And then I shall be home in no time.'

No time, according to what Sister Shelton had told her, would be a good month or two but Eve didn't dampen his enthusiasm.

'I'll come and see you as soon as I know where you are,' she promised, 'but in the meantime do as you're told and don't try to do too much.' The sister had told her only that morning that they had caught Caleb attempting to get out of bed because he had a fierce distaste for the bedpan he was forced to use at present.

'Yes, ma'am.' He grinned at her and she smiled back. And then he caught her hand, his voice soft as he said, 'Thanks for staying, Eve. I don't know how I'd have got through the last week without your visits to look forward to. In the middle of the night . . . Well, you know. Things always seem at their blackest then.'

She was trembling deep inside. She always trembled when he touched her. Even before he had gone to war it had been the same. She wetted her lips. 'That's all right.'

'It must have cost you a fortune in that boarding house. I'll make it right when I come home.'

'Don't be silly. I'm not exactly destitute.'

'It will seem strange tomorrow when you don't come.'

She didn't think she could stand much more of this without flinging herself on him and that would never do. 'Look, that's the bell. I must go.' Even to her own ears her voice sounded throaty. She saw his eyes narrow. 'I'll give your love to your mam, shall I? Say you sent her a big kiss?'

Her attempt to lighten what had become a tense few moments worked. 'Not if you want us to remain friends,' Caleb grunted. 'But give Nell a hug from me, OK? And tell her I'm looking forward to seeing that bairn of theirs.'

'It'll be two bairns soon.' He had let go of her hand and she stood up. 'She looks ready to pop, bless her.' Friends, he had said. Did he see her as a woman at all? 'Goodbye, Caleb.'

'Goodbye, Eve. And thanks again for everything.'

Outside in the summer sunshine she stood still for a moment or two, composing herself. Two women came out of the doors of the hospital, one crying bitterly and the other trying to comfort her. As they passed her she heard the first one say, 'This war! What's glorious about a man with no legs, you tell me that,' and then they moved out of earshot. Eve stood and watched them until they disappeared from view, the blazing sunshine mocking the tragedy. How many more women were facing the same sort of thing, their loved ones crippled or blinded or maimed beyond recognition. Thank God, oh thank God that Caleb was out of the war now. Lloyd George might give his rousing speeches but the reality of the conflict was in the building behind her and they were the ones who had survived, if you could call it survival for some of the broken bodies she had seen in the last week. The war that had been supposed to end that first Christmas was going on and on, what would be left at the end of it?

She began to walk, knowing she had to hurry if she wasn't going to miss the train.

She wished she didn't have to go back to Washington and leave Caleb here, but although he saw her only as a friend they had grown closer over the last days. And love could blossom out of friendship, given the right circumstances. She would be able to visit him often when he was moved north and once he was home again anything could happen. She wasn't going to give up, somehow she would make him love her. She didn't mind how long it took and now he was safe, time was on her side.

By the time the horse-drawn cab she'd caught outside the station dropped Eve at the inn she felt like a wet rag. The moon was riding high in the sky but it was still quite warm and muggy, not so much as a breath of wind moving the sluggish air.

She entered the inn by way of the back yard and as she stepped into the scullery she was immediately greeted by a whine. 'Jack, is that you, boy?' The next moment she was almost knocked off her feet by a rapturous shaggy shape. 'What are you doing out here by yourself?' she murmured as she fussed the ecstatic animal. 'Why aren't you keeping Ada and Winnie company?'

She left her travelling bag where it had fallen and opened the door into the kitchen, only to freeze as she took in the scene in front of her. Nell was sitting at the kitchen table and Ada was stirring something on the range, but it was the golden-haired girl opposite Nell who claimed Eve's attention.

Mary had come home.

Chapter 15

'I tell you, Toby, there's something funny about all this.' It was the next morning and Nell and her husband were sitting having their breakfast before he had to leave for the pit. 'When Winnie came to fetch me yesterday and said Mary had turned up at the inn, I didn't know what to expect, but not what greeted me, I can tell you. She's . . . different.'

'Well, she would be, she's been gone a couple of years.'

'Aye, I know, but it's more than that. She says her husband's an officer away fighting and she's dressed nice, beautiful, but why would she choose to come and pay a visit now, her expecting an' all? Don't that seem strange to you?'

'When did she say the bairn was due?'

'October. But like I said, there's something funny going on.'

Toby sat back in his chair. 'What is it you're saying, lass?'

'I don't know.' Nell gave a weak smile. 'I don't know what I'm saying. Oh, perhaps I'm being silly. Put it down to my condition.' She patted her huge stomach, the baby was due in four weeks at the end of August.

Toby didn't smile. 'You're never silly,' he said slowly. 'If you think

169

there's something wrong then there probably is. What does Eve say? Does she agree with you?'

'We didn't have a chance to speak privately. She didn't get home until I was ready to leave. I'll try and have a word on the quiet with her today.'

Toby nodded, standing up and picking up his bait tin from the table. 'I don't want you worrying,' he said quietly, 'not with the babbie an' all. You've enough on your plate looking after Matthew and it being so hot. Whatever is wrong, if something *is* wrong, we'll sort it. All right? She's back in one piece and according to you doing very nicely thank you. Whatever it is, it can't be that bad, pet.'

Nell nodded, and then as they heard Matthew call out, she said, 'Let me get him quick and then you can see him for a minute before you go. He likes that.'

The next five minutes were filled with the child but once Toby had left for the pit and Matthew was settled in his wooden high chair eating his porridge, Nell found herself going over what had happened the evening before. Toby was of the mind nothing much was wrong but she wasn't so sure. May God forgive her if she was wrong, but she didn't believe Mary's story of a husband and a big house down south and all the rest of it. Something didn't sit right. And her clothes. They were bonny, fancy, and must have cost a packet, but . . . Nell couldn't find the words to describe the way Mary had been dressed. If she had been more wordly she would have known the colours were just a little too garish, the cut of the bodice of the dress a smidgen too low. As it was, the unease in the pit of her stomach wouldn't go away.

Eve was experiencing the same thing. Owing to the fact the three spare rooms at the inn were occupied by paying guests, Mary was sharing her room which was more than big enough for two with a large double bed and small writing bureau and chair as well as a small sofa under the bay window. Mary seemed to have filled the room with her bags and clothes, but what had really shocked Eve was her sister's nightwear. She couldn't bring herself to use the word indecent but the transparent black negligées and nightdresses, along with Mary's under-wear, had caused her mouth to fall open. She had spent all night telling herself she was probably being stuffy and old-fashioned, that she had no idea what the middle-class and upper-class fashions were or how high society behaved, but nevertheless she felt perturbed and uncom-fortable. And Mary herself, she was so brittle, so gay. It didn't seem natural, not with the uncertainty of a husband at the front and a baby on the way.

Eve had risen early and come down to the kitchen where she'd had her breakfast with Ada and Winnie and caught up with the local gossip and how things had gone in the last week while she had been away. Jack hadn't left her side, but now as she prepared a tray for Mary who was still sleeping, he made no attempt to follow her as she left the kitchen. Ada had told her Mary had made a great fuss about shutting the dog out because he had growled at her when she had first arrived. 'I think it was the fur coat she had draped over one of the suitcases,' Ada confided. 'Apparently she didn't want to pack it in case it got squashed. I think Jack thought it was some sort of animal.'

'It was once, more than one,' Eve said flatly. Mary had told her with some pride the coat was mink and had cost a fortune. She had seemed to set great store by it.

On reaching the bedroom she entered quietly and placed the tray by the side of the bed. Mary was fast asleep, her hair spread out over the pillows and her breathing quiet and even. She didn't look like a married woman who was expecting a baby in three months' time. Asleep like this beneath the covers, Mary was her baby sister again, fragile and appearing far younger than her seventeen years. 'Mary.' She shook one slim shoulder gently and as her sister opened her eyes, she murmured, 'I've brought you a breakfast tray.'

Mary rubbed her eyes and yawned. 'What time is it?'

'Seven o'clock.'

'Seven o'clock? Heavens, Eve, it's still the middle of the night. I usually sleep the mornings away.'

'You do?' Eve stared at the sleep-flushed face. 'That's a funny way to run a household, isn't it?' Her sister had told her she had a housekeeper and maid at home.

Mary pouted her lips for a moment. 'Not really. Things are done differently down south. I – we entertain a lot.'

'But not when your husband is away surely?'

Mary stretched and yawned again. 'Life doesn't stop when he's not there. And we have lots of mutual friends.'

'Have you a photograph of him or a small portrait?'

'Not . . . not with me. I meant to bring one but I forgot.'

'And his family are from where?'

'Sussex.'

'I thought you said Surrey yesterday.'

'Surrey, Sussex, it's all the same.' Mary sat up in bed and now she appeared every one of her seventeen years and more besides, the sheer material of her nightdress clinging to her body as the covers fell to her waist.

Eve took a deep breath. She had to ask. If she was wrong and mortally offended her sister she'd beg her forgiveness but she had to ask. She placed the tray on Mary's lap and then sat at the end of the bed as Mary began to drink her tea. There was no easy way to say it. 'Are you really married to this man?' she asked quietly.

Mary placed the cup back on its saucer. Eve had expected outrage or at the very least a vehement protestation, but as Mary's blue eyes met hers she saw the lovely face was wary. For answer she held out her left hand on which a wedding ring nestled beside a pretty ruby and seed pearl ring.

Eve's voice was low when she said, 'Anyone can buy a ring, Mary. You know that as well as I. Look, if . . . if you're in trouble, I would rather know now, not find it out later. I'm asking you as your sister and because I love you but I won't be lied to. There will always be a home for you here, you know that. Caleb – Caleb wouldn't see you in need and Mildred has always favoured you, but even she wouldn't like being made a monkey of. Tell me the truth. Are you married or not?'

There was a long silence and Eve's heart rose up in her throat, its beating choking her. She had known. The minute she'd walked in this house last night and seen her sister sitting there, she had known something was very wrong.

'I said I was married because I didn't think you'd want people to know with me being . . .' Mary touched her rounded stomach. 'A husband at the front sounds acceptable.'

Eve's eyes widened and her lips opened and shut without emitting words a few times before she could say, 'So you are not married.' It was worse having it confirmed.

'No, I'm not married.'

'What – what does the father of your child intend to do for you? He'll support you, I hope.'

'Do for me?' Mary laughed harshly. 'Oh, Eve.'

It was as though she had said something terribly naive. 'He knows? About the baby?' As Mary nodded, Eve felt as though she was wading through treacle. 'Then he has to face his responsibilities to you and the child surely? Is he married? Is that it? You can tell me, Mary. I'd rather know it all.'

Mary's façade had cracked. She was biting on her lip now, her head drooped. 'If I tell you you'll hate me.'

'I could never hate you, whatever you've done.'

Mary did not speak for a few moments but continued to gnaw on her bottom lip. 'Are you sure you want the truth? Sometimes it's better not to know.'

'Tell me. Tell me everything from the day you left this house. It can't be worse than what I'm imagining right now.'

At the end of five minutes Eve knew she had been wrong. It *was* worse. Numbly she rose from the bed and walked over to the window, looking out into the sunshine. This room was at the front of the inn and overlooked the village square. It was a pretty view, especially on such a lovely summer's morning. Aware her mind was escaping into trivia, she forced herself to turn and look at Mary. 'And this last man, this Bernard, he's refusing to acknowledge it's his child?'

'He wants nothing more to do with me. He's stopped payment for the rent, I . . . I was literally turned out into the street with just my belongings. He maintains the baby could have been fathered by any one of a number of men but that's not true. He said I'd tried to trap him but I wouldn't do something like that. When I knew I was expecting I tried—' Mary stopped abruptly.

'What? What did you try?' Eve stared at her sister.

'I took something, something the maid got me from one of the old wives who know all about that sort of thing. It made me ill for a week but it didn't work. Nothing did.'

'Mary, you could have died.'

'Well, I didn't.' There was a trace of the old defiance in Mary's voice. 'When it didn't work she, the maid, said she knew someone who would take it away but I didn't dare do that, not have surgery. One girl I know, a girl in my position, was crippled last year like that and her gentleman didn't want to know after. They don't care, not really. All they're concerned about is their good name and their families and their standing in their clubs. I wasn't going to be left like Gracie with no control of my bodily functions.'

She was speaking like a woman of the night, a common prostitute, Eve thought. Her face must have reflected something of her thoughts because now Mary said, and with some heat, 'You said you wanted to know the truth.'

'I did, I do.' They stared at each other for a moment.

'Are you going to tell Nell?'

'I have to tell Nell. You must see that.'

There was a small silence. 'And Caleb and Mildred?'

Eve drew in a long breath. 'They will need to know you are not married but the rest is up to you. Nell must be told it all, that's only right, but if you don't want Caleb and his mam to know the rest of it, then Nell and I will respect that.'

'I don't. I . . . I want to make a new start here.'

'All right.' Eve's head was pounding. 'So do I take it you're back for good?'

'Yes. I'm done with the south. It's out of my system now.'

'But how were you going to explain staying here for good? With this story of a husband and all?'

'Men are dying all the time in the war, aren't they?'

She was still such a child in some ways. But not in others. Oh no, not in others. Knowing she was going to cry, Eve said thickly, 'Eat your breakfast, I'll be back in a while,' and left the room swiftly. In the passageway downstairs, she paused for a moment, straightening her shoulders, and then walked into the kitchen, clicking her fingers at Jack as she said to Ada and Winnie, 'I'm taking him for a walk, I've got a headache and need to clear the cobwebs.'

She didn't stop until she reached Nell's back door and then she again straightened her shoulders before entering the scullery. Nell was in the kitchen, wiping Matthew's face which was heavily caked with porridge, and she raised startled eyes to her sister, saying, 'What's the matter? You look awful, lass.'

Eve tried to say something but all that emerged was a strangled groan and then Nell's arms were round her and she didn't have to be strong anymore.

Mary lay in a pool of sunlight. She had finished the breakfast Eve had brought and had slipped down under the covers again but now she raised herself slightly, glancing round the room. It was pleasant, comfortable. Not in the same league as what she had been used to over the last two years, but still nice. She had often peeped into these guest rooms when the daily from the village had finished cleaning them and thought how bonny they were, certainly compared to the attic room.

And now Eve had this room as her own. Of course Mildred's was better and Caleb's would likely be in line with his mother's. With the jewellery she had sold once she had known Bernard intended to be rid of her she had a nice nest egg to furnish a room, a couple of rooms, if need be, exactly how she liked.

Slipping out of bed she walked across to the window and peered outside. Could she stand living here? There would be no dinners out, no dancing, no shows and parties. But if she married Caleb she would be mistress of this inn and she could persuade him to drive into Newcastle now and again for a night at the theatre. Yes, she could do that. And as mistress of this place she could take her ease. The child could be cared for by Eve or that young girl in the kitchen. Certainly with a bairn hanging round her neck like a millstone she couldn't go back to her old life. Or she could leave the child here and disappear. She'd done it once before, she could do it again. But she didn't have to decide now.

Oh, how could she have been so foolish as to get caught in this way? Her mouth tightened. But Bernard hadn't been like Clarence. Bernard had expected her to take care of that side of things but he hadn't always given her due warning of his visits, turning up more than once when she hadn't been prepared. He had been a pig of a man, Bernard. She wasn't sorry to be rid of him in some ways.

Padding back to bed she slid under the covers, her hands resting on the mound of her stomach until a movement in her belly caused her to remove her hands, her nose wrinkling with distaste. She couldn't wait to own her body again. How some women could choose to subject themselves to this she didn't know. But for the moment there was nothing she could do about it except bide her time. But she would be comfortable here while she waited. That was the important thing.

'She's back?'

'Yes, yes she's back and expecting a child like I said. There's . . . well, there's no easy way to say it, Caleb. She isn't married or betrothed to the man. He's married and now that she's in the family way he has denied all responsibility. He's quite well off, I understand, but in spite of that has refused to help her in any way.'

Eve watched him struggle to take in what she had said. It was the second time she had visited Caleb since he had been transferred to the hospital in Sunderland but the first time, a few days ago, he had been in pain and too exhausted from the journey to hear about Mary. She had also, she admitted silently, wanted one last time with him without Mary there between them. Instead she had filled the time talking about Nell's baby which had arrived early, a little boy they'd named Robert, and inn business. But today he was sitting up in bed and looked rested and so she broke the news immediately she sat down. She had wanted it over and done with.

'He's abandoned her?' Caleb ground out grimly. 'Was she living with him or is he still living with his wife?'

'I think she lived in her own apartment.'

'She was his mistress.' His jaw clenched. 'A kept woman.'

'I suppose so.'

'Did she know he was married from the beginning?'

'Caleb, you'll have to ask her these things.' On the way to the hospital she had decided that as she wasn't going to lie for her sister but she couldn't tell Caleb the truth, not all of it anyway, that was the stance she would take. 'She . . . she wants to come and see you if you are agreeable.'

He said nothing to this, staring into the distance for a few moments. His face was brooding, withdrawn.

'I said she could stay at the inn for as long as she wants to. You don't mind?' Even as she said it, she was railing at herself for hoping he might show some reluctance.

Caleb roused himself. 'Of course I don't mind.' *Mary.* Back at the inn and in the family way. He had imagined she was gone for ever, he'd told himself he would never see her again. It had been the only way he had been able to come to terms with losing her, to try to forget her and block her out of his mind. And now she was back. His heart was pounding so hard it hurt. 'This man, he seduced her and then led her up the garden path. Something must be done about it.'

'I don't think it was altogether like that.'

'Of course it was like that.' He saw the look on her face and realised his voice had been too sharp. He said quickly, 'I'm sorry, Eve, but these hooray-Henry types are all the same. I'd have the lot strung up if I had my way. When . . .' he paused, rubbing his hand across his mouth, 'is the baby due?'

'Not for three months.'

'Thank heaven she had the sense to swallow her pride and come home. Is she well? Apart from the baby?'

'Yes, she is very well.'

Her lips scarcely moved as she brought out the words and Caleb stared at her for a moment before putting out his hand and placing it over hers. 'Don't worry, everything will be all right. She's home, Eve. That's the main thing.'

'So I'll bring her with me next time.'

Caleb nodded. He didn't know how he was going to feel seeing her again, especially with another man's child swelling her belly, but he was going to have to face it sooner or later if she was going to be living at the inn when he got out of this place. One thing was for sure, she was no more the young innocent girl she had been two years ago than he was the same man he'd been before the war. He had loved her then, he'd nearly driven himself mad in those first days after she'd gone, thinking of another man touching her, kissing her. Since then he'd had more than one woman; he'd discovered some lassies would do almost anything for a bloke in uniform and French girls were no different to English in that respect.

He became aware that Eve was waiting for him to say something. He looked into her face, the face he no longer saw as plain but as reflecting the inner woman, the kind, gentle, inner woman, and tried to bring his thoughts to order. Again he said, 'Don't worry. This can be sorted out, OK? But don't you worry anymore.'

'I'm not.'

'That's all right then.' He didn't know what else to say. She didn't seem herself, but then she wouldn't, would she, after such a shock. 'What has she told folk at the inn?'

He watched her Adam's apple move up and down as she swallowed. 'She's told everyone she's married with a husband at the front because of the baby. In due course she's going to say she's heard he's been killed.'

'That won't fool anyone. People aren't daft.'

'No, I know that but it's up to her, isn't it?'

'How has my mother taken all this?'

'Oh, you know your mam where Mary's concerned. What's happened is everyone and anyone's fault but Mary's.'

Her tone surprised him. He stared at her for a moment and she stared back at him, her green eyes challenging. He had thought he knew all her moods but he couldn't fathom her today. Quietly, he said, 'She's barely seventeen, Eve.'

'I was five years younger than Mary is now when I was running my father's household.'

For the second time in as many minutes he didn't know what to say. After a moment or two, his voice low, he said, 'Aren't you glad she came back rather than ending up in the workhouse or somewhere similar?'

For answer Eve said, 'I fought to keep her out of there when my father and brothers died so I don't think that is a fair question to ask me, Caleb.'

'No, no, I'm sorry. It's just that you seem . . .'

Her eyes tight on him, she said, 'Angry? Upset? Grieved? Disappointed? Aye, I'm all of those things if you want to know and I'm not going to apologise for it either. I don't like what she's become. There, you have it.' She rose to her feet, her face white. 'But she's my sister and I will support her all I can for as long as she wants me to. I'll bring her with me next time and you can ask her all you want to know. All right?'

'You're not going already? You've only just arrived.'

'I've things to do.' She was pulling on her gloves as she spoke.

Caleb stiffened. For crying out loud, anyone would think all this was his fault, the way she was carrying on. He had agreed to see Mary, hadn't he? Said she could stay at the inn for as long as she wanted to. What more could he do or say? 'Don't let me keep you then. Goodbye, Eve.'

'Goodbye.' She stared at him for a moment before turning away.

He watched her walk down the ward and out of the door and she didn't look back and wave as she normally did.

'Didn't stay long today, did she?'

The man in the other bed, a rough-spoken northener who was the comedian on the ward, nodded in the direction Eve had gone.

'She said she'd got things to do.' Caleb was miffed and it showed. 'Couldn't wait to leave, quite frankly.'

'Oh, they've always got things to do, women. Mine's the same. And if she's not doing with her hands, she's talking the hind leg off a donkey. Recites the shopping list in her sleep. Used to drive me mad, she did. Mind, I wouldn't be without her and she's been good about this lot.' He waved his hand at his scarred face. Caleb knew the burns extended over large parts of his torso and one hand had contracted into a claw. 'Me poor old mam fainted clean away when she first came in to see me. I said to her, I never was what you'd call good-looking so what you've never had, you don't miss.'

He grinned at Caleb and Caleb smiled back. 'You look all right to me,' he said quietly.

'Aye, but that's because you're an ugly blighter yourself, mate.'

They continued with the banter which spread to neighbouring beds, but at the back of his mind Caleb was thinking about both Mary's return and the way Eve had been that afternoon. He didn't know which end of him was up, he admitted silently. One minute everything had been straightforward and now he was in turmoil. Why did life always seem to rear up and bite you on the backside when you least expected it?

Chapter 16

When Eve brought Mary to the hospital the next day and watched her sister with Caleb, she knew nothing had changed. And it was clear Mary's power over the male sex extended beyond Caleb; most of the men in the ward couldn't take their eyes off her but Mary only had eyes for Caleb. She cried a little but prettily, told Caleb what she thought he wanted to hear and parried any probing with a tremulous mouth and fluttering hands. By the end of the visit she had him eating out of her hands.

As they left the hospital, Mary said thoughtfully, 'He took it very well, didn't he, me and Bernard and everything. And if anything, he's more attractive than he was before the war. I was worried he might be, well, scarred or something. Like that man in the next bed. But you'd never know there was anything wrong with Caleb.'

'I think if you saw his legs you wouldn't say that.'

'Oh, his legs.' Mary waved her hand. 'They don't matter, it's not like his face, is it? You have to look at someone's face all the time if you're living with them.'

Eve stared hard at her sister but Mary was looking straight ahead.

'Even if he was scarred as badly as that poor man you spoke of, he would still be Caleb, wouldn't he?'

Mary shrugged. 'I might have known you'd look at it like that. You're so nice, our Eve.' She made it sound like a failing. 'But anyway, he's not scarred or anything so that's all right.'

Eve felt sick. Would she be able to stand it? The thought had kept her awake all night. When Caleb was home and she had to endure seeing them together, would she be able to stand it? Well, she'd have to, at least until Mary's baby was born and she knew her sister was all right. After that, once everything had settled down and a routine had been established, there would be no need for her to stay if she didn't want to. And she suspected she would not want to.

Six weeks later at the end of September, Caleb came home.

He had made quite remarkable progress, the doctor at the hospital told Eve on the day of Caleb's departure. Quite remarkable. But that happened sometimes when patients were moved closer to their families and loved ones. It gave them the spur they needed to push themselves, you see, and of course he hadn't seen his mother for a long time, had he? With her being bedridden and unable to visit him. Likely that had motivated him more than a little.

Eve smiled and nodded her head. She knew who had been the spur the doctor spoke of and it certainly wasn't Mildred. After that one visit to Caleb, Mary had announced she felt too embarrassed in her condition to go into a ward full of men again and would prefer to stay at home when Eve visited. Staying at home consisted of staying in bed most of the time, eating chocolates, reading Mildred's magazines and only coming downstairs for her meals, when she invariably managed to upset Ada and Winnie with her high-handed manner. Things improved a little once Caleb was home. Mary was on her best behaviour for one thing, and Eve was spared the visits back and forth to the hospital. Caleb had to rest in the afternoons and he often spent these talking to Mary in her room.

The child was born ten days after Caleb returned. Whether this was early or not was debatable, Mary had not seen a doctor and seemed unsure of her dates. What was certain was that the baby, a little boy, was sickly. He did not cry when he was born and when the doctor, a portly, kindly man whom Eve had called in when Mary's labour had become protracted and the midwife had been unable to cope, told Eve to put him to Mary's breast, he would not suckle.

Taking Eve by the arm, the doctor led her from the bedroom and once they were standing on the landing with the door closed, he said, 'Has your sister been seriously unwell at any time in her pregnancy? There is a school of thought that this can effect the child in the womb.'

Eve stared at the doctor. She was remembering the first morning after Mary had come home when she had admitted she had taken some brew or other to rid herself of the baby and had been ill for a week. 'She might have been but she only came home some weeks ago so I wouldn't really know.'

He nodded. 'Well, it's by the by now. In such cases I've found the only answer is mother's milk and warmth.'

'He-he won't die?' The doctor's voice had been sombre.

'Only God knows that, m'dear. Just do all you can. If he persists in refusing the breast then try spooning a weak broth into him which you've strained through muslin.'

'My other sister has recently had a baby and has milk to spare. Would he be able to have that?'

'Yes, yes, ideal. But again, if he won't suckle, you may have to spoon it into his mouth, a drop at a time. And frequently. Very frequently. Day and night. Do you think you could do that? It will be tiring.'

'Of course.' She would do anything. He had looked such a sweet little baby in the brief glimpse she'd had of him before the doctor had handed him to the midwife but very different to Nell's strong, lusty boy.

After paying the doctor his ten shillings she saw him downstairs and left him talking to Caleb in the kitchen. She sent Winnie to fetch Nell and then flew back upstairs. The midwife was seeing to Mary when she entered the bedroom and the baby was lying quietly in his small crib. Eve had purchased this along with some baby clothes and blankets a few weeks ago when Mary had admitted she had nothing for the baby. She picked him up in the snug cocoon the midwife had made of the blanket and as she did so one little hand became free and the tiny fingers wrapped round her thumb.

'Hello,' she murmured into the milky blue eyes looking up at her. 'I'm your aunty.' He was beautiful, she thought wonderingly. Not like most newborn babies she had seen who were invariably red and blotchy and squashed looking. He was perfect, like a porcelain doll, with his tiny features and miniature face. 'You're going to be all right,' she whispered softly. 'I'll make sure of it. We're going to feed you up and keep you warm and in a few months you'll be playing with your cousins. How about that?' He was so small and so needy and the surge of love which overwhelmed her for this little scrap of humanity was like nothing she had experienced before.

Nell arrived as the midwife left and when she had expressed some milk Eve sat and fed it to the baby a few drops at a time. He had only had a tablespoonful by the time he wouldn't swallow anymore and it had taken her half an hour to get that down him. Mary was fast asleep after her long labour and Nell sat watching Eve cradle the baby until he was asleep. 'You can't keep this up by yourself day in, day out,' she said worriedly. 'Everyone will have to take a turn. You've got to be sensible, our Eve.'

'We'll sort something out.' Eve smiled mistily at her sister, knowing she was going to take sole care of the baby until Mary was well enough to have him and he was feeding properly. She wouldn't dare trust him to anyone else, he was already too precious.

When Mary awoke, Caleb and Ada and Winnie came in to see her and the baby but only stayed for a few minutes. Nell left enough milk to tide the baby over until she could return later that evening and went to collect her children from her mother-in-law. Eve had just persuaded the baby to take another tablespoonful of milk and had settled him among his blankets, when Mary said, 'Would you take it downstairs, Eve? I want to go to sleep.'

Eve glanced at her sister in surprise. The child hadn't cried since he was born and had barely made a sound. 'Go to sleep then, I'll be here in case he needs feeding.'

'I don't want it in here. I can't relax.'

'But we need to keep trying him to the breast before I feed him just in case he suckles. Your milk would be best for him, I told you what the doctor said. It's important we keep trying.'

'*I don't want it.*'

'What's the matter?' Eve asked flatly.

'What do you think the matter is? I've just had a baby, haven't I? I'm entitled to some rest.'

'Mary, you know the doctor was worried about him. He's very small and this is a crucial time.'

'I don't care what that old goat said.' Mary's lips began to tremble and her eyelids blinked rapidly before tears began to run down her cheeks. 'I don't want it in here. I never thought it was going to be so horrible, the . . . the having it. I thought I was going to die, the pain was so bad.'

'I know and you were very brave, the doctor said so. But it's over now and you have a bonny baby boy—'

'Don't patronise me.'

'I beg your pardon?'

With tears streaming from her eyes and her face flushed, Mary glared at her. 'You always think you know best about everything but you don't. I said I don't want it in here and I meant it. And . . . and if you leave me alone with it I won't be responsible for my actions.'

Her face white, Eve stood up with the child in her arms. 'Don't talk like that, I won't have it, but for your information I had no intention of leaving this baby alone with you. He needs someone to look after him and all you are interested in, all you've ever been interested in is number one. Has it even crossed that selfish little mind of yours that the reason he's so weak and poorly might be because of what you took to get rid of him?'

The minute the words had left her lips she regretted them. She didn't know if that was the case, besides which Mary had just been through a long and difficult labour and here she was making things ten times worse. But in spite of how she was feeling inside, she couldn't find the words to make amends.

'I hate you.' Mary's voice was in the nature of a hiss. 'I wish I'd never come back.'

Eve was unable to speak because her throat was blocked. Half choking, she left the room with the baby, only to bump into Caleb on the landing, causing him to stumble and almost drop the stick he used to assist his walking.

'What's the matter?' He stared at her. 'What's wrong?'

'We've . . . we've had an argument.' She couldn't wipe away her tears because she was holding the baby and sniffed inelegantly.

'Who? You and Mary?'

Eve nodded. Then between gasps, she said, 'She doesn't want anything to do with him. The bairn. She told me to take him away and . . . and I lost my temper with her.'

'You lost your temper?' His tone was reproachful. 'She's just had a baby, Eve. Couldn't you have let whatever she said go for once? I'm sure she didn't mean it, she must be exhausted.'

'She meant it all right.'

'You don't know that. Give her time.'

She just checked herself from saying, 'All the time in the world will make no difference but you'll never see that, will you?' Instead she repeated, 'She meant it, Caleb.'

'I don't understand you, Eve.' His face was stiff. 'You're normally the first one to give someone the benefit of the doubt. Can't you apply that to your own sister? You've been different the last weeks.'

It stung. Raising her head, she looked him full in the face. 'When was I different, Caleb? When I was running back and forth to the hospital visiting you? Or when I was waiting hand and foot on Mary? Or was it when I was taking your mother her trays and seeing to everything in there because she won't allow Ada or Winnie to see to her? That on top of doing the ordering for the inn and dealing with any problems it throws up. When, exactly?'

'I had no idea you resented your lot so much.'

Her chin rose. 'I don't.'

'It sounds like it to me.'

Biting back the words hovering on her tongue, she said, 'I have to see to this baby,' and left him standing on the landing. In the kitchen she explained her tears to Ada and Winnie as a reaction to the ups and downs of the last hours. It was clear they didn't believe her weak excuse but they were too polite to press her further. She sent Winnie upstairs to bring down the rest of the milk Nell had expressed into a jug, along with the baby's crib and some clothes, and then set about the laborious task of getting some milk down him. It was clear the little mite didn't want to swallow but eventually he took a little through her persistence.

'He don't look very well, lass.' Ada had come to sit with her at the kitchen table as she cradled the now sleeping infant. 'There's a blue touch to his lips if I'm not mistaken.'

'The doctor said if we keep him warm and feed him he'll be all right.' He had to be all right. Anything else was unthinkable. 'And it will be better down here with the range and all, especially tonight. The bedrooms can get chilly.'

'I take it Mary's passed him over to you to look after?'

'She's weak after the birth.'

Ada made a sound in her throat that could have meant anything but said no more.

At five o'clock that evening Eve sent for the doctor again. He stood looking down at the child in her arms, his round face troubled. 'He's not even managing as much as he was this morning now, doctor.' Eve didn't look at the doctor, her eyes were on the baby. 'All he wants to do is sleep.'

'You're doing all you can, lass. Take comfort in that.'

'But there must be something more we can do. You said food and warmth and he's got that. Why is he getting worse?'

'No two babies are the same. They're individuals, same as we are. And . . . and there could be something wrong with his heart.'

'But . . .' She couldn't go on.

'I can't wave a magic wand, m'dear.' He glanced at Ada and Winnie who were standing by the table looking stricken, then at Caleb sitting in his armchair in front of the range with Jack at his feet. Caleb still tired easily and his right leg was liable to give under his weight if he was on his feet for any length of time. It was to Caleb he said, 'I think you had better prepare yourselves for the worst.'

'No.' Eve was still looking down into the child's tiny face. He didn't even have a name yet, she thought brokenly. She would call him William after their brother until Mary decided what she wanted. 'No, he'll be all right. I know he will.'

William died just before five o'clock the following morning as a pink and silver dawn bathed the sky. He was in Eve's arms where he had been all night and she was stroking the small silky forehead with the tip of her finger as he gave a quiet little sigh and didn't take another breath. He looked as though he was still sleeping and for a while Eve wouldn't believe he had gone. Caleb had insisted on sitting up with her and was fast asleep in his armchair in front of the range. She looked across at him, so stricken with grief she couldn't make a sound to alert him to what had happened.

She moved the blanket and William's little jacket and felt the tiny chest. It was quite still. He was warm but life had gone. Tears creeping down her cheeks, she made him snug again, rocking him back and forth as she whispered sweet nothings against the downy head. She kissed the little eyelids, his mouth, his little hand that he had liked to have free of the blanket, and felt she couldn't bear it. For long minutes she prayed God would work a miracle, that He would infuse life back into him along with her kisses, but nothing happened.

'I'm sorry, little man. I'm so sorry.' He had touched her life so briefly but she would always love him. She hadn't given birth to him but she felt as though she had. It wasn't right that he should die before he'd had a chance to live, it was so unfair, wicked. Life was horrible, a monstrous joke.

She sat for the next hour until Ada and Winnie came downstairs, just holding him close to her heart and looking at his sweet little face now and again. She wanted every tiny feature imprinted on her mind for ever. He deserved someone to remember him like that, he was a little person, a little boy. He couldn't be forgotten.

Just before Ada and Winnie bustled into the kitchen, she looked across at Caleb. He was still fast asleep and he looked tired, even haggard. She had tried to mentally distance herself from him over the last weeks but now with her emotions so raw and tender over the child she knew she hadn't succeeded. She would never succeed while she stayed within sight and sound of him, she loved him too much. And so she would leave here. There was nothing to hold her now. Maybe if William had lived she would have stayed to take care of him if he had needed her, even if Mary and Caleb had married. But now she was free to go where she would.

'Oh, William, William.' She kissed the transparent tiny forehead one last time and then as the door opened and Ada walked into the kitchen, she straightened in her chair and prepared herself to tell them the sad news.

PART FOUR

1918 – To Everything There is a Season

Chapter 17

Howard Ingram's warm brown eyes twinkled as he surveyed the hot face of his housekeeper across the dinner table, although she could scarcely be termed such these days, he thought to himself. He had employed her as housekeeper eighteen months ago, but Eve had swiftly become his wife's companion and nurse and a friend to them both. Within two months of her joining their small household, Esther had insisted Eve join them at mealtimes and he had not objected to this. On the contrary, he liked the young woman who had brought a new lease of life to his poor Esther. He liked her very much. She had a keen mind and a ready wit and he appreciated both in a woman.

'So,' he said quietly, 'you think the Germans are the only ones to have concentration camps?'

It brought the response he had anticipated. 'Of course not, I didn't say that. Merely that they don't treat their prisoners of war as we treat ours.'

'And you know this how?'

'By reading the newspapers and listening to the reports on the wireless.'

'Ah, I see. And you trust these reports implicitly, do you? In spite of our discussion about war propaganda the other day? Or is it only the Germans who twist the truth to suit them?'

'Howard, please,' Esther intervened, her soft voice reproving. 'Don't tease Eve.'

'I'm not teasing her, m'dear. We're merely having a conversation. Is that not so, Eve?'

Eve stared at the man she had come to like and respect greatly. He was a good man, a good husband and a good employer, and in spite of being one of the leading lights of the town of Newcastle he had no side to him whatsoever. She'd known she had landed on her feet when she had arrived here, bruised and raw in spirit a month after William's funeral at the parish church in Washington.

She had seen the advertisement for the post of housekeeper to a Mr and Mrs Howard Ingram three weeks before this in the *Sunderland Echo*. At her interview she had felt it was the place for her, should she be offered the post. She had been offered it and had accepted with alacrity, immediately informing Caleb of her intention to leave so he had time to find her replacement.

Ada and Winnie had promised to take care of Jack for her, but the big dog was devoted to Caleb and so she hadn't felt so bad about leaving him behind. Only Nell knew her new address. She'd divulged it to no one else, wanting a complete break from her old life. Nell was the only person she corresponded with.

She knew she'd mortally offended Caleb. First by leaving his employ, then by refusing to give him her address. This could not be helped. And when, three months later, Nell had written to say Mary and Caleb had become betrothed, it had been all the confirmation she needed that she had done the right thing. Even when Mary ran true to form and disappeared again a few weeks later, it did not change her mind about returning to Washington. She was done with that life. Nor had she weakened when Mildred had passed away with a massive heart attack. There had been no love lost between Caleb and his mother, he would not need comfort for his loss and she was sure the last person Caleb would wish to see was herself anyway.

And she was content in Newcastle. Not happy exactly, but content. And that was enough for the present.

She was brought back to herself by Howard saying, 'Well, Eve? What say you on the matter of propaganda?'

'I know it happens, of course.'

'It certainly does. Take the South African war with the Boers. A tiny nation of farmers, in effect, but unfortunately for them the Afrikaner republic of Transvaal just happened to be situated on the richest gold-field in the world. Britain waging war against them showed us as bullies in the eyes of the world but you would never have thought that from the newspaper reports here. And it was Horatio Kitchener, m'dear, the great British commander, who conceived a new tactic to bring the Boer people to their knees, the concentration camp.'

'Is that true? That we thought of it first?'

'I'm afraid so. Not Britain's finest hour.'

'But you—' She stopped abruptly. She knew Howard had fought in that war, that was where he had lost his left arm.

'I was part of that army which devastated the countryside and rounded up thousands upon thousands of Boer women and children for the camps, yes. As I said, not our finest hour and certainly not mine.'

'But you were just a young man out of officers' school,' Esther protested. 'And you were only over there the last six months.'

Howard nodded. 'Yes, I was, but is that excuse enough? I think not. The trouble was I didn't think for myself in those days and thinking is vitally important for both men and women. Never forget that, Eve. For men and women.'

She nodded. Education was a bee in Howard's bonnet and she had gained much because of it. Shortly after she had come here a chance remark of hers one day had started a discussion about the reasons for the war, and by the end of it she had been mortified to realise how ignorant she was. But her employer had not belittled her, foolish though some of her statements had been in retrospect. The next morning he had taken her aside and inquired if she had any desire to learn. Not ladylike accomplishments such as painting on glass or doing fine tapestry, he'd added impatiently, but *real* learning. History, politics, social reform – things that mattered. And Eve had answered yes, she would like to gain a knowledge of such subjects. And so her education in this house had begun.

Most afternoons after lunch when Esther took her nap and the cook and maid Howard also employed were busy about their duties, he delayed returning to his engineering business in the middle of town to give her an hour's instruction. As time had passed Eve had begun to appreciate that in the class and society to which he belonged Howard Ingram was one of those rare creatures who truly had the working class's best interests at heart. He had been a great advocate of the school leaving age being raised to fourteen which had come into effect three days ago on 13 March, and he was known far and wide as the best employer in Newcastle.

With this in mind, Eve said quietly, 'I can't believe that even as a very young man you would have done anything cruel.'

They were having Sunday lunch and Daisy, the maid, bustled in at that point with their pudding. Howard waited until it was just the three of them again before answering. 'I wish I could say your faith in me is justified but it is not.'

Esther, her voice low but penetrating, said, 'I hate it when you talk like this, Howard. Whatever you did, you did under orders. Why must you torture yourself with such thoughts?' She turned to Eve, her once pretty face, which was now marked by the years of suffering she had endured with a chronic and progressive disease of the nervous system, reflecting her distress. 'He is the kindest and best of men. You know this, Eve.'

Howard leant forward, taking his wife's hand and pressing the frail white fingers. 'Don't upset yourself, m'dear. We will talk of this no more except to say I learnt things at that time I could not have learnt in any other way so it was not all loss.'

What trite things he said on occasion to ease her mind. As his wife's face relaxed and she smiled at him, his answering smile hid the contempt he felt, not for his wife but for himself. From a small child his father, a military man, had instilled in him a desire to follow in his footsteps and those of several generations of Ingrams before him. The army had been held up as representing everything that was good and fine about England, and he had not questioned this in his youth. After a good education followed by officers' school, he had been thrust into this fine and noble world. It had nearly been his ruin, and the loss of his arm had been the least of it. He had been sickened by what he had seen and done, a hundred lifetimes would not be long enough to assuage the shock of first-hand experience of man's inhumanity to man. Esther had been his life-saver, he knew that. They had become betrothed just before he had left for South Africa and on his return, when he had been sick in mind and body and his parents had become irritated and then angry with what they perceived as his weakness, Esther had stood by him. Theirs had been a happy marriage, in spite of the onslaught of this vicious illness of hers which now saw her confined to a wheelchair.

Pressing Esther's fingers once again before releasing her hand, he looked down at his treacle pudding. 'That looks tasty enough in spite of the butter rationing,' he said in an effort to lift the sombre mood. His tongue ran away with him on occasion, the more so since Eve had joined the household. He had got into the habit of speaking his mind freely and sometimes he forgot Esther's delicate constitution.

'That comes from having a cook whose sister happens to be married to a local farmer.' Eve wrinkled her nose and smiled.

'Don't tell me.' Howard held up his hand in mock protest. 'I don't want to know. That way when I'm taken to account by the authorities I can say in all honesty I wasn't party to such carryings-on.'

Eve raised her eyebrows. 'But I thought you told me the other day I should examine my conscience in all matters.'

'Absolutely. And you must do as I say, not as I do.'

Esther was laughing as she gazed at the faces of the two people she loved best in the world. She often had to remind herself it had been only eighteen months since she had met the woman who was now such a necessary part of her life. It was hard to recall a time when the days hadn't been brightened by Eve's presence. When Eve had replaced the elderly housekeeper who had been with them since their marriage, she hadn't expected to find a friend. No, more than a friend. Much more. Her sisters and the friends of her youth had gone on to have children and grandchildren, and although they were always kind when they visited, it was with a faintly patronising air. From the first she had sensed a wealth of understanding in the young woman whom society would deem was beneath her. But as Howard always said, the British class system needed to evolve and this wouldn't come about so much by laws being passed as by men and women in all stratas of society accepting that no human being should be considered better than another by the mere accident of birth.

It had been this school of thought, along with Howard's strong views on decent education for the masses and the right of women to have the vote, among other things, which had finally alienated them from his family. She had shed no tears about this. His parents were very much lord and lady of the manor, with a large country estate in Durham and a town house in London, and she had never cared for them or Howard's three older brothers and sister.

Her parents had held Howard in high esteem. As their only child, she and Howard had inherited her father's engineering business and a great deal of money on their untimely demise in a yachting accident whilst holidaying abroad shortly after she and Howard had got married. Within a matter of months she'd begun to show symptoms of the disease which now racked her body. But she had much to be thankful for. She hugged the thought to her as she smiled at Howard and Eve's banter. Not least a husband who loved her and for the first time in her life a friend she could talk to about anything. She hadn't realised what had been missing from her life until Eve had come to live with them, but she knew now she couldn't do without her.

Howard was now on his favourite subject of the Labour Party's elaborate scheme for the political organisation and education of women through the Unions and the Co-operative movement. Few if any in their social circle held similar views and it made for some interesting dinner parties. She caught Eve's eye at one point and the two women smiled at each other. Yes, thought Esther. She had plenty to be thankful for.

Very early the next morning Eve was woken by a sharp knock on her bedroom door. She pulled on her dressing gown, thrust her feet into her slippers and padded to the door without bothering to light the gas mantle.

'Can you come quickly?' Howard's face was white in the light of the oil lamp he was holding. 'She's worse, much worse. Something's happened. I've sent for Dr Wynford but she wants you. Something's dreadfully wrong, Eve.'

As soon as Eve entered the dimly lit bedroom, she could see the change in Esther. 'Eve.' Esther drew in three short breaths and then as Eve took her hand, looked up at her husband. 'Please . . .' She struggled for breath, her face becoming contorted for a moment. 'Please, Howard, leave us for a few moments. I-I wish to-to talk to Eve alone.'

Howard bit his lip but when Esther murmured once more, 'Please,' he nodded.

'I'll be waiting outside,' he said to them both. 'Call me if you need me.'

When the door shut behind him, Eve bent over the frail woman in the bed. 'What is it, dear?' she asked softly, dropping the more formal 'Ma'am' she used if anyone else was present.

'I must-must ask you . . .'

'Don't talk anymore, wait until the doctor comes.'

'No. Eve, I know – I know the time is short. I've known for-for weeks now. I've felt – different.'

It was painful to witness such pain and be powerless. Tears in her eyes, Eve whispered, 'What is it you want to ask me, dear?'

'Howard. He's – not as he presents himself to the world. Not inside. Vul-vulnerable. Needs – you.'

'I'm not going to go anywhere, Esther. And in a little while you'll feel better and things will be back to normal.'

Ignoring this, Esther's fingers tightened on hers with a grip surprising for such a sick woman. 'Promise me you – you will – stay. Take care of him. To-together. Want to think of you together.'

Eve's eyes widened. 'I'll stay on as long as he wants me to, as long as you both want me to. You know that.' Esther couldn't be suggesting . . .

'He – admires you.' Esther's head sank into the pillow, the white of the cloth emphasising the grey pallor of her skin. 'And he is kind. Suc-successful marriages are built on such – qualities.' She gasped, making a sound in her throat as though she wanted to cough but instead, to Eve's horror, she began to choke.

Eve screamed out for Howard and he rushed into the room. They raised Esther into a sitting position. This seemed to help but as the choking stopped, a thin stream of blood began to ooze from her mouth and her head fell heavily against Howard's chest.

It was over very quickly. By the time Dr Wynford arrived, Howard was sitting in stunned silence by the side of the bed and Esther was at peace. Eve had wiped her friend's face and pulled the coverlet up to her neck, concealing the bloodied nightgown, and to all intents and purposes Esther could have been sleeping. In death the lines of pain and exhaustion had smoothed away and she appeared much younger.

After a brief examination, the doctor confirmed what they already knew. Gently, he said to Howard, 'She died in her own home with you at her side. That was always the way she wished it. Be grateful for that.'

'Grateful?' Howard stared at the doctor who was also a friend. 'The last years she's suffered dreadfully with this foul thing. What is there to be grateful for?'

'This last stage could have gone on for days, weeks. She was spared that, Howard.'

Howard rose to his feet. 'You mean well, John, but I would like some time with my wife alone.'

'Of course.' As Eve led the way out of the bedroom, John turned at the door. 'If you need me, call.'

'I need no one.'

In the hall, the doctor paused. His voice low, he said, 'He will take this very hard, Eve. You are aware of that? He needed her every bit as much as she needed him.'

She nodded, feeling numb. It had happened so fast, she couldn't take in that Esther had gone.

'If you're worried about him in any way, please call me, night or day. Try and persuade him to take these.' He reached into his black bag and brought out a small phial of round white pills. 'One at bedtime for a few nights. They are a strong sedative so no more than one with a glass of water.'

'Yes, I'll do that, doctor. Thank you.'

'In cases like this where the couple have been very close and there are no children, it's doubly hard,' the doctor said sadly. 'Goodbye for now and don't forget what I said. Call at any time. And . . . and keep the pills in your possession, Eve.'

Eve stood alone in the hall for a few moments. She knew Daisy and Elsie, the cook, were in the kitchen waiting to hear what the doctor had said. She ought to go and tell them their mistress had passed away.

They both cried. Elsie had been with the Ingrams as long as the former housekeeper, and Daisy for nearly five years. She was the newcomer, Eve thought as she retraced her footsteps up the stairs and stood outside Howard and Esther's room on the wide carpeted landing, not knowing what to do. And then she heard it. A groaning that sounded as though it was wrenched up from the depths of him.

She stood for some moments more and when she turned and made her way back to her own room to get dressed, she found the sound had unlocked her own grief and her face was awash with tears.

Chapter 18

It was almost six months later. New Allied tactics had got Germany on the run and the character of the war had changed, tanks and planes now being used in large numbers against the enemy. The character of life had changed at 47 Penfield Place in the heart of Newcastle too.

The first month after Esther's death Howard had been inconsolable, spending most of his time in his study when he was back from the engineering works. He had barely eaten anything in spite of Elsie rustling up all sorts of delicacies to try and tempt him. When he had begun to eat a little again, he had also begun to drink heavily. He had always had a glass of wine or two with his meal when his wife was alive, but now it was more in the nature of a bottle or two and this was often followed by him disappearing into his study where Eve knew he kept a bottle of brandy.

Eve said nothing about this, she did not feel it was her place. With Esther's going, something had changed in her relationship to her employer. The old easy familiarity had gone. At first she had thought this was a result of his grief and the fact that she saw so little of him now compared to before. The hour of instruction had ceased the day after Esther had died and although she had half expected it to resume again in the following months, it had not. But as time had gone on she had come to feel Howard was deliberately holding her at arm's length. It was not just her, he treated everyone the same, refusing to accept any social invitations and shutting himself away each evening. When visitors called, and there had been quite a few in the early days although only John Wynford had continued to persevere, Howard's manner could only be termed wooden. He was a changed man.

But for her promise to Esther, Eve would not have continued in the post of housekeeper. From her first day at the house, so much of her time had been tied up with Esther that now she felt the hours dragged. She had never experienced boredom before and her nature did not lend itself to sitting about doing nothing. Consequently, with Howard's blessing, she got involved in voluntary war work. For two days a week she gave six hours a day at the local town hall, handling some of the paperwork generated by rationing, and on the other four days assisted at a Newcastle organisation which aided families who had lost their breadwinner. She always made sure she was back at the house in time to eat with Howard and in the evenings busied herself until bedtime with her duties as housekeeper. She had little or no time to herself but she did not mind this. Exhaustion was an opiate; it prevented endless post-mortems in her mind regarding Caleb and Mary and little William, for which she was thankful.

It was in the first week of September that the Spanish flu epidemic which had swept the world began to take its toll in a war-weary Britain, and Elsie and Daisy went down with it within days of each other. Around the globe this virulent strain of influenza had already caused millions of deaths and doctors were predicting more people would die of the flu than would be killed by the war. Eve did not dwell on this, she had more than enough to cope with. With the cook and maid confined to bed, the full weight of the household was on her shoulders. Between seeing to the invalids, she cooked and cleaned and washed and ironed but there were simply not enough hours in the day. And then Howard succumbed to the illness. He came home from work one day looking like death warmed up but although Eve tried to insist that he stay at home the next morning, he left the house as usual. At eleven o'clock there was a knock at the door and two of Howard's office staff practically carried him into the house.

'He collapsed on the factory floor,' Ned Duckworth, Howard's manager, told Eve once Howard was in bed and the doctor had been called. 'Out like a light, he was. Mind, I've seen it coming for some time. Thin as a rake he's gone since his missus died. If it hadn't been this flu that got him, something else would have. Know what I mean?'

Eve did know what he meant and so did Dr Wynford when he came. After examining Howard, he checked Elsie and Daisy before spending some minutes talking to Eve in the drawing room. 'I can't do anymore for him than I've been doing for Elsie and Daisy,' he said soberly, 'but whereas they want to get better, with Howard I don't know.' They stared at each other for a moment. 'Get plenty of fluids down him and make sure he stays in bed. And be firm with him, Eve, if you have to be.'

'I will.' She nodded. She had come to like and trust John Wynford over the last months. In spite of the fact she was just the housekeeper, he had always been very pleasant.

'Let's hope you don't get sick too. This thing can run through a household like wildfire.' John shook his head. 'They're saying London's central telegraph office is crippled because seven hundred people are down with the flu, a complication the war effort doesn't need. And it'll get worse before it gets better, you mark my words. Half my patients are weakened by wartime hardships and couldn't fight off a cold, let alone this flu. How do you feel, incidentally?'

'All right. I know I don't look it but I'm quite tough.'

'Sore throat or headache?'

'No.' She smiled at him. 'I'm absolutely fine, really.'

'Good.' He smiled back, his hazel eyes warm. 'But if you start to feel ill, don't try to be brave and soldier on. This flu doesn't let you do that.'

'I'll remember.'

Holding his black bag in one hand, he patted her arm with the other. It was a light touch but his voice was soft when he said, 'It was a good day when you came to this house, Eve. Esther thought the world of you, as do we all.'

She blinked at him. 'Thank you.'

'I'll call and see how he is tomorrow.'

She saw him out but after she had closed the front door behind him, she stood for a moment, staring at the brown painted wood. No, she was being ridiculous. She shook her head at herself. Dr Wynford would never think of her in *that* way. She thought back to one or two occasions recently when the doctor had called socially to see Howard and she had felt – not exactly uneasy in his presence, more flustered. And it had been when he'd looked at her like he'd looked at her a minute ago. She stood a little longer before giving herself a mental shake. She couldn't stand here daydreaming, she needed to see to the soup for lunch. Elsie and Daisy hadn't been able to tolerate solid food but they had swallowed the nourishing broth she'd made at regular intervals. Perhaps Howard would take a little too.

Seven days later Daisy was back on her feet and Elsie was able to sit wrapped up in the rocking chair in the kitchen, giving orders to the little maid regarding meals, because all of Eve's time was taken up with Howard who was a very sick man.

John Wynford didn't try to conceal his concern from Eve. 'He's got to try.' They had just left Howard's bedroom and were standing on the landing in the semi-light of late evening. 'He's relinquishing his hold on life without a fight. It's as though he is willing the illness to take him.'

Eve nodded. That was exactly what Howard was doing. He had begun the process the night Esther had died. Quietly, she said, 'I'll talk to him.'

'I've talked to him.' John Wynford's irritation with his inability to get through to his friend was plain to see. 'It's getting him to listen which is the problem. I've known him since I started practising, Esther was one of my first patients and I'd have sworn on the bible that apathy was not part of Howard's make-up.'

'Grief is a strange thing.' In the days after William's death, when Caleb's only thought had been for Mary, she had wanted to die too. Looking back, she had barely been rational.

'He's forty-nine years old, Eve. He's got years and years ahead of him in which to enjoy life, to meet someone else. Esther was a fine woman but it would be a crying shame to see him follow her so soon. And it needn't be, that's the thing. If Elsie with her weak chest can come through unscathed, I'm damn sure—' He stopped. 'Sorry,' he apologised. 'I'm quite sure Howard can recover with a little fighting back.'

'I'll talk to him,' she said again. 'As soon as you've left.'

'I hope you have more success than me.'

Two minutes later she entered the bedroom and went straight to the bed. Howard was lying propped against several pillows to aid his breathing and his eyes were shut. It was he who spoke first. 'I suppose he told you he thinks I'm giving in.'

'Dr Wynford didn't have to tell me that. It's obvious to everyone. The flu has provided a wonderful excuse for you.'

Her tone was not gentle and his eyes snapped open. 'What did you say?'

'You heard me.' Her voice grim, she continued, 'I perhaps should have said this a long time ago but I didn't consider it my place. But now I think it is necessary. Esther would have been horrified, horrified and disappointed to see the man you have become since she died. She would have expected more of you.'

Howard clearly couldn't believe his ears. He had been lying very still, his arm resting on top of the bedclothes, but now her words acted on him like a bucket of cold water, so much so that the sharp movement he made to sit up caused him to cough and gasp for air.

When the paroxysm was over, Eve spoke before he could. 'She fought her illness every step of the way, you know she did, and for you to simply give in must be the worst insult you could pay to her memory. She loved you and she wanted you to go on—'

'*Be quiet.*' It wasn't a shout, he didn't have the energy for that, but nevertheless the tone of his voice brought Eve's head jerking upwards. 'Please, Eve, be quiet.'

'No, I won't. I won't be quiet. I've been quiet long enough.'

'What do you mean, you won't. I pay your wage, remember.'

It was the first time he had ever said such a thing and although she told herself he was reacting out of the black anger evident on his face, it hurt. 'I know that but I have to say this whether you are vexed or not. It's–it's what Esther would have wanted. You don't want to hear it but it's true.'

'Don't presume to tell me what Esther would have wanted.'

'Someone has to.' She took a deep breath. 'And I would be failing in my duty to her if I didn't speak out.'

'I suppose John put you up to this?'

'Dr Wynford is concerned about you, yes, but I'm saying it because it's the truth.' Her voice had risen. 'The past months you have been so different. When–when you've had a drink, Daisy is slightly afraid of you. Did you know that?'

'*What?*' Again he reared up like a scalded cat.

He looked dreadful, as pale as lint but for the two red feverish spots of colour burning his cheekbones, but Eve did not allow her pity to weaken her. 'It's the truth.'

'I don't believe you. Daisy has been with us since she left school. She would never be frightened of me.'

Eve looked at him but she did not speak.

After a moment he lay back against the pillows, grinding his teeth. When his jaw stopped working, he muttered, 'I've got the influenza like half the nation. What's that got to do with having a glass of wine in the evenings? This is ridiculous.'

'You drink one or two bottles a night before you retire to your study. Then you turn to brandy—'

'Enough!'

Sick as he was, his voice resounded like a pistol shot, making Eve jump. Her voice shaking, she said, 'Well, don't you?'

'I don't have to explain my actions to you.'

'No, you don't.' She stared down at him, taking a deep breath before she was able to say, 'You are answerable only to your conscience and perhaps the memory of a sweet, brave lady who would never have taken the coward's way out. I'll go and get your medication and a hot drink.'

She turned and had reached the door before his voice came, saying, 'You don't understand. I miss her . . .'

'I do understand.' Her voice was soft but firm. 'You aren't the only one who has lost someone but shutting everyone out, Dr Wynford and the rest of your friends, isn't the answer. Neither is drinking too much.'

He coughed again, hard, racking sounds, and she went to him, reached for the glass of water on the bedside cabinet and held it to his lips as he took a few sips. When the spasm subsided, his voice came as little more than a whisper. 'What was the answer for you?'

She didn't pretend not to understand. 'To say goodbye and move on. It's not easy but it is the only way, believe me.'

'And it worked? For you it worked?'

'Mostly.' Her voice was very low.

He nodded. 'What about the times when it doesn't?'

'Then you weather them. And eventually you come through.'

'I don't know if I can, not without a prop.'

She looked at him, pity filling her. 'Then let me be your prop, not – not the wine. You can always talk to me, night or day. I made Esther a promise I would be here for you and I will, but you have to let me in. If not me, then someone.'

He waved a weary hand. 'It would be much simpler to join her. I want to be with her, wherever she is.'

'I doubt you'd get the reception you expect. Like I said, she wouldn't approve of your conduct over the last months.'

'That's true enough.'

She thought she detected a note of amusement in his voice even though his expression had not changed. It encouraged her enough to say, 'Will you fight? Not just the flu but this . . . depression? Will you at least promise me to try?'

'Oh, Eve,' he closed his eyes, 'you make it sound so easy. I don't know if I've got the strength or the inclination. That's the truthful answer.'

'I can provide the former but not the latter. That's up to you. But I will stand with you every inch of the way.'

'I might not get over this flu. Millions haven't.'

'You'll get over it.' She smiled faintly at him. 'What was it you used to say? Only the good die young.'

'I'm not young though.'

'Of course you are.' She meant it. Before Esther had died, she would have said he had the most youthful, inquiring, open mind of anyone she'd ever met. 'And Britain is going to need men like you when this war is over.'

'Men like me?' He stared at her, sweat gleaming on his brow although his hand had been cold when she had helped him drink. 'Britain can do very well without men like me, Eve.'

'I think not.' She looked at him in silence now, then moved her lips one over the other before she said, 'You have no idea of the esteem in which you're held, not just by Elsie and Daisy and me but by your friends and those who work for you at the factory. Esther used to tell me about all the people you've helped, quietly and without fuss. It's no wonder your employees think so much of you. Most men in your position look on the men and women who work for them as little more than scum.'

'I'm no saint, Eve.'

'No, you're not a saint, Mr Ingram.' She put her head on one side, her smile wide. 'No one could ever accuse you of sainthood, you're too human for that. But you're much nicer than you give yourself credit for. And now I'm going to bring you a bowl of soup with your medication and I expect you to eat the lot. All right?' She left the room quickly, pretending she hadn't noticed the moisture swimming in his eyes.

Howard lay still for some moments and then he wiped his wet eyes with the back of his hand. She had said he was held in esteem, that people cared about him. She'd also said Esther would be disappointed and horrified to see him now. She was right in that at least. He shook his head, his lips moving in a brief grim smile. And Esther would have let him know it too.

Was he drinking too much? The answer was clear and again he shook his head, which was pounding. After that he lay staring up at the ceiling.

When Eve returned with the tray holding a bowl of soup and a freshly baked soft roll, the smell of the food made him faintly nauseous but still he sat up and made an effort to eat. He didn't touch the roll but drank half the soup.

'That's better. You see, you can do it if you try.'

She had stood and watched over him like a mother with a recalcitrant child and her voice reflected this. In answer he said wryly, 'After the talking-to I've just received I didn't dare do anything else to bring your wrath down on my head.'

She smiled. He had noticed before how her smile changed the whole of her face, lighting up the green eyes and giving her nondescript features a charm that made the onlooker want to say something more to make her laugh. Their conversation that morning had made him realise he really knew very little about her. Esther had told him there had been a man involved in Eve's decision to leave Washington, unrequited love or something of that nature, but he had not pressed to know more. Perhaps Esther had not known anything more. Suddenly, though, he needed to hear her story and he would not have a better opportunity to ask. Feeling slightly ashamed of the way he was using her concern for him, he said, 'Would it pain you too much to tell me about the person you spoke of earlier, the one you lost?'

It was some seconds before she answered, 'There is not much to tell.

He – we weren't – what I mean to say is, it wasn't like you and Esther. We weren't even betrothed.'

'Was he killed in the war?'

'No, no, nothing like that. He was injured, but he recovered before I left. My sisters and I worked for him. He was the innkeeper I told you about when I applied for the post of housekeeper.'

Howard nodded. 'He took you in when you left the village where you had been born, if I remember correctly. Why did you leave there? I don't think you ever said.'

He could see the indecision in her face and knew she was wondering how much to say. Then she sat down in the chair at the side of the bed. 'How much do you want to know?'

'All of it. If you want to tell me, that is.'

Again there was a pause; and then, her words clear but her voice low, she began to speak.

It was a full twenty minutes before she became silent, and Howard had not interrupted her. He found her story remarkable but he did not comment on this. What he did say was, 'You are worth more than being second-best. You know this, I hope.'

Her chin lifted. 'Aye, I do. That was never an option.'

'You haven't said how you feel about Mr Travis now, after so many months have elapsed.'

Her voice was small as she said, 'I shall always have a regard for him that time and distance won't change. I-I think that's the way I'm made.'

Yes, he could see that. What a pity she had chosen to give her love to a man who did not appreciate her rare qualities. 'And your sister, Mary. You have no idea where she is or what she is doing?'

'None. Nell would write and let me know if she heard anything. To date there has been no word whatsoever.'

'You must miss Nell and her family.'

'Aye, I do. We write every week but it's not the same as meeting. But she is happy and that's the main thing. She had a little girl a few weeks ago and I would like to see her before she is much older, but,' she shrugged, 'I don't want to go to Washington and it would be difficult for Nell to make the journey to Newcastle. But it doesn't really matter.'

'That is a shame when you clearly value each other so highly. I have siblings but we haven't spoken in some time and we were never what you would call close. It was not encouraged in the house in which I was born. It was, I suppose you could say, run on military lines. Affection had little place in it. In fact, any show of emotion was considered a weakness.'

'That's awful. All children need plenty of love.'

'Looking back now I would agree with you but at the time I considered it normal. One's environment and the way one is brought up has a lot to do with the finished article, don't you think? Give me a child until he is seven and all that.'

She considered this for a moment. 'Partly, but character will out too. The way you've described it I can imagine your family as being a little cold but you are not like that.' And then she blushed furiously, rising to her feet as she said, 'I have to see to things downstairs, Elsie is still very weak and Daisy does her best but . . .'

'Of course.' When he was alone again, Howard closed his eyes. She had said character would out. After the Boer War when he'd suffered the mental breakdown and his family had been so appalled at what his father had declared was lack of moral fibre, his low opinion of himself had never recovered. Esther had tried to bolster him up, bless her, but his family's verdict had trickled its way into his very bones. All his life he had been trying to rise above it but according to Eve others saw him quite differently. They perceived what his family labelled weakness as kindness.

He swallowed hard. With Esther's going he had felt bereft; she had been his rock, his mainstay for so long. Which was funny when you thought about it because most people thought that was exactly what he had been for his wife. Only he had known the truth, that without her unswerving faith in him he felt himself reverting to the spineless creature his family had branded him to be.

His breathing laboured, he moved his aching limbs in the bed. His remorse for what he had seen and had to do in South Africa had separated him from his family for ever but that was no bad thing. He was not like them. He did not want to be like them. Why had he never seen it so clearly before?

He wiped the back of his hand across his eyes again. He had cried in those weeks and months when he'd first been back on English soil, and sometimes he had been unable to contain it to the night hours when he was alone. The atrocities he'd witnessed, atrocities carried out on innocent women and children by so-called civilised men, had haunted him to the point where he had attempted to take his own life, and that had been the final straw for his father. He would never forget the contempt on his father's face or the things he had said when he'd come to see him in the hospital. It had been the beginning of the end, they had both recognised that. But there had been Esther. Sweet, gentle Esther. And now . . .

He gave a shudder and opened his eyes. Now she was gone and he had to let her go. Eve was right. And drinking himself into a stupor each night was no answer to anything. After South Africa, he had never felt he had the right to live on and be happy, not when so many children had died so horribly because of a country and army he was part of. If he had been able to bring one child back by dying himself he would gladly have done so. But he couldn't. Remorse was one thing, self-pity quite another, and he had been indulging in the latter for too long. But no more.

His head was throbbing and he couldn't remember ever feeling so ill, but his mind was clearer than it had been for years. He believed God had forgiven him. Now he had to forgive himself.

Chapter 19

Victory Day, 15 November, began quietly under sombre, granite skies. It was a bitterly cold morning in Newcastle but when, at eleven o'clock precisely, the armistice took effect, giant maroons – hitherto used as warnings of impending disaster – were fired and the population poured onto the streets in scenes of wild rejoicing. Church bells began to ring, Boy Scouts cycled through towns and villages sounding the 'all clear' for the last time on bugles, sirens went off and men, women and children cheered in the highways and byways, waving flags and loosing off fireworks. Every serviceman within reach was hoisted shoulder high and carried triumphantly through the streets, folk danced cakewalks in the city centres and squares until the early hours, street lights were uncovered, blackout curtains ripped down and shop windows blazed with light for the first time in years. The country went mad and the pubs were packed until they ran out of beer.

For Eve the day was one of double rejoicing. Unbeknown to her, Howard had arranged for Nell and Toby and their children to be picked up and brought to the house where they would stay the night. They had arrived just as the maroons were fired and when Eve saw her sister standing in the hall with little Lucy in her arms and Toby and their two boys standing behind her, she burst into tears. There followed a wonderful day made all the more special by the noise and hilarity filtering through the windows from the street. Toby and Howard got on like a house on fire, something which clearly amazed Nell. Not so Eve. She knew Howard was equally at home with rich and poor, master and servant. It was one of the things she liked best about her employer.

It wasn't until late in the evening, when Toby was settling Matthew and Robert down in their room and Eve was sitting with Nell while she fed little Lucy prior to dinner that the two women were alone. Nell glanced round the guest room, her eyes lingering on the expensive furnishings and wide, comfortable four-poster bed. 'By, lass, this is some place,' she said softly, her hand stroking the downy head of the baby at her breast. 'And yet he's got no side, Mr Ingram, has he?'

Howard had asked Nell and Toby to call him by his Christian name but it was clear Nell found this uncomfortable.

Eve smiled. 'He's a nice man. An unusual man.'

'Oh aye, I'd agree with you there. I couldn't believe me eyes when his letter came saying he wanted to bring us to see you as a surprise, and that he'd arrange everything.' Nell paused. 'You've landed on your feet here, lass.'

'I think so although I still miss Esther.'

'An' her, his wife. He's getting over it a bit, is he?'

Eve nodded. She hadn't told her sister about Howard's drinking, feeling it was somehow a betrayal. She had just indicated in her letters that he was finding it hard.

'An' the way he talked to my Toby, like he was his equal,' Nell said. 'I might as well tell you, lass, Toby was in a right two-an'-eight about coming. He only did it for me. He was for staying home with the bairns an' me bringing Lucy.'

'I can understand that.'

'But he's not what you'd expect, Mr Ingram, is he?'

216

'No, he's not.' Eve hesitated a moment. 'You-you didn't mention to anyone else where you were going?'

Nell looked at her, a straight look. 'Toby didn't even tell his mam an' da in case it got back, lass, so don't worry.'

She had promised herself all day she would not ask. Now she found herself saying, 'How is he?'

'Caleb? I don't really know, to be honest, lass. Once Mary scarpered there was no reason for me to go to the inn. He came to the house to tell me she'd gone but from that day to this I've exchanged no more than the odd word with him if I've seen him out. He's . . . different. That much I do know. Everyone says it.'

Eve's heart was thumping hard. 'In what way?'

'He don't smile no more. He's not up for a laugh like he used to be. Mind, being made a fool of like he was is enough to make any man keep himself to himself. I asked him, when he come to tell me Mary had gone, if he was going to try and find her and bring her back, and do you know what he said?'

'What?' She wasn't sure if she really wanted to know.

'It'd be as easy to find where the wind blows. That's what he said. It's sort of poetic, isn't it?'

Eve stared at her sister's round homely face. She wanted to ask if Caleb had asked after her on the odd occasion Nell had spoken to him but she had a good idea what the answer would be. He had been outraged when she had refused to tell him where she was going when she'd left Washington. She could understand it. As far as he was concerned he'd taken them in when they were desperate and always been a good friend to her and then she had thrown his kindness back in his face by insisting she wanted a clean break. And she couldn't tell him why, she couldn't say she loved him so much it was a matter of self-preservation to ensure their paths didn't cross. And so she'd made the excuse that she looked on this new stage of her life as a fresh beginning without the burdens and impediments of the past continuing to hang on and complicate things. She would always be grateful to him, she had said, but now this was *her* time to do what she wanted and what she wanted was to start afresh. Trite words, but he had accepted them at face value.

Nell reached out and took her hand for a moment. 'He's a fool, lass. I've always said it. An' you're worth better.'

'We're both fools if loving someone who doesn't love you makes you a fool.' Eve smiled sadly. 'I think it's more a case that life doesn't come in neat packages for everyone, Nell. And you can either rant and rave and wear yourself out crying for the moon or get on and make the most of what you do have.' She glanced at little Lucy sucking lustily and softly stroked the baby's head. 'You're lucky, Nell.'

'I know it. My Toby might not be everyone's cup of tea but we suit each other down to the ground. An' I tell you something else that makes me lucky. I've got a sister who's a diamond. I don't know what we'd have done without what you give us each month, lass, and I mean that. You'll never know the difference it's made. There's been weeks we'd have been desperate.'

'I'm glad I could help but you'd do the same for me.'

'Course I don't let on to Toby how much it is. I say you've sent a couple of bob for the bairns an' mostly leave it at that. If he's like his da and the rest of them in one thing it's in this pride of providing for your own, you know? An' so I let him think I can make a penny stretch to a pound and he's happy. His mam's clicked on though.'

'She has?'

'Oh aye, she's canny, is Mam. "Right good sister, you've got," she said the other day, and she's said the same more than once. She knows what Toby earns to the penny, them all being miners see, but the men don't know two figs about housekeeping, do they? Most of 'em anyway, and certainly not my Toby.'

'No, I suppose not.' Eve felt a bit uncomfortable to be the cause of Nell's duplicity but it was for Nell to do what she thought best.

Her sister must have read her mind because, with a slow smile spreading over her face, Nell said, 'You'd have to tell him if it was you, wouldn't you? You'll never make life easy for yourself, our Eve. You can be too honest, you know.'

Eve smiled back, glad Nell hadn't taken offence. 'We're all different. It's what makes the world go round, after all.'

'That's for sure but there's not many to the pound like you.' Then suddenly she bent forward, causing the baby to lose her grip on the nipple and squawk in protest, and again took Eve's hand. 'I know you think a lot of Caleb but there's other fish in the sea, lass. If something – *someone* – comes along, don't miss the chance to get wed and have bairns. You're a natural mother. Look how you brought me an' Mary up.'

Eve stared at Nell, taken aback by the urgency in her sister's voice. 'I don't think there's much chance of that,' she said after a moment. 'The men aren't exactly queueing up.'

Nell looked as though she was about to say something more but as Lucy's protests grew louder, she settled back in the chair. 'You don't know your own worth, lass. You never have.' Then, as though following on from their previous conversation, she added, 'I like the way you're doing your hair now, it suits you.'

Eve patted her hair which, instead of being pulled back in a tight bun, was now coiled in shining loops. 'It was Esther's idea,' she admitted softly. 'When I started here she said she needed to take me in hand.' Dear Esther. She so missed her. Rising to her feet, she said, 'I'm just going to check everything is in order for dinner. Come down when you're ready.'

Nell continued to sit still, the baby at her breast, when Eve had left the room but her outward calm belied the racing of her mind. So it had been the wife who had instigated the change in Eve she'd noticed the minute she'd set eyes on her sister. The way she did her hair, the pretty clothes she was wearing, the neat leather shoes on her feet. Unconsciously Nell tucked her feet in their ugly servicable boots further under the chair. And Eve had filled out a bit, she wasn't so straight up and down now. And it suited her.

Lucy drifted off to sleep. Nell adjusted her clothes and fastened the buttons of her blouse, but she did not get up. Eve had told her the gist of Esther's last words but whereas Eve seemed convinced Howard's wife had just been asking her to stay on and run the household, Nell wasn't so sure. She sat on for some minutes more before settling the sleeping child in the crib Howard had thoughtfully asked Daisy to purchase the day before, without Eve's knowledge. He really had thought of everything, Nell told herself, and would you do that just for a house-keeper? Of course by his own admission Eve had been a rock for him after his wife's death, but still . . . Bringing them here just to please her, making them so welcome, treating them like family. It made you think, didn't it?

She said the same to Toby much later that night when they had retired to their room after an excellent dinner. Howard and Toby had sat enjoying a glass of port in the dining room after she and Eve had gone through to the drawing room. Oh, the drawing room . . . She had never seen anything like it. The gold drapes and furnishings, the wall-to-wall carpeting in dove grey and the beautiful ornate fireplace. She had been frightened to sit down when she had first entered the house and she hadn't known a moment's peace until the lads were in bed and couldn't break anything. And then Eve had shown her the dining room and the morning room and the library and Howard's study . . . The house had gone on and on.

Snuggling up to Toby in the big four-poster bed, Nell whispered, 'I can't believe our Eve is in charge of running this place, Toby, and him being so nice to her and everything. I mean, what employer would bring us here for the day and put us up an' all? Howard's not a bit like I thought he would be.' She had finally succumbed to calling him by his Christian name some time near the pudding stage of the evening meal.

Toby nodded. 'He's a good bloke.'

'Do you think . . .' Nell paused. 'I mean did he, Howard, say anything when you were having your port?'

'And cigar.' In the light from the glowing embers in the fireplace, Nell could see that her husband was smiling. 'Cigar and port, lass.

I thought I'd died and gone to heaven. The lads won't believe me when I tell 'em.'

'Aye, well, don't let your tongue run away with you. Don't forget no one knows where she moved to. All right?'

'Aye, don't fret. I won't let on, lass.'

'So did he? Say anything?' Nell asked again.

Toby peered at his wife. 'Course he said something, we didn't sit in silence, did we? We talked about the bairns and football and the unions. He's all in favour of the unions. Could have knocked me down with a feather when he said.'

'What about the war?'

Quietly now, Toby said, 'No, lass. We didn't talk about the war. It didn't seem the day for it somehow.'

There was silence for a moment, interrupted only by the odd crackle and spit from the fire. Then Nell said in a low voice, 'So that's all you and him talked about? Our bairns and football and the unions an' that? What about Eve?'

'What about her?'

With a sharp wriggle of irritation, Nell twisted to face him. 'Did Howard talk about Eve? Did he mention her at all?'

'No. At least I don't think so. No, no, he didn't. Why?'

Sighing at the dimness of men and her husband in particular, Nell kissed his bristly cheek. 'It doesn't matter.'

'If all that was a confluentin' way of asking me if I think he likes her, then the answer is aye, I do. All right?'

'You do?' Nell shot up in bed. 'Really? You do?'

'Lie down, woman. What's the matter with you? Aye, I think Howard's fond of Eve. Certainly he admires and respects her, you only have to see 'em together to understand that. Whether it's anything more . . .' Toby shrugged. 'It's early days, lass.'

'Aye, in a way, but his wife has been gone nearly nine months.' Nell snuggled down beside him again.

'That's nowt though, is it? Nine months.'

'Oh, it is. How can you say that? It's nearly a year.'

Toby said nothing. Under any other circumstances, with anyone else, Nell would have been shocked to the core at the merest suggestion the bereaved husband could be looking elsewhere so soon. The baby began to stir and he watched as Nell climbed out of the bed and brought the infant back to feed her. Once Lucy was on the breast, Nell said thoughtfully, 'Of course our Eve has got to like him too. That's the thing.'

'Lass, you're in danger of putting the cart before the horse here.'

'I'm not. How can you say that? You said yourself you think he likes her and inviting us here proves that, if nothing else. Going to all that trouble just to please her.'

'They're from different backgrounds, lass. Different worlds. You know that as well as I do, now then. He's from the gentry, however he seems.'

'But he's not like them, you know he isn't. And our Eve could rise to whatever was expected of her. She's got an air about her, she always has had.'

She'd got the bit between her teeth. Recognising the signs and knowing from past history he couldn't win whatever he said, Toby kept quiet.

'Well? Couldn't she carry herself anywhere? You saw her tonight and how she was. Like a lady to the manner born.'

'Aye, I'm not saying she's not able, lass.'

'So what's to stop them? With him being like he is an' all?'

Stifling his growing impatience, Toby reached out and stroked his daughter's downy head. 'Lass, there's no one I'd like to see settled and happy more than Eve, but even if he does like her, and we don't know that for sure, what if she don't want him?'

Nell's eyes narrowed as she glanced towards the glowing fire. 'She admires him very much, she's said that. And he's nice looking and smart and kind. She'd have him if he asked, I feel it in my bones.'

'Oh well, that's settled then if you feel it in your bones. We can all go to sleep knowing there's nowt to worry about.'

'And don't try to be sarcastic. It doesn't suit you.'

Chapter 20

It was the day before Christmas Eve. Although the war was over, the new and deadlier enemy, the Spanish flu, was still in the business of taking the lives of men, women and children throughout Britain. Fear of the epidemic had instigated strict hygiene measures for crowded public places in all the big cities, but still the relentless culling of the weak, the elderly and the very young went on. Most folk were hoping the bitter weather would kill off the spread of the infection but to date this had not happened.

As Caleb crossed the inn yard he was not thinking of the influenza outbreak, his mind being fully occupied with the subject that had dominated it for months now: Eve's whereabouts. He couldn't have put a finger on exactly when it had dawned on him that it was not Mary's absence that was affecting him but Eve's departure. Certainly it had not been for two or three months after Mary had broken their engagement and left him again. He had been desolate at first or, more precisely, he had thought he was. It had taken finding an old pair of Eve's gloves at the back of a drawer before the realisation had hit him that the void she had left with her going was consuming. It had taken him a further few weeks to admit he was aching to see her face, hear her voice, watch her as she busied herself in the kitchen but when he did, he'd called himself every kind of fool. He hadn't seen what was under his nose and now it was too late.

He paused at the gates into the yard, watching a woman alighting from a cab on the other side of the road but his mind was miles away. Why hadn't he realised his love for Mary had burnt itself out long before Eve had gone, even before Mary had returned to Washington? Perhaps he had but hadn't been able to admit it to himself, feeling it made him fickle, inconstant. His love for Mary had been a schoolboy kind of emotion anyway, he realised, a love which placed the beloved on a pedestal, which refused to see anything but perfection. And when Mary had returned pregnant and in need, it had brought out the protective side of him which had always been a strong element in his feeling for her. Eve didn't need protecting in the same way, Eve was strong, gutsy. Theirs would have been an equal union, mentally as well as physically.

Why was he thinking like this? He took off his cap and raked his hand through his hair before pulling the cap back over his forehead. Eve had always regarded him as a friend, nothing more, and a friend she had found it easy to wipe out of her life at that. Furthermore, she had witnessed his infatuation with her sister at first hand and must faintly despise him for his weakness where Mary was concerned. She'd washed her hands of them all.

Scowling to himself, he turned out of the yard but he had only gone a step or two when he froze.

'Hello, Caleb.' The woman from the cab had crossed the road and was now standing a few feet away, a cloth bag in her arms. 'I know I have no right to expect you to take me in but I have nowhere else to go.'

'Mary?' As he spoke he saw her sway but before he could pull himself together, she had fainted at his feet.

An hour later Mary was lying in bed in one of the guest rooms and Caleb was sitting in a chair at her side. He could hardly believe his eyes on two accounts. One, that Mary should have returned to Washington once more, and two, that she was so changed as to be almost un-recognisable. The woman lying so pale and still in the bed looked to be forty if a day, so thin she was skeletal. Her once glorious hair was thin and brittle, with no life or colour left in it, and this, more than anything else, had transformed her looks. Clearing his throat, he said, 'I've called the doctor. He should be here shortly.'

'You needn't have bothered. I could have told you what he will say and none of it will be good.'

It was Mary's voice coming from the skull's head, in which only the eyes were the same. There followed a silence. It was broken by Caleb saying softly, 'You're ill.'

'Yes, I'm ill.' She took a breath. 'I'm very ill.'

'I'm sorry.'

'I believe you are which is . . . amazing considering how I have behaved. You should be pleased to see I've got my just desserts.'

'Don't talk like that.'

'Why? It's the truth and we both know it. The only excuse I have to offer is that I couldn't help myself, which is no excuse at all really. I've always liked you, Caleb. Always. But to stay here in this little back-water was beyond me. I thought I could perhaps manage to do it after William died, I was genuine in that, please believe me, but as the weeks went by I felt stifled. I couldn't breathe. It wasn't you, it was me. I needed more than there is here.'

'More than me.' He smiled to soften the words, surprised how little they hurt. 'I could never have been enough, could I?'

'Oh, Caleb.' She stared at him for a moment and then spoke the very thing he had come to understand over the last months. 'You never really loved me, just an image of someone you wanted me to be. I could never have lived up to it. You always looked at me as though I was an angel or something, I could see it in your face. But I'm no angel, Caleb. Unless it's a fallen one.'

'Mary—'

'No, let me speak. Please. I-I don't want to lose your regard but I have to say it.' She looked for a moment longer at the tender expression on his face and then shut her eyes tightly. 'I've done things I'm ashamed of, Caleb. Bad things. It — it didn't begin like that but that's how it finished. Everyone, if they knew the truth, would say I've got what I deserve.'

'Not in my hearing.'

'No?' Her voice was soft. A whisper.

'No.'

'Thank you.' The tears were seeping from her closed eyelids. 'But you wouldn't say that if you knew.'

Leaning forward he reached for her joined hands which were lying on top of the eiderdown. The bedroom was warm, there was a roaring fire in the grate and Daisy had warmed the bed with stone hot-water bottles, one of which Mary still had at her feet, but her hands were icy cold. 'Open your eyes,' he said. And when she obeyed he stared into the swimming blue pools. 'I'm not the young lad wet behind the ears I was when you and your sisters first came here. I went away to fight and,' he smiled, 'I sowed my wild oats. You won't shock me, Mary.'

'You-you won't hate me if I tell you? I couldn't bear that.'

He looked at her solemnly. 'I can promise you I won't. OK?'

'When I left here, the-the last time, I went back to London but it wasn't the same. The man who had been keeping me had said things to his-his associates. A girl in the same house where I'd lived before said I could share her flat. Men came . . .' She moved her head on the pillow. 'They were vile, some of them. But I felt trapped. I didn't know where to go.'

Caleb kept his gaze on her. She would never know the effort it took. Whatever he had expected, it was not this. She was saying she was no better than the dockside dollies or the girls in Ma Skelton's place in Gateshead. Not that he had availed himself of the services of either but he'd heard the talk of men who had. He rubbed her hands which were lying limply in his because the pain tearing through him had to have some expression. His voice was throaty when he said, 'Why didn't you come home?'

'I couldn't, not after running out on you the way I had.'

Her eyes were tight on him and he knew she was looking for a sign of the shock he had promised her he would not feel. But he was shocked. And repulsed. And angry. He had to wet his lips before he could say, 'How did you get ill?'

Again she shut her eyes as though she could not bear to witness what she might read on his face. 'I got pregnant again. I thought I'd been careful but one night there were a group of men, young mostly, who almost broke the door down so Sarah, the girl I lived with, let them in. They-they were drunk. One of them was a regular of hers but the others . . .' She turned her face into the pillow. 'They came into my room. I had been asleep until they started banging on the door. I tried to make them leave but there were five of them . . . After-afterwards I wanted to go to the police but Sarah laughed. She said they'd never take the word of two . . . of us against some toffs, one of which was the son of a lord. When I found out I was expecting I went to someone. I couldn't go through a birth again.'

Again he wetted his lips. 'What happened?'

'It worked but after I didn't stop bleeding. I-I didn't dare go to a doctor, not for ages. Sarah was good, she looked after me but from the beginning I knew.'

'Knew what?' He stared at her. 'Knew what, Mary?'

She was staring fixedly at him now. 'A life for a life.'

'Don't talk like that.' He shook his head.

'It's true, Caleb. Even before I had it done I knew something would go wrong. Sarah had an abortion a couple of years ago and something happened. She-she has to wash all the time or . . . she smells.'

Dear gussy. He remained very still, just looking at her. 'If you knew that why did you go through with it?'

'I don't know. I suppose I thought I might be all right and I just wanted to get rid of anything to do with that night. And I was scared of the pain of having a baby. It's–it's awful.'

'All right, all right, don't cry.' He shook her hands gently. 'Look, we'll sort this. The doctor will be here in a minute. This might not be as bad as you think.'

'I saw a doctor yesterday. He told me what to expect. That's why I've come home. I didn't want to die so far away and Sarah's not well herself. Do you mind very much?'

'This is your home, it's always been your home and I want no more talk of dying, all right? You're going to get better.' The shock and anger was gone but now he was having to fight the overwhelming feeling rising up in his chest and blocking his throat, a feeling that made him want to shout out his pain and shame. Pain for her, and shame that he was a member of a sex that could take something so beautiful and innocent and turn it into the broken woman in the bed. Forcing out the words, he said, 'Say it, Mary. I'm going to get better. Say it out loud.'

She was looking at him almost pityingly now. 'I'm going to get better.'

'You will, I promise you.' He patted her hand and stood up. 'I'm going to get you something to eat and drink now so just lie quiet.' Mary nodded and closed her eyes. He went out of the room and crossed the landing to the stairs, but once on the ground floor he did not go directly to the kitchen. Instead he made his way to the privy in the yard and it was there he brought up the contents of his stomach.

The doctor had been and gone. He had given Mary a strong sedative. She would sleep, he had assured Caleb, until late the following morning and once she woke she could have a smaller amount of the same medicine every eight hours. It would help with the pain and keep her in a relaxed state. Other than that he could do very little for her. Whoever had been responsible for butchering her – and that was the only word for what he had discovered – had done such a thorough job, there was

228

no hope of recovery. Perhaps if the patient had sought help within a day or two of the procedure which had torn her womb and damaged her bowel and done goodness knows what other mischief, there might have been a chance. As it was . . .

Caleb had thanked the doctor and paid him. After showing him out, he had made his way to the kitchen and told Ada and Winnie enough to let them know that Mary had come home to die. When he sat down at the kitchen table with his head in his hands, they had come either side of him, patting his shoulders ineffectually while Jack whined at his knees.

When Caleb left to inform Nell and Toby that Mary had returned, Ada made a pot of tea. 'Whatever next is going to happen?' She stared at Winnie. 'Nothing has been the same since Eve left, you know that, don't you? And now this. I won't pretend I've ever had any time for Mary but she's not twenty yet. It don't seem right, does it?'

Winnie shook her head. 'Do you think Eve'll come and see her?' They had long been of the opinion that Nell knew where Eve had gone.

Ada nodded. 'She'll come.' She raised her eyes to the ceiling as though she could see into Mary's room. 'But she won't have to dally.'

Caleb was saying much the same thing to Nell at that very moment. 'I know you must correspond with Eve, she wouldn't have gone without letting you know where she is but if she wants to see Mary alive there's not much time.'

Nell stared at Caleb. She had been in the middle of making a batch of mince pies when he had knocked at the door. 'How much time?' she asked bluntly. 'Did the doctor say?'

Caleb shrugged his broad shoulders. 'A few days, maybe even a week or two, the doctor wasn't sure.'

Nell's mind was racing. It had been a while since she had been face to face with Caleb and seeing him afresh she could see what attracted her sister. He was a very masculine man, not exactly good-looking but with an appeal that went beyond handsomeness. And Eve loved him.

If she came back now, would she be tempted to stay and comfort him after Mary died, hoping he would turn to her? It was possible. And then this other thing would be finished. And there was no guarantee Caleb would ever return her affection; in fact, it was highly unlikely.

Nell drew in a long breath and let it out again before she said, 'It's not as simple as you'd think. The people Eve works for think a lot of her and they have gone away for Christmas and they've taken her with them.'

'Are you sure? Would they have left already?'

Nell wasn't a natural liar but her voice was firm when she said, 'They left a day or two ago.'

She watched him move his head frustratedly. 'Where have they gone? Have you any way of contacting her?'

'No. I just know they'll be away for two weeks or more.' It was nearly time for Toby to come home after his shift and she prayed Caleb would be gone before he returned. She would need time to talk Toby round to her way of thinking on this.

'Mary might not have two weeks. In fact it's highly unlikely.'

Mary. Always Mary. And then Nell felt ashamed of herself. Quickly, she said, 'I'll come and see her tomorrow when she's awake. Toby's mam'll have the bairns for a bit, they'll be on their best behaviour with it being Christmas Eve and wanting their stockings filled come morning.'

Caleb's face was grim. 'Are you sure you can't let Eve know? She would want to see Mary. You know she would.'

Guilt made Nell's voice sharp. 'You're probably right although Mary's brought her nothing but grief all her life. All she did for Mary and never a word of thanks in return.'

They stared at each other, a dart of hostility between them. 'I don't think this is the time to go into all that, Nell, do you? It won't help the present situation.'

Nell's chin rose. 'I'm saying it as it is, that's all. You know me, I always speak me mind.'

Caleb fought down his impatience. 'If you could see Mary you wouldn't be angry,' he said simply. 'She's not the same.'

'That's as may be, but if I don't know where Eve's family has gone, I don't know. I can't wave a magic wand and produce her out of thin air.'

'I know, I know.' Caleb reached out as if to touch her but let his hand fall to his side. 'I'm sorry, Nell. I didn't mean . . .' He shook his head. 'You'll come tomorrow then?'

Nell nodded. 'Once I've sorted the bairns.'

'She'll be asleep until late morning with what the doctor gave her.'

'I'll make it early afternoon then.' She wanted him to go. If Toby came back and put his foot in it . . . Moving towards the door, she said, 'I'll see you tomorrow then.'

Once she had closed the door behind him she stood for a full minute staring across the room. Everything was the same as it had been before Caleb had knocked on the door. Lucy was asleep in her crib to one side of the range and it was peaceful for once, the lads having gone sledging in the snow with their friends. A winter twilight was falling outside and the glow from the fire made the room cosy and warm, the paper chains Eve had bought for the boys the Christmas before strung from the ceiling and the steel-topped and brass-tailed fender shining in the dim light. She had been happy minutes before, thanking God for all she had and praying that before next year was out Howard Ingram would have spoken. All of a sudden she felt shivery and slightly sick, and had a great desire to cry.

When Nell arrived at the inn the following afternoon she was paler than normal. This was the result of the row which had erupted when she had told Toby what she had said to Caleb. But in spite of their sitting up until three in the morning, by which time they had both said things they regretted, she was still sure she was doing the right thing. Even after she had persuaded Toby to say nothing and they had gone to bed, she hadn't closed her eyes, and she knew he hadn't slept a wink although they had remained perfectly still and inches apart.

Toby had gone off to work that morning without kissing her,

something he had never failed to do since the first morning they were wed. She had felt it like a knife in her breast and cried for an hour or more, but it had not weakened her resolve. She was sorry Mary had come to this pass, of course she was, and she felt sick when she considered she was keeping all this from Eve, but the alternative was worse. Eve had a chance of making a good life for herself, a life far above anything any of them could have dreamt of years ago, but Caleb was her Achilles heel. And before yesterday he had never even asked after her. Now that spoke volumes, didn't it? Eve could waste the rest of her life working in that inn and waiting for him to notice what a wonderful person she was, whereas Howard Ingram . . .

Ada and Winnie were in the kitchen when Nell walked in, up to their eyes in preparing food for the evening and following day. They both looked up when she entered and Ada said quickly, 'It's right sorry we are about Mary, Nell. And at Christmas too.'

Nell nodded. During the morning, in an effort to justify herself, she'd asked herself if Mary was really as bad as Caleb thought she was. Mary had always been one to make the most of feeling bad. Mind, the doctor had seemed to think it was serious. And to come back at Christmas of all times – but that was Mary all over, selfish through and through. She had been born thinking of herself and nothing had changed. So her thoughts had churned over and over and now she had a thumping headache on top of everything else. 'Where's Caleb?'

'With Mary. She's in the end guest room. He's just took her a bite to eat.'

So she was eating. Well, she couldn't be that bad then, could she? She still wouldn't put it past Mary to come back here and cause ructions and then skedaddle again. Slipping off her winter coat and felt hat, Nell smoothed her hair before making her way upstairs. She paused outside Mary's room but there was no sound from within. She knocked twice on the door and it was Caleb who called, 'Come in.'

As soon as she stepped into the room she noticed the smell. It wasn't strong but it was unpleasant, like meat gone bad. And then she saw her. For a minute she thought, that's not her, that's not our Mary. There's been some sort of a mistake.

'Hello, Nell.' The figure in the bed smiled but the action stretched the once full lips tighter and increased the impression of a skeletonised head still more.

Her face straight and tense, Nell walked over to the bed. Caleb stood up from the chair he had been sitting in, saying, 'I'll leave you two to chat for a while. Try and get her to eat something, Nell. I had no success.'

Nell didn't answer or acknowledge she had heard him. Her eyes on her sister, she murmured, 'What have you done to yourself, lass?' as she sank into the chair Caleb had vacated.

Mary smiled faintly. 'It's too late for recriminations, Nell. Much too late.'

Nell's lips were quivering now, her eyes were blinking. 'I wasn't going to have a go at you.'

'No, I know.' Mary reached out a hand and Nell took it in her own. 'I know that, Nell.'

'You're cold. Like a block of ice.' Nell chaffed the thin fingers in her own warm ones. 'Do you want me to go and fetch a hot-water bottle?'

'There's two in the bed already.'

'Oh, lass, lass.'

'Don't cry, Nell. I think I'd rather you shout at me than cry. Now you didn't ever think you'd hear me say that.'

'I can't help it, you're my sister.' But Eve was her sister too. Wiping her face with the back of her hand, Nell said, 'Has Caleb explained about Eve being away?'

Mary nodded. 'I'd have liked to have seen her before . . . you know. But I don't suppose it matters really. Little does.'

What should she do? She couldn't pretend to herself that Mary wasn't dying, it was as clear as the nose on your face. But no one knew Eve like she did. When Eve loved, she loved without restraint, it was the way her sister was made. In most people there was some sort of in-built self-protection, a tiny part of them that required something back from the beloved before they would be willing to put all on the altar. But Eve wasn't like that, she hadn't been like it with Mary and herself and she wasn't like it with Caleb.

Nell ran her hand over her wet face again. Much as she loved Toby, she knew she wasn't like Eve. She didn't want to be like her. She wasn't as selfish as Mary had always been but she wasn't like Eve either.

Forcing herself to speak with regret, she said, 'She'll be gone a while, Mary. And there's no way of contacting her.'

'But you're here. And Caleb.' Mary squeezed her hand. 'You'll come every day? Promise me you will, Nell.'

'As much as I can.'

'Caleb said Toby's mam is happy to have the bairns and I need you, Nell. I-I get frightened when I'm by myself.'

For the first time Nell caught a glimmer of the old Mary. It enabled her to take out her handkerchief and blow her nose, smooth her hair back from her damp face and say quietly but not unkindly, 'It's Christmas, lass, and I have a family to see to but I promise I'll come as much as I can. All right?'

There followed a long pause while they stared at each other. Then Mary said, with what could have been a catch of laughter in her tone, 'You were the only one I couldn't wind round my finger, Nell. Remember when you used to say that to me? "You can't wind me round your little finger, Mary Baxter, so don't try."'

Nell was remembering a lot of things but most of all how bonny Mary had been. Brokenly, she muttered, 'Don't, lass.'

'It's all right.' Mary squeezed her hand again. 'Since I've had that medicine the doctor left, the pain's much better. I can sleep now. You don't know how wonderful sleep is until you can't have it. Some people say death is just a long sleep, that there's no heaven or hell but just what we have down here. I used to listen to Clarence talk, he was the man I ran away with when I first left here, and he seemed so sure we just go back to the earth and that's that. Do you believe that, Nell?'

Nell caught the thread of fear in her sister's voice. Her eyes soft, she said, 'Have you made your peace with God, lass? I mean have you said sorry for all the bad things you've done in life and meant it? For-for the last baby and William too?'

Mary nodded. 'For them most of all.'

'Then He'll hear you. This Clarence might have been a toff but half of them are so far up their own backsides they're no earthly good to man or beast. They can go to their universities and spout off about this and that but what do they really know about living, Mary? Have any of them had to rely on their Maker when they're crawling on their bellies under tons of rock and slate with matchsticks holding the roof up? Well, my Toby has and he knows there's a God. Most of the men and women hereabouts don't go on about it but they know all right. But them that have everything don't have to rely on no one and that's when they get these fancy ideas. You ought to have told this Clarence to stick his daft talk where the sun don't shine.'

Mary sighed. Closing her eyes, she said drowsily, 'Aye, I should have. I should have done a lot of things I didn't do and not done what I did do. Don't go yet, lass, will you? I-I feel safe when you're here.'

Nell swallowed hard. Safe, she'd said. She was still little more than a bairn at heart, there was a part of Mary that had never really grown up. And yet in some ways it was as if she had always been as old as the hills. 'You have a little sleep,' she said softly. 'I'm not going nowhere for a bit.'

Chapter 21

Howard Ingram stared at the man who up until a moment or two ago he would have sworn he knew through and through. Such was his surprise at what John Wynford had revealed, he had to clear his throat a number of times before he could say, 'I had no idea you were thinking along those lines, John. I don't know what to say. Is she aware of your feelings?'

'I'm not sure. I don't think so. I certainly haven't spoken to her if that's what you mean. I thought it only right to inform you of my intentions first.'

'Yes, yes, I see. And of course I appreciate that.'

'Let me be frank, Howard. I wanted to know if you would have any objection if I pursued this.'

A little stiffly now, Howard said, 'I don't follow you.'

'I think you do.' John sighed deeply. 'Look, man, no one knows better than me how much you cared for Esther. Damn it, I thought you were going to follow her for a while after she went. But it has been over a year now and things move on. It's natural. Healthy. And no man is an island.'

Howard was sitting very straight now. 'What exactly are you suggesting?'

'Nothing at all. I merely need to ascertain if I have your blessing to approach Eve and ask for her hand in marriage. That is all. I have no wish to offend, Howard. Far from it.'

Howard looked hard at his friend. 'And if you haven't my blessing to proceed?'

'Then I shall not press my cause. You're my oldest friend, more than a friend, something of a father figure, if the truth be known. I haven't forgotten the way you welcomed me into your home and oiled my way when I first came here. There were those who were wary of a young new doctor. Those first few years could have been very different, I'm aware of that, but for you and Esther taking me under your wing.'

Howard had relaxed as his friend had spoken and now he reached for his glass of port. They had enjoyed a fine dinner at their club and had taken their port through to the members' reading room where they were ensconced in two armchairs before a roaring fire. Although it was the first week of April, the weather was bitter and it had snowed earlier that day. Quietly, he said, 'You are asking me if I care for Eve. Is that it?'

'Do you?' John asked, just as quietly.

Howard did not reply immediately. After a moment or two, he murmured, 'Can I ask you if she has given you any reason to think she would welcome your advances, John?'

John took a sip of port then wiped his lips with the back of his thumb. 'She's always very pleasant, and on the occasions we speak we get on very well, but no, not really. As I intimated, I have not yet made my feelings plain.'

'And what are those feelings? Do you love her?'

John took another sip of his drink, settling back in his chair before he said, 'I think she would make an excellent doctor's wife. She has a way with people, have you noticed that? And she is discreet, personable and able to run a household efficiently. Those are fine qualities in any woman.'

Howard nodded. 'I agree, but that's not what I asked.'

John smiled. 'I don't think I'm built to indulge in romantic flights of fancy, Howard. I'm not made that way. I like and respect her and that would be enough for me. I would care for her and protect her to the best of my ability and provide a comfortable home, and in return I'd expect her consideration and loyalty.'

Howard's face had taken on a slightly blank expression but behind it his mind was working rapidly. He had been wondering what to do, hadn't he? Asking for a sign. And maybe this was it because, dear friend though John was, he'd want to punch him on the nose if he so much as laid a hand on Eve. But would Eve look on either of them favourably, that was the thing? He knew full well there would be those who would say he, and John to some extent, were looking beneath their station, but he wanted little to do with such people. And he knew Eve would not be influenced either by his wealth or John's position in the community. Of course John was much nearer her age and whole in body. Would Eve be repulsed by the stump where his left arm had been? But no, he didn't feel she was squeamish. And Esther had been very fond of her. He didn't doubt she would be happy for them. The times she had tried to make him promise he would marry again after she went had been without number. He had always replied there would be no other woman who would suit him as she had, but now . . .

He sighed and leant back against the chair. Since he had begun to recover from the influenza, something had changed in his relationship with Eve. Or perhaps it was simply that he himself had changed. He had started to feel as he had never expected to feel again and although he had fought it for all sorts of reasons, the feeling had grown. And it sure as hell wasn't the somewhat lukewarm emotion John had described. He wanted Eve for his wife, not some glorified assistant. Of course John was a fine fellow and everyone was different . . .

He became aware John was looking at him, waiting for him to speak. His voice low, he said, 'I appreciate your frankness and I will be frank with you in return. It is true that over the last little while I have begun to see Eve in a different light. Having said that, I have no idea how she feels which is perhaps the nub of the issue. For both of us.' He smiled wryly and John smiled back. 'Added to which, in my case, society would frown on my looking elsewhere so soon after Esther's passing.'

John drained his glass. 'The war has changed a lot of the old prejudices, Howard.'

'Not as many as I would like.'

'And you would care? You'd care what people like the Strattons or the Clarks said behind closed doors?'

'Not for myself, but for Eve, yes.'

'I hate to point out the obvious, but just the fact that Eve is your housekeeper would be scandal enough and that will still be the case however long you leave it.'

'Yes, I know. I do know that.'

'But I meant what I said. The war has caused the wind of change to blow with some gusto through England's green and pleasant land. Who would have thought that women would take over men's jobs? Not only take them over but in some cases increase productivity a hundred per cent. And all those men and women who used to be in service, can you see them returning under the same conditions now? The divorce laws are changing, Queen Mary's opened a women's extension of the London School of Medicine and in December women got the vote—'

'All right, all right.' Howard held up his hand, half laughing. 'Why are you trying to convince me? I'd have thought it was in your best interests to keep quiet.'

John leant forward and now his voice was quietly emphatic. 'Not at all. I prize our friendship above all things, certainly a woman, even Eve.'

'I appreciate that sentiment, John, I do assure you, but I have to say where Eve is concerned I am not so magnanimous,' said Howard, his voice dry.

'In that case, my dear fellow, I think we both have our answer.'

They continued to sit in a silence that was companionable but Howard knew that this conversation, which had come like a bolt out of the blue, was a milestone in his life. He was sure Esther would have given him her blessing so why was he hesitating for the sake of how it would look to others? He had never been a mealy-mouthed man, in fact there were many instances in his life where things would have gone more smoothly if he had been less forthcoming. And he wasn't as young as he once was. All right, fifty wasn't over the hill and he wasn't ready for his bath chair yet, but he didn't have time to waste.

He would ask her. He finished his port, his heart racing. She would have already retired by the time he got home tonight but tomorrow morning he would ask her to be his wife and to hell with the consequences. Of course she might not accept him. This Travis fellow still had a hold on her affections, she had been clear about that, but she had also been adamant she knew there was no hope in that direction. And she must want children, you only had to see her with her nephews and niece to know she had a way with little ones. Children. A son . . . He had given up any dreams in that direction long ago when Esther had become ill but now there was a chance he might one day see a child of his flesh. But he was running away with himself here. And of course there was another thing to consider. If he openly declared himself and she refused him, would she find it awkward to stay on as his house-keeper? Possibly. More than possibly. And suddenly he knew he had to keep her in his life.

'Penny for them?'

John's voice was quiet as it intruded on his thoughts and Howard did not look at his friend but into the flames of the fire as he said, 'I was just thinking I might have a lot to lose if she can't bring herself to see me as a future husband.'

'Then you had better make sure she can.'

When Howard arrived home he was surprised to see there was a light burning in the drawing room. When he visited his club and Eve knew he was going to be late, she normally left the hall lights on but the rest of the house in darkness. As he approached the drawing room, the door – which had been ajar – opened fully and Eve stood in front of him. He could see immediately she was in some distress, even before she said, 'I've been waiting for you to come home, Howard. I need to talk to you, if that's all right.'

'Of course.' He followed her into the room and when she stood with her back to the banked-down fire, wringing her hands and biting her lip, concern made his voice sharp. 'What is it? What's happened?' When he had left the house first thing that morning, she had been her usual contained self. This was a different woman.

'I had a letter this morning.'

'A letter? From whom?'

'Toby. Nell's husband.'

Howard nodded impatiently. He knew who Toby was. 'Is she ill? Has something happened?' Pray God it wasn't one of the children because Eve set great store by her niece and nephews. 'It's not the baby?'

'No, Lucy's fine. They're all fine. Well, in a fashion.'

'Sit down.' He virtually pushed her down on the sofa and then sat beside her but without touching her. 'Tell me.'

'I . . . I had a letter.' Tears filled her eyes and then she thrust her hand into the pocket of her skirt, saying, 'I can't . . . Read it, Howard. Please.'

Howard took the letter without betraying the fear that had gripped him. If this missive was calling her home, if she was going to leave him . . . The pages were crumpled and he took a moment to straighten them on his knee. Then he began to read the large round letters which could have been written by a child.

Dear Eve,

I'm writing this without Nell's knowledge or permission but I shall tell her the minute I've posted it and it's on its way so she'll know by the time you read it. I need to tell you something, something that's put a wedge between Nell and me that won't be done away with until it's out in the open. Nell was going to leave it until she sees you next but as I said to her, that could be months and I'm not prepared to go on living as we are. Mary came back just before Christmas, lass, and she was bad. Dying. She'd fell for a bairn and had it taken away and it had gone wrong. The quack said she'd only got a couple of weeks but as it turned out it was more like a couple of days. She died the day after Boxing Day. Peaceful it was. Nell told her you were away for Christmas and couldn't be reached and she did that for you, lass. She thought you coming back here and seeing how Mary was would break your heart and upset the apple-cart all over again. To be truthful we argued about it but you know Nell when she gets the bit atween her teeth. Mary had fallen low, lass, down there in London. She told Nell all about it and it weren't pretty. No one knows the story except Caleb and he'll say nowt. Mind, I reckon most folk have put two and two together. Anyway I just want to tell you Nell did what she did because she loves you and has your best interests at heart. Worrying about it has fair broke her up, she's skin and bone and that's not my Nell. I'm sorry to write like this and I tell you straight I didn't see it like Nell did, but that's by the by. What she did, she did for you. That's all I can say. Right or wrong, she wanted the best for you. I hope you can find it in yourself to write and put her mind at rest but I've told her you might look on it different. I'm sorry, Eve. Heart sorry.

Your brother-in-law,

Toby Grant

Howard continued to stare at the last page of the letter after he had finished reading. His mind was amassing the facts contained in Eve's brother-in-law's letter but overall he was conscious of feeling a great sense of gratitude to Nell. This Travis fellow was in Washington and Eve still cared for him. If she had gone back, who knows what would have occurred? Aware he could say none of this, he raised his head and met the green gaze trained on his face. 'I'm so very sorry,' he said softly.

'I can't believe she wouldn't tell me, that she would keep something like this from me. I thought her letters were odd since Christmas and she's only written three times instead of every week, but I thought she was perhaps tired, what with Lucy and everything. I never dreamt . . .'

As her voice trailed away, Howard reached out and took her hand. 'I don't know all the ins and outs of it, Eve, and it's none of my business but I do agree with Toby that Nell would have been thinking only of your best interests.'

'How can you say that?' She laid her head against the back of the sofa and turned her face from him but did not remove her hand from his. 'She prevented me saying goodbye. That's unforgivable.'

'You might not have been in time if she had told you, it only being a couple of days.'

'That's not the point.'

No, it wasn't. Searching his mind, he said quietly, 'I think Nell thought you had been through enough. She perhaps thought it would bring William's passing to the fore again. You have shouldered such a lot during the last years, Eve. I think she was attempting to spare you more heartache. When you said goodbye to Mary before you came here she was as you'd always known her, pretty and well and regaining her strength after the birth of William. I'm sure Nell thought it best you remember her like that. You could have done nothing, and she was not alone. She had Nell and her family and . . . and Mr Travis.' He had to force himself to say the name but when there was no response, he added, 'Mary knew how much you loved her and that you would have been there if you could, you know that.'

Now she did look at him. In a small voice, she said, 'I don't know if she did. We . . . we didn't part on bad terms but it wasn't the same as it had once been.'

'How could it be?' He pressed her fingers. 'Nothing stays the same, Eve. Relationships change and evolve. She had come back to Washington pregnant and then the baby died. I'm sorry to speak ill of the dead but she didn't want the child, you know that, and you must be clear about this now in view of what's happened. It would appear it was the same predicament and her handling of it that caused her to become ill.'

Her fingers jerked but when she would have pulled her hand away, he did not let her. 'You're saying she brought this on herself. That she deserved to die because she killed her baby.'

'Don't put words in my mouth, Eve. No one deserves what happened to Mary but with every choice we make in life there are consequences. I'm sorry if that sounds judgemental but it is the truth. I'm also deeply sorry she chose the life she did because she was your sister and you loved her, but it *was* her choice. You told me that yourself. She had every chance to reform, she did not want to. I am not standing on high moral ground either, how could I? I have done things of which I am so ashamed it took me years to face up to them.'

'The . . . Boer War?'

'Just so.'

They sat in silence for a full minute. Eve retrieved her hand and wiped her eyes with the white linen handkerchief Howard gave her. He wanted to draw her close to him and comfort her, to take away the look of desolation on her face and tell her everything would be all right, but he checked himself. Now was not the time. And then his control was put to the test when she said quietly, 'You must think we are a terrible family but she wasn't a bad girl, Howard. I know it looks as though she was, but my father used to call her fey and he was right. She was so beautiful and fragile, like a lovely butterfly drawn to the bright light that will devour it. I didn't protect her enough. In the beginning, with Josiah, I didn't protect her enough. I should have known . . .'

Her voice ended on a wail and as she fell against him, the tears flooding her face, his arm went out to hold her close. 'Mary, oh, Mary. I'm sorry, I'm sorry.' Her cry was agonised and cut through him, causing his jaw to clench against the pain she was feeling and which he was powerless to do anything about. All he could do was hold her tight and let the grief pour out.

It was a long time before she became quiet and even after that he continued to stroke her hair and murmur soothing words above her head. He thought she might have fallen asleep with the exhausting emotion which had racked her, but then a small voice whispered, 'I'm sorry. I didn't mean to do that.'

'I'm glad you did. I'm only sorry I was out all day and not here when you needed me. You should have put a call through to the works or, failing that, the club this evening.'

'I wouldn't do that.' She sat up, smoothing the pleats of her skirt in embarrassment.

He handed her his handkerchief once again, eyeing her tear-ravaged face tenderly. 'I want you to promise that if you ever need me again, that's exactly what you will do.'

His tone must have conveyed something of what he was feeling because she appeared startled and a little embarrassed. 'I . . . I don't suppose I shall need you again.'

'Don't say that.' Telling himself he was every kind of fool and doing exactly what he had promised himself he wouldn't do, he said softly, 'I want you to need me, Eve. Because I need you. Just how much I didn't realise until tonight when I held you.' And then, at the look on her face, he added quickly, 'I love you and I want you for my wife.'

Dear gussy, had she thought . . . But he hadn't expressed himself very well. He should have had a ring ready and gone down on one knee. He had never imagined she might think he was propositioning her to be his mistress.

Eve's head was spinning. She looked down at her hands, not to play the coquette but because she couldn't hold his gaze. She had wondered, yes, she had to admit she had wondered what she would do and say if this moment should occur. Tucked up in her solitary bed at night she had allowed her mind to wander and play out the fanciful idea that Howard might want her for more than his housekeeper. But at the bottom of her she had dismissed the notion. He was kind and generous and that was why he was so good to her, she'd told herself over and over again. She was getting well above herself to imagine anything more. And pride went before a fall. Every time. But now it had happened and she didn't know what to say. Raising her head, she looked into his face. It was a nice face. Not handsome but possessed of a certain charm. A distinguished face. Hesitantly, she said, 'We come from such different backgrounds. People would be horrified.'

'Do you think I care one jot about anyone but you and me? And anyone who doesn't see you as the wonderful woman you are will not be welcome in this house.'

'I'm so much younger than you.'

'Or perhaps we should say I'm so much older than you, but what does it matter? I know many couples where there is a significant age gap and they are very happy.'

'People, your friends, everyone would say it's too soon after Esther's passing.'

She was saying all the things except the one that really mattered. She was aware of this even as he answered, 'It's been over a year and all that matters is that Esther would understand. You do know that, don't you? That she would be pleased for us?'

Eve bowed her head. She had never told him what Esther had said to her as she had been dying. 'Yes, I know that. But,' she paused, 'you know why I left Washington.'

'Because of this man. Caleb Travis.'

'Yes.' She looked at him. Her face was burning, suffused with a deep red. 'And nothing has changed in regard to my feelings for him. It wouldn't be fair to you to say otherwise.'

'Perhaps not, but that doesn't mean you can't learn to love me, Eve. There are all kinds of love, I've come to understand that. Even between a man and a woman. Esther was and always will be my childhood sweetheart and ours was a natural progression into marriage. She was a very different woman to you but I loved her and I love you. You do like me a little, don't you?'

'You know I do.'

'And I don't . . .' He cleared his throat. 'This,' he touched his empty sleeve, 'it doesn't repel you? Please be truthful.'

Her colour would have deepened if it was possible. 'Not for a minute, how could you think such a thing?'

'I hoped not but I must be frank. I love you and I want you for my wife but not merely as a companion. I would like children in the future. Do you understand?'

Eve nodded. She wasn't so naive as to imagine he had been suggesting a marriage without physical closeness.

'But let me make one thing clear. If children were denied us for whatever reason, I would be content with you and count myself blessed. It's you I want. You I need. And I do need you, Eve. So very much.'

She gazed at him, finding it amazing that this attractive and cultured man should be in love with her. And he was attractive, she thought. Nell had called him a fine figure of a man and she was right.

'I should not have sprung this on you tonight of all nights.' Howard took her hand. 'It was wrong of me.'

'No, no, it's all right.'

'Will you think about it? I don't expect an answer right away. And if you cannot consent then we will go back to how it was before. There will be no embarrassment or awkwardness between us, I will insist on that.'

Eve would have smiled if her heart hadn't been so sore about Mary. This was so like Howard, insisting on something which would be impossible. It was then, as she looked into his kind brown eyes, she thought, I don't want to have to leave him. He had enriched her life in so many ways and her daily lessons were just part of it. Life would be empty without his sense of humour, his gentleness, his kindness, even his stubbornness. But she didn't care for him as she did for Caleb. She must be honest with herself. And would this feeling she had for Howard be enough? Enough for marriage? More importantly, enough for the marriage bed?

Howard drew her to her feet. 'You must be exhausted.'

She was tired, and unbearably sad. Hearing about Mary had brought all the anguish about William to the fore. Howard had said he wanted children and so did she, she ached for bairns of her own. After she had left Washington she had imagined she would live life as a spinster but it wasn't a path she would have chosen or wanted.

'Go to bed and tomorrow we will decide what to do about the letter. You will think clearer when you've had some sleep. This has been a great shock and I haven't helped, have I?' He smiled ruefully. 'But we'll sort it out together, you aren't on your own. If you wish to write to Nell, I'll see to it she receives the letter immediately, or we can go and visit her if you prefer it. Whichever you would like.'

'Thank you.' He knew as well as she did that Mary had become a prostitute before she had died. That alone would be enough to cause most men to run a mile. The scandal of associating with someone who'd had such a sister would be bad enough, but to suggest marrying them! And despite her new hairstyle and clothes, she was still as plain as a pikestaff. And yet when Howard looked at her, there was something in his eyes that made her blush. He cared for her. And she wanted to be cared for in that way. She might not love him as she loved Caleb but he knew all about that and he still wanted her. And she didn't want to lose him. She wanted, just by one person in her life, to be adored.

Drawing on every scrap of courage she possessed, Eve reached up and took his face in her hands. And then she pressed her mouth to his.

Chapter 22

Howard took Eve to see her sister three days after Eve had received the letter. Eve had needed the time to set her thoughts in order and decide how she felt about the decision Nell had taken. She and Howard had talked it through incessantly and this had helped her to see things more objectively. Something, she admitted to herself, she would have been unable to do without his guidance. She had been so angry with Nell, so disappointed and hurt.

The interval also meant that by the time the taxi cab deposited them outside Nell's front door, Eve was wearing an engagement ring on the third finger of her left hand. The morning after he had proposed, Howard had insisted on visiting the best jewellers in Newcastle. Eve had chosen a dainty ring consisting of three diamonds on a gold hoop. It had not been the most elaborate or expensive ring in the shop, but it was the one she had fallen in love with.

Eve had not protested at Howard's urgency but she had been a little surprised by it. He knew this, but when she had expressed a desire to return to Washington and see Nell face to face, he'd felt his engagement needed a solid base. Hence the ring. Something everyone – including Caleb Travis – could see.

Now, as they stood together outside the small terraced house, he kept his arm tightly round her. 'It will be fine.' He smiled at her. 'Stop trembling.'

It was Toby who opened the door to their knock. Eve saw his eyes widen and then he stood back, saying, 'Eve, lass, and Howard. Come in, come in. I'm off work at the moment, crushed me fingers an' the quack won't let me back yet, daft so-an'-so. Sure sign he ain't paid by the hour.' And then he stopped abruptly as though he had become aware he was talking too much.

Eve looked across the room to where Nell had risen from the table, the vegetables she had been preparing in a bowl in front of her. Matthew and Robert were sitting on the clippy mat in front of the range, playing with two little cars fashioned from wood, and Lucy was in her high chair gnawing on a crust. It was a homely scene, cosy, but Eve could see that all was not well with her sister. As Toby had said, she'd lost weight. 'Hello, lass,' she said quietly.

It was a moment before Nell whispered, 'Hello,' and then her voice was small and didn't sound like hers.

Eve looked into Nell's eyes. They seemed altogether too big for her face. Any remaining hurt was swept away by the expression in them. Without a word Eve moved forward. As she opened her arms, Nell flew into them and the next few minutes were lost in unintelligible murmurings and sobs.

Once they were all seated at the kitchen table with a cup of tea, Nell took Eve's hands in her own. 'I'm sorry, lass, I am. I thought I was doing the right thing but then the minute she died I knew I should have told you. It was too late then though and—'

'I know, I know. It doesn't matter. Will you come with me to the grave later before we have to go?'

Nell nodded, fresh tears sliding down her cheeks.

More to stop Nell breaking down again than anything else, Eve held out her left hand, waving it under her sister's nose. 'You haven't noticed, have you?'

'Eve!' Nell grabbed her fingers, her voice rising as she said, 'You're engaged! Toby, they're engaged.' And then, quickly, she looked at Howard.

Laughing, he said, 'It's all right, you haven't put your foot in it. I am the lucky man.'

As Toby shook Howard's hand, Nell kissed her sister. 'I am so pleased, lass, I can't tell you. When I saw you together in Newcastle I knew there was that spark.'

Eve smiled. She wanted to confide in Nell that she was feeling, if not exactly frightened then bewildered by the speed with which every-thing had happened. But she couldn't. And so the four of them chatted and she gave the children the little presents she had bought for them, and after lunch she and Nell put their hats and coats on to walk to the cemetery in the grounds of the church in the village centre. It had been agreed that Toby and Howard would stay with the children to enable them to have some minutes at the graveside alone.

As they walked to the churchyard, Eve was trembling in the pit of her stomach. Mary's grave was covered with snow but when Nell brushed the headstone clear, she read, 'Here lies Mary Baxter. Beloved sister of Eve and Nell. Safe in the arms of God.' They said a prayer and cried a little and then stood for a while, lost in memories.

It was as they left the churchyard that she saw him. Caleb had come out of the inn and was standing looking across the space separating them.

She had known this was going to happen, she told herself. How had she known? She couldn't have. But she had. As he came towards them, she felt Nell's hand tighten on her arm and it was as much to herself as to Nell that she murmured, 'Don't worry, it's all right. I need to thank him for taking Mary in that one last time anyway. He was good to do that, Nell.'

He looked older than when she had left. Thinner. And his hair was longer. It suited him. Thoughts whirled in her mind and then he was standing in front of her, his rugged face unsmiling. 'Eve, it *is* you. I thought my eyes were deceiving me.' He took her gloved hands in his own. 'You've been to the grave?' he asked softly.

She nodded. She wanted to say something but the lump in her throat was preventing words.

'I'm sorry.' He shook his head slightly, his eyes not leaving hers. 'About Mary, you being away, everything. But there was nothing you could have done.'

'I know.' The muscles of her throat contracted and she swallowed hard. 'And I want to thank you for what you did. It–it was kind of you in the circumstances.'

'I'm glad she came home in the end.'

He had not left go of her hands and other than pull them away she did not know what to do. She knew her voice had trembled and she prayed he would put it down to her grief about Mary. Was he wondering why she hadn't come to see Mary's last resting place before? She wanted to tell him she hadn't known her sister was dead but that would put Nell in a difficult position and so she remained silent.

Softly, he said, 'You look very well.'

'I am well. And you?'

'Tolerable.' She watched him take a deep breath. 'But nothing is the same—'

'Eve is here with her fiancé.' Nell's voice was louder than theirs had been. 'Show Caleb your ring, lass. It's beautiful, lovely. And he's such a nice man too. A real gent, you know?'

Caleb relinquished his hold as Nell jostled for Eve's hand, whipping her glove off and showing him the ring. 'There, isn't it bonny? She's done right well for herself.'

'*Nell, please.*' Eve's face was scarlet.

'What? You have. I'm only saying, aren't I?'

The muscles of Caleb's face had tightened but his voice was pleasant when he said, 'Congratulations, Eve. I assume your fiancé is someone you've met in Newcastle?'

She nodded. Aware she couldn't leave it at that, she said, 'Howard is the man I was housekeeper to, actually.'

'Great big house he's got and his own business and everything.' Nell wouldn't shut up. 'Own cook and maid she'll have, won't you, lass?' She dug Eve in the ribs. 'One of the toffs, you'll be.'

'Don't be silly, Nell.' If the ground had opened and swallowed her, she'd have been thankful. She had never felt so embarrassed in her life.

'I'm pleased for you.' Caleb smiled but it didn't reach his eyes. 'I wish you both well.'

'Thank you.' He was pleased for her. That said it all really. Praying she would reveal nothing of how she was feeling, she said quietly, 'How is Jack? I miss him.'

'He's fine. My constant companion most days. We go on long walks together or perhaps I should say he takes me for a walk. Invariably he leads and I follow.'

She forced a smile. 'Your legs are better then?'

'Much better.' Their eyes held for a moment. 'Are you staying in Washington?' he asked after a moment's pause.

'No.' Suddenly she wanted to be gone. This was too painful, coming on top of seeing Mary's grave. They were talking like polite strangers. They *were* strangers. She couldn't bear it. 'No, this is just a fleeting visit to see Nell and Toby.'

Caleb nodded. 'Well, I mustn't keep you. Not in this weather. No doubt you will want to get back in the warm. Goodbye.'

His glance included both women and simultaneously they said, 'Goodbye.'

As Caleb walked away, Eve noticed he had a slight limp. It brought a physical pain to her chest and she wanted to run after him, to say she was sorry he was unhappy, she was even sorry he had lost Mary and was all alone. But she didn't. Instead she walked in the opposite direction with Nell. As they passed the village blacksmith, the smithy was shoeing a horse. Forever after the smell of the hot shoe on the hoof, the smoke rising from it followed by the hissing as he placed the shoe in water to cool would bring to mind the desolation she felt that day.

They were walking along Spout Lane, treading carefully because of the frozen snow, before Eve said quietly, 'You shouldn't have made me show him my ring like that, Nell. It wasn't very tactful after Mary and all. He must be feeling dreadful now he knows she's gone forever. He loved her so much.'

Nell said nothing. She was not concerned whether it was tactful or not. She had accomplished what she'd set out to do the minute she had spotted Caleb. Eve's soft heart could be the ruin of her. Caleb would only have had to express a desire for her to return to the inn and her sister would have been at sixes and sevens. She wouldn't put it past Eve to call off her engagement to Howard. Never mind that all Caleb wanted was a dogsbody to help him run his inn and that one day he was sure to take up with some lass or other. Eve wouldn't see it like that. And Howard was so right for her. He would love her and take care of her and whatever happened in the future, Eve would be set up for life.

As they approached the house, Nell said, 'Are you going to say we bumped into Caleb?'

Eve hesitated, then said, 'I don't see why not. Howard knows why I left here.'

'He does?' Nell looked at her in surprise.

'I've no secrets from him and I don't want to start now. He's accepted how I feel but he also knows Caleb is part of my past. Howard is my future.'

'And you're sure about that? That Caleb's in the past, I mean?'

Eve looked at her sister. They stared at each other for a few moments and then Eve put her hand on her sister's arm. 'That's why you did it, isn't it? Stopped me from coming back and seeing Mary? And showing him the ring today. You were worried if I returned I wouldn't go back to Howard. Oh, Nell.'

'You ran that inn for him when he was away at war and looked after that old devil of a mother of his and he took it all for granted. Used you as a workhorse. And then Mary came swanning back and it was all moonlight and roses again.'

'Nell, stop it. Look, let's get a few things straight. I stayed and took care of the inn because that was what I wanted to do. No one twisted my arm. And he didn't take advantage, you can't say that. Where would we have been if he hadn't taken us in in the first place? I won't pretend I didn't hope that one day, with Mary gone, he might start to see me differently, but it didn't happen. It wasn't his fault, anymore than me loving him was my fault. He's not a bad man, Nell.'

Tears were sliding down Nell's face. 'You're daft, our Eve. Anyone else would have been only too pleased to show him they'd done very nicely thank you and he could do the other thing with knobs on.'

In spite of how she was feeling, Eve had to laugh. She hugged Nell for a moment and then pushed her away, saying, 'If I'm daft so are you, so there's two of us. Come on, we'd better go and help the men with the bairns. They're probably at their wits' end by now.'

Nell dried her face and smiled at Eve. As she moved ahead to open the door, Eve glanced behind her down the lane. She had seen him and she had survived it, but there would be no need to repeat the experience. She wouldn't be coming back to Washington in the future.

When Caleb entered the inn, he walked straight through the kitchen without speaking to Ada and Winnie. It was only when he reached his own room and had shut the door behind him that he breathed out a shuddering sigh. He sat down in the big armchair in front of the fire and leant forward, his hands on his knees as he stared into the flames. She had come back and she would have left without seeing him. He didn't understand that anymore than he understood why she had been so adamant about not giving her address to anyone. And she was engaged to be married, to some bloke who was rolling in it, by what Nell had said. A cook and a maid. Well, well, well. And he had thought he knew her.

He became aware he was grinding his teeth and stood up, beginning to pace the room. He had been stupid to waste a minute thinking about her, he saw that now. All along she must have had her sights set on catching a rich husband; why else would she have left Washington? She had been comfortable here, she had lacked nothing but it hadn't been enough for her. She had aimed high and she had got what she wanted. He swore softly before flinging himself down in the armchair again.

He was glad he had seen her today. It put an end to a period of his life that should have had a line drawn under it a long time ago. There were plenty of other fish in the sea, for crying out loud. He knew more than one lass who would be willing, and he wouldn't be chary about making hay while the sun shone from now on. He didn't need her. He didn't need anyone. He had come through the war against all the odds and he was the owner of a prosperous inn. Everything was going his way.

When he left the inn a few minutes later, he didn't admit to himself what he was about. It wasn't until he had found a spot in Spout Lane where he had a clear view of Nell's front door but could not be seen that he acknowledged he had to see the man who was now her fiancé, at least once.

Twilight was beginning to fall when the taxi came along the street. Caleb was frozen, the icy chill had penetrated his very bones but still he had not moved from his vigil. He narrowed his eyes as the front door opened and light spilled out into the shadows. They had obviously been watching for the taxi.

And then his eyes fastened on the man who had stepped out of the house. He was vaguely aware of Eve hugging Nell in the doorway but all his attention was concentrated on the well-dressed figure waiting on the path. He couldn't distinguish his features clearly but he could see the man was taller than he was and held himself with almost a military bearing. And he was older than he had expected, middle-aged, but a youthful middle-age from what he could see. His hair, although greying, was thick and he didn't look to be overweight.

He watched as Eve left her sister and joined the man, who immediately put his arm round her. They were saying something to Nell and Toby who were standing arm in arm in the doorway, but he could not hear what. He did hear them all laugh, though, and as Eve and her fiancé climbed into the taxi, Toby called, 'Whenever it is, we'll be there. You can count on that.'

And then the taxi drew away and he watched Nell and Toby wave for a few moments before they went back inside the house. Although he could now go home, Caleb continued to stand in the deepening twilight until it was pitch black. The lights from several windows glowed cosily in the frosty darkness and once or twice a dog barked somewhere close. He had never felt so alone in all his life.

When he began walking he was so stiff, his limp was more noticeable than usual, causing an uneven jerky gait that had him swearing under his breath more than once as he nearly went headlong. When he reached the inn yard, he stood for a moment, looking up into the dark sky studded with stars. From this day forth he had to get used to the idea that she was with someone else. Somewhere she would be laughing, eating, sleeping, talking, and all without a thought of him. He'd had her in his grasp and he had let her slip away, and there was no one to blame but himself.

Four months later Eve and Howard were married at the small parish church which was a stone's throw from Penfield Place. It was a quiet wedding. John Wynford was Howard's best man and Nell, Eve's matron-of-honour. Eve looked lovely in a simple gown of ivory silk and she carried a posy of pink rosebuds. Including Nell's children, there were twenty people at the wedding breakfast. Both bride and groom had wanted it that way.

They were honeymooning at a hotel in Hartlepool and arrived there in time for dinner. It was a lovely summer's evening, mellow and warm after a scorching August day, and after they had eaten they went for a walk along the promenade before retiring. On returning to the hotel they went straight upstairs.

As Howard closed the door to their suite, Eve walked to the window and stood looking out. She was nervous. The day had been more tiring than she had expected and she found it hard to take in that she was now a married woman. She still felt just the same. But she wasn't the same, she was a wife, and for the rest of their lives she would sleep in the same bed as her husband.

'Don't be frightened.' Howard had come up behind her and now he drew her to the chaise longue standing at the end of the big four-poster bed. He sat down beside her. 'Not of me.'

'I'm not, not really.' She tried to smile. 'But this is all new to me.'

'Would it surprise you to know I am nervous too?'

'You?' She stared at him in surprise.

'Yes, me. I find myself in the privileged position of having a young and beautiful wife and I am neither young nor beautiful.'

She laughed as he had hoped she would. 'You're handsome, though. And very distinguished. Everyone thinks so.'

'I don't think so.' He smiled, but then his face straightened as he said softly, 'I have never regretted the loss of my arm so much as at this moment. I want to hold you properly, with two arms. Love you.'

She had sensed the need in him for reassurance that the loss of his arm would not be repugnant to her several times since their engagement, but never so strongly as at this moment. He had not voiced it directly, he never did, but the expression on his face spoke volumes. And it was in answer to that unspoken plea that she lifted her face and for the second time in their acquaintance kissed him first.

PART FIVE

1925 – Different Kinds of Love

Chapter 23

Eve had been married for six years and it would be true to say she was a different woman to the one who had stepped off the train at Newcastle Central on the day she left Washington. Many changes had occurred in her life and also in the country in general. The Great War had cast a pall of mourning over the last year of the previous decade. The litany of sombre place names, Ypres, Loos, the Somme, Verdun and Passchendaele, had been on everyone's tongue. But then 1920 had dawned. A new era, and one in which women were coming to the fore in a way which horrified the old traditionalists. Women had proved they could take on men's jobs and do them exceedingly well during the war, and now these same women were demanding the right to spread their wings. A revolution was afoot, albeit one aided by the giddy flapper with her tassels and beads.

For Eve the changes had been mixed. The transition from house-keeper to wife had been a big one, but for the first time in her life she was experiencing the happiness involved in coming first with someone. From their wedding night, when Howard had proved himself to be a selfless and adept lover, her affection for her husband had grown and grown. And love had begotten love. Within weeks of her marriage she had known she loved Howard. Maybe not as she loved Caleb, but this love was solid, warm and reliable, and one that she could wholly trust in.

Four months to the day after they were wed, she found she was expecting a child. Oliver Howard Ingram was born in June the following year. Three years later, Alexander William made his appearance. Both boys were strong and healthy, with curly hair and blue eyes. It was remarked on that if they'd been born nearer in age, they would have been mistaken for twins.

Their characters were quite different, though. Oliver was a determined, outgoing little boy with a sunny disposition and a ready laugh. Alexander was altogether more retiring and never so happy as when he was at his mother's side. Howard unashamedly worshipped both his sons, but partly because Oliver was the older child Howard tended to have more to do with him than with Alexander. But they were a close and happy family unit, so happy that sometimes Eve felt guilty her life was running so smoothly when outside the four walls of her home unrest was spreading like wildfire through the country. The slump was making itself felt and the dole queues were lengthening. The bitterness of the working class was reflected in strikes at the docks, on the railways, in the shipyards and the coal mines. One in five of the working population was out of work and they were desperate.

Not long after Alexander was born, Eve started a soup kitchen in the parish church hall for families whose breadwinner was out of work. This had come about through Daisy. Eve had found the little maid in tears one day and had discovered her sister and the sister's husband and three children had been forced into the workhouse a few days previously. The husband had been a stretcher-bearer in the war and had won the Military Medal for bravery, but on demobilisation he had had to go straight into the dole queue through no fault of his own.

Howard had seen to it that the man was given a job at the engineering works, which had enabled the family to rent two rooms in a terraced house close to the works, but the whole incident had set Eve's mind working. With Howard's blessing she had spoken to several of the wives of his friends, and together they had banded together and opened the soup kitchen. In addition to making sure those in need had one good meal a day, they also distributed clothes and boots and blankets. When it became apparent that nits, ringworm, impetigo and fleas were rife, Eve arranged for a friendly school nurse to be loaned to them one day a week. Bad cases of infestation were dealt with at the cleansing station, a small room at the back of the vestry which Eve commandeered for the purpose. There the children's heads were shaved.

Both Oliver and Alexander accompanied Eve now and again to the soup kitchen. She and Howard didn't want their children to grow up in a privileged bubble as so many of Howard's friends' children did. They wanted their boys to be aware of poverty and the effect it could have on families from an early age.

On a sunny Saturday morning in late September, Eve glanced across the breakfast table at her sons. Oliver was eating his boiled egg and soldiers and Alexander was doing the same in his high chair next to his brother. 'I'm going to be handing out some picture books and crayons to the children this morning, Oliver. Would you like to come and help me?'

Oliver looked up, his blue eyes bright. 'Daddy said we could go and sail my boat on the river. Didn't you, Daddy?'

Howard smiled ruefully, 'Sorry,' he said to Eve. 'I didn't know you would be working today.'

'No, it's my fault.' Since Oliver had started at a small prep school at the beginning of the month, Eve had tried to make sure one of the other women, not all of whom had young families, took her place on a Saturday so she could spend the weekend with her family. 'We're short-handed today, Annabelle Sheldon and Verity Alridge are attending a garden party and Gladys Owen has gone abroad for two weeks.' She wrinkled her nose as she spoke. Gladys was all right, but the other two women, both prominent members of Newcastle's high society, never missed an opportunity to let her know she was not one of them. She was tolerated, for Howard's sake, but she was not of their class and therefore socially inferior. The scandal of Howard marrying so far beneath himself might have been replaced by other, more recent gossip, but Annabelle and Verity made sure it was not forgotten.

Eve would have liked to say that the prejudice she met from these two women and others did not bother her, but in all truthfulness she could not. It was hurtful. Not that she let them see when they wounded her. She would rather walk through Newcastle stark naked. Most of the time, and certainly within these four walls, she felt fulfilled and content, but there was the odd moment when she longed to throw off the mantle of sedateness that went with being Howard's wife and tell Annabelle and Verity and one or two others exactly what she thought of them. They might have been born with silver spoons in their mouths but they were the sort of upper-crust women Nell would have described as being up their own backsides.

'What are you thinking about to put that look on your face?'

She realised Howard was still looking at her and said hastily, 'Nothing, just how Annabelle and Verity have gone on about their new hats all week. They are desperate to outdo each other.' She had never revealed to her husband how she felt. In the early days of their engagement she had told Nell she didn't intend to have any secrets from Howard, but it had not taken her very long to understand that that was naive. Only then had she fully understood why Nell had not burdened Toby with the knowledge of the money she gave her sister each month. If she told Howard of the numerous but subtle slights that came her way, he would be both angry and upset. He would cut himself off from his friends and in doing so not only deprive himself of companionship and social acceptance, but probably endanger his business too. Because, say what you like, it wasn't what you knew but who you knew that counted in this town. Probably every town. Their circle included shipyard owners and mine owners as well as a Sir or two. Oh yes, it wasn't what you knew but who, she thought grimly.

'Those two.' Howard's voice was scathing. 'Flibbertigibbets, the pair of them. They haven't got a brain cell between them. Do you remember that last dinner party at the Alridge's, when they were discussing the Zinoviev letter? How they imagine a letter from the Communist International to British Communists just happened to mysteriously fall into the hands of the Tories so they could publish it just before polling day beats me. Of course the Tories romped home after that. And if that letter's not a forgery, I'll eat my hat. I didn't know whether to laugh or cry when Verity said Tory politicians wouldn't dream of showing such bad form as to sabotage the Labour Party.'

'If I remember rightly you neither laughed nor cried but were some-what rude.'

'Believe me, I could have been a lot ruder.'

Eve smiled. 'I'm sure you could,' she said soothingly.

'Mammy, can I have all my hair cut off?' Oliver brought his parents eyes to him as he dunked a soldier into the yolk of his egg.

'Why on earth would you want to do that?' Eve asked helplessly. Since he had been able to talk Oliver had had the knack of completely disconcerting any adult he was with. He asked the most perturbing questions for a five-year-old.

'Because then it wouldn't get tangly.'

'I see.' She glanced at Howard. 'But you wouldn't look so nice then, would you?'

'Those children at the church have their hair cut off.' He dug into his egg with his spoon. 'You let them so why can't I? Don't you think they look nice?'

Oh dear. Howard's mouth was twitching but he said not a word to help her out. 'Well, those children have to have their hair cut because . . .' She wondered how to phrase it. She had learnt the hard way to be very careful what she said to her son who had a habit of repeating her words at just the wrong moment.

'Because the nurse who comes to the church thinks it is necessary,' Howard said, straight-faced. 'When it isn't necessary, it is not done.'

'And she wouldn't think it was necessary with me?'

'Definitely not.'

Oliver made a face. 'I don't like that nurse.'

'Now, now, we don't say things like that, do we?' Eve said quickly as Howard turned away to hide his smile. 'The nurse is a very kind lady.'

'To some children but not to me.'

She wasn't going to win this one. 'If you've finished your breakfast, go and wash your hands and get ready to go out with Daddy.' She looked at Howard. 'Are you taking Alexander too?'

Alexander had been following the conversation and now piped up, 'Stay with Mammy.'

Howard shrugged. 'I'll take him if you want but you remember the last time I did that when he said he didn't want to go.'

She did. It had been a disaster. Looking at her two-year-old's pretty little face, Eve smiled. Alexander might not be an extrovert like Oliver but he was just as determined in his own way. She knew one or two of their friends blamed the child's fear of being parted from her on her refusal to have a nanny for the boys. It had caused eyebrows to be raised when Oliver had been born and she had said she was going to take care of her baby herself. It just wasn't done, several of their so-called friends had murmured. She had replied it was done because she was doing it and that was the end of that. It had been the first time she had really shown her mettle since her marriage and Howard had backed her one hundred per cent. Dear Howard. Her smile included him. 'He can come with me, it will be all right. I'll take Daisy with me and she can keep an eye on him.'

Once Oliver was ready and stood clutching his boat which had been his birthday present that year, Eve kissed him. 'Be a good boy for Daddy, won't you?'

'He's always a good boy, aren't you, son?' Howard ruffled Oliver's curls as he spoke. They were waiting for the taxi cab Howard had ordered. Due to his disability they did not have a motor car as most of their social circle did, but this did not hinder them at all.

Eve knew where Howard was making for, it was one of their favourite picnic spots in the summer when they took the boys out for the day. The Tyne curled and wound its way past Newcastle's industrial factories and shipbuilding yards and chemical works to emerge westwards near Ovingham and Harlow Hill as a far more gentle and picturesque river, with many streams and small natural lakes. There the boys could run to their heart's content in the meadows thick with wild flowers, climb trees and sail their toy boats in tiny rivulets.

'I wish you were coming too, Mammy.'

It wasn't often Oliver said such a thing, he was the antithesis of his brother in that respect, and for a moment Eve was tempted not to go to the church. But they really were terribly short-handed, and so she bent down, took his face in her hands and kissed him again as she said, 'We'll all go together next week, I promise. All right? And for the whole day with a picnic. Would you like that?'

He nodded, smiling, and as she did every day of her life, Eve counted her blessings. She hadn't known what love was until she had her boys, she reflected. The maternal love that had sprung into being the first time she had seen Oliver's little face had outdone any feeling she had felt before then for anyone. Apart from William perhaps. But she hadn't borne him, hadn't had the wonder of carrying him inside herself for nine months, feeling him move, kick. It was such a different kind of love to what she had felt for Caleb and which she felt for Howard. But then that was natural, she supposed. The feeling one had for one's parents, sisters, brothers was different too.

'Here's the taxi.' Howard kissed her and Alexander who was clinging to her skirt.

On impulse she went into the dining room once the door had closed behind them and from the window watched the taxi draw away. It was a beautiful day, she thought wistfully. Probably one of the last really warm days they would have before autumn's chill made itself felt. She hoped Howard wouldn't let Oliver eat too many wild blackberries. Of course part of the thrill for Oliver was picking the ripe fruit himself. He thought himself such a big boy.

'Come on.' Eve whisked Alexander up into her arms, making him squeal with delight. 'Let's get you ready. And once we are finished at the church, we might have time for a walk in Leazes Park to see the ducks. Would you like that?'

When she arrived at the church hall with Alexander and Daisy, the other women were busy putting up the trestle tables on which they would serve the thick meat and vegetable soup and shives of bread, followed by treacle pudding, which was the meal that day. The doors of the hall were opened to the public at eleven o'clock, and Eve knew a long queue would have formed by then. A round table at the back of the hall held a collection of second-hand clothes, boots and blankets, along with a pile of baby clothes, and the same woman was in charge of that most days. Although most of the folk who took advantage of the soup kitchen were what Eve mentally termed respectable poor, a few from the worst area down by the quayside wouldn't be averse to taking the items to sell on in return for drink and tobacco. They'd found if the same person kept charge of the stall each day, they recognised the opportunists.

Once the doors were open, Eve made sure Daisy was in charge of Alexander and began to help serve the food to those who shuffled in. The queue was orderly, it always was. There were usually lots of elderly couples and young mothers with children, and most of them were too thin and tired looking to do more than stand and patiently wait their turn. The church's privy, situated outside the hall's back door in the small yard, always had a long queue too. The communal lavatories in the teeming filthy tenements where most of their customers lived were often shared by twenty or more families. They were so nauseating that many women suffered constipation rather than use them. And Eve knew that some of the women she saw each day only ate the meal they provided and customarily went hungry the rest of the time for the benefit of their children.

As the numbers began to dwindle near two o'clock when they shut the doors and began to clear up, Eve glanced at a group of children playing with the colouring books and crayons she had brought in that day. They were sitting with Daisy in a corner of the room and it was with a pang to her heart that she realised only Alexander had shoes on his feet. They would have to obtain some boots for the children for the winter, she thought, making a mental note to bring the matter up at the next committee meeting. There were several pairs of adult boots and shoes on the table at the back of the hall, but the children's sizes were always gone in a flash, probably because mothers who were too proud to take boots for themselves would receive them for their bairns.

At half past two the hall was restored to its usual neatness and everything was washed up and cleared away in the kitchen leading off the front door. After sending Daisy home to assist Elsie, Eve took Alexander to the park as she had promised.

They had a lovely afternoon in the late September sunshine. They sat by the ornamental fountain and Alexander had a nap on her lap while she watched other mothers stroll by with little ones in baby carriages and older children running here and there. She would like another baby, she thought drowsily, as one rosy-faced little cherub under a parasol was wheeled by. Maybe a little girl this time. She would call her Angeline, that was a pretty name. Or perhaps Rebecca. Nell had had another little girl three years ago and Betsy was a poppet.

It was just as Alexander woke up that she saw Daisy coming towards her, and something in the little maid's face alerted her to the fact that all was not well. A long time afterwards she realised that that moment in time would forever be crystallised in her memory. The warm gentle breeze, the sound of children's laughter, the young mothers in their summer dresses and her feeling of well-being. And then everything changed in one second of time. For ever.

'What is it?' She stood up at Daisy's approach, holding a sleepy Alexander in her arms. 'What's wrong?'

'Oh, Miss Eve . . .' Daisy was so worked up she had reverted to addressing Eve as she'd done before Eve had married Howard. 'There's two policemen at the house. They want to talk to you.'

'What about?' She was already walking swiftly, holding Alexander to her and causing Daisy to trot at her side.

'I don't know, they wouldn't say. Only that they had to talk to you and it was imperative they speak to you straightaway. I said I thought you'd be somewhere here and they said to fetch you but not to worry you,' Daisy gabbled.

'They gave you no indication what it was about?'

'No, miss − ma'am − they just said they'd wait till I come back. I looked over by the aviary first but you weren't there, and then I thought that master Alexander likes seeing the water in the fountain so I come here.'

'It's all right, Daisy.'

'Elsie, Elsie's made them a cup of tea,' Daisy panted.

'Good, good.'

Eve was on the verge of collapse by the time she reached the house although it was only a short walk from the park. But Alexander was heavy and the afternoon was very warm. Her mind had been screaming all the way home but even her worst fears could not have prepared her for what she was about to hear.

One of the constables sat her down and the other saw to it that Daisy took Alexander to the nursery and Elsie was sitting beside her, holding her hand, before he said, 'There has been an accident, Mrs Ingram.'

Eve stared at him, her eyes dry and wide. 'My son?'

'It appears from witnesses at the scene that your son was sailing his boat when it got caught by the current and was swept away and out into the main swell of the river. They said your husband called to the boy to stop but the youngster overbalanced and fell into the water. Your . . . your husband jumped in after him.'

Eve continued to stare into the constable's face. It was a sad face. Was it normally sad? She asked herself, or was it sad because of the news he had to impart? And then a voice she didn't recognise as hers, said again, 'My son?'

'I'm afraid your son and husband were recovered too late, Mrs Ingram. It was the current. Their rescuers were keen swimmers and even they had a battle to stay afloat. I am very sorry.'

She heard Elsie make a kind of whimpering noise at her side but it didn't penetrate the void in her head. 'No, you're wrong. My son and husband will be home shortly.'

When John Wynford appeared in the room, she didn't realise for a moment that the policemen must have arranged it so. She looked up into the familiar face. 'John, they are saying . . .'

'I know.' He knelt down in front of her. 'And you must be very brave.'

'No.' It wasn't true. Oliver couldn't be dead. He was just a little boy. 'No, they will be home in time for tea.'

'Eve, it was an accident.'

'No.' It couldn't be true. Just a few hours ago she had stood in the hall and kissed them both. They had been warm and alive and breathing, they couldn't be dead. It wasn't possible. She thought she heard John say, 'She's going, give me my bag quick,' but then the rushing darkness surrounded her and she let herself fall into it.

When she came to, she was lying on the couch in front of the fire in the drawing room where she had spoken to the constables, only they weren't there. John was sitting by her side, holding her hand, and immediately she opened her eyes, he said, 'I want you to swallow this, Eve. It will help you sleep.'

'I don't want to sleep.'

'Yes, you do. Drink it down, it won't hurt you.'

She swallowed the draught rather than argue with him. 'It's not true, John. They're mistaken.'

'Lie back and shut your eyes.'

'I don't want to shut my eyes. I have to sort this out.'

'In a little while.'

'No, now.'

She made to move from the couch but he took her hands, his voice firm as he said, 'Eve, listen to me. They are gone, there is nothing you can do. Howard died trying to save his son which is the way he would have wanted it. It was an accident, a tragic accident.'

'No.' There was a feeling rising up in her which had no expression, so violent was it. She felt her body wasn't strong enough to contain the grief and rage and horror, that she would break into a hundred pieces. 'No, I have to get to them.'

'Howard would have wanted you to be strong for Alexander.'

What was he talking about? Eve snatched her hands away. 'I want to see my son. I have to see Oliver, he needs me.'

She swung her feet off the couch but as she tried to stand up she fell and would have pitched into the fire but for John catching her. 'Sit down, that's a strong sedative. Just relax, that's all you have to do.'

Was he mad? She had to sort out this terrible mistake first, she couldn't sleep. Her voice a moan, she said, 'I want my baby, my Oliver. You have to help me.'

'I'll help you. Of course I'll help you. But first you must rest, all right?'

'You promise? I have to see them, John. Now.'

'Yes, yes, I know.'

A heaviness was blanketing her limbs, a weight on them she couldn't fight. Through the incredible feeling of exhaustion she heard Elsie's voice say, 'Oh, Dr Wynford, how is she?' and John reply, 'I've given her enough to knock out a horse, she should sleep until tomorrow morning.' And then the whirling in her head took over and she was spun away.

★   ★   ★

When she next opened her eyes she was in her own bed and the room was in semi-darkness, the blinds drawn. She turned her head and looked to the side of her. Nell was sitting on a chair. Her sister's eyes were shut.

It was true. The terrible dreams she'd had. Oliver had drowned in the river. Howard too. That was why Nell was here. They must have sent for her. Now, far from fighting the sleeping draught, she let herself fall back into the heavy softness, knowing she wanted to sleep forever.

When she next came to, the light on her closed eyelids was bright. She lay for some moments without opening her eyes, her mind dull but still aware of what had befallen her. Then she forced her lids open. Nell was still sitting in the chair but now she was awake and looking at her.

'You're awake,' her sister said softly. 'That's good.'

'Where's Alexander?'

'He's all right. Daisy is playing with him in the nursery. How-how do you feel?'

Eve didn't answer this. Struggling to sit up, she said, 'I have to see Alexander.'

'I promise you he's all right, lass. He doesn't know anything about what's happened.'

Eve shut her eyes tightly. 'I can't bear it, Nell. I can't. I'll go mad, I know I will.'

The next moment she was gathered up in Nell's arms. 'I know, I know. I don't know what to say, lass. It's cruel, cruel.'

Yes, it was cruel. And wrong. Oliver was only a little boy. And Howard, he had been so kind, so good. 'I want to die too, I want to be with Oliver.'

'But you won't because Alexander needs you.'

She clung to Nell as the tears came in a flood that poured out of her eyes and nose and mouth. She couldn't breathe, she didn't want to breathe and yet life went on even though she wanted it to stop. But

273

how was she going to get through the rest of her life without her baby? Never to see his little face again, to hear his laugh. She couldn't do it, she couldn't. She would go mad, insane.

It was a long time later before she was still and they continued to sit wrapped in each other's arms. 'I can't bear it, Nell. I can't. Even for Alexander.'

'You can.' Nell moved her away slightly, her own face red and puffy. 'And you will. I know you better than you know yourself.'

'How could Howard let it happen? How could he let him fall into the water?'

'Lass, it was one of those things, an accident. There were some blokes on the other side of the river and they said Oliver ran along the side of the stream shouting for his boat and just didn't stop when he reached the river bank. Howard had been shouting for him to stop but it was like the lad didn't hear him.'

'He was so proud of his boat,' Eve said dully. 'He would have been frantic at the thought of losing it. But we would have bought him another.'

'I know, I know. Anyway, Howard jumped straight in after him and was holding him when the current took them away. It happened real fast, they said. And these blokes went in an' all and between them they got them out but it was too late. One of these blokes nearly copped it an' all apparently.'

Eve was resting with her back against Nell's chest, her sister's arms tight round her. 'What am I going to do, Nell?'

'I don't know, lass, but I do know Alexander needs you. He's been asking for you all morning.'

'What's the time?'

'Gone eleven.'

'Eleven o'clock?' Eve sat up straighter. 'He always likes to come into our bed for a morning cuddle. Oliver too.' She made a tortured sound in her throat. 'How am I going to tell him? He adored his daddy and brother.'

'I'll be with you, lass, all the time, and I'll stay as long as I'm needed. Toby's mam's took the bairns and she'll keep 'em for as long as I want. They'll be all right with her.'

'He had just learnt his numbers up to twenty. He was the first one in his class to do it.'

'Oh, lass.'

Eve turned into her sister's embrace again and now she hung on to Nell as though she would never let her go.

Chapter 24

The funeral was over. The black carriage pulled by black plumed horses had carried Oliver and Howard to the church where Eve and Howard had been married, and the cortège had been endless. There had only been one coffin, Eve had wanted father and son to be buried together. The previous night she had spent in the morning room where Howard and Oliver were laid out. Only Nell knew that Eve had lifted her son from his father's side and held him close to her heart through the night hours. It was the last time she would see his little face, his dimpled hands, be able to stroke his thick curls and touch his lips. He had looked as though he was peacefully asleep but it was a cold, frozen sleep, but still she had held him, praying for a miracle the whole time. Praying that somehow his little heart would start beating again, that he would open his eyes, that warmth would flow back into his body.

But now everyone who had come back to the house had left and only Nell and Toby remained with Eve. Howard's parents and one of his brothers had put in an appearance at the church, but Eve had barely spoken two words to them. They had cut Howard from their lives when he was alive and it was too late now to show remorse. Not that they had. They had been very cool and distant, three aloof cold-eyed figures who had neither offered comfort nor appeared to need it. It had been the first time Eve had laid eyes on any of Howard's family and when they had introduced themselves at the graveside she had inclined her head and thanked them for coming and moved on. She wanted nothing to do with them.

Contrary to what she knew was expected of her, she had not brought Alexander to the church. Neither had she made her son kiss his father and brother when they had been laid out in the morning room, as was the custom. She didn't care what people thought, she knew Alexander better than anyone and he was unlike Oliver in that he was highly strung and sensitive. She had sat him on her knee the day after the accident and explained his daddy and brother had gone to heaven together and that she and Alexander had to look after each other now. One day they would all be together again but until then Mammy would always be here for him. He had been satisfied with this. Anything else she did not consider necessary for a two-year-old.

'Eve, you must eat something.' Nell was holding her hands as they sat on the couch in the drawing room and Toby was sitting in an armchair opposite them, his rough big-nosed face troubled. For a moment at the graveside he had thought Eve was going to throw herself into the ground with her son and husband. Indeed she looked as though she had died herself. She had never had much flesh on her bones but now her skin seemed as though it was stretched to breaking point over her nose and cheekbones, and her green eyes were almost black with the depth of her suffering. He knew Nell was worried to death about her sister.

'I'm all right, dear.' Eve squeezed Nell's hands. 'I couldn't eat right now.'

'You haven't eaten for days, just the odd bowl of soup won't sustain you.'

'I'll eat tomorrow.' And then Eve seemed to rouse herself as she said, 'You must go home with Toby today, Nell. Your bairns need you and you can do nothing more here. I don't know how I would have got through the last few days without you and I can never repay you for your care and love, but I have to get on with life now. For Alexander.'

'I'm staying a bit longer.' Nell glanced at her husband who nodded. 'Just until . . .' She had been going to say until Eve was more like herself, but would she ever be herself again after this? 'Until you're eating a bit and sleeping again.'

'There's no need, Nell. You can't leave the bairns any longer. It's not fair on Toby's mam.'

'Lass, I'm not budging for a while. All right? Toby's mam's coping fine with 'em. Apparently she's got our Betsy out of nappies in the day and I've been trying to do that all summer. I'm staying a bit longer and we'll see how things go.'

'You're very good.' Eve glanced at her brother-in-law. 'Both of you.'

'Good be blowed. You're my sister and I love you,' Nell said stoutly.

Toby cleared his throat. 'Nell will stay as long as you want her to, lass. We're agreed on that. A week, a month, it don't matter, so don't fret.'

The kindness in his face brought tears to Eve's eyes but she blinked them away. She had cried an ocean over the last week. She had to try and pull herself together. At least during the day. At night when she was alone she could cry but it upset Alexander if he saw her weeping.

'I'm going to have to be away.' Toby got to his feet. There had been two strikes at the pit already this year and they couldn't afford for him to lose more than one day's pay. Mind, with the owners having backed down on their demands for longer working hours for less pay due to this subsidy the government had brought in, there'd be more trouble ahead. What happened when the nine-month period was over? Nowt would have changed. But now wasn't the time to be thinking of all that. As he looked at Eve's white, strained face, the thought that had been with him all day surfaced again. He had a lot to be thankful for.

Eve and Nell stood up too, Eve leaning forward and kissing her brother-in-law on the cheek. 'Thank you so much for coming, Toby. Do something for me, will you?'

'Aye, lass. Anything.'

'Take this for your train fare and for your mam to help out with having the bairns.'

As she stuffed the notes into the pocket of his jacket, Toby turned bright red. 'Eeh, no, lass. No. I couldn't do that.'

'Please, Toby.' As he made to fish the money out of his pocket, Eve put her hand on his arm. 'I've got it, you know that, and it will make me feel better about having Nell here because I do feel bad at keeping her from you. I . . . I don't know what I'd have done without her and then you coming today . . .'

'Don't cry, lass.' Toby looked helplessly at Nell. 'It's the least we can do. We're family, aren't we?'

'Then if we're family and you look on me as a sister, please take it. You'd do the same if the positions were reversed, and . . .' she gulped in her throat, wiping the tears from her face with the back of her hand, 'what's money, Toby? It's nothing compared to people, is it?'

There was a moment of deep silence. 'No, lass, it isn't,' said Toby gruffly. 'And if it makes you feel better then I'll say thank you most kindly. Me mam's struggling a bit if the truth be told, this'll be a godsend sure enough.'

Nell's eyes mirrored her thanks to her husband. Only she knew what it would have cost him to say what he had. Leaving Eve in the drawing room, she saw Toby out. They clung together in the hall for long minutes. When he eventually disentangled himself, he said softly, 'Come on, old girl. Dry your eyes.'

'It's so sad and it don't seem fair.' Nell scrubbed at her face with her handkerchief. 'Why our Eve? You answer me that. And the bairn,

Toby. She worshipped him, same as she does Alexander. You-you make sure you tell our lot how much I love 'em when you get back, all right?'

'They know, lass. They know.'

'Aye, but tell 'em, won't you?'

'I will, I do.'

'And you. You take care of yourself.' Again she was clinging to him. 'Promise me you won't take any chances what with them cutting corners on safety and the rest of it. What do the owners care if the roof comes down as long as they're all right in their big grand houses. Promise me, lad.'

'I promise.' It was a futile promise and they both knew it. Some of the lads at the pit were good talkers and clever with it, and they'd told anyone who would listen about the history of coal mining and the struggles of the working class and the Labour movement. They knew that the Earl of Durham owned 12,500 acres and got more than forty thousand pounds every year from royalties just because coal was mined under his land, for instance. It had shaken Toby when he'd heard that. Especially in view of the fact that even the most basic safety procedures had been whittled away over the last years until every damn mine in the country was a death trap. They'd save a pound for their pockets and take a man's life and think nowt about it. That was what they were up against. He said none of this, however, holding Nell tight one last time before gently moving her to arm's length. 'Goodbye, lass,' he said softly. 'Try and not worry too much. Your Eve is a fighter, she'll come through.'

'I know, but at what cost?'

Toby opened the front door. It was a cool night but pleasant. Nell watched him walk away until he reached the corner of the street where he turned and waved, then he disappeared from view.

She wiped her eyes again and straightened her shoulders. Then she shut the front door and went in to her sister.

★   ★   ★

The solicitor called the following afternoon. He was a quiet, sympathetic individual and spoke in plain terms. Mr Ingram's will was very straightforward. Mrs Ingram inherited everything. 'Everything' consisted of the engineering works, this house and all it contained, a number of stocks and shares and a sizeable amount in the bank. There were also several insurances and things of that nature which would add up to a substantial sum. But he would not burden her with too many details at present.

He took a sip of the tea Daisy had brought in and cleared his throat.

Perhaps when she was feeling a little better she would like him to call again. They would need to discuss how she saw the future with regard to the engineering business and other matters that would not wait too long. But for now she could rest in the knowledge that she was financially secure for the rest of her life.

Eve thanked him and he left. As he was to say later to his wife over tea, you would have thought he had been discussing the weather, so little interest did Mrs Ingram show.

It was three weeks after the funeral and Nell's first evening home. She hadn't wanted to leave Eve but her sister had insisted. 'She said she had to get used to being on her own with Alexander at some time,' Nell said to Toby as they sat in front of the kitchen range having a cup of cocoa together before bed. 'And with Elsie and Daisy living in, she said she'd always have someone to talk to if things got too bad.'

'Well, she's right, lass.'

'But it's not the same as your own flesh and blood, is it?'

'No, but what were you going to do? Live there for the next umpteen odd years? I know it's hard but the bairn and Howard are gone, lass. It's done.'

'Believe me, no one knows that more than Eve. The loss of Oliver hit her immediately – well, that's natural, isn't it, with your own bairn.

But I don't think she'd realised how much she was going to miss Howard. He was such a nice man.'

'Aye, he was.'

'She's . . . well, she's sort of lost, Toby. I've never seen our Eve like it, not even in the worst of times.'

Toby reached out and took his wife's hand. 'Like I said before, she'll come through.'

Nell looked at him, a quiver in her voice as she said, 'It's frightened me, all this, Toby. I know I lost me mam and then our da and me brothers, and poor Mary, but this is different somehow. I can't explain it but it is. Perhaps it's seeing Eve so crushed, she's always been so strong and unmovable. I feel like nothing is solid. Aw,' she made a flapping movement with her hand, 'you must think I'm daft.'

'Course I don't.' He put his cup of cocoa down and stood up, pulling her out of her chair. 'Come here,' he said softly. 'You don't know how much I've missed you, me an' the bairns. Nothing's been the same.'

'Let's go to bed.' Nell cradled his rough face in her hands. 'I've missed you too.'

They were at the foot of the stairs when there was a knock at the back door. 'Who the dickens is that?' Toby looked at her in surprise. 'It's nigh on ten o'clock. Look, you go up and I'll get rid of 'em, all right?'

Nell was still standing in the hall when she heard Caleb's voice. When she entered the kitchen he was saying, 'I just wondered how she was, that's all, but it'll do tomorrow.' And then he looked at her. 'Oh, hello, Nell. I'm sorry, I should have come earlier but I only just found out you were back. I was wondering how Eve was.'

'You've heard then? About the accident?'

'Yes, I heard. You wouldn't expect anything else in this place, would you? You can't blow your nose but someone times how long.'

Nell stared at him. He sounded bitter but if half the stories about him were true, it was more than enough. He'd played fast and loose with more than one lass, had Caleb, since Mary had gone, and that sort of carry-on was bound to get about. You shouldn't speak ill of the dead but how a man like Caleb hadn't seen Mary for what she was, she didn't know. But that was men. A pretty face and they were like bees to a honey pot. Quietly, she said, 'She's none too good but then you'd expect that, wouldn't you, losing her bairn and man in one fell swoop.'

'There's still another child, isn't there?'

'Aye, and I thank God for it else I think she'd have followed Oliver and Howard, the way she's been since it happened.'

'I'm sorry.' He stood for a moment, biting his lip.

It was Toby who said, 'Sit yourself down, man. Me an' Nell have a cup of cocoa about this time, do you want one?'

'No, no, I won't keep you.' Looking directly at Nell, he said, 'Pass on my condolences next time you speak, would you?'

Somewhat stiffly now, Nell said, 'Of course.' Caleb had turned to go when she added, 'Course the only good thing in all of this is that he's left her a small fortune, set up for life, she is. She could buy and sell anyone in this town ten times over.'

'Is that so?' Caleb's voice was flat.

'Aye, it is so. Mind, that don't help when you're grieving like Eve is grieving, but she'll be beholden to neither man nor beast for the rest of her life so that's something, isn't it?' She waited for a response but he just stared at her. 'Howard, her husband, saw the worth of her, that's the thing. Doted on her, he did. On the family an' all. He knew he'd got a diamond in Eve. Which makes it all the more unfair now.'

Their eyes joined and held, and it was Toby who broke what had become a tense silence by saying, his voice over-hearty, 'Are you sure you don't want a drink, Caleb? There's tea if you'd prefer it. Cocoa isn't to everyone's taste.'

'No thanks, I'd better be going.'

'Well, we'll tell Eve you called, man, and thanks for coming. I'm sure she'll appreciate it.'

Nell said nothing. She stood and watched as Toby ushered Caleb out.

She was still standing in exactly the same position when he came back into the kitchen. 'Why?' He stared at his wife, his face angry. 'Why, Nell?'

She didn't try to prevaricate. 'Because he'd got it coming. Eve don't need him or his inn no more.'

'He came round here to offer his condolences, you heard the man. Why be so prickly?'

'Oh, Toby.' She rubbed her forehead. 'You don't see, do you?'

'No, I damn well don't, so enlighten me.'

'Eve's always liked him. Caleb. Always. But he'd got eyes for no one but Mary. Eve worked in that inn from dawn to dusk and he took full advantage of her willingness. Look how she ran things when he went to war. And then Mary comes back and Eve's—' She stopped abruptly. Taking a deep breath, she said, 'I want him to know she's rolling in it, that she don't need the likes of him. He's always looked on her as some kind of a workhorse. Oh, it's true, say what you like,' she flapped her hand at Toby, 'I know, I've seen it.'

'So that's why . . .' Toby sat down suddenly on one of the hard-backed chairs. 'That's why you didn't want to tell Eve when Mary came back. You thought she'd stay here because she loved him.'

'She would have.' Nell's chin was jutting out but her bottom lip was trembling. 'I know Eve better than anyone and she would have stayed if she thought he needed her and she could help. And then the same thing would have happened all over again. She was worth better than that and I knew Howard liked her, I could tell. She would have thrown that away and then be left with nothing.'

'Why didn't you tell me? How Eve felt, I mean.'

'I couldn't. I shouldn't have now.'

'And does he know? Caleb?'

'I don't think so. No, I'm sure he doesn't. Whatever he is, he's not that bad. I think if he'd known how she felt he wouldn't have flaunted Mary under her nose like he did. But the fact remains she does love him, Toby. Still. I'm sure of it. And he'll never feel the same way about her.'

Toby's brow was wrinkled. 'But she married Howard.'

'Which was absolutely the right thing to do,' Nell said vehemently. 'Just because she loves Caleb it don't mean she couldn't love Howard too.'

Toby stared at his wife as though he didn't know her. His voice deep, he said, 'If I caught you looking at another man—'

'Oh, don't be daft.' Nell walked up to him and put her arms round his neck. 'You an' me are different.'

'I should damn well hope so.' Toby shook his head. 'I don't understand women, I never have.'

'Good. I wouldn't want you to understand me, well, not completely. There'd be no mystery left then and if all the magazines are right, it's mystery that holds a man.'

'I can't believe you read such rubbish and actually believe it.' Toby's hands had found their way to Nell's ample buttocks. 'Give me a bit of this any day and to blazes with any mystery.'

They pressed into each other, their kiss long and deep, and it was a minute or so before Toby said, 'Come on, lass, let's get to bed before I take you right now in front of the range. Mystery! You're a one an' no mistake.'

After leaving Nell's back yard, Caleb didn't immediately walk on but stood in the narrow dirt lane staring blindly ahead. The October night carried the chill of autumn and the full moon cast a cold white brilliance over his surroundings. He found his hands were knotted into fists and he consciously forced himself to relax his fingers, one by one.

So Eve was a wealthy woman, was she? But of course she was. He had known that before he had spoken to Nell. Only it hadn't struck him in the same way somehow. Perhaps it was how Nell had put it to him, as though she thought he was after Eve's money. He shook his head. Or was he imagining things?

No, no, he wasn't. Look at Toby, he'd been embarrassed, he'd seen it in his face. Toby had cottoned on to what Nell was inferring. He looked back at the house. For two pins he'd go back and make her spell it out. He didn't understand why, but it was as if she'd got a beef against him all the time. And what had he done to upset the woman? Nowt. No, all he'd done was to take the lot of them in years ago and then be a patsy ever since. First Mary treating him like dirt and then Eve taking herself off without so much as a by your leave. And then Mary had come back and he'd taken care of her when most blokes would have told her to sling her hook, ill as she'd been. He'd fallen over backwards for the lot of them so why Nell was so antagonistic he didn't know. Considering the three of them had lived at the inn for years under his protection, it was the most natural thing in the world for him to offer his condolences for Eve's loss, wasn't it? And Nell had made him feel like some scrounger on the make when all he'd wanted to do was say he was sorry.

Was he? Was he sorry?

Aye, course he was. He was. For a bairn to be taken like that, it was terrible, terrible. And him, the husband. He wouldn't have wished that.

He began to walk, his hands thrust deep into his pockets and his head bowed. He had seen how the death of Mary's little bairn had affected Eve; what she must be feeling now, he couldn't imagine. He stopped, clenching his teeth as a groan deep inside brought him hunching his shoulders. And he couldn't go to her, couldn't even offer a word of comfort. Not only did he not feature in her life but now the gulf between them was unbridgeable.

He reached the end of the back way and stepped into Spout Lane but again he stopped, staring about him in the blackness. He had made a mess of his life. Somehow, somewhere, he'd taken a wrong turn and had blundered along ever since. As soon as he had realised how he felt about Eve he should have gone and found her and never mind she didn't want to know. If he had done that, sat her down and told her how he felt, at least he would have the satisfaction now of knowing he had done everything he could. But he had been hurt and offended at her wanting to cut him out of her life and so he had taken the line of least resistance. Like his father had always done. Looking back, their lives could have been so different if his father had stood up to his mam and worn the trousers. He had always blamed his mam for the rotten family life they'd had, but if his da had been a man and kept his mam in order, things would never have reached the pitch they did. Aw, what was he thinking of his mam and da for tonight? Fat lot of good that was going to do.

He walked on, and as the inn came into view, he thought, would Eve have stayed and been content to be mistress of the inn and his wife if he had had his wits about him in those days? Or had she always set her sights on something grander than being the wife of a village publican? He made a disparaging sound in his throat. He'd never know, would he? He was years and years too late wondering. But one thing was becoming clearer, he didn't intend to spend the rest of his life in Washington. Or even England for that matter. Years ago he'd had itchy feet, but then Eve and her sisters had come to the inn and he'd got caught up with life and responsibilities. And there had been his mam like a millstone round his neck. But life had changed. Even Jack had died the year before. He had no ties here.

He stood in the inn yard and stared up at the building. He would sell this place come the spring, take as much as he could get for it what with the slump and all and leave for pastures new. France perhaps. Or even further afield. Why not? He was still a young man, he was only thirty-four. He'd heard fortunes could be made in Australia, maybe that was the place to be looking at. One thing was for sure, he didn't intend to stay here and turn into his father. Or get hitched up with some lass or other. And that's what they were all angling for. He always made it clear he wasn't in it for the long haul but sooner or later they'd get that look in their eyes.

He breathed out slowly, and as he did so he noticed he could see the white fan of his breath in the air. The nights were drawing in, winter would be upon them soon and the old-timers were predicting a bad one this year. But come the spring he'd set wheels in motion and by the summer he should be free of this place. And free of all the memories that tied him to her. And that was what he wanted now.

Chapter 25

The winter was long and cold. Looking back on the months after Oliver and Howard's passing, Eve saw them as one dark continuous vacuum. Her only motivation for getting up in the mornings was Alexander, for his sake she picked up the threads of their life and forced herself to go on. He mentioned his brother often in the natural way very young children had. His father he spoke about only occasionally. This was not surprising. Howard had been gone for a large part of most working days but until Oliver had started school three weeks before the accident, the boys had been inseparable.

Day followed joyless day. Weeks passed. Christmas came and went. Eve would gladly have ignored the season but for Alexander's sake she invited Nell and Toby and their children to join them for the festive period. They arrived Christmas Eve and she was glad she'd made the effort when she saw how much Alexander enjoyed having his cousins to stay. Nevertheless it was a difficult time and she wasn't altogether sorry when they had to leave on Boxing Day afternoon because Toby had a shift the following day. On New Year's Eve, once Alexander was asleep, she took a sleeping pill and went to bed early, there to cry herself to sleep as she did most nights.

One of the things that helped her to keep going on the darkest days was her work at the soup kitchen. Things were going from bad to worse in the country as a whole, and the queue was getting longer each morning. It was all very well each year on November the eleventh at eleven o'clock in the morning to have a two-minute silence for those who had died in the war, but that did not put food into children's bellies.

January and February were raw months with deep driving snow and bitter winds that cut through to the bone. One afternoon as Eve was about to close the door to the church hall and lock up, she noticed one of the regular visitors to the soup kitchen waiting for her. Verity and Annabelle and the two other women who had helped her that day had already left; he clearly wanted a word with her alone. Mr Hutton was an ancient old man with skin like crinkled leather and only the week before she had noticed his cloth jacket was so threadbare it was hardly holding together. The next time he had come to the hall she had quietly passed him a thick overcoat she'd bought, along with a warm muffler. He had been so touched he hadn't been able to say more than a muttered, 'Bless you, ma'am.' Now he said in a low voice, 'Can I talk with you a minute? It won't take long.'

'Of course, Mr Hutton.' Eve stepped back into the hall. There was the smell of snow in the wind and although there was no heating of any kind in the hall it was considerably warmer than outside.

'There's a young lass in the house where I live, nowt but fourteen or fifteen, an' she's in trouble, ma'am.'

'You mean . . .'

'No, no, not that. At least not yet. She's a good lass but no thanks to her da. He's a rough un' an' handy with his fists. Knocks his poor wife about somethin' rotten an' the bairns an' all if they get in his way. Over the years afore me wife died we'd have the bairns in ours when he started an' I suppose Tilly, she's the little lass, looks on me like a granda. We lost our only one with the fever when he was five years old an' the good Lord didn't see fit to bless us with any more.'

'Oh, I'm sorry, Mr Hutton. I didn't know.'

'Aye, well, I don't talk about it but I knew you'd understand, what with your misfortune an' all. Right sorry everyone was to hear about that, ma'am.'

'Thank you, Mr Hutton.'

'Anyway, I knew there was somethin' wrong with young Tilly an' last night she slipped in to see me. Her mam an' da have got the upstairs an' I'm in the two rooms downstairs, see.'

Eve nodded. In some parts of the city it wasn't unusual for three or four families to be living in one house.

'Tilly works at the Grand in Market Street as a chambermaid,' Mr Hutton continued. 'But her da's sayin' she don't bring enough in. There's eight of 'em upstairs an' another bairn on the way. Mind, he's never done an honest day's work in his life, her da.'

'I don't quite see . . .'

'He's after puttin' the little lass on the game.'

Eve stared into the rheumy old eyes. She knew what Mr Hutton meant but she could hardly take it in that a father would do that to his own daughter.

'Tilly's scared to death of him, they all are. One minute she was talkin' about runnin' away and the next doin' herself in. She reckons if she scarpers, her da'd find her an' bring her back an' skin her alive. An' she's got nowhere to run to. The mam an' da come across from Ireland when Tilly was a babe in arms, they've got no one here. No one except me.'

'But the mother? Surely she wouldn't allow it?'

The old man shook his head. 'Bess'll do what she's told.'

Oh dear. She really didn't want to get involved in this, she had enough on her plate. Then Eve felt ashamed of herself. It was obvious she had to do something if this child wasn't going to be forced into a life of degradation, but what?

Mr Hutton brought her attention back to him. 'I'd be much obliged if you would talk to the lass, ma'am.'

Eve nodded. 'All right, Mr Hutton. Why don't you bring Tilly here tomorrow?'

'Oh, I can't do that, ma'am. She works during the day at the Grand, like I said. Her da takes every penny she earns an' he'd know if they dock her pay for bein' off an' be sure to take it out of her hide.'

'Well, I suppose you could bring her to my house in Penfield Place. It's number forty-seven.'

'Today?' he said quickly. 'I could meet her out an' bring her along then an' her da would be none the wiser.'

'Very well.' What had she let herself in for? After watching the old man shuffle away, Eve locked the church hall door and made her way home, taking care not to slip on the icy pavements. It began to snow again as she reached the steps leading up to her front door, and the sky was low and heavy, with more to come. It was only the last week of February, Eve thought wearily. There were weeks and weeks of bad weather to get through yet, and already Alexander was tired of being confined to the house. Of course he had always had Oliver to play with in the past. *Oliver.* Oh Oliver, Oliver.

Alexander came running down the hall like a small whirlwind to meet her as she entered the house, Daisy trailing after him. She knelt down and opened her arms and he flung himself into her, squealing his delight she was back. She played with him for an hour before Daisy got his tea, and then read him picture books until it was time for his bath in front of the nursery fire. She had only just lifted him into the warm water Daisy had prepared when the maid returned to say the visitors she had been expecting had arrived.

Leaving Daisy to oversee Alexander's bath and dress him in his night-clothes, Eve walked downstairs. Mr Hutton and a small thin girl who didn't look to be more than eleven or twelve were sitting side by side on two hard-backed chairs in the hall. They stood up immediately they saw her and Eve noticed the girl was so nervous she was visibly shaking.

'You must be Tilly.' Eve's smile included Mr Hutton. 'Let's go through to the drawing room, shall we? There's a nice fire in there.' Once in the drawing room Eve indicated a two-seater sofa placed at an angle to her armchair. 'Sit down, please.'

The two sat. It was clear that for once Mr Hutton was overawed, as he had not spoken a word, merely glanced round the room once and then sat down with his gnarled red hands placed palm down on the knees of his worn trousers. Eve looked closely at the young girl in front of her. She was poorly dressed but clean with two bright blue eyes staring out under her faded felt hat. Thin as she was, her coat looked to be a couple of sizes too small and her hands were blue with cold.

'Mr Hutton has informed me of your circumstances, Tilly,' Eve said when it became apparent the old man was tongue-tied. 'He's very concerned about you.'

'Yes, missis.'

'Ma'am.' Mr Hutton spoke for the first time. Tilly looked quickly at him. 'You say ma'am to the lady, lass.'

'It doesn't matter.' Making up her mind on the spur of the moment, Eve said, 'Would you like a cup of tea? It's very cold outside, you must be frozen.'

Tilly glanced at Mr Hutton and it was he who said, 'Thank you right kindly, ma'am.'

Rather than ring the bell, Eve said, 'I'll just go and see cook about a tray. Daisy, the maid who let you in, is seeing to my son's bath.'

In the kitchen she instructed Elsie to make up a tray with toasted teacakes and jam and fruit cake. The pair of them looked as though they were half starved. She had only just walked back in the drawing room and was saying, 'Now, perhaps you can tell me a little about yourself, Tilly,' when the door opened and Daisy walked in with Alexander in her arms. It was clear he had been crying.

'I'm sorry, ma'am, but he wants to see you,' said Daisy, red in the face.

Eve sighed inwardly. She had told Daisy to be firm with him if need be but Alexander, young as he was, knew he had the upper hand and always led Daisy a dance. She held out her arms for her son and then placed him on her lap, saying, 'You be a good boy while Mummy talks to her visitors, all right?'

Alexander took his thumb out of his mouth and looking straight at Tilly, said, 'I'm Sander. What's your name?'

For the first time Tilly smiled. 'My name is Tilly and this is Mr Hutton.'

And then Alexander completely disconcerted everyone by adding, 'Ollie's not here. He lives in heaven.'

Tilly's face straightened. She nodded solemnly. 'I've got a sister and brother who live in heaven too. I miss them. I suppose you miss your brother too?'

Alexander stared at her. A child of instant likes and dislikes, he now struggled off Eve's lap and held out his teddy bear to Tilly. 'This is my bear. You can play wiv him.'

Recognising the honour, Tilly said softly, 'He's a grand bear.'

Eve swallowed hard. For a ridiculous moment she felt she was going to burst into tears. Then Elsie bustled into the room with the tray, and Eve turned to Daisy who was standing behind her chair. 'Would you take Alexander to the nursery and read him a story in bed? I'll be along shortly.' And when Alexander opened his mouth to protest, she said firmly in the voice she used for such occasions, 'You will go with Daisy, Alexander, and Mammy will come in a little while if you are a good boy. Daisy will give you your milk and biscuit. All right?'

Once Tilly and Mr Hutton had a plate of cake on their laps, Eve said quietly, 'You have a way with children, Tilly.'

Again the girl smiled and Eve thought what a difference it made to the sad little face. 'I'm the eldest at home, ma'am, an' I've helped look after our lot 'cos me mam's often not well. She . . . she suffers with her stomach.'

Eve could imagine her father's fists had a lot to do with that. 'And you say you have lost a brother and sister?'

The smile dimmed. Tilly nodded. 'Our Jed was nigh on three an' me sister, Jinny, nine months when the influenza took them. She . . . she was me only sister. All the rest are lads.'

'You work as a chambermaid. Do you like it?'

'Like it?' It was clear Tilly had not been asked this before. Then she shook her head, adding quickly, 'But I was lucky to get it, ma'am, I know that,' as though Eve had accused her of being ungrateful.

'What is your wage?'

'Six and six a week, ma'am.'

Six shillings and sixpence a week, and for that she would be worked to death, no doubt. 'How old are you, Tilly?'

'Fifteen come the summer, ma'am. Me . . . mam can't remember exactly when but I was born one day in the first week of June.'

Eve nodded, keeping all expression from her face as she thought, poor little mite. Her gaze dropped momentarily to Tilly's hands. They had turned bright red as she had warmed up and were chapped and sore, but her fingernails were short and clean. Until she heard herself say it, she wasn't conscious of having made the decision. 'How would you like to come and work for me as a nurserymaid, Tilly? You know my circumstances from Mr Hutton, I'm sure. Until now I have looked after my boys,' she stopped abruptly and took a deep breath, 'my son, largely myself, but on the occasions I am out Daisy finds him hard to manage. And she was not employed for this purpose, of course. I feel it would be good for Alexander to have someone with him all the time, someone he can play with as well as care for him. Do you understand me?'

Tilly's eyes were wide. 'Aye, yes, ma'am.' She glanced at Mr Hutton but he was staring at Eve.

'I would want you to live in and a uniform would be provided.' She thought rapidly. It would be in the child's best interests to have as little contact with her father as possible. 'You would have one half day a month off when you would be free to do as you please. Oh yes, and your wage would be ten shillings a week, paid monthly.' She now turned to Mr Hutton and pretended not to notice his glistening eyes. 'You would be more than welcome to call and see Tilly when you are passing, Mr Hutton.'

'Thank you, ma'am.'

Her eyes returned to Tilly and she saw the young girl's face was shining. 'So? Do you think you could fit into my household?'

'Oh aye, yes, ma'am. I would, I could. Thank you, thank you, ma'am. I can't believe . . . Thank you.'

Eve smiled. 'When can you start?'

Tilly hesitated. 'I could come right away, ma'am, but they won't give you a reference then. I'm supposed to work a month's notice. An' me da, well, he's expecting me money.'

'Do you feel obliged to work a month's notice?'

Tilly stared at her uncertainly.

'What I mean is, suppose I give you your first month's wages in advance to give to your mother' – she could not bring herself to say father – 'and you start work here tomorrow, would you feel happy to do that? Would that make things . . . agreeable at home?'

'Oh, ma'am.'

'That is what we will do then. Mr Hutton can assist you to bring your belongings here tomorrow morning at nine o'clock.' Eve's voice softened. 'Don't cry, Tilly. Everything will work out, I'm sure. Now eat your cake.'

Over the next months Eve was to look back on that cold snowy day in February as the start of the next stage of her life. Within days of Tilly arriving at Penfield Place, it was as though she had always lived with Eve. Alexander adored her and Tilly handled her charge beautifully. Daisy was glad to be free of the responsibility of Alexander when Eve was out and she got on very well with the new nurserymaid, as did Elsie. Tilly was so visibly thrilled and grateful to be part of the household that she would have won the hardest heart over.

In the spring, Eve bought a motor car. It was something she had been thinking about for some time and would give her a degree of independence hitherto unknown. She received only scant instructions from the salesman, but after several somewhat scary forays in the very early morning when few folk were about, she grew in confidence. There were few rules and regulations to adhere to on the whole, and she found driving mostly a matter of common sense.

So it was that during April on fine afternoons, once she had finished at the church hall, she and Alexander and Tilly would go for a ride in the country. She took Mr Hutton with them on one or two occasions. Since he had been calling at the house to speak to Tilly once or twice a week, Eve had discovered she liked the irascible old man very much. And he was lonely. He never said this himself, but because since Howard had died she had moments of loneliness, she recognised it in others. All her busyness, however, couldn't keep her mind off the worsening situation in the country between the miners and the government. She knew Nell was worried to death and she had every reason to be. Eve had thought about going to see her once or twice but the possibility that she might bump into Caleb restrained her. She was still feeling so raw and fragile after the loss of Oliver and Howard that she didn't know how she would react if she saw him, and the last thing she wanted to do was make a fool of herself and embarrass him.

And then what everyone had been expecting happened. On 30 April, the coal owners closed every pit in the country and locked the miners out. Their terms to the miners amounted to pre-war wages and an extra hour on the working day. Their terms to the government now the subsidy had ended amounted to no state interference in the running of the mines, all strikes to be made illegal and the state to take over control of all funds belonging to trade unions.

It was war, but this time on England's soil between the upper classes and the working class. And Eve was bang smack in the middle. For the first time since her marriage to Howard, she was brought face to face with the stark reality that she could not have a foot in both camps. The government had been shrewd enough to see what was going to happen and they had made plans for combating widespread industrial action. A huge force of middle-class volunteers was ready and willing to keep essential services running, so on 4 May when the unions backed the miners by calling for a general strike throughout the nation, a civilian army was ready to drive trams, buses and trains, distribute food and join the police specials. When Verity and Annabelle approached her to, as they put it, 'do her bit', she replied she would not be part of a strategy to rob miners of their rightful living wage. The terms to the miners were a disgrace, she said, and for Churchill to call the men who had slaved under the ground for coal during the war the 'new Red threat' and 'worse than the Hun' was unforgivable.

The result of this was that the instrument Eve had always been faintly suspicious of but which Howard had loved – namely the telephone – rang less, she received fewer callers, and invitations to soirées and other engagements markedly declined. All of which worried her not a jot. She was far more concerned when, after nine days, the TUC halted their action and the miners were left to fight on alone.

By the middle of September she knew she had to go and visit Nell and give her sister what encouragement she could. She had asked Nell and the children to come and visit several times but Nell had always replied that her place was with Toby while the lock-out lasted. And although Nell was still accepting the money Eve had been in the habit of sending her sister each month, she would not take any extra. Eve surmised, rightly, that Toby had forbidden what she knew he would term as 'hand-outs'. He had long ago become aware of the arrangement they had, but when Nell had explained it away by insisting Eve was sending money for the bairns in her role as aunty, he had capitulated. But he would go only so far and no further.

Eve didn't want to come between man and wife. But she was worried. From the talk at the soup kitchen and from miners who were now regularly knocking on doors asking for any work, however menial – 'I'm a dab hand at grooming dogs, missus, or sweeping chimneys' – she knew each week was becoming harder than the one before. And the lock-out showed no sign of ending. Even the most sympathetic of the miners' supporters were getting fed up with donating and lending and helping.

Although it would have been very convenient, she knew she couldn't travel to Washington by car. To arrive at the colliery town in a shining new motor car in the present desperate circumstances was unthinkable. So it was by train and cab she made the journey to see Nell one Tuesday in the last week of September. She'd left Alexander at home with Tilly. She didn't know what to expect when she arrived and had warned Tilly and the others she might have to stay overnight.

It had been a surprisingly hot and dry September. The day was very warm. After the taxi cab had driven off in a cloud of dust, she stood looking at Nell's house. She had expected . . . Well, she didn't know what she had expected, but certainly not this curious lack of activity. She pulled her hat off and fanned her face as she glanced about her. Where were all the bairns? Then the front door of Nell's neighbour opened, and a woman appeared in the doorway. Eve recognised her, and she said, 'Hello, Mrs Ramshawe. I'm Eve, Nell's sister.'

'Aye, I know who you are, lass.' The woman's voice was not unkind. 'It was right sorry we were to hear about your man and the little lad. We all said a little prayer for you in church.'

'Thank you.'

Eve walked up the path to Nell's front door and Mrs Ramshawe said, 'They're not in, lass. Did she know you were coming?'

Eve shook her head. 'No, I thought I'd surprise them.'

'The men have gone on one of their marches, Durham way.' Mrs Ramshawe's tone seemed to suggest she was not in favour of the march. 'An' quite a few of the women and bairns have gone tattie and turnip picking. Farmer Brown at West Pelton and Farmer Kirby on the south side are paying in swedes and kale and other vegetables. It might not be pounds, shillings and pence but it fills the bairns' bellies.'

'When will they be back?' Eve asked politely.

'Not afore nightfall, lass. Leastways I shouldn't think so.'

Eve was mentally kicking herself. She should have said she was coming but she hadn't thought for a moment Nell wouldn't be in. She nodded her thanks to the neighbour and opened Nell's front door, knowing it wouldn't be locked. No one locked their doors in Washington. She walked past the front room where she knew Nell and Toby now slept, the lads having one of the upstairs bedrooms and the two little girls the other.

In the kitchen she stood looking around her. It was cool; for once the range wasn't on. She supposed there was no coal now to keep the fire going night and day, it would only be lit when necessary. Everything was spick and span as always but it was a cleanliness that spoke of poverty. The kitchen shelves had little on them and the table's oilcloth was devoid of even a crumb.

Eve placed the heavy bag of groceries she had brought with her from Newcastle on the table. Sorting through, she lifted out a joint of ham and slab of butter and some cheese which would need to be put on the cold slab in the pantry, the rest she could leave for Nell to put away. When she opened the pantry door, however, she stood quite still for a shocked moment. The pantry was all but empty. She stared at the bare shelves in dismay.

Returning to the bag, she now swiftly packed away the food she had brought, her mind made up. She would go and buy some more groceries. If the food was packed away when Toby came home he might not notice too much, besides which there would be nothing he could do about it. They hardly had anything to eat in the house, she had to do something. And Nell with four bairns. Her sister must be at her wits' end.

Biting her bottom lip, she snatched up the empty bag. She should have brought more with her, she would have been able to if she had come in the car. She could have piled up the back seat. But no, it would have looked bad, it was better she'd arrived by train. She was well aware her good fortune would have labelled her an upstart in some quarters, she didn't want to add fuel to the fire. It wouldn't be fair on Nell and Toby.

Leaving the house, she didn't look to right or left. She knew Mrs Ramshawe would be peering out of her window, the woman was one of life's natural busybodies, and no doubt Nell's neighbour would clock in the groceries when they were delivered but it couldn't be helped. Walking quickly, Eve made for the Spout Lane branch of the Co-op at the junction of Front Street. She could get most of what she needed there; the shop had its own butcher, grocer and hardware department, besides millinery, tailoring, crockery, and boot and shoe sections. And they would deliver a big order immediately, which is what she wanted. Besides everything else, she intended to buy a sack of potatoes and a sack of flour and she couldn't carry those herself. She would also make sure a cartload of logs for the range was delivered from Hobsons who had their yard at the far end of Front Street.

In the big sprawling shop she took her time making her purchases. There was no need to rush. Nell and the bairns wouldn't be home until twilight, so she wouldn't be going home on the train tonight which wasn't altogether unexpected. She could sleep on the settle in the kitchen for one night. She needed some time with her sister.

After paying for her order which the assistant promised would be delivered within the hour by the Co-op's trusty horse and cart, she made her way to the timber yard and arranged for the logs to be dropped off that afternoon. Then she began to walk back to Nell's. She had no inclination to dally in this heat. She refused to admit to herself it was more the possibility of running into Caleb that was sending her hurrying back to the house.

She had reached the front door and had her hand on the latch when Mrs Ramshawe appeared on her doorstep like a genie out of a bottle. Eve sighed. She might have known.

'Had a bit of a wander, have you?' Mrs Ramshawe's beady eyes went to the shopping bag holding a loaf of bread and some thinly sliced beef which Eve intended to have for her lunch. 'Had a look round the shops an' that, I suppose.'

It was useless to deny it. 'Yes, Mrs Ramshawe.'

'Aye, that's right. Nice shop, the Co-op. For them that can afford it. Must seem strange coming back, now you live in the city. Everywhere seem small, does it?'

'Not really.'

'There's another one soon to be off but then you'd know all about that, wouldn't you?'

'I'm sorry?' Eve looked more closely at Mrs Ramshawe.

'Caleb Travis. I suppose Nell's told you about him selling up, what with the three of you working for him for so long?' There was a slight emphasis on the last words. Mrs Ramshawe hadn't forgotten this one's beginnings and however high she'd risen it didn't hurt to be reminded of where she'd come from.

Eve stared at the broad flat face, utterly taken aback.

'She hasn't?' Mrs Ramshawe was delighted. It wasn't often she was the first with news. 'Oh aye, he's selling the inn and going abroad, I hear. I couldn't believe it meself when I first got to know. I mean, his da was born an' bred in these parts an' his granda before him, an' that inn was his da's pride and joy. I'd never have thought Caleb would let it go. But there, that's another generation for you. Come too easy to him, if you want my opinion.'

Eve didn't. 'He's leaving? When?'

'Oh, I don't know that, lass. I'm not exactly in his confidence, you know.' Mrs Ramshawe laughed at her witticism but then stopped abruptly when Eve turned from her and entered Nell's house without another word. Well! Mrs Ramshawe glared after her. Didn't that just prove you couldn't make a silk purse out of a sow's ear. No manners, no manners at all. She might be dressed like a lady but that's where it ended.

In Nell's kitchen Eve sat down heavily on the settle and the long shuddering breath she sighed seemed to deflate her body. He was going to leave Washington, leave the country. There would be no chance she would ever see him again. She wouldn't know where he was or what he was doing.

But she had left here, hadn't she? she argued with herself in the next moment. She had purposely cut her losses and moved on, even going so far as to make sure there was no contact between them.

But that was different. Rising from the settle, she walked over to the window and looked out into Nell's back yard. Even though she was elsewhere, she had known he was *here*. She found she was ringing her hands and turned from the window, panic uppermost. He couldn't just disappear. She would have to get an address, know where he was, write to him.

Oh, don't be stupid. The argument went on. How could she suggest writing to him when for the last eight or nine years they'd had nothing to do with each other? He would think she was mad. Worse, he might suspect how she felt about him. But she couldn't just let him go. She moaned deep in her throat. Everyone she loved, she lost. Her mam and grandma, her da and the lads, Mary, William, Howard, and worst of all her darling boy, her Oliver. Was it her? Did she have some sort of curse on her that reached out and touched those she cared about?

A storm of weeping followed and she had only just dried her eyes and washed her face in cold water when the horse and cart from the Co-op clip-clopped to a standstill in the back lane. She had asked them to deliver by the back way, thinking it would attract less attention, but she didn't doubt Mrs Ramshawe, for one, would monitor everything that went into the house.

She tipped the man sixpence for carrying the sack of flour and sack of potatoes into a corner of the kitchen, and when he had gone she put everything away. Then she made herself a pot of tea. She opened the blue bag of sugar the delivery man had brought and had two strong cups of tea one after the other, with plenty of sugar in each cup. Since living in Newcastle she had found she liked her tea sweet, it always seemed to give her something of a lift. And she needed a lift right now.

After making herself a sandwich with the beef and a couple of shives of bread from the loaf she had bought, she had one last cup of tea. The sandwich stuck in her throat and she had to force it down but she knew she needed something in her stomach. It was now gone two in the afternoon and she'd last eaten at eight o'clock that morning before leaving Newcastle. She couldn't afford to feel faint. Not in view of what she was going to do.

Could she carry it off? She sat at Nell's kitchen table, the butterflies in her stomach dancing. Could she manoeuvre things so the last umpteen years were put to one side and it would seem natural to suggest they correspond once he left England's shores? She didn't know, she only knew she had to try or she would regret it for the rest of her life.

She walked over to the spotted brown mirror and peered at her reflection, tidying her hair. She was glad she hadn't been tempted to have her hair cut in one of these new bobs where it was shingled into a permanent wave. At least she still looked like the same old Eve, almost. But she wasn't the same girl who had left Washington all those years ago. She had been married. She had borne two precious children and suffered the worst loss of her life. Perhaps Caleb had changed too. Perhaps she wouldn't feel the same when she saw him.

She shook her head at herself. That was ludicrous. But was she doing the right thing in attempting to maintain contact in the future? Would it cause more pain than anything else? What about when the inevitable happened and he met someone? Fell in love, married?

Enough. She turned away from the pain-filled eyes in the mirror. Right or wrong, she couldn't let go completely. It was as simple as that.

Chapter 26

Caleb stood polishing a glass at the bar. He was quietly whistling to himself. The estate agent had been right, the old goat. All along the man had said not to lose heart when potential buyers had been thin on the ground due to 'the present economic climate', as he'd put it. You only need one, he had said. Be patient. And now that one had come along and he hadn't had to drop the asking price much either. He'd be leaving this country with money in his pocket and the day couldn't come soon enough. He'd had a bellyful of England.

He put the glass down and picked up another. He had been sickened by what he'd seen over the last few months, the bully-boy tactics Churchill and his crew had employed to grind good honest working men into the ground. All the misery and suffering and hatred, and what would come of it? Nowt. Families were eating food that should have gone to pigs and making blankets out of old newspapers, and the heartbreaking thing was, every jack man knew that sooner or later they'd be forced to knuckle under and go cap in hand to the mine owners. For himself, he wanted no part of a country ruled by a government where working men and women were given less consideration than the mine owners' horses and dogs.

Shaking himself mentally, he put down the glass and signalled to one of his two barmaids he was going out the back. He had had a late breakfast that morning and hadn't wanted a bite at lunchtime, but now his stomach was after thinking his throat had been cut. In the corner were a couple of old boys his father had been friendly with, both ex-miners, and they had been nursing a half pint of bitter for the last hour, two mangy fox terriers asleep across their feet under the table. Quietly, Caleb pulled two foaming pints of beer and told the barmaid to take them across. 'Compliments of the house,' he murmured, and then went out the back quickly so they didn't have to thank him.

Ada was in the kitchen. Winnie had been in bed all day with some-thing Ada had described briefly that morning as 'women's monthly trouble'.

He had just sat down at the table and was about to begin eating a bowl of Ada's thick mutton broth, which was second to none, when they heard a knock from beyond the scullery at the back door of the inn. Ada looked at him. 'You expecting a delivery?' she asked as she went to answer it.

'No.' He started on the broth. He heard Ada's voice high and surprised and his eyes narrowed, then she came bustling through. He opened his mouth to ask what was what but the words were never voiced. He looked at the tall, slim woman behind Ada, and said weakly, 'Eve.' He could scarcely believe his eyes.

'Hello, Caleb.'

He got to his feet, the blood rushing into his face. If Mr Baldwin himself had suddenly materialised, he couldn't have been more amazed. 'What-what are you doing here?'

Quietly, she said, 'I've come to see Nell but she's not in. Her nextdoor neighbour said Toby's gone on a march and Nell and the bairns are picking tatties somewhere or other.'

'Aye, they have to take any work they can get, along with scratting for rags to make clippy mats to sell or following the carthorses for the manure.' Talk natural, don't let her see how she's affected you, not with her standing there as cool as a cucumber. 'The bairns' schooling comes second these days.'

She nodded. 'I don't know where it will all end.'

'Oh, I know where it will end. With the rich getting richer and the poor getting poorer, same as always.'

They stared at each other for a moment and it was Ada who broke what had become a tense pause by saying, 'Sit yourself down, lass. I've just made a pot of tea for Caleb if you'd like a cup? It's a hot day for travelling, I'll be bound.'

'Thank you, Ada. I'd love a cup.'

By, she was one of the gentry now. He dare bet her clothes, plain as they were, had cost a pretty penny. Their colour reminded him of her loss and his voice was softer when he said, 'I was sorry to hear about your husband and son. We all were.'

Again she said, 'Thank you.'

His stomach was turning over, he couldn't eat the soup. Pushing it to one side, he said, 'It's been a long time, Eve.'

'Yes, it has. Some six or seven years I think.'

Had she always been this cool and composed? Probably. Of the three sisters, Eve had been the quiet one.

'I hope you don't mind me coming, Caleb, but I find myself in something of a difficult position. I didn't expect to find Nell out, I should have checked beforehand, I suppose, but I wanted to surprise her. As it is we'll have no time together if I leave this evening as I'd planned to do. And I couldn't impose on them for the night, you know how they're placed. I wondered if one of the guest rooms here is free. I would pay the going rate, of course.'

Whenever he had imagined seeing her again, and he had imagined it, he admitted to himself, nights without number, he had seen himself taking the initiative. He'd strike just the right note, he'd be courteous but let her see she meant as little to him as he did to her. Now his guts were writhing and he had an anger welling up within that was so strong it frightened him.

He took a sip of the tea Ada had placed before him before he could trust himself to say coolly, 'Of course you can stay, and as my guest. I wouldn't dream of taking payment from an old friend.' He glanced at her handbag. 'You have no luggage?'

'No, I didn't expect I would be staying the night, as I said.'

And no doubt she would have come and gone without him knowing but for Nell being out. Damn it all, what had he ever done that she should treat him this way? He didn't understand it. He didn't understand *her*. He had no false modesty about his attraction where the opposite sex were concerned. He didn't class himself as handsome, he never had, but going away to war had opened his eyes to the fact that he had something women liked. He didn't know what it was but nevertheless it enabled him to have feminine company when he wanted it, and without paying for it either. But he could have been fashioned from a lump of wood as far as Eve was concerned. And even the friendship he'd thought they'd had and which he had prized so highly, looking back, had proved to mean little to her.

'Your old room is unoccupied.' He didn't add that he hadn't let that room since she had left because he was, in truth, ashamed of the sentiment behind it. 'Would you like me to show you up now so you can rest while you wait for Nell to come back?'

'Drink your tea first.' For a moment a glimmer of the old caring Eve was there.

'It's all right.' He stood up and she rose with him. 'I think there might even be a couple of your old books still in the room. Would you like Ada to bring you a tray in a minute?'

'No, no, I've recently eaten.'

He opened the door of the kitchen and let her precede him into the passageway which led to the stairs to the upper floors. As she passed him, he became aware of the scent of her, a composite of fresh, newly laundered clothes, and clean skin and hair. There was something else too, a faint smell of roses or something similar. Whatever, he felt himself harden and his voice was gruff when he said, 'I wasn't thinking, the bed won't be made up but it won't take a minute for me to do.'

'Oh no, I'll do it. I've made quite a few beds in my time.'

'But not in latter years.'

They had reached the landing and as she paused to let him lead the way, she said quietly, 'No, not in latter years.'

When they reached the room he did not open the door immediately. Instead he turned and looked at her. 'How are you, Eve? The last year must have been very hard for you.'

For the first time since she had walked into the inn, she appeared slightly discomfited. Stammering a little, she said, 'I-I am better than I was at-at first.'

He nodded. 'Is it still too painful to talk about?'

There was a faint touch of colour in her cheeks and her green eyes seemed to dominate her face. He wondered how there had ever been a time when he had not noticed her unusual beauty. But that was it, it was unusual. You had to look for it, it was not obvious and brash as Mary's had been.

She lowered her lashes. 'No, not really. Alexander, my younger son, has helped in that regard. He talks about his brother often, they were very close.'

There was an ethereal quality to her these days that hadn't been there before. Perhaps grief had done that. He had the mad impulse to take her in his arms. Not for any other reason but to comfort her. But she wouldn't want his comfort. She was a self-contained and mature woman, not the young lass he had once known. And a wealthy woman to boot. Clearing his throat, he opened the door to the room. 'He's at home? Your son?'

'Yes, Alexander is at home.'

She did not elaborate. Perhaps she did not consider it any of his business. He walked across to the window and flung it open – the room smelt stuffy. When he turned, she was still standing in the doorway looking about her, and something in her face made him say self-consciously, 'Not much changes here, as you can see.'

He saw her swallow. Then she said, 'That's not quite true, from what I hear. You're selling the inn, I understand.'

'Yes, I am. Who told you? Nell?'

'No, it was Mrs Ramshawe.' She gave a small smile. 'She took great pleasure in telling me something I didn't know.'

'Aye, I can imagine. There's more than one like that round here. We don't need no telegram service in Washington.'

She looked down at her joined hands. 'Where are you thinking of moving to? Anywhere near here?'

'Abroad.' She said nothing, merely raising her eyes to his face, so in spite of himself he felt compelled to say, 'I was thinking of Australia at one stage, there's lots of opportunities out there, but on further investigation' – he liked that, further investigation, it made it sound as if he knew what he was on about, which in truth he didn't feel he did – 'I favour New Zealand.'

She inclined her head. 'What will you do out there?'

'What I know. Open an inn. Leastways, that's the plan.'

He expected her to say something more but when she merely stared at him, he raked his hair back from his forehead as he always did when at a loss. 'I'll leave you to it if you're sure you don't want me to make the bed.'

'No, no, I'll do it. Of course I'll do it.'

'Will you be wanting a meal tonight?'

'I-I don't know. No, perhaps not. I shall go and see Nell later. She should be home once it starts to get dark. I'll probably eat with her. In fact I might go soon and get something ready for them for when they come in.'

He stared at her. Bluntly, he said, 'Is there anything to get a meal with?'

'Aye, yes, I've taken care of that. I . . . I got some things delivered earlier today from the Co-op.'

He nodded. 'Right.' Lady Bountiful. How would Toby take that? And then with a feeling of shame he said to the bristly wounded part of himself, Nell's her sister, of course she would help out. 'Well, I'll leave you to it then.' He walked across the room and she stood aside for him to leave.

On the landing, Caleb screwed up his eyes and breathed out hard through his nose. Dear gussy, what was he going to do now? Why did she have to come back? He felt like beating his hands against the wall or screaming, anything to express the raging feeling inside him. He had been settled, he had known what he was going to do and how he was going to go about it, and then she had to turn up like this. *Damn it!*

He strode along the landing. And the way she'd strolled in, as bold as brass. Anyone would think the last eight years hadn't happened. What did she think he was? Something to be picked up and dropped whenever she felt like it?

The feeling inside him had to have some expression and as he reached the top of the stairs he kicked out at the wall with his good leg, nearly breaking his toes in the process. The pain provided a focus and after a moment or two when he was in danger of throwing up, he made his way downstairs to the kitchen. Ada turned from the range. 'I've just made a fresh pot of tea. That other was stone cold.'

He nodded and sat down at the table. 'Thanks.'

'That was a turn-up for the book, her arriving out the blue.'

Without looking at Ada, he said, 'It's perfectly natural. She used to work here and we have guest rooms.'

'Aye, mebbe, but without so much as a by your leave? I'd have thought she'd have let you know.'

'You heard what she said. She didn't expect she'd be staying the night.'

'All seems a bit cheeky to me but then, what do I know?'

'Leave it, Ada. All right? Just leave it.'

'Well, we don't hear anything for years and then she swans in like—'

'*I said, leave it.*'

Caleb jumped to his feet, his face as black as thunder, and disappeared into the scullery. A second later Ada heard the back door bang.

She stood for a minute gazing after him. Then her eyes moved upwards as though she could see through the ceiling to the rooms above. 'Well,' she breathed out softly. 'So that's the way of it. Who would have guessed?'

Chapter 27

Eve had purposely not bought any sacks of coal. She had imagined that might serve as a red rag to a bull as far as Toby was concerned. She knew how the miners regarded blacklegs, whether or not they were drafted in from other counties, and it would be blacklegs who had mined the coal, in Toby's opinion. But the logs from the stack now piled outside were blazing and a pot of thick beef stew was simmering in the range oven when Nell walked in as it was getting dark.

Nell stood in the doorway, the children clustered wide-eyed behind her. She looked at the warm kitchen, the table set for dinner and smelt the stew. Her eyes fastened on Eve who was smiling uncertainly. Then she burst into tears.

For a minute or two all was consternation and bustle. The children weren't used to seeing their mother break down. She was the corner-stone of the family. But eventually Nell was laughing and smiling and they all sat down to a hearty meal. Once they'd finished, the children licking their plates clean, Nell sent her offspring up to bed. Betsy was asleep on her feet as it was. The two sisters sat at the table drinking their third cup of tea and talking quietly.

'I can't believe what you've bought.' Nell reached out her hand and grasped Eve's tightly. 'I tell you, lass, today was my worst day yet. It was such hard work in the fields, not for myself but the bairns I mean. They're all pale and washed-out looking but they worked the whole time with not one word of complaint. Our Robert's got a mouthful of ulcers and the lassies' impetigo just won't clear up.' She stopped, shaking her head. 'I looked at the four of them and, well, I despaired, I suppose. And then on the way back the lads took it in turns to carry Betsy on their backs. No one asked 'em to, they just did it, and that more than anything . . .'

'Oh, Nell, don't cry.'

'I told meself I couldn't go on. We had no food in the house and nothing to light a fire with. The vegetables we got from Farmer Brown I thought we'd have to eat raw. And then I come in and you were here.'

'Please let me give you more money, Nell. Please.'

'No, lass. You know what Toby's like. What he'll say when he sees what you've bought, I don't know, but,' Nell sniffed and straightened her back, 'I'm glad you did, lass. We were desperate and I'm not too proud to say it.'

'Oh, Nell. What's mine is yours. What's the good of me having money if I can't help you when you need it most? I'm going to say that to him when he comes. Would you mind if I did? He must let me help more, it's the least I can do.'

'You say it, lass. If you can persuade him to accept help, I'll dance a jig. It's funny 'cos me and Toby are all right, I mean we are, really, but he don't see it like I do. To me the bairns are more important than anything, but his pride . . . But then all the men are the same. Well, most of them.'

'But this isn't like charity or accepting help from virtual strangers. We're flesh and blood, family.'

'I don't know what we would have done without what you send for the bairns, Eve. It's helped me pay a bit off the back of the rent now and again, enough to stop us being put out. The Lees were evicted a month ago, living rough by the old quarry, they are, but they won't be able to keep that up with the cold weather coming. It'll be the workhouse. The Crofts went in last week and her with a newborn baby. Pitiful, it was.'

Eve let her sister talk, sensing Nell needed to spill out her fears and worries. Nell was so strong for the children and for Toby too, but she couldn't constantly keep everything bottled in. Nell talked for nearly half an hour but at the end of it she looked brighter. It was then she said, 'Toby can sleep on the settle tonight, lass. You can bed down with me.'

'It's all right.' Eve took a deep breath. She had a good idea what Nell was going to say next. 'I'm staying at the inn.'

Nell's face straightened. 'No, lass. Oh no. Have some sense. Don't start that, seeing him.'

'It's all right,' she said again. 'It was my decision. Mrs Ramshawe told me about Caleb selling up and, well, to be truthful, I had to see him, Nell. I know you think I'm daft but I can't help it.'

'I do think you're daft,' Nell said flatly. 'The man's poison where you're concerned. Rat poison, in my opinion.'

'That's a bit strong, lass.'

'Look here, Eve—'

Whatever Nell had been about to say was cut short by the sound of a knock at the back door. It was thrust open to reveal Toby being supported by two other miners. He had dried blood over his face and one eye was closed, the flesh so distorted on that side of his face it was like a football. But it was the state of his right leg that brought Nell to her feet, moaning, 'Toby, Toby.' His trousers were in shreds below the knee and the bone of his leg was sticking through his flesh.

The miners carried him to the settle, one saying, 'It was the law, lass. Great big so-an'-sos on horseback. They were waiting for us an' we never stood a chance. Peaceful march, it was, but they weren't having it.' Toby said nothing. He had passed out.

Once they had laid Toby gently on the settle, the two men straightened. They were both bloody, one had a gaping flap of skin hanging down from his cheekbone. Nell knelt at Toby's side, her face awash with tears.

'They went berserk, Nell. Some of the lads had brought their wives along, but men or women, they didn't care. Leathering into us with their truncheons and the horses trampling folk down. Lonnie's been arrested and a couple of the other lads.'

'He would never let me go on the marches,' Nell whispered. 'He said they were no place for women.'

'He was right an' all. That's been proved the day.'

'How did you get back?' She raised her head. 'You didn't carry him all the way from Boldon?'

Both men nodded. 'Aye, lass, what else?' the first one said. 'Look, that leg's bad, you'll need a doctor.'

Eve had been standing with her hands pressed over her mouth. Now she roused herself to say, 'I'll see to it. Can–can I get you a drink?'

'Aye, lass. Mine's a double whisky,' said the man who was doing all the talking with grim humour. 'Look, we need to be away, Nell. Me brothers were on that march and we all lost sight of each other with what was going on. I want to check they're back and everything's all right.'

'Aye, aye, you go, Joe. An' thanks. Thanks, Ronald. I'm grateful. You're good pals to Toby.'

'It's nowt, lass. Toby'd do the same for us.'

When the door closed on the two men, Eve knelt down by her sister. 'I'll get a doctor. Do you want me to help you first? Shall I get some hot water and disinfectant?'

Nell's face was chalk white. 'He's unconscious, Eve. What if that blow to his head has done for him?'

'He's fainted with the pain. Do you hear me, Nell? He's going to be all right but I need to go for the doctor. Look, I'm going to wake Matthew.' At eleven Matthew was a chip off his father's block and very protective of his mother. 'He'll come and sit with you until I get back.'

Nell made no answer but when Eve came downstairs with a sleepy

Matthew, Toby's eyes were open and Nell seemed to have pulled herself together. 'Hello, Eve,' Toby said weakly. 'Bit of a to-do, this.'

'I'm going for the doctor, Toby. You need to get your leg seen to. I won't be long but just lie still.'

'No, no doctor. I don't want no doctor, I'll be all right.'

Eve stared into the grey face of her brother-in-law. 'If you don't have a doctor you're likely to lose your leg,' she said steadily. 'Do you understand me? If you do nothing else for your family for the rest of your life, Toby Grant, do this for them now. Let me help you. I have more money than I will ever need and apart from my son, Nell is my only flesh and blood. Who knows but that I was meant to marry Howard for just this moment? Please don't shut me out.'

He closed his eyes. 'You're a good woman.'

'Howard used to say I was too bossy.'

When he opened his eyes she was smiling at him. 'Aye, well that aside . . .'

'I won't be long.' She pulled on her hat and coat and hugged Nell who was crying again. 'I'll be as quick as I can.'

'There's a new doctor, Eve.' Nell followed her into the hall. 'The old one retired a few years back. This one's Dr Hogarth and he lives two doors up from the police station.'

Eve flew down Spout Lane but as she reached the square, she hesitated and then detoured into the inn yard. In the kitchen, she said to a surprised Ada, 'Would you go and fetch Caleb for me? Tell him it's urgent. It would cause less interest if you go in, Ada.'

Caleb was back with Ada in seconds and she swiftly put them in the picture, adding, 'Would you go to Nell's, Caleb? Toby's leg's bad and I think it would be good for another man to be there. I don't know what the doctor will want to do.'

They left the inn yard together, Eve to fetch the doctor and Caleb running in the direction of Nell's house.

Thankfully Dr Hogarth was at home. His wife showed her into a small room off the hall which was furnished as a waiting room, but she didn't have to wait more than a few moments. He proved to be a young man with the broad physique of a labourer rather than a professional man. She quickly acquainted him with the facts and even as she talked he was reaching for his black bag to which he added a few bits and pieces. He left the house with her, and as they walked she said breathlessly, 'Please do whatever is necessary, doctor, regardless of expense. I shall meet the bill immediately you present it.'

'And you are?'

'Nell's – Mrs Grant's sister. My name's Eve Ingram.'

'Right. And Mr Grant got knocked down by a runaway horse.'

For a moment Eve didn't understand. 'No, doctor, I told you. They were on a march and—'

'I have to report any injuries as a result of conflict with the law during this strike, Mrs Ingram. A runaway horse is a different matter. Accidents with horses happen all the time.'

She was trotting to keep up with his long legs but flashed him a grateful smile. 'It was a horse that did the damage, doctor.'

'I thought so. They can be lethal when they run wild.'

It proved to be a long night. When Dr Hogarth had examined Toby, he pronounced he was not at all happy with the nature of the break and the injury to surrounding tissue. He had a colleague with a private practice on the outskirts of Gateshead who was the man for this job. He would telephone him and inform him he was bringing Mr Grant to see him tonight if Mr Travis could assist him.

Mr Travis could.

Within a short while Nell had cleaned Toby up as best she could after Dr Hogarth had given him a strong painkiller and fixed the leg in a splint for the journey. The doctor would not allow him any food or drink because he was almost certain the patient would need an anaesthetic. If it was possible, Toby went even greyer at this point. Once the doctor had brought his car to the front door, he and Caleb carried Toby out of the house. Eve and Nell stood on the doorstep with Matthew and watched the car disappear from view.

'Oh, Eve, lass, this is going to cost a packet.' Nell was wringing her hands as Eve closed the door and led her sister into the kitchen. 'I'll pay you back somehow.'

'Don't even think about that, I can afford it, Nell.' She didn't add that since being back in Washington she had almost felt ashamed of her wealth when she saw how Nell was placed.

Once Matthew had gone back to bed, the two women sat in front of the fire talking quietly and dozing a little. At one point just before dawn, Eve got up and made a pot of tea. As they drank their first cup, she said, 'You know, lass, it's occurred to me that this might be a blessing in disguise.'

'It's a darn good disguise then.'

'Hear me out. Reading between the lines of what Dr Hogarth said, I can't see Toby being able to go back to crawling along tunnels on his belly even if his leg does heal well.'

'And you call that a blessing, lass? I wouldn't want to be involved in what you'd term a disaster.'

'But perhaps it's time for him to do something different. For you both to do something different. What I mean is, I've been thinking for a while now that I can't stand Newcastle much longer, and this lock-out and the way Howard's friends, our social circle, reacted, showed me I'll never fit in there. I don't think I've ever really wanted to but I made the effort for Howard and the boys. I knew Howard wanted Oliver and Alexander to follow him into the business and move in his circles, but it's different now. I've sold the business, it's gone.'

Nell peered at her sister, her mind momentarily diverted from Toby. 'What are you saying exactly?'

'Exactly?' Eve grimaced. 'I don't know. But I do know I want to be with folk like Mr Hutton and Tilly and you and Toby, and not the likes of Annabelle Sheldon and Verity Alridge. I suppose in the back of my mind I've been thinking of buying a big place that can be converted into a school as well as a home, for bairns like Tilly and maybe those who have lost their da in the war and their mam's unable to look after them. Or orphans. There's plenty of those about. But I'd want a place where there's ground to build workshops and things, so I could employ people to teach the bairns a trade if they're so inclined. Academic opportunities in the school but for those who are good with their hands more practical instruction once they're old enough to leave the school. And they could make things to sell while they're learning so the place could be productive financially. And we could grow all our own vegetables, keep our own hens and pigs and cows. Even set up a market garden and sell produce. The place would be run on the same principle as the Co-op, everyone a part of it together, but it would be a big family.'

She stopped for breath. She hadn't realised all this had been bubbling inside her for months.

'Blimey, lass,' said Nell. 'You don't do things by half.'

'It could work. I know it could work.'

'It'd cost a fortune.'

'I've got it, Nell. I'm what I suppose you could call a financially independent woman of considerable means.'

Nell smiled as she was meant to. 'And you see me and Toby fitting into this set-up?'

'I don't suppose I had before tonight,' Eve said honestly. 'But this accident, well, it makes you think.'

'Aye, you're right there. It does.'

They stared at each other. 'It would need some cottages separate from the school for workers who had families like you and Toby, and me and Alexander, but there'd be other staff who would live in the home itself all the time.'

'So it would be like a little community?'

'Aye, I suppose so, but one which prepared the children for the outside world. Think of it, Nell. Bairns who had nothing and nowhere to go being loved and cared for. Oh, I know it would only be a drop in the ocean when you think about Newcastle and Gateshead's dockside tenements and the workhouses and the brothels.'

'Not for the bairns who would come under its protection, it wouldn't,' said Nell softly. 'For them it would be home.'

Somehow Nell's words panicked her. 'It would be an enormous undertaking.' Could she do it by herself? If she had been contemplating something like this with Howard at her side, it would have been different. Could she, a woman on her own, take on the responsibility for so many lives, bairns and adults alike? She had Alexander to consider, after all. But what use was her money in the bank? It just gathered interest and made more money, it didn't *do* anything. There were so many Tillys, so many bairns like she and Nell and Mary had once been. Desperate, afraid. 'I'd have to look into it properly but it's something to think about.'

It was just after seven o'clock when Caleb tapped at the back door and walked in. Eve had finally persuaded Nell to go and lie down a little while ago, and the children were still asleep, worn out by their work in the fields the day before. It was a beautiful autumn morning, mellow and warm, and Eve felt more tired than she could ever remember feeling.

It was the first thing Caleb said. 'You look tired.'

'I am. How is Toby?' She had just made yet another pot of tea to try and keep herself awake and, without asking, she poured Caleb a cup.

'Asleep.' He ran his hand round his face. His chin was bristly and his hair tousled. 'It was a long old business. Dr Hogarth assisted this friend of his and all I could do was wait. It wasn't just one break, apparently. Coming back, Dr Hogarth said anyone other than his friend would have amputated. The knee was damaged and,' he took the cup from her, 'it was a mess. But this friend is a marvel, apparently. Recently qualified and as keen as mustard. Rich father, which helps. You ought to have seen his place.' He took a long sip of the tea, scalding hot as it was. 'He said Toby will always have a stiff leg but at least he will have his leg.'

Eve stared at him. She wondered why it was that a woman looked tired and that was all she looked, whereas on a man it made him doubly attractive. On Caleb, at least. Trying to concentrate her wandering mind, she said, 'Where is he? Toby?'

'Still there. This bloke wants to keep an eye on him for a day or two. I think it's some kind of hospital, private like, for the toffs but,' he shrugged, 'Dr Hogarth said this bloke thinks he's an interesting case. Because of how bad it was. Gave him a chance to try out a couple of things.'

'But Toby will be all right?' she asked with faint alarm.

'Aye. Aye.'

'What is it? What are you looking like that for?'

'He won't be able to go down the pit again, Eve. I don't know how he'll take that when he knows.'

Perhaps it was because she was so exhausted that in her relief she didn't think about what she was saying. 'Is that all? Oh, I think we can get round that. Nell and I have been talking and I want to—'

Her voice was cut off abruptly as Caleb got to his feet so suddenly his chair skidded on the flagged floor. 'Is that all? *All?* Have you considered that he might not want to be beholden to you for the rest of his life? You come here in your fine clothes flinging your money about like Lady Muck.' He drew in a deep, ragged breath. 'Oh, to hell with it. Tell Nell I'll be along this afternoon about three. She can go and visit Toby then.'

Eve had gone white. 'Caleb, I didn't mean – Nell and I had been talking, that's all, and I was trying to reassure her that if the worst came to the worst I'd got a plan in mind.' That sounded worse. 'Something that would still give Toby his dignity,' she said desperately. 'I wouldn't be giving them money. It's not like that, really.'

'It's none of my business, Eve.' His eyes were black and hard. 'I'll be along later.'

He saw a quiver pass over her face as he turned away but he did not hesitate, continuing out of the door which he shut quietly behind him. Out in the back lane he walked a few yards before stopping. It was very quiet, there were no bairns playing out yet. He stood staring at the dusty rutted ground beneath his boots and then lifted his eyes up to the blue sky. There was a faint smell from the privies at the end of the terraced yards but the sky was high and wide and clean looking. A bird was drifting on the air currents far above him, circling lazily and then gliding on, free and untroubled.

What had he had to say that for? He remembered the look on her face and groaned. Of course she would want to help Nell, that was her nature, it was nothing to do with how much money she had. She had been the same when she'd had nothing. And it was time to face something. Knowing Eve as he did, she would have married her husband for love. And that was what stuck in his craw. If she had married him for money he would have found that easier to come to terms with. So what did that make him?

He began to walk. He didn't like what it made him. He knew he had faults but he had never considered himself a small-minded man before this moment. Stubborn, aye, and arrogant on occasion, but never petty or small. And there was another thing. Loving her as he did, he ought to be able to say her wealth didn't matter. Wasn't love supposed to surmount all obstacles if it was true? Of course if the boot had been on the other foot as it always had been until she'd left Washington, if he had been the wealthier one, that would have been all right. That was how it was supposed to be. No one looked down on a woman for marrying a rich man.

Was he worried what people would think? Again the answer wasn't to his liking and he clenched his teeth, his jaw rigid.

Anyway, it was all irrelevant. She had never by word or action indicated any interest in him in that way so why should she be inclined to do so now? Even if he did pluck up the courage to say how he felt. Likely she'd look at him with those great green eyes of hers and gently – because she would be gentle, she wasn't cruel, not Eve – inform him he hadn't a hope in hell. Well, he knew that, didn't he? Aye, he did. She had her life, a life with her son and her rich friends and a position in society, and he couldn't match that. He might one day, he might make his fortune in New Zealand and end up a rich man, but it would be too late to make any difference to Eve.

At the end of the back way he stood for a moment before stepping into Spout Lane. He wasn't going to think about this anymore, thinking never did anyone any good. She would probably have left to return home to her boy by the time he went back that afternoon. And that was fine, just dandy. If by any chance she came to the inn to rest in her room beforehand he would be polite. No more outbursts. He would keep it civil. Perhaps even apologise for his tetchiness. Not that he thought she would come after how he had behaved.

She didn't. Until he left in the horse and cart for Nell's at three o'clock that afternoon, Caleb was on tenterhooks. Every time the door to the inn opened, his eyes sprung to it, and each time one of the barmaids brought food through from the kitchen, he tensed in case it was her. But no tall, slim woman with hair the colour of warm chocolate and green eyes came to hear the apology he had been mentally practising.

The afternoon carried a thick mugginess that spoke of a storm brewing, you could feel the pressure behind your eyeballs. As the horse ambled down Spout Lane, Caleb knew that if she had already gone back to Newcastle he would have to go and see her before he left the country. He didn't want their last meeting to be one of discord. And he couldn't forget the look in her eyes.

There were a number of children playing in the field opposite the houses in Spout Lane, and as he drew up outside Nell's, Betsy detached herself from the others and ran into the house calling, 'Mam, Mam, Mr Travis is here.'

Caleb sat on the long wooden seat of the cart waiting. He felt extremely irritable and weary and at odds with himself. This changed the moment Nell stepped out of the door with Eve at her side. She hadn't gone. His heart gave a bound.

'Eve thought she would come with me and see Toby for a minute or two and then take a cab from Gateshead, if that's all right,' Nell called. 'She's more than halfway home from there.'

'No need, I'll take you home,' he said gruffly, his eyes meeting Eve's. She nodded her thanks but did not smile.

'This is so good of you, Caleb.' Nell climbed on to the seat beside him and Eve sat next to her sister. 'And last night an' all. I appreciate it an' I know Toby will be grateful. Eve went to see Dr Hogarth earlier and settled up with him.'

'Good.'

'He was ever so kind, wasn't he? Mind, I don't know what his friend will charge.' For a moment Nell's chatter ceased. 'Dr Hogarth said to Eve his friend's a surgeon but he's an inn-innov—'

'Innovator,' put in Eve quietly.

'Aye, that's it, an innovator an' all. That means he's all for new methods and ideas. Not like some, Dr Hogarth said. His friend is a great one for keeping everything clean. Sprays carbolic acid all over the place and he uses some drug or other, what's it called, Eve? I'm no good on names of things.'

'Pyocyanase. It's an antibiosis, I think that's right. It fights infection.'

'Aye, well, his friend uses this on all his patients. He's written in medical journals and everything. Apparently down south, in London and them places, there's lots of work going on but Dr Hogarth said his friend is one of the first up here to set up the way he has. We . . . we were lucky.'

From the corner of his eye Caleb saw Eve reach across and squeeze her sister's hand. 'He'll be fine. Stop whittling.'

'I can't help it, I shall feel better when I see him.'

Nell continued to talk non-stop all the way to Gateshead. It was with a great sense of relief that Caleb saw the tall spires of the great residence where Dr Hogarth had driven them the night before, near the outskirts of the town. The road followed a high stone wall for some three hundred yards before reaching two massive wrought-iron gates which were open. Caleb drove the horse and cart on to a long drive bordered by well-tended grounds and after a minute or two the house appeared in front of them.

He pulled up at the bottom of a series of wide circular steps which led to the studded front door. He got down from the cart and helped Eve and then Nell to descend. 'You go and see him, I'll wait with the horse. She gets skittish anywhere new.' This wasn't true but he was feeling distinctly uncomfortable. It had been different the night before, he had been with Dr Hogarth and it had been dark. Even then he had been overawed. Now, in the bright light of day, he could see just how grand a place this was. There were two motor cars parked to one side of the drive and his horse and cart couldn't begin to compete. It wasn't even as if he was driving a carriage and pair.

He climbed back into his seat and sat staring stolidly ahead. He hadn't missed the air of assurance with which Eve had led her sister into the building. She'd be used to grand houses and hobnobbing with the gentry. She'd know all the right knives and forks and which glass to use. A few weeks back he had gone into a top hotel in Gateshead after visiting the solicitor who was dealing with the sale of the inn. He'd wanted to celebrate that he'd finally got a sale. He had sat there in the fancy dining room and looked at the row of cutlery in front of him and the four different glasses – four, mind – and wanted the ground to open up and swallow him. And the waiter had been a snotty so-an'-so. He'd been polite enough but his tone had suggested Caleb had strayed into the wrong place. Just to show him, he had had the full dinner, a bottle of wine and two brandies after. He hadn't felt so bad when he'd left, even if he did walk over to the only horse and cart tied up in the courtyard. He grinned to himself. Having done it once he had told himself it wouldn't be so bad the next time. Not that there would be a next time.

His stomach was in knots by the time Eve came through the front door twenty minutes later. He jumped down from the cart and helped her up into the seat, his nose drinking in the scented smell of her which was faintly mixed with carbolic now. 'How is he this afternoon? Feeling a bit better?'

She looked at him. 'He – he didn't seem like Toby. He was in bed and so tired. They said it was the effect of the anaesthetic. Do you think it was?'

'I'm sure it was.' Even to himself his voice sounded over-hearty. More quietly, he said, 'He'll be all right, Eve. Don't worry about them, you've done all you can. I don't know where they'd have been without you.'

'Caleb—'

'I'm sorry about this morning.' He said it quickly, before he lost his nerve. 'I spoke out of turn, lass, and I should have known better. Me and my big mouth. And it wasn't even true, that's the thing. You're not like that, not a bit of it.'

She said nothing. When he glanced at her he saw her eyes were shut but two great tears were sliding down her cheeks.

'Oh, Eve.' Remorse flooded through him. 'Eve, don't cry, lass. I'm sorry, I am. I've got a mouth the size of Glebe pit.'

She made a little ineffectual movement with her hand.

'Please, lass, don't cry. I'm a brute, I know it, but I lash out when' – he had been about to say when I'm hurting but changed it to – 'when I'm tired. That's no excuse, of course, but I'm far from perfect as you well know.' He passed her his handkerchief, thanking his lucky stars he had put a freshly laundered one in his pocket earlier.

She mopped her eyes, sniffed, then said, 'I'm tired too and I always get weepy when I'm tired.'

'It's nice of you to let me off the hook, I don't deserve it.'

'No, you don't.' She looked at him and gave a small smile.

It made him feel like a worm. He cleared his throat. 'You're the last person I want to upset.'

She lowered her eyes and passed the handkerchief back to him. He

327

stared at her for a moment and then said quietly, 'What's happening with Nell? I presume she's staying with Toby for a while.'

'Oh, yes, yes, I was supposed to tell you. They've said she can stay as long as she wants. They're so nice.'

Aye, that was as maybe but no doubt Eve would be paying for their 'niceness'. He did not voice this, however, but said, 'That's good. Did she say what time she wants me back?'

'Not really. Any time. Toby's mam is at Nell's looking after Betsy and when Lucy and the lads get home from school she'll give them their tea and stay on till Nell's back.' Eve hesitated. 'You don't have to take me home, Caleb. If you take me into town I'll get a taxi cab. I don't mind.'

'Don't be daft.' He clicked at the horse and she obediently ambled in a semi-circle and off down the drive. It wasn't until they were back on the road that he glanced at her again. 'You know what day this is, don't you?'

Her brow wrinkled. 'It's Wednesday.'

'Aye. What else?'

'I'm sorry, I don't follow you.'

'This very day seventeen years ago I went to the hirings at the Michaelmas Fair.' Her astonishment caused him to smile.

Then the smile was wiped away when she said in a low voice, 'You must have regretted that day many times.'

'Regretted it? Of course I haven't regretted it.' And then, when she said nothing but kept her eyes on her hands which were knotted tightly on her lap, he said, 'What made you say that, Eve?' She shook her head in a dismissive way. 'Eve, I need to know. Why would you think that?'

'I don't want to rake up old wounds.'

'You won't.'

'It's just that I know how much Mary must have hurt you. You were so kind to her, right to the end.'

After a short silence during which only the sound of the horse's hooves on the dusty road and the twitter of birds in the trees lining the avenue could be heard, he said quietly, 'She did hurt me, yes. But not to the end. I had realised long before she came back that last time that what I'd felt for her was the idealistic puppy love of youth. It bore no resemblance to the real thing. Mary herself told me I had never seen her for what she was and this was true. I was dazzled by her beauty and zest for life, I suppose. But I'm glad she came to me at the end. We became friends. It's what we should have been all along. If I had seen this from the start I might have been able to protect her from herself.'

'I don't think so. I don't think anything any of us could have done would have prevented what happened. I blamed myself right up until Oliver and Howard died, I suppose, and then a little while after they had gone I realised I was doing the same thing again. If I had gone with them that day, if I had jumped into the water after Oliver, if, if. But life can't be lived looking backwards.'

'That's very wise.'

'No, not really. It boils down to the old saying that hindsight is a wonderful thing. But all we can do is make judgements and decisions in the present and then live by them.'

'That's harder than it sounds.'

'Yes, it is. Especially when those same judgements and decisions hurt those we love.'

His voice tender, he said, 'I'm sorry you've been hurt so much, Eve. If I could bring your son back, I would.'

'Don't.'

Her voice was choked and it caused the muscles of his face to tighten. In that moment he knew if he could give his own life for the child's, he would have done so. The force of his emotion clamped his teeth together and neither of them spoke again for some miles. Then he saw her start when he said, 'It's Michaelmas Day, the fair will be at Saltwell Park. Do you fancy going for old times' sake? We can stay as long or as short as you like.'

She stared at him, her green eyes wide under her bonnet. 'But-but it will delay you and there's going to be a storm.'

'Damn the storm. Do you want to go? I'll take you home after-wards.' He found he was waiting for her answer with bated breath. When it came, the whispered 'Yes' caused him to let out a shuddering sigh. 'Good, that's what we'll do then.' He grinned at her and she smiled faintly back.

Chapter 28

The fair was in full swing when they reached the park as an early sombre twilight took hold. Caleb tied up the horse and cart in the same fishmonger's yard he had used all those years ago, but now the fishmonger's lad was a grown man with a wife and a bairn.

The raucous noise of steam organs and hurdy-gurdies was borne on the muggy air as they approached, walking side by side but without touching. They passed the brightly painted wagons of the Romany showmen first, a couple of dogs barking but without any real energy. Even they seemed sapped by the thick stillness that precedes a storm. And then they reached the shooting galleries and coconut shies and side shows: a bearded lady, performing dwarfs, the 'snake' woman with live pythons, sword swallowers, gypsy fortune tellers and a huge man built like a brick outhouse who was challenging all-comers to a boxing match.

They stood watching some screaming children on the swing boats for a moment or two, and then walked past the helter-skelter and colourful merry-go-round to the stall selling roasted chestnuts. Caleb bought Eve a bag and a couple of toasted muffins dripping with butter for himself. He couldn't have described how he was feeling. Elated, nervous, brave, joyful, panicky, his emotions were changing by the second and leaving him tongue-tied. He didn't really want the muffins but needed to give his hands something to do to stop himself taking hold of her. That's what he really wanted to do, to capture her in his arms and kiss her until she was breathless. But likely that would signal the end of this tentative closeness that had sprung up.

He wiped his hands on his handkerchief when he had finished the muffins and they continued to stroll, his hand now and again dipping into the bag of chestnuts she was holding. They passed a blind match-seller and he dropped a few pennies into his tray.

He could hardly believe he was here with her like this. He caught her looking at him and forced himself to smile and say jocularly, 'Who would have thought all those years ago we'd be walking round the fair again like this? And you with enough behind you now to buy and sell anyone here a hundred times over.'

She didn't smile back. Neither did she drop her eyes when she said, 'I'm still the same frightened girl I was then, deep inside, Caleb.'

He stopped walking. 'You, frightened?'

'Don't you think I'm capable of feeling frightened like any other woman?'

He had offended her in some way, he could see it in her face but for the life of him he couldn't think how.

She had started walking again and he took two long strides to reach her side. It was then she said in a low voice, 'Contrary to what you may think, I am capable of feeling fear and longing and joy and–and love like–like the beauties of this world. More so, in fact, because when you look like I do—'

'What do you mean, look like you do?' He caught hold of her arm now, swinging her round to face him and not gently. His voice had been rough, too, almost angry.

Taken aback, the colour flooded her face. Why had she said anything? Why? Stammering a little, she said, 'I . . . I was trying to explain that my emotions don't match my looks, that's all. People . . . well, they expect plain women to be cold and,' she swallowed hard before bringing out, 'passionless.'

Two bare-footed little ragamuffins ran by, shouting excitedly and almost knocking the bag of chestnuts out of her hand. Eve seized the momentary diversion to begin walking once more but was again brought to a standstill by his hand on her arm. 'Is that how you see yourself? As plain?'

She stared into the deep brown eyes. She couldn't bring herself to speak but inclined her head. This was the ultimate humiliation and she had brought it on herself by agreeing to come to the fair with him. She would have to watch him trying to be kind now while she read the pity in his face. She had loved this man for as long as she could remember because the time before she'd met him had shrunk to the blink of an eye, such was her feeling for him, but the one emotion she couldn't bear from him was pity.

The faraway rolling of thunder was becoming louder and the sky was charcoal dark except when it was split by distant lightning. Eve was conscious of this on the perimeter of her mind but her senses were taken up with watching the dawning expression on Caleb's face. Her emotions heightened to breaking point; the only way she could describe it to herself was as though he had removed a mask and she was seeing him as she had never seen him before. And she knew it wasn't pity in his voice when he said huskily, 'You're beautiful, Eve, beautiful. So beautiful.' She did not resist him when he caught hold of her hand and drew her closer, the chestnuts falling to the ground unnoticed. 'I know you could never feel the same way, I do know that, and I understand, well, in part, but to me you're . . .'

She was gazing into his eyes and he into hers. Her voice was no more than a sigh in the air when she whispered, 'What am I?'

'Perfect. Beautiful and perfect and everything a man could ever want.'

'You . . . you loved Mary.'

'As a boy. As a man there has only been you. Will only be you . . .'

Emboldened by the fact that she had not rebuffed him thus far, he seized the moment and put his arms round her. He felt her trembling and when she allowed her body to fall against his, he drew in a long shuddering breath before taking her lips.

As though nature had orchestrated the moment, a streak of lightning directly overhead followed by a mighty crash of thunder which had folk screaming was followed by torrential rain. People were running hither and thither, stallholders were whipping their produce away and dashing for cover, and all was mayhem and confusion. In the midst of it all they continued to stand locked together, their arms round each other, their lips moving over each other's faces, brows, eyes, cheeks as first one and then the other feverishly sought to merge closer. Gasping and murmuring, their frantic kisses interspersed by half-formed words of love, they stood lost in a place where time had no meaning, her bonnet hanging down her back by its ribbons and their eyes blinded by the pouring rain.

How long it was before Caleb gained control he didn't know. It could only have been a matter of two or three minutes, but when he lifted his head and held her tightly against his breast, he was aware they were both soaked through and the water was running off the parched ground in a tide. 'Eve, we have to get out of the rain.'

She nodded, half laughing, and he laughed with her. She cared for him. How long she had cared he didn't know but in one way it didn't matter. Nothing mattered but that she was in his arms at last. Everything else could be worked out, he would make sure of that. She spoke, but another blast of thunder drowned her words. He bent his head. 'What did you say?'

'The fair's over.'

He turned with her to look at the scurrying people and the stallholders salvaging what they could, and again the urge to laugh was strong. Whisking her up in his arms he twirled her round and round before he allowed her feet to touch the ground again, and then he kept her within the circle of his arms. 'How soon will you marry me?'

She made a small movement with her head. 'It's only a year since Howard—'

'I don't care.' His voice was thick. 'I've waited years for you.'

When she lifted her hands and cupped his face, bringing his mouth down to hers, he groaned softly, but when the kiss had ended, she said softly, 'Caleb, there's Alexander to consider. I would like him to get used to you before – before we tell him.'

'How long will that take?'

'I don't know.'

The rain was like a sheet and now he tucked her into his side, saying, 'Come on, you'll catch your death. I'll take you home and then we can start the process of him getting used to me there and then. But, Eve,' he caught her to him again, his voice dropping so low she could scarcely hear him, 'say you love me. Out loud. Say it.'

'I love you.' She smiled and in that moment she was radiant. 'I've loved you from the first moment I saw you and I'll love you till the day I die and beyond. Through all eternity. Will that do?'

'For now.'

Epilogue

Eve and Caleb were married nine months later. On the eve of her wedding, which was to be a village affair at Washington's Trinity Church, Eve visited the churchyard where Oliver and Howard were buried. It was a beautiful June evening, the birds singing in the trees surrounding the churchyard and the air still scented with the May blossom which had been late that year.

She went alone. She had wanted it that way. It would have been Oliver's seventh birthday the week before and now she stroked the steam engine made of flowers she had brought to the grave that day. His steam engine had been his favourite toy.

'I love you, my precious baby.' She pressed her hands against her chest to contain the pain. 'My sweet, precious boy. My darling one.'

After a while she lifted her wet face to the sky. For months after they had died she had found herself raging at Howard every time she came to the churchyard. She had been so angry, so full of rage that he could have let their son die. But lately the anger had gone, to be replaced by a sad acceptance that her husband had loved his son with all his heart and had given his life trying to save him. It had been an accident, that was all. A tragic, senseless accident. And with the acceptance had come a measure of peace.

A deep twilight had fallen by the time she closed the gate to the churchyard behind her, and then she gave a little cry as a shadow close to the stone wall moved. Caleb stepped forward, taking her in his arms as he murmured, 'I thought I'd find you here.'

She clung to him, the tears falling again. 'I know he's in a better place but I want him here, with me. He was only a little boy. A little boy, Caleb.'

'I know, my love. I know.' He let her cry for a while and then dried her tears. They had agreed not to see each other the night before the wedding, but he had felt compelled to come, suspecting she might visit this very place. He held her close, his heart aching for her. He would make her happy, he vowed silently. Whatever it took, whatever he had to do, he would make her happy.

The next day half of Washington's residents were there to throw rice and rose petals when the couple emerged from the church to the peal of church bells, the groom's stepson held tight in his arms. No one, looking at Eve that day, would have labelled her plain.

When the newlyweds returned from their week's honeymoon, they set in action the plans they had talked over during their engagement. After consolidating their assets into one pot, they purchased a property on the edge of Gateshead not far from the establishment where Toby had received his treatment. The enormous old manor house was ideal in that its extensive grounds boasted three barns and a number of outbuildings as well as a large stable block. The stable block was transformed into a comfortable four-bedroomed bungalow and once it was finished Nell and Toby and their family moved in. Toby's days down the pit were over, his leg had healed but the damage to his knee in particular meant the limb was stiff and inflexible. Instead he was to manage the staff who would work in the workshops, vegetable gardens and orchard, and the animal husbandry section of the estate once it was all up and running.

While Toby supervised the remodelling of the barns and other outside work, Eve and Caleb presided over the alterations to change the manor house into a children's home-cum-boarding school. This included a one-bedroomed apartment in the basement for Mr Hutton whose official title was that of caretaker. Once the school was up and running, however, it was clear he had become everyone's grandad.

Along with the changes to the original building, a new west wing was added. This provided Eve and Caleb with a large family home in which Tilly had her own sitting room and bedroom next to the nursery suite. Tilly's duties were added to sooner than Eve had expected. In the midst of all the work, Eve discovered she was expecting Caleb's child.

Luke Caleb Travis was born on a windy October morning four weeks after the Oliver Ingram-Travis home for boys and girls was officially opened. Caleb wept unashamedly when he held his son in his arms, and Alexander was delighted with his new baby brother. If it had been a girl he had intended to see it was sent back.

Twin boys followed eighteen months later, and then on Eve's thirty-sixth birthday, with Nell urging her on and Tilly holding her hand, Eve's longed for daughter arrived. When the news was announced in the morning assembly, the huge family the school had become cheered and stamped their feet so hard Eve heard it in the west wing.

The December day was bitterly cold and through the window of her bedroom Eve could see it was snowing heavily, but inside all was snug and warm. She glanced across the room to the roaring fire in the grate, then her gaze travelled over the pleasant furnishings and rested on the big framed portrait of her precious boys that Caleb had painted as a surprise for her birthday. He was gaining a reputation as a respected artist these days and regularly sold his paintings for a considerable amount of money.

Finally her eyes settled on Caleb who was sitting in a comfortable chair nursing his tiny daughter. The expression on her husband's face was all Eve could have wished for.

She smiled softly and lay back on the pillows, shutting her eyes. She was richly blessed.

DININE⁸⁰/
MN

X

Lb

RAR

AB

JR

DW♥